# Sovereignty of the Dragons

# Sovereignty of the Dragons

Karen Hulene Bartell

**Five Star**
**Unity, Maine**

This novel is a work of fiction. Names, characters, places, and incidents are either the product of the author's imagination, or, if real, used fictitiously.

Five Star First Edition Romance
Published in conjunction with Karen Hulene Bartell.

Cover design by Peter Bartell.

June 1999

First Edition, Third Printing

Standard Print Hardcover Edition.

Five Star Standard Print First Edition Romance Series.

The text of this edition is unabridged.

Set in 11 pt. Plantin by Al Chase.

Printed in the United States on permanent paper.

**Library of Congress Cataloging in Publication Data**

Bartell, Karen H.
Sovereignty of the dragons / Karen Hulene Bartell.
— 1st ed.
p. cm. — (Five Star first edition romance series)
ISBN 0-7862-1887-8 (hc : alk. paper)
I. Title. II. Series.
PS3552.A7475S68 1999
813′.54—dc21 99-13671

**To Peter Bartell, my fellow flotsam along life's meandering stream.**

# PROLOGUE

"Wong's dying."

The two listeners glanced furtively about Beijing's Great Hall of the People, assuring themselves tonight's guests had all emptied into *Tiananmen* Square. Two thousand business allies and members of the National People's Congress had just finished dining in the elegant main hall, toasting Hong Kong's return to China. Until now, none had dared voice the thought preying on everyone's mind.

"Tsai's the heir apparent," said President Zheng. "If we don't move quickly, we'll lose all we've worked toward."

Convinced they were alone and unwatched, Ho Yu-lin nodded in tacit agreement. He glanced at his associate for confirmation, then faced Zheng.

"The Congress is gaining momentum," said Ho. "It was a rubber stamp in past decades, but now it has the power to ride the tiger. As Speaker of the Congress, you have my support."

Nodding, Zheng's jowls wobbled. Turning toward the well-heeled businessman, he fixed him with a hawkish, unwavering stare.

"With Hong Kong's recovery, the People's Republic needs three things for super-power status: improved international trade, Taiwan's reunification and Tsai's. . . ." Zheng paused prudently.

Finding a euphemism, Chen Da-wei filled in for him. "Fall from grace."

The three cackled mirthlessly. Brushing imaginary lint

from his silk, tailor-made suit, Chen hid his smirk as he continued. "My business contacts can increase the PRC's share of global markets, and my political connections in Taiwan will bring about reunification. I guarantee you'll achieve the first two goals. The Mainland's power struggle is no secret, Zheng. Your personal stakes are high. What can you offer me for helping crush Tsai?" Before the Congressional Speaker could answer, Chen grinned shrewdly. "After all, when a man gets power, even his chickens and ducks should rise to heaven."

"Of the US delegates, who's the most likely to support us in the trade agreement?" As Chen grilled his aide on the flight back to Macao, the stocky man shuffled through the manila folders.

"The profile on Governor Burkener shows a certain fondness for Asian boys. We could cater to his preferences." When Chen shook his head, the aide offered, "Or threaten to expose him."

Chen considered it, then discounted it. "He'd vote no to acquit himself. Who else have you got?"

"Senator MacKenzie has an impeccable record. . . ." The aide fingered another file indecisively. They heard the tinny hum of the plane's engines as he hesitated.

"But what?"

"He recently invested in a state-owned textile company in Guangdong. His entire capital's tied up," said the aide, looking up with a triumphant grin. "In fact, he's running into debt, waiting for Beijing to privatize the company. Spent his wife's inheritance. Is mortgaged heavily. And is rumored to be taking kickbacks." Hoping for approval, he watched Chen expectantly.

Like a stele, his face chiseled in stone, Chen listened attentively, missing nothing. The archetype of inscrutability, he was the consummate businessperson. Powerful in financial and political circles, commanding or charming as he chose, he cut an impressive figure in his expensively tailored suit. Polished professional, he emanated success the way most people perspire.

Handsome in an unconventional way, Chen's features were arresting, more Japanese than Chinese. Dark eyes so piercing, they absorbed all he saw and all who saw him. His unwavering gaze easily held people captive. Contrasted against his white teeth, his complexion was the color of a perpetual tan. With his high cheek bones, rectangular jaw and high-bridged nose, he looked almost western. The thick shock of hair, stylishly cut, bristled and gleamed like a silver-fox tail. Square-shouldered, trim and agile for a man of forty-nine, he carried himself with authority and éclat.

"Anything else?"

The aide flipped through the pages. "Mid-life crisis. His wife just passed away. His daughter's moving to Taipei. His popularity in the polls has dropped. . . ."

His interest piqued, Chen interrupted. "What's the connection between the daughter and Taipei?"

"The mother was Taiwanese, married MacKenzie while they were in college. Now the daughter wants to explore her Asian heritage."

"And the polls?"

"His popularity's slipping," said the aide. "Can't keep his constituency happy *and* protect all his PACs and lobbies. By backing unpopular issues recently, he's been losing voter confidence. Combine that with his state's drought and rising unemployment, and there's no way he'll get reelected next term."

Rubbing his nose thoughtfully with his index finger, Chen made his decision. "Find everything you can on him—and the daughter."

# CHAPTER 1

Twinkling with thousands of lightbulbs, Taipei's Presidential Office Building was an embroidery of incandescent pearls stitched onto painted placards. Its reflection illuminated the limo as it passed beneath.

Lane's father stared through the tinted windows as fireworks blitzed the sky, bracketing the colonial building with immense plumes of iridescent greens, reds and gold. The flash also revealed the gaudy, lacquered panels tacked on the structure for the occasion.

To Lane's western viewpoint, the colors clashed. To her eastern tastes, the primal yellows, reds, greens and blues roused the senses, invited celebration. Towering over all, the billboard-sized Republic of China's flag glowed neon red, white and blue. It was an optimistic beacon.

"Double Ten's to Taiwan what the Fourth of July is to the States," Lane said, taking her father's arm.

He immediately pulled loose from her grip as he leaned forward to see another burst and shower of light. Lane sighed, resolving not to let his mood interfere with her own. Tonight was *hers,* and nothing would spoil it.

She unruffled her brow as consciously as she smoothed wrinkles from her satin gown, ignoring the doubts that pried. She focused instead on the fireworks' dazzling light display reflected on the glossy fabric. Changing from shades of lime to deep-forest green, the shimmering dress' alternating hues complimented her remarkable Anglo-Asian eyes. Almond-shaped and blazing with intelligence, they mirrored the fireworks, flashing a jadeite green as brilliant as Burmese emeralds.

Her mouth relaxed into a half smile as she focused on the night's engagement party. Having met Li only four months earlier, it was a whirlwind courtship in any culture. But to the primly regulated Taiwanese attitude, it was a romance of typhoon proportions.

Remembering Li's mother's urgent requests to postpone her only son's marriage to a *wai guo ren,* a foreigner, Lane smiled, the curve gradually tightening into a grimace. Then she dismissed the thought with a defiant tilt of her chin. She was glad they had gone ahead with the plans, being too much in love to delay any longer.

Infatuated with their dual cultures as much as each other, they had planned to celebrate Chinese-style with a boisterous dinner party of close friends and family. Instead, her father had insisted on a formal announcement, inviting members of his diplomatic corps from the Dixie Trade and Investment Office, her colleagues from the de facto consulate and hundreds of other ambassadors, diplomats and business people.

Exasperated, she had finally agreed out of a sense of duty, anything to ensure harmony, even sharing her special moment with strangers. Angry words rose in her throat but just as quickly were swallowed along with her resentment. It was her father's *job* to entertain dignitaries, she consoled herself, her green eyes resting on him affectionately.

She stared at him, old habits dying hard. Childhood behavior patterns still dictated, and she saw him through the eyes of an awed daughter. Sitting next to him, she couldn't help thinking how regally handsome he looked, the perfect image of a diplomat. Authority rested on his shoulders like an ermine cape. His graying blond hair gleamed silver and gold, more stately than a crown. Senator MacKenzie was an imposing figure; his rigid posture and jutting jaw revealed his unyielding nature.

Despite her father's disturbing need for control, Lane knew he loved her—in his own self-serving way. But tonight she was so filled with love for her fiancé, it overflowed to include everyone, even her father, *especially* him. Her heart swelled with the tenderness of a daughter realizing the first man in her life has been replaced. Then with a shiver of anticipation, her thoughts returned to Yang Liu—Li.

She smiled, remembering Li's straight black hair, parted at the center, sweeping his brow like ravens' wings. She loved how it brushed against her face, tickling when he bent to kiss her. Taller than most Chinese, he had to stoop to reach her lips, even when she stood on tiptoe. Clasping her hands tightly, wishing they were holding him instead, she couldn't believe that after tonight they'd belong to each other.

The Trade and Investment Office was holding a small reception in their honor, her father having skillfully arranged it. His administration would finance the cocktail party in exchange for the consulate sponsoring the expensive formal dinner.

*That's* why he invited everyone, she suddenly recognized, to make them obligated. Successful at manipulation, he was less adept at covering debts. Though he played the role of prosperous senator and entrepreneur, her father was living on extended credit.

Again she shook off the negative thoughts, concentrating instead on the night to come. She and Li had agreed to meet at the reception, have a drink, then leave for the Grand Hotel, where they'd host their engagement dinner for four hundred people.

If less than intimate, their party would at least be politically correct. More importantly, its location would be next door to the American Club, where her father would inevitably retreat with an entourage of business associates to discuss the trade agreement. Then she and Li could be alone.

Flushing, she remembered a rainy Taipei afternoon six weeks before when one heated kiss had ignited the next. With a frustration born of twenty-seven years of denial, Lane had surprised them both with her ardor.

Her hands, feverishly pulling at the buttons of his shirt, had swept their long fingertips across his lean, muscular chest. He responded by tenderly kneading her breast, first through her blouse, then under her lacy bra, molding her flesh, beading her firm nipples into dimpled tips of excitement. With a relinquishing whimper, her lips eagerly sought his.

Despite impassioned kisses in the past months, they had curbed their hunger for each other, waiting at least until the engagement was official. But the restriction had only whetted their appetites. They had tasted and nibbled until only a feast would satisfy them.

Never taking their eyes from each other, they had undressed quickly. His black eyes following the contours of her nude body for the first time, he whispered hoarsely.

"You're lovely, like carved white jade."

As he crushed her to him, she felt his maleness press against her. With a sweet shudder, Lane trembled as his fingers explored the cleft of her legs. Slowly he worked his hand within her until she closed around his fingers, moving against them, with them. As if she were candy, once he penetrated her sugar coating, he felt her creamy, melting center.

Barely restraining himself, he had continued to satisfy her until he could wait no longer. Then with a cry of wonder, he entered her, feeling her velvet muscles ripple for the first time. The two rose and fell and met again and again. Finally they arrived at a release that left Lane at such an emotional peak, she sobbed, not from pain or remorse, but from relief. She was freed of that resistant sheath protecting her virginity, isolating her within a gossamer sack like a baby within a caul. She was emancipated.

"Lane!" Her father's voice jolted her back to the present. "Wave!"

Startled, she reacted automatically, nodding and waving on cue. Looking out the window, she suddenly realized they had arrived at the Trade Office. Then she noted the attractive man's arresting smile and formal Asian bow.

"Who is he?"

"David Chen from the Macao delegation. He's heading the commission to strengthen ties with Taiwan, more to the point, to improve trade."

MacKenzie stepped out of the car hurriedly, only pausing to lend Lane an impatient hand when he saw her struggling with her long skirt.

"Chen," he called, "a real pleasure to see y'all."

"As dawn comes to a bleak night, the pleasure's mine."

Dressed fastidiously in a tailored white tux, the distinguished-looking man approached their limo like a male crane strutting and preening for a hen. Reaching for her hand, he smiled warmly at Lane and noted her trim figure sheathed in green satin. Though his silver-black hematite eyes remained on her, he addressed her father.

"You haven't introduced me to your charming daughter."

She studied him with interest, noting his handsome, raw-boned face framed with silver-shot hair. But it was his mesmerizing black eyes that held her captive. Not waiting for MacKenzie's response, Chen seized the moment.

"I'm David, and you—Lane, isn't it?—are as green and fresh as a sunlit bamboo forest."

She blushed at the compliment despite her instinctive distrust. Having been around phonies all her life, she smelled insincerity. And excessive flattery raised her suspicions, no matter how attractive the man.

"Are you always this *poetic?*" she asked.

"Only in the company of beautiful women." Whether he noted her cynicism or not, the smile remained on his lips. Releasing her hand, he gripped her elbow. "Allow me the privilege, Senator, of escorting your daughter."

"The honor's mine. Say, Chen, we could use your know-how with the Sino-North American trade offer." Sidling up to the Chinese, Percy MacKenzie fawned as only a career office-seeker can.

Chen's lip curled contemptuously. "Careful, Senator, you know the old joke about *honor* and *offer,* don't you?"

MacKenzie's bland expression was his answer.

"In the Ching Dynasty, the emperor married off his daughter to a scholar. Not used to courtly ways, the young man asked how to approach the marriage bed. 'She will offer you her honor,' he was told, 'and then you will honor her offer.' All night long it was honor and offer, honor and offer."

MacKenzie and Chen laughed loudly at the ribaldry, while Lane tried to pull her arm away. She kept her eyes focused on the marble floor as they entered the reception area, disguising her irritation at his off-color humor.

To the assembled dignitaries, her entrance looked otherwise. They saw a stunning woman arm-in-arm with a man obviously charmed by her. The women noticed her lustrous, coffee-brown hair contrasting against her luminous, ivory-colored complexion as translucent as rice-porcelain. The men noted how her shimmering dress accentuated each curve and hollow of her lithe body. But it was not until she lifted her spectacular eyes that the people recognized her unique beauty. Combining the elements of classic western and Asian features, hers was a beauty that appealed to both sets of ideals.

At that moment Yang Liu spotted her and swallowed quickly, a lump suddenly in his throat. His love for her was as genuine as his fear. What was Chen doing here? He left his mother's side and crossed the room.

As soon as he came into view, Lane's crystal green eyes shone for him alone. They followed him as he approached, silently expressing their love. Anticipating his reaction to her news, she decided against waiting until after dinner. Instead she would find a stolen moment and squirrel him away. Then a bold impulse shouted, Why not now? The secret was too exciting to keep to herself. She took a step forward to kiss him hello but felt herself suddenly pulled back.

Tightly gripping her elbow, Chen was the first to speak. "Li, I read your report on the monetary exchange rates. Well done."

Li's first reaction was irritation at his employer's interference with his fiancée's kiss and their engagement party. Still he hid his feelings, remembering his position. His dark eyes blazing, he nodded respectfully. He then shook hands with MacKenzie, his expression softening.

"Good evening, sir."

"Li." MacKenzie answered him in his good ole boy politician drawl.

As Li's eyes turned to Lane, they smiled ever so subtly, merely creasing at the corners to anyone's scrutiny but hers. Only she saw the love.

Leaning into his kiss, she felt the restraining hand. This time she shook it off. Daring Chen to intrude, she kissed Li fully on the lips. Then linking arms, they excused themselves. Once out of earshot, she whispered excitedly.

"Li, there's something. . . ."

"Before we get. . . ." The two began speaking at the same time, then laughed. "You first," he said.

"No, you." She had been bursting to tell him since morning. Then she remembered they had a lifetime ahead of them. She could wait another minute.

His expression suddenly grim, his eyes bored into hers. "There's something you have to know. . . ."

Suddenly distracted, he stopped speaking. She followed his line of vision and saw his mother motioning. Her gesture looked like a small child's good-bye wave, but it was the Chinese signal for *come here.*

"My mother wants me," he said.

Li responded much too quickly for Lane's taste. The American side of her rebelled at his mother's grip, at his blind obedience toward the woman. Except for his threat to elope when she had barred their marriage, Li never challenged his mother's authority or opinion, and it irked Lane. After one particularly bitter argument, his eyes had penetrated hers with their poignancy.

"Your main reason for coming to Taiwan was to explore your Chinese heritage, find your roots, wasn't it? This is the Chinese way. Sons respect their mothers. It's natural I feel this way. Who gave me life? Who fed me? Who took care of me?"

"But that's what parents *do* for children. It's their job. Then when children grow up, they cut the umbilical cord."

Lane's counter evoked a scornful smile. "That's the western way. Here mothers give their sons everything. Then they expect payment in kind. Do you know the Chinese character for happiness?"

Lane shook her head.

"A woman holding her son."

"What about daughters?" she asked.

"Mothers don't get as attached. Girls don't belong to their mothers. They're brought up for their husbands' families."

"You're kidding!" Lane raised her eyebrows as her mouth fell open in disbelief.

"Chinese think females are bad investments," said Li. "No matter how much interest is staked in raising them, the returns go to the husbands' families."

Lane thought of this as they approached Li's mother and her friend. She tried to put on a face of daughterly devotion but was hard pressed to feel any emotional attachment. Yang *Taitai* did not speak English, and Lane's Chinese was rudimentary at best. But even if language were not a barrier, communication would have been improbable. Li had to translate every word exchanged between them.

"*Ni hao ma?* How are you?" Lane asked them politely, coming to the end of her conversational Mandarin repertoire.

"*Hao*. Good."

Both older women wore pained expressions as they answered her. Then Mrs. Yang broke into a lengthy discourse in a rapid dialect, leaving Lane far behind. All she could do was watch the body language. After several uninterrupted minutes, she asked Li to translate. He rolled his eyes, then threw up his arms in frustration.

"I can't. There's too much. *Feng shui*, loosely translated, wind/water. They're worried. We didn't hire a geomancer to choose an auspicious day for our engagement. My mother's friend said today's date will bring bad luck."

Lane chalked it up to one more bias to overcome in her prospective in-laws' eyes. She took a different tact.

"Tell your mother she looks lovely in her new pearl necklace."

Secure in the knowledge the woman liked pearls, she had given her a string of matched Malaysian pearls. Wearing a smile, Lane waited patiently for the translation. Another five minutes of Taiwanese passed. Neither son nor mother was smiling.

"She says thank you."

Judging from the woman's expression and repeated gesture of wiping the pearls with a tissue, Lane disagreed.

"I know the words for thank you, and she didn't use them. What did she really say?"

Shrugging, Li took her hand. "She loves them, just like I love you. But before we join the guests, I have to tell you something."

"Wine?" offered a waiter, interrupting.

As they each took a glass, a squat man approached in a mismatched suit, the jacket a deeper shade of blue than his shiny-bottomed trousers. Helping himself to a glass of wine, he addressed Li in Taiwanese. Lane smiled and nodded politely, oblivious to what was being said.

Finally he ended in English. "This who?"

"Lane," said Li.

"Lanne, good to know. Today—ah, my English not well—good day to engagement!" He held up his thumb to stress his point. "No work today, everyone no work, memory your day." He tapped his forehead. "Today Republic of China day. Wuchang Revolution, Ten, Ten."

"October tenth," said Lane, "Double Ten."

Then eyes twinkling, he gave her a mischievous grin. "Lanne, three thing Chinese man want. You know?"

She shook her head, not sure she wanted to hear the punch line. He held out his wrist.

"Rolex, Benz. . . ."

"Mercedes," Li filled in.

"And Japan wife," he finished. "Chinese very like tradition wife."

Not to be outdone, she asked, "And what do Japanese women look for in a husband?"

"Education, income." The short man paused as he looked up at Li. "And length."

As Lane flushed, Li hastened to explain. "He means height."

"Yes, height. Height much important! *Ganbei!*"

He clapped Li's shoulder, then held up his glass with both hands, waited for them to do the same and downed his drink.

"I very like wine . . . wines. Which? Countable? Non-countable?"

"Depends on how many you've had."

"You very fun lady. Good day to engagement!"

He gave a hearty laugh and shook Lane's hand. Then he waved as he crossed the room.

"Who was that?" she asked.

"No one, just a member of the Legislative Branch."

"I like his attitude. Today is a good day, *feng shui* or no *feng shui!*"

She chuckled until she saw his mother wipe her pearls again with a tissue. Then Lane's brow creased skeptically.

"What is she doing?"

He hesitated only a beat. "Wiping off hairspray."

"Your mother doesn't use hairspray. What's she doing?"

"All right, you might as well know. She said a film rubbed off the beads." He hesitated. "She thinks the pearls aren't real."

"Aren't real?! I . . . I bought those myself . . . last. . . ."

Before she could sputter a response, Li interrupted with a kiss. "Don't take it personally. She criticizes everything. Look at it this way. She's wearing them. If she really didn't like them, she'd leave them in a drawer, right?"

His comical smile made her laugh. "Right."

But as she kissed his indented nose, his smile suddenly sagged. "We've got to talk. Now, before someone else interrupts."

He snatched her hand, jerking her unceremoniously behind the refreshment table. His abrupt change alarmed her as the hairs on the back of her neck tingled with a mixture of curiosity and apprehension.

Her fitted satin skirt rustling, Lane was forced to take short steps, struggling to keep up with his fast pace without appearing to hurry. One thing her father had instilled in her: appearance is everything. As they huddled near the wall, her green eyes opened wide with anticipation.

"What's the big secret?" she asked.

"How do you know Chen Da-wei?"

"You mean David Chen? I don't. I just met him."

"He seems to know you." Li's withering expression revealed his opinion of her entrance on Chen's arm.

She shrugged. "He's a business associate of my father. Something to do with the trade agreement." Then taking the offensive, she asked, "What's he to you?"

"For starters, he's CEO of our company." He chewed his lip; then mincing words like a cat stepping on a wet floor, he continued. "Lane, he's a powerful man, and where there's power, there's danger."

The small smile playing at her lips burst into a grin. "Li, are you jealous?"

"Of course not!" His chin jerked indignantly. "I can't explain now; I can only advise your father to be careful. There's more to Chen than meets the eye."

"He's just another bag-of-wind puffed up with himself." Dismissing him with a wave, she used her raised hand to lightly stroke Li's forehead. "And I advise you not to worry so much. You're getting lines."

"The Chinese say lines are a sign of wisdom." Grabbing her hand, he drew her to him and spoke under his breath. "I'd rather you stroked something else."

His hot breath tickled her as much as his words. She laughed for the sheer pleasure of being near him. Then she remembered her news. Whispering, her lips brushed his ear.

"Close your eyes. I have a secret. . . ."

A woman screamed.

They heard, but cocooned in their own world it took a moment to realize what was happening. Pandemonium broke loose as someone began shouting in Taiwanese. Li's eyelids sprang open. As he searched for the sound's direction, he broke away from Lane.

"Mother!"

They rushed back to see his mother's crumpled figure on the floor. When a young woman in a wispy aqua dress saw Li, she pointed at him and let out with a stream of Taiwanese, inciting the crowd. For a moment, she faltered as Li's angry eyes met hers.

Then the mother's companion joined in, alternately prompting the girl and goading Li. Ignoring the stereophonic harangue, he lifted and carried his mother toward a row of upholstered chairs.

"What happened? What are they saying?" Lane shouted above the din, but he couldn't hear. The old woman and the girl in aqua had begun screeching at him. When Lane looked at his face for a clue, she saw his jaw clenched tighter than his mother's grip on his heart.

He propped his mother on a chair, and she began regaining consciousness. Before her eyes focused, she shook her head to rouse herself, then rejoined the argument.

Lane stared at the three women, sensing their problem concerned her. She watched their jade-braceleted wrists slash the air and their painted, firecracker-red lips spew out words. She heard the abusive tones but failed to understand the meaning.

Finally the young one pointed at Li, shouted something, then raised a handkerchief to her tear-stained face and began to sob, her frail shoulders shaking pathetically.

His mother cried, "Aaayyah," then stared wordlessly at her crony.

Silence followed. Everyone's eyes turned to Li.

After a long, embarrassed pause, Lane spoke in a small voice. "What is it?"

His face stony, he said nothing. Dreading what she may learn, Lane stared at him, her eyes mutely begging him to answer. Chen stepped beside her and spoke to the crowd. With tacit nods, they seemed to agree with his words and moved away from the scene. Her father planted himself between Li and Lane.

Livid, MacKenzie demanded an explanation in a slow southern drawl. "What's goin' on here?"

When the young man's pale lips gave no answer, Chen turned to MacKenzie. "Why don't we use your office?" Chen gestured toward Lane with his chin. "For privacy."

She felt she was seeing a video of the scene, not participating. She sensed her future hinged on the drama's results, yet she felt detached, removed. Watching dully, she noticed the older woman had sat down beside Li's mother, the two whispering conspiratorially, while the sniffling girl in aqua sat at a cautious distance.

Lane scrutinized each crisp detail of the actors, especially the girl's. She saw the gauzy dress, the spike heels. She noted her tiny frame, fine bone structure and thick mane of velvet-black hair. She saw the tears spilling down her face but noticed that the girl's curved, wide-set eyes were clear, not blood-shot from grief. Frozen with fascination, Lane couldn't look away, even when the bright eyes met hers with an unmistakable gleam of victory. As MacKenzie bounded toward his office, Chen wrenched Lane from the trance and steered her after him.

Li stood paralyzed by the scene, unable to leave the three seated women. He stared at the girl who looked almost prim compared to her usual self. He remembered the first time he had seen her in tight, red-sequined hot pants worn over a sheer black body-stocking. Her matching red-sequined bolero had done little to hide her breasts, large by Chinese standards. He had been unable to keep his eyes off her then, too. Was it only six months ago?

He and Chen had been entertaining Japanese clients at an upscale KTV karaoke bar on *Shuangcheng* Street when he noticed her. After exchanging several lingering glances, the girl had sauntered over to their group and suggestively pressed a microphone into his hands.

"I need a partner for the duet," she said.

Speaking directly, she focused on him those exotic eyes that tipped up at the corners into graceful whorls. He felt self-conscious, flattered and disturbingly aroused, as well.

They read the words from an over-sized screen, singing along with the music video. To Li's relief, the reverberating sound system compensated for his melodic shortcomings. She sang in a husky contralto, her sexuality wafting from her like her Hermes' cologne. Her eyes danced, playing to the men at the bar when she sang solo, then returning to his when they harmonized. As another customer's selection appeared on the screen, Li passed him the mike, then suggested she join their group for a drink.

Before he could introduce himself, Li heard Chen's arrogant voice.

"Who is this lorikeet?"

As a familiar grin crossed Chen's face, Li watched them. The girl's wide cheekbones rose higher as she subdued a knowing smile and slid a child's hand along Chen's necktie. He promptly pushed it away.

Not until MacKenzie roared his name did Li rouse himself from his musings and follow. After he shut the door, MacKenzie turned to the young man. "What's going on out there?"

His mouth dry, no words came out on Li's first attempt to speak. He swallowed and continued. "Mei-ling announced. . . ."

"Oh, Mei-ling, is it," her father sneered, crossing to his desk.

". . . that she's pregnant," Li paused, furtively glancing at Lane, "and that I'm the father."

Lane found she was unexpectedly distant. She could remain calm only because she felt numb. She was watching a tape. This was not happening.

"I could have you shot for this." MacKenzie's eyes bored into the young man's. Then he took a deep breath, filling his wide chest, and asked the inevitable. "Is it true?"

"I doubt it," mumbled Li, "but it could be."

"Damn! How could y'all be so stupid?!" MacKenzie's fist pounded the desktop.

Li closed his eyes as he whispered hoarsely. "If it's true, it happened accidentally."

"How could anyone in this day and age get pregnant accidentally?!" MacKenzie looked apoplectic.

Lane was not able to stifle a nervous giggle. She had the irresistible urge to laugh at this joke life was playing. As she looked from one shocked face to another, she could contain herself no longer. Her giggle became a chuckle, then grew to an hysterical laugh accented by sobs, the sound echoing in the silence of the cold marble room.

"Stop it! Y'all want everyone to hear? You're making a spectacle of yourself like *Mei-ling!*" Her father spat the name contemptuously, then adjusted his lapels. "We have guests to consider!"

"Guests?!" Once Lane's emotions surfaced, they ignited. "Is that all you can think of? Perceptions?!" Adrenaline fueled her fury, increasing her outcry as each new idea emerged. "That's all you care about. What will people say? Well here's what I say. I don't care! Do you hear me? I *don't care!*"

Li raced to her side. "Lane, I know how this must sound, but try to believe me; I love you. No matter how it looks, it's you I love. It has been since the day we met."

Her anger evaporated at the sound of his voice. Her body still shaking, she nodded weakly. Though the joy was gone, her love remained. Li reached for her hand, but before he could clasp her fingertips, MacKenzie rushed him.

"Don't lay a finger on her!" he said, grabbing Li's arm. "Don't touch my daughter again!"

"She's my fiancée," said Li, wrenching his arm from MacKenzie. "We're engaged!"

"Not yet, you're not," said Chen softly. For the first time Lane became aware of him still holding her elbow. He looked at MacKenzie meaningfully. "Officially no one knows. No one *has* to know. . . ."

"What y'all have in mind?"

"Announce the engagement as planned," said Chen.

"After *this?*" roared MacKenzie. "So everyone can laugh? Not on your life!"

"The Chinese are masters at saving face," Chen continued. "Announce your daughter's engagement. To me."

# CHAPTER 2

Although he remained silent, Lane could hear the well-greased wheels turning in her father's mind. She spoke before they sealed her future, once more pulling away from Chen's grip. "You're crazy if you think I'd ever marry you!" Her eyes defiant, she said simply, "I love Li."

"You *love* a man who cheated? Knocked up some cheap China-doll he can't remember?" asked MacKenzie. "Even if y'all could kiss and make-up, how can you ever trust the sonofabitch again?!"

Her father's words beat against her brain like gongs. She turned her glare toward him, and his tone softened.

Reasoning, he spread his hands. "He did it once; he'll do it again."

"That's not true!" Li looked at her earnestly. "I was ending the relationship with Mei-ling when you moved here four months ago. After our first date, I never saw the girl again. It was over, finished. I . . . I had no idea she was pregnant. If she is," he muttered under his breath. Then he turned to her father, appealing again. "I would never do anything to hurt your daughter. I love her."

His eyes glowing with the truth, Li urged the group to believe him. When Lane stepped toward him, Chen sensed the changing mood in the room. Pulling her back sharply, he regained control by assuming the air of protector.

"This is very touching," said Chen, "but it's not helping the very person you *say* you love. Nor is it helping her family's name. Do you want people to laugh at Lane and her father?"

Chen eyed the young man sternly, watching Li's forehead crease as his conviction faltered. Only then did Chen turn his attention to MacKenzie.

"And you, Senator, can you afford to be made a laughing stock, especially when the trade agreement with the US, Macao, Taiwan and Mexico hinges on personalities and impressions? A man who can't control his own family is hardly a man to head an international coalition." Chen's eyes penetrating, he spoke in somber tones. "Being seen as a weakling won't help you at the bargaining table."

The senator stroked his chin thoughtfully before answering. "This plan of yours, would it keep this . . . calamity under our hats?"

As MacKenzie gestured toward Li with his chin, Chen nodded, smiling wisely. "Like gunpowder and fireworks, saving face is a Chinese invention."

"All right. Shoot."

Her father's approval shocking her into action, Lane's sharp voice pierced the air like a bullet. Her gaze fell first on Chen. "Have you forgotten what century this is? Emperors don't give daughters to scholars." Then as she looked from him to her father, her green eyes threw sparks. "Nor do people arrange marriages anymore. You can't give me away like an industrial contract! I'll marry whoever I please!"

"Lane, you misunderstand." Chen's words flowed as smoothly as a silk scarf waving in the breeze. Releasing her arm, he looked at her benevolently. "This is for appearances *only*. There'll be no wedding, just an official announcement of engagement for the 'audience' tonight. This is a formality, nothing more."

"I'll be honest. I don't trust you." Unconvinced, she stared him down.

Then forgetting his suave public mien, her father exploded. "Lane! I won't have you insulting your elders."

"I'm a twenty-seven-year-old woman. I'll be damned if I'll let you or him bully me into a marriage of convenience!"

As if she hadn't spoken, Chen continued. "Think of this as a press release, a reason for the people to be here tonight. They're expecting an announcement. Give them one! No one will remember if a wedding follows or not . . . only if an expected announcement *doesn't* take place. *That* they'll never let you forget." He looked at MacKenzie deliberately, passing the torch.

"You never have to actually marry Chen, just pretend you will." Her father resumed the argument, then looked quickly to the idea's author for support. "Isn't that right?" At Chen's formal nod, MacKenzie continued. "This would buy us time. You walked in on Chen's arm. That alone should show he's your fiancé. Makes damned good sense. Fine idea! I like your way of thinking."

As he clapped Chen on the shoulder, Chen smiled, first at MacKenzie, then at his voluptuous daughter. In her fitted, green dress, Lane looked as juicy as a cluster of grapes, ripe and ready for pressing. Catching the glint in his eye, Li moved quickly, shouldering his way between his employer and fiancée.

"This is preposterous!" said Li. "Lane and I are in love. If you go through with this scheme, we'll elope. Only *then* would you lose face." He put his arm around her waist possessively.

"You bastard! I told you to keep your hands off her!" Nearly thirty years older but fifty pounds heavier, MacKenzie easily pulled him from his daughter. Before Li could resist, he sent an upper cut to the young man's jaw, knocking him backward.

"Stop it!" Lane rushed to Li's help. She steadied him,

then gently wiped the trickle of blood from his chin. "Are you all right?"

Li nodded, turning to face her father. "Mr. MacKenzie, I love your daughter. I want to marry her." He placed one arm protectively around Lane as the other gingerly worked his jaw. "There's no loss of respect for you or your name."

"But there is for a girl who's been jilted," said Chen. "She loses face. What about her?" Pointing to the door, Chen's eyes glinted roguishly. "I didn't realize what an ambitious man you are, Li. Two women. What did you plan to do? Keep one for your *xiao taitai?*" He laughed derisively. "Which one?"

"What's a *xiao taitai?*" MacKenzie's scowl deepened the creases in his forehead.

As if explaining to a student, Chen answered patiently. "*Taitai* means wife. In earlier times, Chinese kept several wives, but only the first was *taitai,* literally 'great-great.' The rest were *xiao taitai,* little wives, concubines. Today it roughly translates to mistress."

"Why did you ask which one would be his mistress? He's a jackass, but he obviously wants to marry my daughter." Suspicion coarsened MacKenzie's dignified features. When Chen hesitated, pretending discretion, MacKenzie pressed him. "Spit it out!"

"Li didn't tell you everything." After another deliberating pause, Chen challenged the young man, his eyes calculating. "I'm offering you a last chance to tell them yourself." Li remained silent, eyes down, as Chen addressed the senator. "He's already married to Mei-ling."

Lane's mouth fell open as she stared at him in disbelief.

His upper lip sweating, his eyes bulging, MacKenzie turned to Li. "What were y'all thinking, you sonofabitch bigamist? Keep 'em both as long as they stayed out of each other's sight? Thanks to you, Lane and I are the laughing stock of Taipei's diplomatic community."

"Mr. MacKenzie, the whole thing's a misunderstanding." Li swallowed hard. "She *thought* we were married, but we never signed anything." He turned to Lane. "Believe me, this can all be explained. The girl's from Tainan, a city in southern Taiwan."

At her puzzled expression, he took a deep breath. Looking from face to face, Li clarified. "The Tainanese get engaged twice. Once at a little engagement, when the couple tells their friends, and again at a public engagement—like tonight. At a party four months ago, after too much wine, she told our friends we were getting married. To save her embarrassment, I didn't deny it."

MacKenzie glared at him.

"Nor did I confirm it," Li added quickly. "That's her basis for her saying we're married. She's either kidding herself or deliberately lying."

"What about her witnesses?" asked Chen. "She said they'll testify."

Li stared him in the eye. "Those are the friends I mentioned. She has no proof, no marriage contract."

"According to her, you talked her out of it, said you didn't want it recorded. If your passport read *married*, you told her you couldn't apply for a US green card." Chen appraised his quarry, then struck. "Maybe Lane was your ticket to citizenship. Marry her, keep her in the States and keep Mei-ling in Taiwan. . . ." Chen let his words hang.

"That's not true!" Li's dark eyes defied Chen's, then tensely searched Lane's.

She bit her lip in confusion. Though she wanted to believe him, the circumstantial evidence was mounting. Despite her qualms, she still grimaced a half-smile, and Li grasped her hand as if it were a lifeline.

Chen sniffed and nodded in the door's direction. "Do you think that girl will take this passively?" He shook his head. "If she's come here tonight, she means to have you, one way or the other."

"How do you know so much about her? To hear you talk, you've already met." Lane eyed him skeptically, strengthened by Li's steady grip.

Smiling benignly, Chen answered with a chuckle. He walked to the door and paused, his hand on the knob, his black eyes challenging hers.

"I know the mentality of Asian women, their reasoning, their manner of thinking. But see for yourself." With that, Chen called to Mei-ling in Chinese.

Lane shuddered as she watched the girl enter the room hand-in-hand with Mrs. Yang. The gloating, older woman followed close behind. Mei-ling's spirits seemed as high as her rhinestone heels and chiffon hem-line. Her tears, long vanished, had left behind a pair of clear, hauntingly curved eyes that focused jubilantly on Li.

Unnerved as much by the girl's brazenness as his mother's evident approval, his jaw went slack, and his hand fell from Lane's. As if an icy ghost had stepped between them, Lane began shaking. Without his reassurance, she felt unprepared to meet the girl's triumphant eyes. Instead she concentrated on Li's beaming mother and the older woman. She watched them greet Chen with nods.

They conducted the discussion in Taiwanese, Chen acting as arbiter. Lane felt left out and stood by her father, again watching but unable to participate. At one point Li pointed at her but appeared too caught up with the debate to notice her nervous smile. She heard his mother say something about a *wai guo ren,* but could make out little else.

Trying to understand, Lane watched the body language. The older woman touched the girl often, pointing to her face, her body, especially her belly. With so much handling, she seemed Mei-ling's champion, promoting the girl's assets, fending off Li's verbal assaults.

As the decibel level increased alarmingly, Lane worried the discussion was becoming a riot, then reminded herself that even polite Taiwanese conversations can sound like shouting matches. Grimacing, she gave MacKenzie her best imitation of a smile, trying to exude a confidence she far from felt.

He shook his head dolefully. "Lane, if you won't think of yourself, think of my position. My political career could be ruined over an international incident like this."

Before she could answer, they heard Mrs. Yang cry out. Appalled, they watched her tear off her necklace and throw it at her son. As the pearls clattered about his feet, Li reacted as if he had been slapped.

His face blanched. His jaw clenched and unclenched, biting back bitter words. He stared mutinously at his mother, his eyes blinking in disbelief. Then he glared at the old woman and Mei-ling contemptuously, as if they could read his thoughts. His eyes passed over Chen once, openly flashing hatred, and rested again on his mother. Finally Lane watched his chest heave and heard him draw a deep breath as he turned to her.

"Lane," his voice croaked, "can I speak to you over here?" He nodded toward the far corner.

"Oh, no, you don't! Anything you have to say to my daughter, you can say in front of me!" The senator stepped between them, characteristically belligerent.

"Mr. MacKenzie, this is between Lane and me." Li struggled for self control. "All I'm asking is a moment's privacy."

"And all I'm saying's *no,*" shouted MacKenzie. "Say it like a man, out in the open. Don't go traipsing behind women's skirts like a yellow-bellied coward!"

MacKenzie and Li eyed each other dangerously. Only the young man's heavy breathing could be heard as the pause lengthened. Finally MacKenzie's mouth twisted cynically.

"Y'all got something to say, boy? Or not?"

Resigning himself to his fate, Li slumped. His expression drooped; his shoulders sagged. With a contemptuous sniff, Lane thought he looked like one of Taipei's street dogs. If he'd had a tail, it would have been tucked between his legs. He spoke faintly, as if the wind had been knocked out of him.

"All right, Mr. MacKenzie. Families are what life's about. You have a right to hear this, too." He looked at Lane with a puppy's sad eyes. "Since you're not Chinese. . . ."

"I am."

She peevishly contradicted him, distaste rousing her anger. He closed his eyes and started again.

"Because you're only *half* Chinese and you've been brought up with western values, I don't expect you to understand what I'm going to say."

Lane braced herself for what was coming, straightening her spine, lifting her graceful head high. His words provoked both dread and rage in her.

"Don't you dare condescend."

He scratched his head and began a third time. "Because of five thousand years of Taoist ancestor worship, Chinese are bound by tradition to do as their families say. Confucian ethics stress filial piety, duty, especially for the first-born son."

"What has this history lesson got to do with me?" She did not try to hide her impatience.

He looked into her clouded face, saw the storm brewing

and looked away. "The strongest bond in our culture is between mother and son. It's natural. It's the original relationship, the first a man has. Even when a Chinese man marries, his loyalty's expected to remain with his mother. Besides being the eldest son, I'm the *only* son. Because of that, I have a greater responsibility toward my mother than most. I can't forget my duty."

He looked into Lane's wide green eyes and flinched at the unspoken malice he saw. He paused and took a deep breath, as if he did not have the energy to continue. Then swallowing, he persevered.

"My mother's friend is Mei-ling's matchmaker. She believes Mei-ling and I agreed to marry and, in effect, *are* married." The volume of his voice increased. "We aren't, I swear!" Then he returned to a weary whisper. "We had . . . an affair, but it wasn't a marriage, and there never were any papers or promises. Still Mei-ling's convinced my mother that she's my wife, my pregnant wife. And I have to respect my mother's wishes when. . . ."

"Just like that, huh?" Lane snorted and snapped her fingers. "You're going to let that, that . . . *xiaojie* . . . come in here and ruin our lives?! And you're not so much as raising your *voice* to stop it?"

His moist eyes pleaded with hers. "Lane, I asked my mother for time to . . . to resolve this problem. . . ."

*"Ask?"*

She shook her head, not believing the weak logic she heard. Because his eyes could not meet hers, he focused on his hands.

"She . . . my mother . . . has threatened suicide if we announce our engagement."

"What?!"

Lane could not believe the irrationality of the threat. He

felt miserable but could think of no other plan than to simply repeat what had been said. Still concentrating on his hands, he rubbed them together slowly as if warming them.

"My mother's friend told her you're a 'scheming foreign devil.' Now my mother won't listen to reason. Since she believes I'm already wed to a Taiwanese with a baby on the way, she won't let me disgrace the family by marrying you."

Lane looked at him with loathing as she spoke. "Maybe my father's right. Maybe you are a coward hiding behind women's skirts: hers," she pointed to Mei-ling, "and your mother's. Are you a man or a mama's boy?!"

"She said you wouldn't understand." He shook his head, slowly raising his eyes to meet Lane's. Then snickering, he answered in a monotone. "My mother was right. It's no secret she objected to our marriage, but she yielded to my love for you. Now she doesn't know what to believe. She's sick. Tonight's events have been a shock to her. I'm sorry for causing you pain, but I have to think of my mother's health. I can't ignore her wishes. Until this is resolved, she won't consent to our marriage. You'll have to be patient."

Speechless, like a great beast gathering its might before attacking, Lane lifted herself to her full stature. Then marshaling her forces, she spoke with cool authority, her voice low, intense.

"How old are you? Twenty-eight or eight? Get out of here before your weakness infects me, too." She stared at him with rage-blinded eyes. Then glimpsing the three women staring back scornfully, she sneered at him. "Take your *skirts* and hide behind them. Just get out of my sight!"

Wordlessly he turned and joined his family. As he walked away, his mother leaned heavily on his arm. The other two women dogged his heels.

Though Lane closed her eyes against the sight, his echoing

footsteps danced a tango with her pulse. Time crept forward frame by frame, like a movie reel in slow motion or stop-frame animation. Before he had reached the doorway, she made her decision.

"Wait!" she called.

Like pausing a tape, the scene froze. Action suspended.

In that instant, Chen looked from daughter to father, reminded of MacKenzie's words at their introduction six months earlier.

"Wait!" The perspiring trade-development aide hurried down the steps, two at a time. Though out of breath, he struggled not to wheeze. Mopping his brow, he controlled his breathing. "Senator, I'd like you to meet Macao's chief delegate in the Sino-North American trade coalition, Chen Da-wei."

"David Chen," he corrected, extending his hand.

The grip firm enough to impress a foreigner, the inevitable gold Rolex hung slack at his wrist, Asian style. Like Hong Kong itself, he was a blend of east and west. His smile as congenial as shrewd, it was ruthless in its intensity.

MacKenzie brayed in his profundo basso southern drawl. His gold tooth glinted from his practiced smile, even as his eyes lit up with dollar signs. Pumping Chen's hand with his right arm, he clapped him on the shoulder with his left.

"So you're the man heading the commission," said MacKenzie. "I've heard mighty fine things about y'all. Mighty fine."

Standing on the steps of the Hong Kong Convention and Exhibition Centre in the Wan Chai District, the two men regarded each other. Each assessed what he could gain before the afternoon conference began.

"Perhaps you'd join me for lunch, Senator?"

"Fine idea." Still clapping him on the back, MacKenzie dismissed his car. Chen's limo immediately pulled up, so glossy it repelled dust. The aide slunk away unnoticed.

"So, Senator. . . ."

"Mac," he said, settling onto the plush leather seats.

"What's your long-term prediction for the PRC's economy?" asked the Asian. "Supercharged growth or hyper-inflation?"

"The ROC's growing at a slower rate, but the GDP. . . ."

"No, the PRC, not the ROC."

"Which is which again?" Grimacing, MacKenzie scratched the back of his head.

"The PRC's the Communist mainland," said Chen. "The ROC's Taiwan, the island Chiang Kai-shek fled to in '49 with China's gold reserves. Taiwan considers itself the capital of China, while the mainland still thinks of it as a renegade province."

Nodding in recognition, MacKenzie chuckled. "Called it Formosa when I was in school. All those Made-in-Taiwan labels changed that. My wife's family hailed from Taiwan, you know."

Chen smiled politely. *I know.*

Recalling past marital squabbles, MacKenzie grimaced. "Damn! It used to stick in her craw, but I never could keep all those letters straight: PRC, PC, ROK, ROC. They all sound the same."

"Think of people," Chen said. "The *People's* Republic of China is the mainland. The Republic of China is Taiwan. Remember, at one and a quarter billion versus twenty-one million, there are more *people* on the mainland than the island."

Chen answered patiently, aware most foreigners confused the acronyms, not to mention the governments. Eastern history wasn't taught in western schools. Although, he grudgingly conceded, even China had conveniently avoided teaching history recently. How could the Party justify its mistakes?

Eager to get on with business, the senator cut short the explanation. He leaned closer, speaking in confidential tones. "Y'all asked my prediction for the PRC's economy. The way I see it, unparalleled growth. After 1999 when Macao reverts to China, the PRC can ride its shirttails into all the foreign markets. That's why I'm here. Any deal made *now* between Macao, Taiwan, Mexico and the US will automatically grandfather in China. Damn right, it will!"

He bobbed his head to make his point. Chen watched him thoughtfully, his index finger stroking his nose. Not wanting to appear eager, he prudently let the senator court him.

"Sounds almost too good," said Chen. "What's the catch?"

Misreading the ploy, MacKenzie wondered why an Asian would be so direct. An uneasy chuckle covered his confusion. "No catch, just a little friendly horse-trading."

"Such as?"

"Using top-grade US cowhide for all shoes and leather goods made in Guangdong's factories. Fine leather at a fair price, now that's a bargain." MacKenzie ran his hand along the limo's upholstery. "What'd be the harm? None, other than generating revenue for my state. And with foreign-trade dollars coming into the state, my constituents would back my decision to lobby for this trade agreement."

"Then your support's conditional?"

"I wouldn't call it that." MacKenzie flinched. "Let me give y'all another example. . . ."

"Just a moment, Senator." Chen interrupted as the car stopped in front of a glass and steel structure. "This is the Hopewell Centre. Ever eat in the Revolving 66 restaurant?"

He shook his head. "But as long as it's got steak, it's fine with me."

"It serves western cuisine," Chen said, hiding a smile, "though the beef's more likely to be Australian than USDA."

"Now there's another example. Reciprocation. Mutual reciprocation. Macao buys US beef; my state lobbies for a trade agreement. Beef and leather for better access to American markets with reduced tariffs and duties."

"What do you want out of this personally, Senator?"

That elicited an embarrassed guffaw. Hedging, MacKenzie chuckled as the chauffeur opened the door. "Why don't we discuss that over a friendly bourbon?"

They settled into a booth along the glass-enclosed wall. As the dining room revolved slowly, Chen pointed out the local sights. "It's just coming into view now. Down and to your right is Queen's Road East. Beyond that is the Hung Shing Temple, built over a hundred years ago to the sea god. . . ."

MacKenzie murmured politely as he craned his neck. Then interest waning, he interrupted, impatiently ending the tour. "Now what were y'all asking me before, Chen?"

"The Chinese call it *guanxi*. I believe you call it political contributions." He rubbed the side of his nose, never pausing. "What is it you want?"

"Like the bride said to the wedding guest. 'Any gift's good, as long as the color's green.' "

Chen smiled distractedly, getting an idea.

MacKenzie's words still echoing in his inner ear, Chen returned to the present. His eyes focused on Lane, terrifying in her proud fury.

"Just a minute!" she called to Li's retreating back. "I'm ready to announce the engagement." Then she turned to Chen, her eyes meeting his defiantly. *"Ours."*

She stood very straight, her arm crooked, holding out her elbow to him. Chen rallied to her like a campaign volunteer to a candidate, while MacKenzie took her other arm.

Li faltered in his stride but kept walking. He never looked back, even as they pushed past him and his female entourage and strode out the office, through the reception hall. Taking command of the situation, Chen motioned his aide to have the car brought around.

Once in the limo, Lane said, "I don't care what you say or do to get us through tonight. Let's just get this travesty over with." Then dry-eyed, she stared glumly out the window as her father and Chen planned the event.

"You'll need rings," MacKenzie said, "for effect."

Agreeing with a nod, Chen became a man of action. "And traditional gifts, at least six of them. They're expected." He rolled down the window separating the passengers from the driver and addressed his aide. "When we get to the Grand Hotel, buy two wedding rings, four necklaces and three bracelets from the jewelry shop."

"What kind?" the man asked, his expression bland.

"The best." Chen turned toward Lane. Referring to the 24k, bright yellow gold, he asked, "Do you like Taiwanese gold?"

She shrugged.

"Buy *jin* and get a glass-topped cash box. Transfer *san bai wan,* three million New Taiwan dollars, into cash. Bundle the money in thirty stacks of a hundred and arrange it in the box." Chen turned to MacKenzie. "Bride money," he said by way of explanation.

"It ain't necessary." MacKenzie went through the motions of a polite refusal but, as was his habit, lost gracefully.

"Ah, but it is," said Chen. "It's the custom. This will reassure the guests about our announcement."

Though Chen was magnanimous, the corners of his mouth lifted in a calculating smile. Then he paused, hand on chin, watching the senator thoughtfully, his index finger stroking his nose.

"Traditionally the money's returned after the ceremony. It's only for display, although there *are* instances when the bride's family keeps it." Chen paused deliberately. "Have you gifts for the guests?"

"Gifts?" His expression remote, the senator peered blandly from under heavy lids. Whether from daydreaming or ignorance of local habit, he looked puzzled.

Chen smiled as he cocked his head toward him. "Another Chinese custom. Each guest takes home a special box of cookies, the more elaborate, the better. How many should we order?"

"Four hundred invitations werc sent," said MacKenzie, "but is this expense *necessary?*"

Chen pursed his lips, hiding his irritation at the miserliness, and spoke to his aide. "Add them to my account. Then see that the hotel delivers them to the banquet room."

Lane barely heard the rushed plans, she was trying so hard to make sense of the events. Half of her wanted to jump out of the limo and call Li, let him convince her it *was* all a misunderstanding. The other half drifted through a fog, sometimes plotting revenge, other times imagining a lonely future, but always wondering how far to let her father and Chen take the night's performance.

Despite the holiday traffic, Lane thought they arrived at the Grand Hotel in record time, until she looked at her watch. An hour? It had seemed like fifteen minutes. Still it had allowed her father and Chen to work out a plausible plan. All she had to do was keep a smile stamped on her lips as if imprinted by a name chop.

As she struggled with her tight skirt getting out the car-door, Chen caught her arm. His smile was genuine, and she rewarded him a surprised, grateful smile. Encouraged, he whispered reassurance.

"Don't worry, I won't let you fall. Everyone slips up now and then, especially in an unfamiliar culture."

His words punctured her armor, and like blood gushing from a wound, her pent-up feelings rushed to the surface. Overwhelmed that someone understood, she suddenly felt simpatico with him and nodded enthusiastically.

"It's true, no matter *what* I do."

Her eyes dewy, she blinked quickly, afraid her carefully governed emotions would erupt at the slightest show of human compassion.

"Coming from Macao," he said, "I know how difficult it is to blend East and West, the oriental and the occidental. Especially when both coexist in such a delightful body."

His eyes met hers, swept across her face, then traveled down her neckline, lingering on her white breasts. When his eyes rose again, they leered.

She gasped at the abrupt change from his sincere persona to his former character. Enraged with herself for almost believing him, her eyes narrowed like a stalking cat's.

"Don't try to con me, Chen. I appreciate your getting me through tonight, but remember, that's all it is: for *tonight*." She scowled as she caught a calculating glint in his eyes. Her green eyes, now dry as gunpowder, blazed with renewed hostility. "Don't expect gratitude. I don't have any illusions about your charity. Nothing's for nothing. You have your own reasons for helping my father and me. I don't know or care what they are, but for tonight they serve my purposes as well as yours. Let's just get this over with."

As she walked boldly into the banquet hall, leaving him a

step behind, she heard his dark laughter float on the wind. Catching up, he took her arm, his touch domineering.

"Bravo! I see you recover quickly." Then he began speaking and bowing graciously to both sides as they passed through the crowd. "Hello, *ni hao,* hello."

She played her part, smiling brightly, nodding as though the man at her side had been her fiancé all along. *Just do it, don't think,* she told herself. Speaking automatically to the guests, Lane looked for relatives of Li's but didn't recognize any.

"Hello, thanks for coming, good to see you," she recited. "Good evening, glad you could come."

She kept up her act so convincingly, Chen asked tongue-in-cheek, "Happy?"

"Thank you for com. . . ." Then under her breath she hissed sarcastically, "Ecstatic."

Once more all smiles, she continued greeting the guests as they crossed the elegant dining room filled with round, lazy-susan tables. When they reached the head table near the dais, they sat next to each other, actors still in character. Her father climbed on stage and used the same speech he had prepared for her and Li, ad-libbing personalized details like the consummate politician he was. They nodded and smiled on cue as if his anecdotes were true.

Dinner was served in traditional Chinese style: legions of platters and tureens placed on the revolving centers of the tables, people helping themselves with chopsticks. As the dishes emptied, waiters replaced them with more local favorites—Buddha-jumps-the-wall, three-cup chicken, *tantze* noodles, minced shrimp wrapped in lettuce, sweet-and-sour soup, and ending with *hongshao yu,* braised fish.

"For luck," Chen explained. "Fish is a symbol of abundance and wealth."

Lane barely tasted the fare, only going through the motions of sampling the various foods. Still when Chen tried to engage her in conversation, she always managed to have too full a mouth to answer. She smiled cordially, congratulating herself on her tact, until he made an announcement.

Pushing back his chair, Chen stood and offered Lane a wineglass. He called everyone's attention, then formally raised his glass with both hands.

"To the woman who will grace my house, the future mother of my children. To Chen *Taitai!*"

"Isn't that premature?" she whispered under her strained smile.

But smiling with eyes bold and self-assured, he ignored her words. "It's customary to toast everyone's health, table by table." In a patronizing tone, he added, "Women usually drink tea."

She heard it as a challenge. Tossing her head scornfully, she refilled her glass with rice wine. "Ready when you are."

None too gently, he took her by the hand and led her to the neighboring table. The eight people stopped eating and stood.

"To your health." Chen raised his glass to the group with both hands. Lane quickly followed suit, and the eight saluted respectfully with their raised glasses and good wishes.

All went well for the first four tables, Lane merely sipping at each toast. But a group of businessmen sat at the fifth table.

*"Ganbei!"* they toasted, laughing.

Lane licked her lips nervously, trying to think of a way out, when Chen goaded her. "Bottoms up!"

Staring him in the eye, she tossed down the drink, remembering that at 44 proof, it was closer to liquor than wine. She immediately felt flushed, her temples damp with perspiration. But she took a deep breath, laughed and held out her glass for a refill. The businessmen cheered.

By the end of the rounds, Lane felt relaxed and oblivious to the night's turn of events. *All's going amazingly well,* she thought, giving Chen a congratulatory smile that he more than returned.

Taking her hand possessively in his, he led her to the raised platform, then told his aide to bring a chair and the gifts. He beckoned MacKenzie with a crooked finger, body language used in Taiwan only for calling dogs and small children, and her father hurried on-stage, ignorant of the subtle insult. Chen spoke into the microphone as a person used to public speaking. He addressed the audience articulately, first in English, then in Mandarin.

"The senator has graciously consented to give me his daughter in marriage. Now let me give my future bride a token of my affection."

Offering his hand, he helped her onto the gilt chair. He motioned his aide to approach, then taking one of the red velvet jewelry boxes from him, opened it and held up a heavy chain of Taiwanese gold. The audience murmured approvingly. After he clasped it around her neck, his aide handed him another gold-embroidered red box. Chen opened it, took out a wider, yellow gold necklace with a jade pendant and placed that on his bride's neck, whispering as he leaned over her.

"They set off your green eyes, shining almost as brightly."

Feeling languidly detached from the scene, almost giddy, she put her hand to her throat to touch the jewelry. Three more times his aide handed him a red box, and he lifted out gold bracelets which he fastened onto her wrists. Endorsement at a price, the audience reaction strengthened with each piece of gold: the more *jin,* the more approval. Chen gestured to his aide to hand MacKenzie a gold velvet box.

"Give that to your daughter," he whispered. "It's her gift to me."

The senator did as directed. Feeling flustered, Lane rose, opened the box and lifted out a heavy gold chain. Chen leaned over to make his neck more accessible.

"You must put it on me."

Still the only way for her to reach was to place both arms around his neck. Uncomfortable at the nearness, her hands fumbled, and she had trouble latching it. Chen covered her hands with his.

"Let me help."

She quickly pulled her arms down and stepped back. He chuckled as he secured the chain, then took the last red box from his aid. When he opened it, Lane gasped at the enormous emerald ring in a setting of baguette diamonds. She squirmed uncomfortably as he tried it on her delicate ring finger. Then when he found the ring too large, he slipped it on her middle finger.

"We'll have it sized."

He whispered so close to her face, she could smell the *jiu* on his breath. She pulled away.

"Don't bother. I'm returning it tonight!"

Plainly unconvinced, he smiled shrewdly. Chen turned to her father.

"If you'll take the gold box and hand it to your daughter, she can place her ring on my hand." He smiled magnanimously. "Then we're officially engaged."

"Uh, Chen, you understand this . . . er . . . arrangement *is* only for tonight."

Chen looked baffled. He gestured to the guests. "Why, Senator, you puzzle me. You wanted them to see an engagement, didn't you?"

"Keep your voice down. Of course I do, but only temporarily." MacKenzie's forehead wrinkled uneasily.

"It's for as long as you like." Chen looked at him evenly. Before MacKenzie could pursue the subject, Chen turned to Lane. "I'm anxious to see your ring, then I can give your father the bride money." Again he turned his gaze to MacKenzie and watched him closely.

"Chen," she began.

"David," he urged, turning back to her. "We're engaged now."

*"Chen,"* she stressed, "tonight this farce ends. Is that clear?"

As he stared, she felt his control blandly begin to strangle her, like the delicate tendrils of morning glories, lightly coiling and entwining until they choke vying plants. She swallowed and set her jaw more firmly, but his hypnotic eyes subdued her into silence. Finally he spoke, breaking the spell.

"The guests are waiting. Put your ring on my finger."

Realizing she still had a role to perform, she opened the box, pretending to go through the motions. Her lips pressed together primly. Lane tried to place the gold band on his right hand, but he presented her his left instead. Not wanting to cause a scene, she gave in. He looked at her, at his ring, then made an announcement.

"After the bride money, the engagement's complete."

Before Lane had a chance to retort, Chen's aide presented her father with a glass-topped box stuffed with thousand-dollar bills.

"Three million NT," Chen boasted, and the audience applauded.

Ever the politician, MacKenzie raised the red-lacquered box over his head, so the guests at the back could see. Then a gleam sparkled in his eyes.

"Of course I understand this is just for appearances. But how much is that in US dollars?"

"At the current rate of exchange, about a hundred and twenty thousand."

MacKenzie's eyes widened. Timing his response like an angler playing his fish, Chen smiled slowly.

"It isn't necessary to return the bride money, Senator. After all, we're *practically* family," he paused, "and there is another matter I'd like to discuss about the trade agreement."

As their eyes met knowingly, MacKenzie shook hands with Chen.

"I've had enough of this pretense," Lane said.

Mortified, she turned away from their satisfied faces, stifling the urge to scream. Instead she politely excused her way through the crowded room, plotting escape. When she saw Chen send his aide after her, she hurried into the relative freedom of the ladies' room.

"Lane!"

She turned and saw Iris following her. "What's wrong?"

The consulate's secretary smiled, small muscles twitching nervously. She clasped Lane's hand. "Li call."

Lane caught her breath. Poised between shrugging it off and begging for details, she whispered lamely, "What did he say?"

"He at hospital. He. . . ."

"What?!" Lane pulled her hand away, accidentally scratching Iris with her ring. "What happened to him? Which hospital?"

"No, no. She . . . *he* not hurt." Iris struggled with her pronouns while Lane glared impatiently. "It her . . . *his* mother. He had heart attack. He . . . *she* at Liming hospital."

"Who? His mother?"

The girl nodded.

Frustrated at her friend's limited English, Lane first had to confirm the patient's identity. When she realized it was Li's mother, she digested the news, surmising his guilt. She knew he would blame himself. Or her.

"Did he say anything else?"

*"Jiang xin bi xin."*

Lane chafed, waiting for the translation. Seeing her expression, Iris quickly explained.

"Confucian saying. Imagine my heart yours."

"Something like, 'Put yourself in my shoes.' " As Lane smiled wryly, contemplating, an old woman in a purple *qipao* with side slits pushed open the door. Instead of going toward the stalls, she stopped and spoke to Iris in Chinese.

Annoyed at the interruption, Lane stood by, wondering if the matron knew how strange her jet-black hair looked against her parchment skin. Then she remembered that Li's mother vainly dyed her hair black, too. "To save face," Li had explained.

Iris turned to Lane and reluctantly began translating while the woman continued to speak. Flustered, the girl confused her pronouns even more.

"Her . . . *she* say she Chen Rong, aunt of your husband. He. . . ."

"Chen's not my husband." Lane smiled stiffly. Then she bit her lip and changed her wording. "Chen hasn't told me he has an aunt."

"Chen Rong help you do family duty."

"Tell her thanks, but no thanks. It isn't necessary."

Through Iris' translation, Chen Rong remained adamant. "She say your husband be anger."

Lane's eyes widened in exasperation. Trying to be polite, she gritted her teeth. "I'm not married. I don't *need* help with any duties to my in-laws because I don't have any." When

Iris' puppy-sad eyes reproached her, she relented. "No husband, so no husband's family."

Iris translated, but such a long discussion ensued, Lane left them to find Chen. As soon as she stepped into the hall, she spied his aide following her.

Her cheeks flushed with rage, she raced through the banquet room of well-wishers. She dimly noted the mountain of red shopping bags, each the size of a briefcase, containing a gift-wrapped box of cookies. When Chen saw her approach, he rose from the table where he was talking with her father over rice wine.

"And here's the blushing bride," said Chen.

"What does your aunt mean about my performing *duties* for my 'husband's' family? Just what kind of tricks should I perform? Jump through hoops? Roll over? Play dead?"

Her face a sarcastic moue, she poured herself a glass of rice wine and downed it. "This charade has gone far enough. I don't know what your game is, but it's over as of *now*." She banged the glass on the table for emphasis.

"Lane, you're not used to liquor. Sit down. Wait 'til the guests leave. We'll discuss this later."

MacKenzie flashed his confidence-inspiring smile and expected to win her vote of approval, just as he had his constituents'. Chen dismissed the incident with a wave of his hand.

"My aunt Chen Rong means well," said Chen, "but she doesn't understand. Please." Pulling out a chair for her, he motioned politely.

She studied his face intently. At last she sat to keep up appearances. "All right," she said, "but don't think this parody will last beyond tonight."

Chen poured her another drink as his eyes met her father's. MacKenzie took his cue.

"Lane, people will talk if y'all break off your engagement too soon."

"This isn't an engagement! It's an act of desperation." Her anger ignited like a roman candle.

Surrendering, her father held up his arms. "I agree, but all I'm saying is don't do anything rash. In fact, don't do anything at all. Chen's going to the mainland for three weeks. Just wear the ring. When he comes back, you can quietly return it."

"And what about these?" she asked sarcastically, touching her necklaces.

Chen looked at the graceful hand at her breast. "Please keep them as a small consolation for tonight's . . . turn of events."

"Here, take your bribes. I'm not interested!"

As she began unclasping them, her father looked around apprehensively. "Lane! Put those back on. Y'all want everyone to see?"

"That's all that's important to you, isn't it?!"

Slapping the gold necklaces on the table, she rose and turned to leave. At Chen's bidding, his aide blocked the way, intercepting her sidesteps as if performing a dance.

"Where y'all going?" Her father's eyes squinted with suspicion.

"To see a sick friend." Corralled, she faced him in an angry standoff. Then she tried to push past the aide.

MacKenzie rose and grabbed her by the wrist. "Y'all fixing to see that two-timing mamma's boy? Sit down 'fore y'all make a scene!"

With a placating smile, Chen tried to make peace. "Senator, this has been a difficult night for your daughter. She needs rest." He addressed his aide. "Take them home in my car."

"But we haven't finished discussing. . . ."

Chen silenced the senator with an upraised hand. His mouth curling in a crooked smile, his narrow eyes implied more than he stated.

"Your daughter's welfare's more important. Take *care* of her. We'll finish our talk when I return."

MacKenzie forced a smile and pulled Chen aside. "I'll keep an eye on her. We wouldn't want the chicken flying the coop now, would we? The deal stands?" He watched expectantly.

"You may not have noticed, Senator, but your daughter's a crane among chickens."

MacKenzie blanched, wondering if he had blundered. Then, the gold Rolex gleaming at his cuff, Chen slowly held out his hand. Relieved, MacKenzie wrung it firmly.

Chen turned to Lane, his bearing changing from imperious to formally gallant. With an affected bow, he leaned forward, his eyes sparkling merrily.

"Until next time."

She glanced contemptuously first at him, then at her father before she stomped away. Laughing, Chen reached for the gold necklaces and held them up.

"She forgot these."

"Lane's got a mind of her own," MacKenzie said, "but she'll come 'round. I'll talk some horse sense into her."

"Do that."

Chen tossed the necklaces on the lacquered money box, gesturing for his aide to carry it. Then the man herded Lane and MacKenzie into Chen's car. Before the limo's door had closed, she turned on her father.

"What's the matter with you?" she asked. "Can't you see what's happening? Are you so greedy you'd sell your own daughter like the aborigines? Maybe I should worry about ending up on *Huahsi* Street as a hooker."

"I'll ignore those remarks since you're distressed."

Her inflammatory speech fanned the fury he felt toward himself until it included her. As MacKenzie struggled to control his anger, she stared at him contemptuously, old wounds festering, her eyes hardening. The rice wine added to her fire.

"Distressed?! Your actions tonight were humiliating, galling! What name should I give your 'offering' me to Chen? Fatherly concern? Love? Or avarice?!"

Her words burned into his conscience like a branding iron. He was disgusted with himself, but he wouldn't take that tone from his daughter. Not thinking beyond stopping her words, he slapped her face.

She gasped. Only a red welt colored her enraged, white lips. Then an angry scarlet spread to her cheeks. In her silence, hatred was born.

The driver looked in the rearview mirror. Riding shotgun, the aide watched out of the corner of his eye, but neither moved. Their interest was idle curiosity, nothing more.

But compounded by her antipathy, MacKenzie misread it as silent reproach. He self-consciously adjusted his lapel, his collar, his bow tie. To ease his frustration, he finally resorted to shouting at her.

"What?! What y'all want? An apology?"

Her cold stare above her hot cheeks confronted him more eloquently than words.

Her unleashed autonomy was a blow to his arrogance. Changing tactics, he appealed to her vanity.

"Lane, I was only thinking of your welfare. Anyone else'd give her eye-teeth to be Chen's wife. He's a man of position, someone who can give y'all the finer things in life, the things y'all deserve."

Her silent scorn called for another tact. He clutched the

lacquered box neurotically as he suggested a compromise.

"All right, I went too far. Of course y'all don't have to *marry* him. Just stay engaged, string him along 'til after the trade agreement's signed."

He chuckled nervously, waiting for a response. When there was none, he tried a new vein: guilt.

"After all he's done tonight for us, for *you,* you can't insult the man. Just keep his ring 'til after the agreement. Lane, please."

She continued to stare defiantly. Depleted of alternatives, he begged.

"If you won't do it for yourself, then do it for me. If I don't pull this trade agreement off, I'll . . . I'm . . . I don't know what I'll do! *Please.*"

Unable to meet her eyes, he looked away, defeated.

After they arrived home, she went straight to her room, locked the door and called the hospital. While she struggled through a series of non-English-speaking receptionists, MacKenzie questioned the housekeeper.

"Any calls?"

The Filipino kept her eyes down submissively, hoping her bearing would earn her a ticket to the States when MacKenzie returned. Though a university graduate with a degree in psychology, she equated financial security with a green card.

"Yes, sir. Three."

"Who?" He lightly stroked the money box.

"Mr. Yang."

MacKenzie cursed through gritted teeth, frightening the woman. "Don't take another call from that jackass, y'hear?!"

"No, sir. Yes, sir!" She swallowed and blinked.

When MacKenzie saw his effect on her, he continued in a

gentler tone. "If he calls again, tell him my daughter's not here, y'all got that?"

"Yes, sir." She nodded, her right eye twitching.

The woman's subservience soothed his crushed ego, his battered conscience. He took a deep breath of relief, feeling almost pleased with the night's turn of events. Then he remembered his daughter's eyes, as sharp as green diamond slivers.

"Let's just keep this between us," he said. "Don't tell Lane!"

Fidgeting with the loose ring, Lane slipped it on and off her finger as she tried to find a hospital operator who spoke English. "What room is Mrs. Yang in? I mean Yang *Taitai.*"

"She ill. Cannot speak."

"No, I want to speak to her son," said Lane. "Can you take a message?"

"Massage?"

Lane's eyebrows formed a *V* of frustration at the girl's doubtful tone. Sighing, she struggled to give her phone number in Chinese. "No, a message. Tell him to call me at this number. Thank you."

She hung up feeling forlorn and lonely. Nothing isolates as much as language. Then she unzipped her dress, letting it lay where it fell. This was the dress made for her. This was the gown she had worn through hours of dull fittings, indifferent to the pin-pricks and tedium only by imagining her future with Li. Now it laid crumpled in a satin heap. As crushed as its velvet trim, she sat in the gloom, morosely waiting for his call.

The phone rang, waking her.

Dazed, she wondered what time it was. She squinted at the morning light, then heard Pearl answer the phone. Looking at the clock, she jumped out of the chair. Nine o'clock! She was late for work. Then she remembered, Li had not called. Li! She called through the door.

"Pearl, who's on the phone?"

"Wrong number," floated back to her.

Lane slumped down in the chair again. Dejected, she dialed the hospital and again tried to leave a message. She called Li's home, but a stranger answered, and she ran into the same language barrier. Rather than sit around waiting for him to return the call, she decided to splash water on her face and go to work. He knew her office extension.

"Congratulations!"

She gasped. The consulate staff was waiting at her desk. Iris handed her a magnificent bouquet of calla lilies, pink roses and orchids, and Lane inhaled deeply.

"Oh, they're gorgeous! Thank you! What are they for?"

The staff looked at one another.

"What are they for?" asked a confused clerk. "Your engagement, of course."

Lane blinked. In her rush to get to work, she hadn't had time to consider the consequences of her charade. Embarrassed, she put her hand to her head and laughed.

"Of course. What was I thinking?"

"Let me see your ring."

As another of the clerks picked up her hand, Lane tried pulling it back. Never having decided whether to leave it on or off the night before, she had forgotten about it in the morning's rush.

A young secretary sighed longingly. "Ohhhhh! It's so *big!*"

Lane looked at her hand and saw the ring was indeed still on her finger. She drew in her breath sharply. Wittingly or not, she was playing along with her father's scheme. Seething, she promised herself to call Li at work and get to the bottom of things. But Iris interrupted her thoughts, pulling her to the file cabinet, proudly showing her a frothy, whipped-cream cake decorated with kiwi fruit.

"Look! Taro, your favorite."

Lane faked a smile, knowing it would be an hour before she could call Li.

When the last crumb of cake was finished and the flowers had been placed in water, the consulate's staff finally left Lane to herself. She waited until they closed the door, then dialed Li's office. Instead of his voice, an unfamiliar one answered.

"No, I'm sorry. Mr. Yang isn't in today. His mother's ill." The tone indifferent, it asked, "Can I take a message?"

"Yes, would you have him call Ms. MacKenzie at 874. . . ."

"Oh, Miss MacKenzie!" The voice rose an octave, jumping to attention. "Mr. Chen said to put you right through. One moment, please."

Before Lane could reply, she heard Chen speaking.

"Good morning. What a pleasant surprise to hear from you so soon!"

The urge to hang up was strong. Debating, she held the receiver halfway to the phone's cradle. Chen's voice sounded tinny through the distance, like cicadas. Then the door opened, and Iris walked in for a file, interfering with her plan to hang up. Irritated, Lane held the receiver to her ear.

"Since I'll be gone for three weeks," he said, "I thought we could have lunch before my flight leaves this afternoon. How does 1:00 sound?"

"Sorry, I'm meeting a friend. Have a good trip."

Chen was the last person she wanted to see. Before he could answer, she replaced the receiver.

When Li did not call the first day, she chalked it up to his having a lot on his mind. But when he had not called by the second day, despite her many messages, she realized their relationship was over. The third day passed quietly, then another and another. Unable to tolerate their misguided well-wishing, she avoided her colleagues. At home she kept to herself, ignoring her father's constant endorsement of Chen. She only left her room for consulate business. Not until Chiang Kai-shek's birthday dawned three weeks later did she socialize, and then only because she had to join the rest of the diplomatic community in paying her respects.

The sky was a typically drab gray, made even drearier by the limo's tinted windows. The first half hour of the drive took Lane and Iris over an eight-lane highway as they sped toward *Taoyuan,* but the fast pace ended abruptly when they met with bumper-to-bumper traffic in *Tahsi.* Iris smiled while their car crept through the narrow lane masquerading as the town's main street.

"See swallow roof? *Tahsi* have very much Chinese building."

Lane listlessly noted the turn-of-the-century architectural styles.

"And best *to-gan.* Have you try?"

"What is it?"

"Tofu," said Iris. "Want to try?"

"Why not? At this pace, we won't even lose time."

Lane grimly noted the non-stop stream of cars, busses, trucks, motor scooters, bicycles, baby-carriages and vendors' carts. Clearing her throat, she breathed through her mouth. The exhaust fumes were so thick, the air was murky. Even with the windows up, the pollution irritated her throat.

They stopped at one of the many small shops and bought dark squares ladled up from a steaming cauldron's vile brew. The shopkeeper sliced the tofu into bite-sized pieces and tossed them in a plastic bag with fresh *jiu-chen-ta,* basil. Spearing the dark-skinned tofu with bamboo picks, the two girls munched on the soft snacks as the car crawled through traffic.

Despite the tortoise pace, they finally arrived at *Tzuhu*, Chiang Kai-shek's tomb at Lake Mercy. Walking through a bamboo grove, they passed the lake, then stopped to gaze at the black swans and paired Mandarin ducks. Lane's brow puckered thoughtfully.

"Don't they mate for life?"

As they passed beneath rows of acacia trees, plain-clothes men lined every inch of the paths. Immaculately-uniformed soldiers conspicuously carried loaded carbines, visual deterrents to any mischief. Lane spotted a group of soldiers playing ball, then dropping for cover.

"What kind of game is that?"

Iris glanced at the troop and shrugged her shoulders. "They practice."

"Practice what?"

"Toss hand grenade."

She nonchalantly ambled toward the small formal gardens, while Lane looked behind uneasily, suddenly feeling vulnerable despite the high security. Finally they reached the sky-blue and brown villa. Although the architecture was ornately Chinese, the intricate fretwork's bright Asian colors had been painted over in a Norwegian motif.

As television crews captured the moment, Lane and the others from the envoy paid their respects to the late President of Taiwan. Each nodding formally, they filed past the dark sarcophagus. Then they gathered outside near a Chinese character fashioned from yellow chrysanthemums.

"What does that character mean?"

"Long life," said Iris.

They stood in their own ranks, grouped with their entourages. Lane saw Li out of the corner of her eye but pretended not to notice. Her posture stiffened as she looked for Mei-ling, then relaxed when she noted he was alone. Seeing him for the first time since their broken engagement, it took all her self restraint not to go to him, confront him, touch him, confess she still loved him.

She felt someone's eyes on her and hoped her expressive face was not mirroring her thoughts. Looking around, she glimpsed Chen staring at her while listening to her father. She looked away quickly, grimly wondering when he had returned.

After the memorial service, the diplomatic group turned and began retracing its steps to the cars. Though Iris had been keeping pace with Lane, swarming crowds temporarily separated them. Despite the chaos, they tried to keep up a polite conversation. The secretary pointed to golden mums the size of cheerleaders' pompoms.

"Memory you of home?" asked Iris.

"Yes. How thoughtful of Chiang Kai-shek to be born on Halloween. US kids would love it to be a national holiday!" When there was no answer, Lane spoke louder. "The kids'd love a whole day to trick-or-treat."

"So would I," rumbled a low voice.

"Li!"

"Meet me by the lake. Tell Iris you've made other plans to get home." He talked without looking at her. Before she could answer, he hurried past, never glancing back. She picked up her pace, dodging the dawdling babies and grandmothers.

"Wait!" Iris called.

Lane turned toward her, hoping to cover Li's retreating figure. She faltered only a moment. "I . . . I'm trying to catch Chen. I promised I'd ride back with him."

The crowds closed around her as she scurried from view. Iris shouted to her unsuccessfully, her voice swallowed by the crowd's din. Only Chen followed the scene. His mouth curling in a smile, he radioed the chauffeur. Then he curtly motioned to his aide.

"Don't let her out of your sight."

Lane searched the lake's shoreline but couldn't find Li. In the process, she noticed the mated swans, swimming side by side, their graceful necks bowing and weaving. She saw the Mandarin ducks, the female tucked inside the male's protective wing. Swift as a gunshot, the pain of separation constricted her throat, and she tried to swallow the lump.

Then she spotted Li beneath a willow at the lotus pond's rim, imperceptibly motioning to her to follow. She nodded discreetly, thinking it a good omen. His name, Yang Liu, meant willow tree. Surrounded by the throng of people, she remained hidden on the winding, narrow trail. But as the path widened into a parking lot, Lane panicked, wondering how she would find him, let alone escape unseen.

Suddenly a silver-gray limousine pulled in front. Chen's aide appeared from the crowd, smoothly opened the door and held out his hand to assist her. At the same moment, she heard a warning from behind.

"Watch your step, Lane."

She turned to see Chen. Wondering if he was referring to her balance or something more sinister, she spoke quickly, struggling to keep her smile bland while she glanced about furtively.

"Beautiful park, isn't it?"

"You enjoy Taiwan's scenery?" To her terse nod, Chen gestured politely but firmly for her to get into the car. "Then let me show you the local sights."

"Thank you, but I've other plans." Her smile stiff, she backed away.

Just then Iris darted from the crowd, gasping for air like a relay runner passing the torch. "Lane, your father say to keep near! What you do?"

"She's accepting my offer to visit *Shihmen* Dam, aren't you?" Chen stared solidly into Lane's green eyes.

Flustered, Iris put her hand to her chest in consternation, addressing him first, then Lane. "Oh, Mr. Chen, I not see you. Yes, you say you riding with her . . . *him*. Sorry. *Dui bu xi.*"

Self-conscious, she excused herself, almost bowing in her hurry to escape. Chen smiled at Lane enigmatically as he helped her into the limo, his silver temples glistening in the sunlight.

"You must be clairvoyant," he said. "How did you know we'd meet this afternoon?"

Lane saw Li's car across the parking lot, wondering what his thoughts must be. Normally she would have ridden with him. They would have laughed and talked, planned their future. But now nothing was normal.

"I didn't know, Chen."

"David, please. After all, we are engaged."

"Only as far as others are concerned." She met his eyes arrogantly.

He chuckled and gave his driver instructions in Chinese. The chauffeur drove along winding roads through the ancient mountains and green valleys until they reached a three-tiered, modern cement pagoda. Behind it, Lane saw a dam as Chen began ordering his driver to park.

"Let me show you something," said Chen. "*Shihmen,* Stone Gate Dam."

They walked in awkward silence, Lane deliberately clutching her purse with both hands to avoid brushing against him. As they crossed the dam, he gently touched her shoulder, directing her view above them. Though she flinched and stiffened, he did not seem to notice.

"This is the Triple Dam. See the other two there?"

She murmured *yes* but was not concentrating, instead keenly aware only of her loneliness. The open space intensified her isolation. The wind whipped her hair into her eyes, giving her an excuse to wipe away the tear.

They walked back to the car, his hand gingerly guiding her elbow. After they had driven by the amusement park, they passed under the largest of the three dams, apparently in the path of any spillover. Lane noticed the narrow road hugged the dam, dissecting both its steep wall and the runoff's descent.

"What happens when water flows over this road? Do they close traffic?" Smiling, he shook his head. "Then wouldn't the cars get washed away?" she asked.

"You'll see it better from above," he said, "but the dam slopes upward, like a ski-jump. The water actually *leaps* over the cars as it crosses the road and continues down below."

They scaled the spiraling road in silence. At the crest, Lane marveled at the vistas. To the left, the dam overlooked a meandering stream in the valley far below; to the right, steep mountains plunged into a chasm. They parked and climbed to the peak's breezy overlook. To steady her on the final wind-swept steps, he caught her hand. She held on, shouting close to his ear, afraid the gusting winds would drown out her voice.

"It's breathtaking."

Smiling, he kept her hand in his. When they had descended, he turned to her.

"Hungry?"

At her nod, he led her back to a restaurant overlooking the 'ski-jump' dam. As they split a liter-sized bottle of Taiwan beer, Chen showed how the dam's angulation caused the water to jump up and over the road.

"This way the runoff flows uninterrupted, yet traffic can pass through," he explained. "Clever design, isn't it?"

"I wonder if motorcyclists get wet?" The mental image amusing her, she grinned without realizing it. As he watched, his own face relaxed.

"It's good to see you do that."

"Do what?" Her large green eyes opened wider.

"Smile." He caught her hand between his, fingering her ring. "It's been three weeks since I've seen you, since. . . ."

"Just . . . don't." She withdrew her hand and bit her lower lip.

"Lane, I've been thinking." As her eyes warned him off, his appealed to hers. "This temporary pact could be more. Have you ever considered marrying an older man?"

"Be serious, Chen—David." Irritated when she saw him gesture, she corrected herself. Then she rose from the table. "I don't know you, and I still don't know your game. But you've got one. I can smell it."

"Lane, hear me out. That's all I ask. Please."

He gestured to the chair politely, but with a certain authority. She sighed, knowing she couldn't leave the dam site without him. Until Chen informed his driver in Mandarin, she was a captive audience. So tentatively perching on the chair's edge, she laid the ground rules.

"All right, but give me credit for some intelligence. I'm not a simple-minded bimbo."

"Point taken. But there's nothing devious in my proposal." He smiled disarmingly, his dark eyes looking at her with open admiration. "You're a very beautiful woman, *intelligent. . . .*"

As he bent forward in a slight bow, her emerald green eyes glittered with a hardness second only to diamonds.

"Don't patronize me," she snapped. "What do you want?"

"And finding myself attracted to you, I want to get to know you." He finished as if she hadn't interrupted, not missing a beat, the glow in his eyes not dimming. "What's the expression? We got off to a bad start. Hello. My name's David." Then he extended his hand.

She shook hands automatically, feeling the pink patches crawl across her cheeks, wondering if she had judged him too quickly. Just then the waitress brought a large platter of sizzling shrimp, and as Lane dealt with her confusion he seized the moment.

"Try these."

He unwrapped her chopsticks and handed them to her, his eyes dancing in the sunlight. Sunlight? She looked out the window. The clouds were sweeping across the horizon, blue sky shining through. Such a change!

She warily accepted the chopsticks. Having started out a fire-eater, she found herself eating her own words instead.

"Sorry, I wasn't thinking. . . ."

"You can't think on an empty stomach!" He waved off her apology.

Eyelashes fluttering, her lips formed a shy smile. She half dreaded, half welcomed an excuse to stay.

"All right, but I really should get back soon."

"Whenever you say. Here, try shrimp the Chinese way."

He lifted one with his chopsticks, then popped it in his mouth, head, shell, tentacles and all. Her mouth turned down in disgust.

"You ate the whole thing! How could you?"

"They're small; the shells are soft. It's like eating crispy fish sticks. Try it!"

He lifted another onto her plate. She tried vainly to remove the head and shell but finally gave up.

"There's nothing to them after they're cleaned."

"Don't think western; think Asian. Don't prejudge. You only *think* they'll taste bad. Go ahead, try them."

As he smiled his encouragement, she cautiously picked one up with her chopsticks, closed her eyes and popped it in her mouth. After several moments of critical analysis, her face lit up.

"They're delicious."

When the waitress brought platters of barbecued chicken with peanuts and stir-fried vegetables, Lane needed no coaxing. She more than ate her share. They finished with a clam soup lightly flavored with ginger that left her refreshed, not stuffed. Then he pointed toward the cruise boats along the shore.

"Would you like a ride?"

"I really should get back. They're expecting me."

She watched the boats bobbing like apples on the water, reminding her of the Halloween game. Suddenly she wanted to cling to her lost childhood, rebel against duties, loyalties, responsibilities. She turned to him with an impish smile.

"Why not?!"

For an hour they plied the water, the dammed river swollen now into a deep lake after the recent typhoons. They sat in the front seats, watching the steeply sloping mountains slip by. Once they walked on deck and stood near the stern, reminiscing about their childhoods, talking quietly of their goals, watching the water's reflections.

On the drive back, they followed the Taiwan Strait, seeing the foamy waves break in the moonlight. Chen told the driver to stop at a temple in Pali. Near the gate, he bought flat red cakes from a vendor. As they tasted the glutinous-rice-and-red-bean patties, he explained.

"*Ang ku kwei,* red turtle dumplings. They were a specialty of *Liao Tien Ding*—before he became a local god." He looked around the empty temple. "It's still too early. This place doesn't get crowded until midnight."

"Why so late?"

"This is the Taoist shrine to *Liao Tien Ding.* Thieves come here to do *bai bai,* to pray for success." He cupped his hands to his forehead three times, a pantomime of offering incense to the gods.

"What kind of god would protect thieves?" she asked.

"He was the Taiwanese Robin Hood, stealing from the rich to give to the poor. People worshipped him—literally—and built this temple."

"They must believe in him, to bribe him so much for favors." She stared up at the gilded and intricately-carved ceiling, smiling wryly, then she looked into his face. "Why did you bring me here?"

"To steal your heart."

His eyes glittered mischievously, and he leaned toward her. She paused only a beat before turning on her heels and swiftly crossing the temple's marble floor to the engraved wooden door.

"Lane, wait. It was a joke, nothing more," he shouted, the sound echoing from the ornate rafters as he rushed after her. Then he caught her by the arm and spun her toward him.

"Here, see if I'm telling the truth or not."

While she studied him dubiously, he led her toward the *chim,* a canister holding long wooden prayer sticks, each etched with Chinese characters.

"I'm going to think of a question, then choose one of these." He smiled. "Divine intervention will guarantee the right choice."

He looked away as he rolled the wooden pins between his hands. Finally he lifted one and read its inscribed number: twenty-seven. His eyes twinkling, he motioned to follow him, then rushed to a wooden cabinet with small, numbered drawers. When he opened one, Lane saw it held narrow paper strips printed with Chinese characters. He began reading the prediction.

"No troubles if there be sincerity." His eyes looked up from the paper only long enough to give her an immodest smirk; then he continued. "Good omen. Regret disappears. A poor beginning gives way to a good ending. Today is an auspicious day for finding lost articles, for seeking a doctor. Favorable to conceive a son." His eyes glinted momentarily in the reflected light of the immense ten-year candles. "You try it!"

Not waiting for a reply, he whisked her back to the wooden sticks. She protested, afraid of calling down heaven's wrath.

"I don't believe in these gods."

"You don't have to. Just concentrate on a question, and fate will answer. Pick one." He spread his hands magnanimously, but she looked unconvinced. Shrugging his shoulders, he used another tact. "Try it for fun!"

She hesitated, then gave in to his urging, handling the sticks gingerly, hoping for some revelation of which stick to choose. When she sensed nothing, she picked one randomly and handed it to him. He held it up to the bare lightbulbs overhead.

"Number three."

"My lucky number!"

He grinned as he noticed her eyes widen with anticipation. Then they retraced their steps to the painted wooden cabinet. She looked over his shoulder as he pulled out the prediction and playfully held the paper against his chest.

"No peeking," he said.

"Read it!"

"Only over dinner."

He put the paper in his pocket and shook his head. Scowling playfully at his primly composed smile, she sighed.

"All right, but then I've really got to get back!"

The limo parked on the main street near a small alley. As they walked into the restaurant, she noted nothing fancy, just low stools and bare tables. A wide-screen television blared in the corner. Yellowed newspaper clippings lined the walls. Although she couldn't read the characters, she recognized the same non-descript dining room in the pictures. Numbered oyster shells hung informally on pegs near the door. He took a shell marked *three* and handed it to the waitress. Then he turned to Lane.

"Your lucky number."

He led her proudly to a table, pulling himself up to his full height. She, in turn, assessed him as she followed, judging him to be about 5'7", her own height. He ordered beer when the waitress brought a heaping bowl of oysters in the shell. Lifting one with chopsticks, he warned her.

"Taiwanese style. They're *hot!* You'll need something to wash them down."

Nibbling cautiously, she tasted one and burned her mouth. The iced beer came just in time. Lane drank deeply then gasped, trying to cool her mouth.

"How many chilies do they add to each oyster? This isn't hot, it's volcanic!"

He laughed and ate another, neatly depositing the shell in a dented metal basin. She picked one gingerly from the shell, her mouth still stinging. This time she avoided the spicy marinade. Nodding his head encouragingly, he helped himself to another.

"That's it."

Once she got used to the taste, Lane enjoyed it. She chose another oyster, skillfully delivering it to her mouth with chopsticks, and another. Within minutes, the first bowl emptied, and the second filled with shells. She smiled through lips still red and pouting from the spices.

"All right, I've done my part. Now do yours. Read!"

He obliged, reaching into his pocket for the slim paper. "Gentle talk, all goes well. Excessive talk, misfortune." He looked up sternly from his reading, his eyes twinkling. "Translation: Silence is golden."

"Forget the interpretation. Just read!"

Stifling his smile, he nodded with exaggerated respect and continued. "Discussion unfinished, the heart's confused. Bride treads on tiger's tail." His smile fading, he crumpled the paper and tossed it on the shells.

"Maybe you should interpret, after all," Lane said, wrinkling her forehead.

"Foolishness, just superstition."

As he motioned for more beer, Lane shook her head *no*. Suddenly seized with cramps, she felt nauseous, and icy beer did not appeal to her. She tried to shrug it off, attempting a laugh.

"Maybe we should take the advice . . . excessive talk, misfortune. I really do have to get home." Looking at her watch, she stood up and twinged.

"Is anything wrong?" His brow creased.

"No, just a stitch in my side."

"A what?"

"Nothing, a small pain. It'll go away."

She smiled to reassure him, and he misinterpreted, linking arms familiarly. Suddenly light-headed, she did not pull away. As they retraced their steps through the dark alley, Lane began perspiring. She tried to dismiss her faintness by unbuttoning her collar. She breathed deeply, but the air was so heavy, it did little to help. Unaware of her distress, he spoke with a self-effacing laugh.

"Restaurants in Taiwan don't believe in wasting money on atmosphere. What they lack in decor, they make up in character. Hope you enjoyed it."

Then turning toward her with a friendly grin, he did a double-take. She was panting. "Are you all right?"

"No, I think I'm going to be sick."

"Over here."

He pulled her into the alley's shadows and led her to a curb. Mortified, she couldn't help herself. Her eyes watering, she began gagging. He thumped her back Chinese-style, bringing on the nausea.

"Oh, this is so embarrassing, I . . . I. . . ."

She retched into the gutter. He continued patting her back, patiently waiting until she finished. Then he silently handed her a pack of tissues.

"Better?"

She nodded sheepishly, shame overwhelming her as they walked back to the car.

"Was it the oysters?"

"Please, I don't want to talk about it." She began gagging.

"Sorry. I could go back and complain, if you like."

Looking contrite in the street-light's glow, he turned toward the restaurant. Under the amber light, her green eyes glowed like a cat's. She lightly touched his arm, restraining him, then dismissed his suggestion with a shrug and a smile.

"It wasn't the oysters. Most things disagree with me lately."

"How long has this been going on? You should see a doctor."

"It's nothing. Just a queasy stomach. This. . . ." Her mouth set in annoyed lines as he interrupted.

"No, you should have that looked at. I'll make an appointment with my doctor tomorrow."

His expression one of genuine concern, he spoke with assurance. The unexpected tenderness in his voice startled her. She looked into his face and noted a gentle warmth about his eyes.

"Please, I insist. It's my fault for bringing you here." Then the arbitrary tone returned, grating on her. "*Tomorrow* you're seeing my MD."

Like a cat, she ignored orders. Squaring off, she took a deep breath, her exhale a controlled whisper.

"Not unless your doctor's an obstetrician."

Her small voice cut the air like a baby's cry, and Chen's eyes fixed on hers. Stumbling, he lost his equanimity.

"You don't mean. . . ."

"I *do* mean."

Her nod dissolved his last vestige of doubt. Hand on chin, he watched her thoughtfully, his index finger stroking his narrow nose. For a moment, neither spoke as each sized up the other. Then in unison they turned and continued back to the car.

"How long have you known?"

"Three weeks." She snorted contemptuously at the irony. "I learned the morning of the engagement."

"It's Li's?"

Instantly defensive, she turned on him faster than a soldier about-faces. "Of course it is! What are you implying?!"

Watching her reaction, he chose his next words more carefully. "It came out badly. I meant, have you told him?"

Her chin dipped toward her chest.

"He doesn't know?" Chen's tone sounded almost gleeful.

"I *tried* to tell him, but there wasn't time, thanks to a certain meddler."

She became defensive again, raising her head defiantly.

Chen studied her shrewdly, pausing, gauging her response.

"You knew, of course, that Mei-ling's pregnant?"

"So she *said*."

"Her baby needed its father."

Lane flinched.

Sensing her wounds, Chen went for the kill. "Have you heard that Li married Mei-ling yesterday?"

"That's a lie!" Hair flying, her head whipped toward him. Then suspicion set in. "Besides, how would *you* know?"

"I emceed."

"Why would you . . . ?" Too bewildered to finish, she stared at him.

"I'm Li's uncle."

# CHAPTER 3

Lane walked the remaining steps to the car alone. Whether from discretion or distraction, he gave her time to herself. Calling his aide to join him several feet from the car, Chen quietly chatted with him. Forlorn, Lane felt more alone than at any time in her life. As she watched dully through the tinted windows, the aide lit the men's cigarettes. All she could see in the dark was the embers glowing like a dragon's eyes, the smoke spurting like its sinister breath.

When they returned to the car, Chen sat beside her silently, waiting for her to begin. His motto was, 'He who speaks first is lost.' Lane bit her lip as long as she could, but impatience was a flaw she had not learned to check.

"He can't be married. I saw him at the ceremony today."

"Really?" Chen feigned his surprise badly, but she didn't stop to analyze his reaction.

"Yes, and he was alone. He *can't* be married!"

"Li takes his responsibilities seriously." He watched her closely, hesitating skillfully. "His position required him to attend today, even if it *were* his honeymoon."

Lane struggled to swallow the lump in her throat. She tried to speak, but the words choked her. Though the silence was painful, she did not want to further embarrass herself with Chen. Instead she willed him to fill the gap until she recovered. He began by whispering soothingly, his voice almost disembodied in the anonymity of the limo's back seat.

"I can understand how you feel: betrayed, vulnerable, alone in this foreign society. I've felt that way myself."

"Really?" She listened for a hollow ring to his words and looked up quickly to see if he were being genuine.

He nodded. Although she hid in the shadows, he noted the tears glistening in her questioning eyes. He answered gently, his voice low, even though his aide and driver in the front seat could not hear.

"How do you think a Chinese feels in Macao? Especially a Mainlander?" A bitter smile crossed his lips as he absently took her hand in his. Too engrossed, she did not object. "Alienation is something I live with. It's like being a stranger in your own home. When I was a child, my aunt and her family came to live with us. Every day as we sat together, she'd ask my uncle and each of my cousins what they wanted to eat. She'd ask those to the left and the right of me, but she'd never ask me. Macao's like that. I feel like a stepchild in my own home. Nothing's as painful as isolation."

He turned to look in her eyes and saw she had started to cry softly. He looked confused for a moment, unsure, then he gently held her to him as she sobbed into his tailored silk shirt. He murmured into her hair.

"It's all right. You're not alone anymore."

She sniffed and wiped her eyes with the back of her hand.

"Remember, I won't let you fall." He smiled reminiscently.

That brought on a fresh round of tears. It had been three weeks since she had felt any sense of belonging. The accumulated desperation engulfing her, Lane began crying. Chen's words opened the floodgates. When the tears finally subsided, she broke the tension with a weepy laugh.

"Not even Shihmen Dam could've held these back."

He laughed so loudly, his aide turned his head to check, then looked away discreetly.

"It's good to see you smile." Chen paused, as if screwing up his courage. "Lane, I'd like to make you happy . . . for the rest of your life. Would you let me do that?" He looked into her dewy eyes. "Would you be my wife?"

Now it was her turn to look confused. "But, you *know,* I've . . . I'm. . . ."

She could not voice the word. Weeks of repression had made it taboo. Gathering her hands in his, he said it for her.

"I've wanted an heir for years. Even if I didn't plant the seed, I'll nourish it. Besides, the baby's of my family's flesh and blood. The ancestral line will remain unbroken."

Embarrassed, she looked down at her hands; the ring sparkled even in the dark. Suddenly she noticed a gleam from his hand, as well. Surprised, she realized he was also wearing his engagement ring. Not sure how to answer, she fingered his ring, stalling.

"I don't make promises lightly," he said.

When she cocked her head, waiting for more information, he spoke softly.

"Three weeks ago I promised to marry you. . . ."

"But that was only for show!"

"Officially, but I have a confession to make. I'd seen you many times before we were introduced. From the first, I wanted you for my wife." He smiled coyly.

"Why would you. . . ." Although she could not put her finger on the reason, his disclosure disturbed her deeply. She blinked, trying to puzzle it out.

"The Chinese language has no equivalent for the word *love,* except *ai,* and that character translates to a dutiful sense of love. Romantic love has no comparable word. Even the idea is foreign. If I told any Chinese I'd fallen in love at first sight, they'd laugh."

He took her in his arms and looked into her eyes, hypnotizing her with his intensity. Distracted, she was unable to refuse.

"Lane, do you believe me?"

Silent, she nodded weakly as he whispered ardently in her ear.

"Then say *yes*."

Suddenly the car came to a halt, and Chen's aide jumped out to open the door. She looked around, surprised to be home but grateful for the refuge it offered. Sitting up straight, she tactfully disengaged herself from his grip. The mood broken, he hid his annoyance at the poorly-timed interruption, helped her from the car and began walking her toward the house.

"Thank you, Chen. . . ."

"David," he corrected, trying to veil his irritation.

Immediately the front door opened, flooding the entrance with light.

"Lane, where have you been?!" Then MacKenzie noticed her escort, and his curt tone became courteous. With a welcoming smile, he stepped back to make space for them. "This *is* a surprise! Come in, come in!"

"Didn't Iris tell you Chen was driving me home?" Lane stood rooted to the spot, wanting only to escape to her room, to think things out. Inviting Chen inside for polite chatter was inconceivable.

"Yes, but I didn't 'spect it to take so long. I thought y'all had met . . . friends." MacKenzie's expression relayed his distrust. Though he had not mentioned Li's name, he might just as well. His suspicions irked her.

"My God, I'm twenty-seven years old. I can take care of myself."

Chen's political astuteness had taught him prudence in family skirmishes. He squeezed her hand.

"Lane, thank you for your company."

"Come on in for a drink," said MacKenzie. The tone was urgent.

"Another time, perhaps, Senator. Good night."

He shook hands with her father, smiled conspiratorially at Lane, and, turning, walked back to his car. MacKenzie ushered his daughter into the house with a false laugh.

"That's a man who won't wear out a welcome. Seems damned considerate, that one."

"Yes, he does." Lane agreed absentmindedly.

"Chen's a fine catch," said her father, noting her mood. He decided to pursue the topic. "You could do worse."

"Oh, Daddy, don't start!" She pushed past him.

"You ain't no filly," he called. "At your age, your prospects are limited."

She stopped in her tracks, turned and met his eyes coldly. "That was uncalled for."

Always a politician, he knew when to strike and when to parry. He smiled boyishly, knowing from experience its endearing effect on voters and daughters alike.

"Lane, I'm only thinking of your welfare. Chen's a man who'll take care of y'all. . . ."

"Take care of *you,* you mean!"

She stared into her father's eyes as an equal. The past three weeks had worn away the patina of childhood awe. She saw through his shallow maneuvers.

He dropped his grin and sat down suddenly, the wind knocked out of him. Then his eyes latched onto hers with a deep awareness that led to a truce. Her insight had cut through his polished veneer like an Exacto knife.

"You're right." He took a deep breath. "I could use a little financial taking care of."

"What do you mean?"

"I dabbled in the Hang Seng Index, gambling on the privatization of a state-owned enterprise in a SEZ."

"What's a *says?*"

"S-E-Z, a 'special economic zone.' This one's in Guangdong, a southern Chinese province. It sounded foolproof, a textile company in the black—just needs management. Once Beijing deeds it to us, the company'll be a money-maker since distribution will be no problem. It's near a port and ready market."

He saw her puzzled expression and explained.

"Guangdong's got one of the world's best harbors, and it's right across the proverbial street from Hong Kong. What with the HK dollar becoming the Canton dollar, it sounded like a sure bet. Acting on the advice of a 'friend,' I invested heavily, expecting a 66% profit by January." MacKenzie grimly shook his silvery head, then got up and paced.

Impressed by the numbers, she whistled. "That's a lot of potential!"

"I know, but the take-over hasn't happened. All my capital's tied up, waiting for Beijing."

"Has this anything to do with Hong Kong and Macao reverting to China?" Politics interested her. Gone was her fatigue and irritation.

As her face became animated, her eyes lit up, their true beauty not the color as much as her intelligence shining through. Despite his agitation, MacKenzie paused momentarily, wondering if he had underestimated his daughter.

"For my investment to show a return, Beijing'll have to do three things. First, drop the phony barriers between Guangdong and Macao. That'll happen when Macao reverts. Next, keep its word not to interfere with Hong Kong's fancy financial and trading services. The third's the biggest pain in the butt; Beijing's got to turn over the factory to our company."

"Are you showing any profit while it's state-owned?" she asked.

"On paper, the company's showing a gain, but Beijing doesn't know how to distribute dividends." Smiling wanly, he bowed to her intellect as he sat down. "And thanks to poor management and bribery, most of the profit's eaten by graft."

Her raised eyebrow was her silent query.

"To answer your question: no, I haven't made so much as a *ren min bi*."

"What about your other investments?" Understanding the cycles of investing, she knew today's washout was tomorrow's windfall. "Aren't they diversified enough to carry you until this one rallies?"

"What other investments? I cashed in my portfolio months ago."

"What about your inheritance? Mother's utilities? Her bonds? The CD's?"

He shook his head at each. Then he rubbed his forehead with both hands and looked up.

"Gone. I followed conventional wisdom and got 'aggressive,' took 'risks.' Win some, lose some, right? My colleagues won; I lost. Why do y'all 'spose I came out here? Every last cent I have is tied up in Guangdong or with this trade agreement. I even sold off the north acreage, and remortgaged the house."

"I'd wondered how. . . ."

Stunned at the idea of losing her great-grandfather's homestead, she pursed her lips to keep from criticizing his market speculations. Unable to sit still, he stood up and poured himself another drink.

"Now y'all see why I'm grateful for Chen's support?" Sipping the bourbon, he steadied himself. "He's a big man in Asia; I need his help to push the agreement through."

"So this all boils down to money, doesn't it?"

She looked him squarely in the eye. Too abashed to admit

it, Mackenzie squirmed at her insight. Softening, she covered her accusing inflection by discreetly lowering her voice, changing her tone.

"Surely your salary and political donations will pay the bills."

He dismissed the idea with a sarcastic sniff.

"And after next election you. . . ."

"My constituents are getting skittish." He watched her reaction as he thoughtfully sipped the liquor. "If I don't have something to show them, like this agreement, there's a good chance they won't reelect me next term."

"I still don't understand how this agreement will help your election." She ran her hand through her hair, thinking, trying to piece his information together.

"International trade," he said with a smile, glad to be on familiar turf, relieved to answer political, not personal, questions. "Let me give y'all an example. Leather from US beef's shipped to China through Macao. Factories in Guangdong make the shoes at a fraction of the US cost. Then Taiwanese trading companies dump 'em in Mexico."

"Why Mexico? Why not the US?"

" 'Cause Mexico has lower duties and fewer restrictions. There they sell 'em wholesale to US jobbers, maybe tack on some bows so they can be labeled *Assembled in USA,* and then retail the shoes at jacked-up prices. Everyone's happy 'cause everyone's making money. And when voters are happy, they reelect."

"Is that why you want me to marry Chen?"

Having timed her words carefully, she watched his response. Her eyes caught his before he dropped his gaze. When he did not answer, she executed an angry about-face and left him to his self-centered schemes. Then as she slammed into her room, the phone rang, jarring her thoughts.

She picked up reflexively, not waiting for the maid.

"Lane? I've been calling all night. Are you all right?"

Li's voice had an eerie effect on her. Except for a brief exchange that afternoon, she had not heard from him in three weeks. He sounded like a ghost back from the dead.

Too startled to be witty, she mumbled *mmm-hmm*.

"Is *that* all you have to say?" His tone accusing, her temper rose like a balloon in a typhoon.

"What did you expect me to do? Wait breathlessly for your call?"

He bit his lip, neglecting to mention the hundreds of calls he had made, messages he had left with the maid, excuses he had been given by the embassy's receptionist during the past three weeks. Had they been following Lane's orders to avoid his calls? Suspecting it, yet unsure, he wondered. Was it Lane or someone else behind the deception? When he spoke, sarcasm hung from his words like the jade pendant from her gold necklace.

"No, but I would expect you to wait five minutes for me to get the car today. Do you find Uncle that attractive?"

"So it's true." She jumped at the connection. "Chen *is* your uncle." She gathered her courage for the next question. "Is it also true he witnessed your wedding yesterday?"

"No . . . well, yes, in a sense, but. . . ."

"This is not multiple choice; it's true-or-false. Did you or did you not marry Mei-ling yesterday?"

"My mother's been very ill, so I thought. . . ."

"Yes or no."

"Well . . . yes, in a. . . ."

She hung up, and, with no more thought than if choosing pink or coral nail polish, she made her decision. Lane found her father in the living room, surprising him with her sudden return. In the background, the phone rang insistently.

"Daddy," she said evenly, "tell Chen I've decided to marry him."

*"Hot Damn!"* MacKenzie jumped up from the chair and gave his daughter a tight hug. "I'll call Chen this minute. Now, if you'll. . . ."

"Mr. MacKenzie," announced Pearl nervously, "there's a call for you."

He smiled conspiratorially at his daughter. "Could it be Chen? Great minds running in the same direction?"

He started toward the hall phone in good humor. Then the maid scampered after him, whispering.

"Sir, it's *him* again."

"Who?"

"Mr. Yang."

Sensing the rage, Pearl lowered her eyes meekly. His smile lines deepened into angry creases as he answered in a stage whisper.

"I told y'all not to take his calls. We're not home, y'hear? Tell him we're not at home. Then call Chen."

"Yes, sir. Yes, sir."

Slippers scuffing, the maid hurried toward the phone. Lane slumped onto a leather chair, exhausted, her energy depleted. She could fight Chen and her father, but not Li, too. Staring through glassy eyes, she started to shake, though MacKenzie was too busy to notice.

# CHAPTER 4

"Traditional but simple," Lane said over lunch the next day. Indifferent about her wedding, she left most of the decisions to Chen. "The engagement dinner was more than enough pomp and ritual for me."

"We'll keep it very personal."

As he smiled roguishly, she instinctively drew away from him and lowered her eyes.

"What? Is anything wrong?" His tone of voice was bruised.

"No, of course not."

As she gave a small, self-conscious laugh, she felt him reach for her hand under the table. Surprised to touch velvet, she fingered the small box he pressed into her palm while he watched her like a proud parent.

"What . . . ?"

"Open it."

"Ch . . . David, you're spoiling me."

She bit her lip, hoping he did not hear her stumble over his name. Reluctantly opening the lid, she drew a quick breath. Then she lifted the heavy chain, inspecting the five-petaled flower in the center of a large, gold heart.

"It's gorgeous!"

"That's a *mei hua,*" he explained, indicating the blossom. "Taiwan's national symbol. It's so hardy, it blooms high in the mountains where it snows." Then he traced the heart with his finger and laughed.

"You're holding both my heart and Taiwan in your hand."

"Does this mean I control your fate?" She tried to make light of it.

"You wield more power than you realize," he said, smiling warmly and taking her other hand in his. "You should have something to remember today by, Lane. I've waited for this moment a long time."

Again his reference to the past made her wary. She looked quickly into his face, but his expression was inscrutable. Still feeling uncomfortable in Chen's presence, she lowered her eyes again and gently pulled away from his grip. As the jewelry glittered in her hand, she stared at the necklace, wondering how much gold he had given her since their engagement. Then remembering her manners, she glanced shyly into his eyes.

"You shouldn't have."

"Of course I should," he boomed.

Embarrassed, Lane looked to see if he were disturbing near-by tables but realized that in Taiwan, no one pays attention to noise. He tugged at her hand to regain her attention.

"You're going to be my wife. Why not show you off?"

"You're too kind."

As she looked away, Chen exploded. Her glib preoccupation was exasperating. His eyes glaring, his face took on a stony appearance, and his voice became icy.

"Kindness has nothing to do with it!"

Then as if to offset his outburst, he took the necklace from the box and opened its catch. Composing his lips into a smile, he spoke in his usual even tones.

"Here, let me put it on you. Lean forward."

To assist, she bowed her head toward him. His face was so close to hers, his breath touched her cheek as he clasped the chain about her throat. Though her aloofness clung to her like cologne, he could not resist the innuendo.

"Are you always so submissive?"

"I help when I can." Stiffening into an upright position, she spoke with injured dignity.

*"Zi qi qi ren."* He regarded her closely, an ironic twist to his mouth. "Self-deception while deceiving others. Wong Xiaoping."

Her eyes darting nervously, she remained silent, not sure how to respond.

"Is there an English equivalent?" he asked finally.

She thought for a moment. "Only its paradox: To thine own self be true. William Shakespeare."

Set for three weeks later, even the wedding's date was a compromise. She had pressed for an earlier one, wanting to marry before she could change her mind. Chen had demurred, wanting more time to arrange his business affairs in Macao. Since her father had already overstayed his official visit, she maintained that three weeks was the maximum time they could wait.

Lane looked on uneasily while Chen consulted the book of favorable dates. His superstition reminded her of Li's mother's beliefs and the ensuing disastrous engagement. Though Lane could not see the wisdom of choosing an auspicious time, he refused to begin the marriage on an unlucky day. When he found one, set for exactly three weeks later, she breathed a sigh, glad to dispense with a long engagement and its accompanying demands of diplomatic protocol.

Foregoing the expected rounds of parties and publicity, she was relieved to get the wedding over with as quickly and quietly as possible. More importantly, while she was racing toward that objective, she was too busy to think beyond. It was a backstop that provided a false barrier to the future.

Looking at his calendar, Chen noted that the soonest he

could return was the fourth Wednesday in November, the day before the ceremony. That their wedding happened to be on Thanksgiving was a coincidence.

After toasting the upcoming wedding, MacKenzie and Chen used their flight-time from Taipei to Hong Kong to coordinate their itineraries.

"I'll have to extend my visa Hong Kong side before meeting up with y'all in Macao."

"Nonsense, Senator, my aide'll see to the paperwork. After my car meets us at Kai Tak, we'll take the jetfoil to Jade Mountain Casino. You'll be my guest in Macao."

Though MacKenzie politely demurred, he gave in with an affable chuckle. "If y'all insist. The taxpayers'd be mighty grateful to y'all for keeping down the overhead. Don't need to fret my constituents with travel expenses or entertainment budgets now, do I?"

Chen knew the reluctance was face-saving. He recognized the senator's type: castrated rooster. The capon liked his gambling risk-free and his politics sterilized. No paper trails, campaign financial disclosures or public scrutiny. Chen made a mental note to present him with complimentary House chips. MacKenzie would leap at the prospect of gambling with other people's money. Then, when he started losing, Chen would extend him a limitless line of credit. He smiled at the possibilities.

"Don't worry, Senator, your presence will be low-profile. Though the trade agreement will boost your state's and the US economy in general, your role in it need be only as public as you wish."

Again MacKenzie's deep chuckle contrasted with the engine's whine. Then he sat back with a slow, wide grin.

"Chen, y'all misunderstand. I'm proud to do my part to

help international trade relations, to bring honest jobs back to the good ole' US of A, to raise political contributions for reelection campaigns. It just galls me to waste taxpayers' hard-earned money, that's all. I'm sure y'all understand."

Their eyes met in mutual comprehension. Lifting his bourbon, MacKenzie proposed a silent toast, but the plane had already begun its swallow's dive between the mountains and the high-rises onto Kai Tak's popsicle-stick runway.

Chen's chauffeur let them off in front of the casino's main entrance. First impressions the most lasting, Chen wanted to dazzle the senatorial bumpkin with his connections and savoir-faire. The tall American in tow, Chen led him into the casino with its flashing lights, two-way mirrors and triad pit bosses.

Rows of "hungry tigers" lined the casino floor like waves of light and color. In this gaudy sea of slot machines stood one cordoned-off baccarat table. Set on a raised platform swathed in velvet, it represented a genteel bastion of elegance against the seedy pachinko-parlor backdrop. High rollers, slots players and crapshooters rubbed shoulders, oblivious of the lack of Vegas glitter or Monte Carlo chic. Window dressing unnecessary, the gamblers had come for one express purpose.

Chintzy carpeting helped subdue the frenzied patois of Cantonese, Mandarin, Portuguese and English being shouted over the bells and whistles of the paying slot machines. Yet energy coursed through the casino like the amphetamine-bolstered ventilation. Feeling a contact high, even MacKenzie felt inexplicably garrulous. As they passed the rows of blackjack tables, crap tables and roulette wheels, he noted several games he didn't recognize.

"What're those?" he asked.

"Chinese diversions," said Chen, pointing first to the

right, then to the left. "*Fan tan* and *dai siu* or Big and Small."

Admiring the scope of the operation, MacKenzie let out a low whistle. "Not bad!"

Swallowing a smile at the understatement, Chen turned his attention to an approaching Chinese. "Senator, this is Mr. Wu, my assistant manager. He'll handle all your needs during your stay."

MacKenzie shook hands with the muscular man, wincing at the man's bear-paw grip. Then Chen motioned the assistant to remove a roll of black chips from his breast pocket.

"Extend an unlimited line of credit for our guest, Wu, to make his stay more interesting. In the meantime, Senator, please accept these as tokens of my good will."

"Right considerate of you," said MacKenzie, pocketing the chips, then following Chen to his private elevator. At the door, Chen pulled a keychain from his vest.

"This is the only key," he explained with a wry smile. "Like you, I also value privacy."

At the top floor, Chen guided him to his office. Heavy mahogany paneled the walls. Rich rosewood furniture and maroon leather upholstery filled the spacious room.

"It doesn't look Asian," MacKenzie said, his eyes contrasting the understated luxury with the casino's ordinariness.

"It isn't. It's Mediterranean. Macao's been under Portuguese rule since 1557, ever since China rewarded Portugal for ridding the area of pirates." He pointed out the window. "That's the Pearl River. The city and those two islands, Coloane and Taipa, make up Macao. We're connected to the mainland by a narrow isthmus, with the *Portas do Cerco* or Barrier Gate separating us."

For once the view held MacKenzie's interest. Few things other than money appealed to him, but the spectacle of red

China within walking distance caught his imagination.

"Never realized China was so close."

"It is in many ways, Senator, much closer than you think."

Startled by the tone, MacKenzie blanched then cleared his throat. "Oh, of course. You mean geographically."

Geopolitically, positionally, financially, militarily, strategically, Chen thought, but his expression remained impassive. He crossed to his private bar and began pouring his guest a bourbon and water.

"Bourbon, isn't it?" The question was as much an afterthought as a formality. He knew what the senator wanted.

"And branch."

Chen smiled to himself as he seized the moment. Again his inquiry was a statement, not a question. "Speaking of branches, governmental branches, that is, aren't you heading the fund-raising campaign for the presidential reelection?"

MacKenzie coughed. "Yes, I'm overseeing contributions to the National Committee."

"A select group of Southeast Asian businessmen is interested in seeing President Dawson reelected. I've arranged for a private fund-raising dinner tonight." Along with the bourbon, Chen handed him the gauntlet.

MacKenzie's eyes swept the room. Of the assembled dozen men, his was the only occidental face. Exuding southern charm, he smiled warmly and wrung each hand firmly as Chen introduced him around.

"Huaqing and Zhu are directors of the Eastern Bank, Ltd." *Along with owners of the off-track betting syndicate and a major share of the CIT manufacturing business,* Chen thought. "Chi and Ng operate the Wok-in/Take-out restaurant chain in Hong Kong, Vietnam and California." *In addition to their string of "barber shop" whore houses.* "Wu and Li own the

Nine-Dragons Shipping Line and an import-export business." *Specializing in opium from the golden triangle of northern Thailand and Myanmar, they also work closely with the rebel Karen tribe.* "Tang and Chiu own and operate the Lucky Tiger Stock Investment Company." *When they're not running their far more lucrative loan-shark business.* "Wang is CEO for the Golden Mountain Tea Export Company." *As well as Chairman of the Chinese Communist Party's State Economic and Trade Commission.* "Cheung is the Chief Director of the Macao legal firm, Cheung, Hwang and Jen." *When he's not acting officially as the National People's Congress Cabinet Minister of Foreign Economic Relations and Trade.*

Who knows most, speaks least, thought Chen, holding his tongue, but he who knows nothing, reveals nothing. What MacKenzie doesn't know can't hurt us.

"Each of these businessmen has pledged a million dollars to participate in tonight's dinner, Senator. We're hoping this modest contribution of ten million dollars will help reelect you and President Dawson."

MacKenzie's eyes never wavered, but his palms began sweating at the unexpected support. Now he had something to show the president: political contributions, solid financing to fund the campaigns. This not only saved him face, it saved his neck. He would earn the president's gratitude as well as his senatorial endorsement. His smile widened at the thought, then as quickly disappeared. Regulations had tightened on foreign contributions since the '96 elections.

"I'm mighty grateful to y'all for your support, but recent, ah, *restrictions* on overseas contributions. . . ."

Chen shared a chuckle with the others. "No need to worry about legalities, Senator. Mr. Cheung's legal firm has a branch in Los Angeles. All contributions will be funneled through ABCs. . . ."

"Come again? ABCs?"

"American Born Chinese. As US citizens, the official contributors meet all legal requirements. No records of overseas transactions will exist. The money will be the sole evidence of contributions, and its paper trail will end with US citizens as the donors."

"How will the Hong Kong dollars be transferred to US banks?"

"That's where Huaqing and Zhu come in. They're the directors of the Eastern Bank, Ltd. They also own forty percent of the Asian Occidental Bank of San Francisco. Each of us will deposit our contributions into a local branch of the Eastern Bank, Ltd. In turn that will be exchanged into US dollars, then transferred to Asian Occidental. From there it'll be deposited into the accounts of ABCs who will contribute the money into PACs."

What Chen neglected to mention was the initial laundering of money through the various legit businesses in Hong Kong and Macao, not the least of which were his casino and trade company. Still, the scant explanation was enough for MacKenzie to grasp. Like connect-a-dot drawings, the incomplete pattern outlined the picture.

With the graphic image of a line chart in mind, the senator understood the cash flow. Now he wondered about his role. His eyes narrowing shrewdly, they crinkled in a practiced, leathery smile.

"This is mighty generous of y'all, but what will you gentlemen expect in return?"

"Good will—yours and the President's. We only want your support on international trade issues, particularly the trade deal we're negotiating between the US, Mexico, Taiwan and Macao.

MacKenzie hid his satisfaction with a self-effacing

chuckle. "Well, I *am* heading the fund-raising campaign for the presidential reelection, overseeing contributions to the National Committee. As long as it's all legal-like, within certain limitations, I'm delighted to accept it in the President's name."

"Better than that, Senator, why don't you call the President? I'm sure he'll find this welcome information. Tell him the good news yourself," urged Chen. "But add that for each dollar contributed to his—and your—reelection, another dollar will be matched in computer investment in Silicon Valley and Tech-xas, creating more jobs and more votes."

MacKenzie's eyes widened at the thought. "With California and Texas electoral votes sewn up, President Dawson's as good as reelected."

"And so are you." Chen let that thought take hold as he motioned to his aide. "Escort the senator to my private office."

MacKenzie nodded dumbly, then stumbled behind the aide. He tried to gather his thoughts, but the image of twenty million dollars' worth of contributions kept him dazed. It was all so unexpected. No matter what they wanted, their money was the answer to all his problems: his own reelection, the president's and the president's gratitude for his fund-raising finesse.

He waited until the aide left, then dialed the private number given him by the White House. Once the connection was made, Chen's men tapped into the call. Initially elated, they lost interest when the presidential staff patched the call through several more numbers, none of which was traceable. If MacKenzie were aware of the subtle clicks and crackles along the line, he didn't let on. Only Chen's aide heard one unaccountable snap, and he made a mental note to sweep later for bugs.

"Yes?"

MacKenzie recognized the presidential aide's voice. "Oscar, I'd consider it a favor it if y'all would put Ken on the phone."

"Sorry, sir, the President's in a cabinet meeting and can't be disturbed."

"Boy, do y'all know who you're talkin' to? This here's Senator Percival MacKenzie. Now go tell your boss, Mac's got news that can't wait."

"Sir, is this a secure line?"

"No, son, but it's one that'll cost you your job security if you don't get Ken on the line!"

The assistant's insolence brought him out of his daze. MacKenzie felt his tongue returning along with his impatience. Three minutes later he heard the president pick up.

*"Ubi ignus est?"*

"What?" MacKenzie hated it when the President used Latin. Dawson's ivy-school veneer was more abrasive than polished.

"Where's the fire, Mac?"

"Under our feet."

"Where're you calling from?" asked the president.

"A fund-raising dinner in Macao." He outlined the proposal. "I'll give you more details later, but I need your confirmation now."

"What's the *quid pro quo?*"

Mac stifled a sigh. "Y'all mean the tit-for-tat, what's our part in this? Only our good will and support on the international issues, especially the big trade deal."

"We've got to think of our constituencies," the President said slowly.

"I am! Hell, Ken, y'all know as well as I do, we need Chinese investment in key states to create jobs before the 2000 presidential elections. Without the financing—and the jobs and votes it'll bring—we both stand a good chance of losing."

Now it was Dawson's turn to sigh as he thought it over. "What've you heard about the Tiaoyutai Islands?"

"Not much, other than Japan, China and Taiwan are heating up over them. Why?"

The receiver amplified the bristling of the President's whiskers as he rubbed his jaw. MacKenzie could almost see the characteristic gesture through the link.

"My informants tell me the islands could have vast resources of natural gas and oil."

"So?"

"With the unrest at Okinawa, our naval forces need a secure base, a stable fuel source."

"I still don't get your drift, Ken."

"Tell your diners that the US Presidential Office will back any nation's claim to those islands if it can produce prior legal and historical rights to ownership. That and grant us unlimited access to the oil through a refueling station."

"Upping the ante, huh?" MacKenzie chuckled. "You're one helluva poker-player, Ken. Y'all ought to be here at Chen's casino."

"I'm just playing out the cards I'm dealt, and you make sure you're covering your bets. Don't lose this hand."

MacKenzie heard the two clicks after he hung up, not caring that the line had been tapped. Rumors were an efficient way to leak information. They saved him the trouble of tactfully divulging official secrets. He purposely delayed going back to the dining room, lingering in Chen's room, reading the newspaper, giving his hosts time to regroup. When he finally returned, Chen and Cheung, Chief Director of the Macao legal firm, had been briefed on the timbre of the phone conversation.

"Sorry I took so long, gentlemen."

"Not at all, Senator."

"Mac."

"Mac." Chen nodded agreeably, escorting him to the round table with twelve place settings. "Rank has its privilege." He indicated the chair to the right of him. "The place of honor is reserved for you."

"Thanks, Chen. I notice the Tiaoyutai Islands have been in the news recently," MacKenzie said as he seated himself. "What do y'all know about them?"

Though mildly surprised the American would broach the topic so bluntly, Cheung took his cue. "Japan's laying claim to the islands, stating the US gave them the authority."

"How's that?"

Cheung motioned to his assistant. "This is George Ma, a junior partner in my firm, who's an authority on the situation. He can explain it far better than I can."

The young man nodded respectfully to Cheung, then politely to MacKenzie. "If you don't mind, Senator, I'd like to furnish you with a little background. The Tiaoyutai Islands are located in the East China Sea, southwest of Okinawa. After World War II they were placed under US administration as part of the peace treaty with Japan. Then according to the Okinawa Reversion Agreement of June 1971, the US returned their administration to Japan. That's when the dispute regarding the Tiaoyutai Islands really began. The US decision spurred protests in Taiwan, Macao, Hong Kong and mainland China since the Chinese viewed it as another example of Japanese invasion of Chinese territory."

"So are y'all telling me the States caused this problem?"

"Not in so many words, Senator. Anti-Japanese sentiment has been around since the Sino-Japanese War in 1895 when China signed the Treaty of Shimonoseki, ceding Taiwan and the Penghu Archipelago to Japan. The Japanese claim the

Tiaoyutais were included in the treaty."

Cheung spoke up. "Beijing's Foreign Ministry contends the islands belong to Taiwan from a geographic and historical point of view, and since Taiwan was *and is* a province of China, Beijing should claim sovereignty. Indeed, Beijing has sovereignty over all of China."

Chen's warning glance silenced him. Turning the lazy susan portion of the table so MacKenzie could reach the shrimp platter, Chen said, "Ma, this is interesting. I've heard rumors, family stories, but haven't known the background of the Tiaoyutais. How does Taiwan figure in?"

"Taiwan claims historical ownership, insisting imperial China never ceded the Tiaoyutais to Japan, and even if Japan ever had a right to the islands, it was revoked when Tokyo gave Taiwan back. Then after the Japanese built a lighthouse on the islets in 1996, anti-Japanese sentiment soared in Taiwan, climaxing on the anniversary of its October 25th holiday, Retrocession."

"What's that?" asked MacKenzie, foregoing his chopsticks for a fork.

"Retrocession marks the end of Japanese occupation of Taiwan and Penghu," said Chen.

"What about the PRC's claim to the islands?" asked Cheung, his chin jutting belligerently. "All of Taiwan and its neighboring islands *and* archipelagos belong to the People's Republic."

"No need to raise cross-strait tensions at the table," said Chen quietly. His face impassive, Chen's eyes smoldered as he cautioned the man to his left.

"As a matter of fact," Ma continued, again playing peace-maker between Chen and Cheung, "mainland Chinese have cooperated with Taiwanese and Hong Kongese to break the Japanese blockade of the islands, landing on the

Tiaoyutais and planting both the ROC and PRC flags."

"So did that convince Japan to withdraw?" asked MacKenzie.

"No, the Japanese immediately tore down the flags. Besides, these protests only slow down negotiations."

"How will this affect bipartisan politics?" MacKenzie helped himself to the ginger beef as he questioned the young man.

Chen hid a smile as he intercepted. "The PRC might consider it bipartisan since it regards Hong Kong, Macao, Taiwan and Mainland all as one big happy family, but Taiwan views it quite differently. The KMT urges the Taiwanese activists to support their government's negotiations with Japan. The DPP warns against political involvement with mainland China."

"How do you feel personally about the issue?" MacKenzie asked Chen.

"I'm very happy the activists landed on the islands."

His eyes heavily lidded, Chen refrained from mentioning his official position, secretly hoping talks between Tokyo and Taipei would collapse, in which case Beijing could initiate talks of its own with Tokyo.

"So let me get this straight," said MacKenzie, "the *only* claim Japan has to the islands is the fact that the US gave it administrative authority?"

"Almost," continued Ma, taking a loose-leaf pocket-notebook from his vest. "Using a time-line, I'll show the historical succession of sovereignty over Tiaoyutai, proving Japan has no legal authority."

"Two ancient records prove the Tiaoyutais were separate from Japan's Ryukyus, a group of fifty-five islands, including Okinawa. Early maps include them as Taiwanese. Then in 1893 in appreciation to an herbalist for treating her illness, the Dowager Empress Ci-xi of the Qing Dynasty granted a *Special Edict,* deeding the archipelago to a Sheng Hsuan-hui and his descendants in perpetuity."

Mouth full, MacKenzie interrupted. "Are any of his descendants alive?"

Ma shrugged his shoulders. "The point's moot, anyway, because the Qing Dynasty ceded Taiwan and Penghu to Japan in 1895."

"Then in 1945 when W.W.II ended, it follows that Tiaoyutai should have been returned to China along with Taiwan and Penghu in accord with the *Cairo Conference,*" said Cheung, still smoldering at his junior partner's conflicting politics. "The Tiaoyutais belong to the PRC!"

"You mean the ROC!" Tang interrupted. "The Nationalists controlled the mainland until 1949."

At Chen's cue, Ma interceded. "Finally in 1990, the US State Department repeated that, according to the 1951 Peace Treaty, Washington had only had administrative authority, so the 1972 transfer to Tokyo was one of *administrative* authority only, not sovereignty. Japan hasn't any legal claim."

"Then who has?" asked MacKenzie. "Taiwan or China?"

"ROC," said Tang.

"PRC," said Cheung.

"Wait, there's one more piece of evidence," said Ma. "Article four of the 1952 *Sino-Japanese Peace Treaty* states all agreements made prior to the 1941 Sino-Japanese Accord are invalid, even the Shimonoseki Treaty of 1895. Legal sovereignty goes back to 1893, when Ci-xi granted Tiaoyutai to Sheng Hsuan-hui."

"So whichever country finds this herbalist's descendants can claim ownership of the archipelago?" asked Ng.

Ma nodded.

The senator spoke in a low voice, as if letting them all in on a secret. "I have it on authority. President Dawson will back whichever nation can prove its claim to sovereignty over the islands."

The men pretended surprise. Chen fell silent, recalling the family story that his mother's line was descended from the herbalist Sheng Hsuan-hui and was legal heir to Tiaoyutai. He began theorizing where such a document might be, if it existed or ever had, and made a mental note to call the Minister of Antiquities at the Chinese National Archives.

In the rafters above the Chula Vista hotel's private dining room, a tall man hunched over, listening in on his receiver. Via four hidden microphones, he heard not only MacKenzie's phone call, but also the diners' conversations.

Alone with his thoughts, the man remembered an event when he had been a boy. His great aunt had shown him an ancient, warped sea chest with salt-water-corroded hinges. Inside had been antiquated papers, yellowed with age and molding from the humidity. She had shown him the threadbare prayer cloth from his ancestors' altar and told him how she had discovered the hidden papers sewn into its lining. Impressing upon him the importance of the documents, she had let him feel the crumbling paper with his childish hands. His eyes widened now, as then, at the possibilities as he speculated about the family legend.

The day dawned an odd mixture of overcast and blue. A fine drizzle reflected the sunlight, making the day seem bright despite the gray. As she peeked through the blinds, Lane watched mist tumble over the encircling mountain peaks like steaming water pouring into the natural basin of Taipei. In the distance, she saw a rainbow over the *Shin Kong* Building. For once, the winds had scoured the bowl-shaped city, whisking away the stagnant pollution. She snickered: Must be a typhoon to the south.

For an inert moment, she allowed herself to contemplate the future. The previous three weeks had been a blur of activity preparing for today. But now, with nothing to distract her thoughts, she had the awesome luxury to wonder:

What about tonight? How do I "honor his offer"? And then what? What about the next forty years? What about my baby?

Suddenly gripped with a fear that attacked the pit of her stomach, she doubled over in pain and nausea.

*My God, what am I doing?*

A rap at the door told her the cosmetologist had arrived. Her green eyes rimmed with red, Lane steeled herself for the three hours of enforced idleness while the woman arranged her hair and painted her face in the classic Chinese style.

The make-up artist was professional, knowing the modern as well as the ancient techniques. Being from Shih Lin, she practiced a unique method of exfoliation. To prepare Lane's face for the pale powder base, she stripped it of all downy hair using a white, gritty powder and twine. Working swiftly at right angles, the woman held the string taut with her teeth and swept it upward between her left thumb and her right hand, peeling dead skin and plucking all facial hair in its path.

Wincing, Lane withdrew from the discomfort and entered the realm of her mind. While sitting through three hours of annoying tedium, she suddenly realized that if she were to survive life's misfortunes, small or large, she would have to tap an inner strength, rise from her own ashes. The answer came to her in the blink of an eye, causing the cosmetologist no little anguish in having to reapply shadow to her left eyelid. In the flash of an epiphany, Lane learned how to triumph. She smiled through her flaming red lips.

Mental preparation was her defense against fright. Once she accepted her changing role, she was able to modify her perspective. She began by identifying her fears, then, one by one, she reasoned them through, systematically replacing vague but debilitating dread with aggressive self-determination. Now with a new resolve, she almost looked forward to life's next venture.

Wearing a traditional red *cheongsam* embroidered with an imperial azure and gold phoenix, Lane surprised even herself. Her expression as serene as the goddess *Kwan Yin's*, she waited tranquilly for Chen's car.

Her new-found composure added another dimension to her beauty. She looked in the mirror and proudly tossed her head, watching the beaded tassels of her headdress swing gracefully. Mirrors don't lie. She knew she looked gorgeous, and, in a spiraling ascendancy, *that* knowledge further bolstered her confidence. Her hair had been swept off her neck in a French twist to expose the intricate teal and turquoise brocade on the high neckline, but it also revealed her strong chin and firmly set jaw. Beneath the porcelain, carefully demure make-up, her eyes glittered like uncut gems, sharp and penetrating.

"You look like a Mandarin empress. You make me proud." MacKenzie spoke with an affirming bob of his chin. Then crossing the marble floor in his long stride, he gripped her fragile shoulders with his wide hands.

"This is the first time you've ever told me that. Is this what it took? Selling myself?" Her expression was placid beneath her traditional headdress. Her green eyes conveying her budding autonomy, her self-control shook his life-long hold on her.

MacKenzie's hands instantly dropped from her embroidered collar. His mouth moved to answer, but a riotous outburst drowned his words. So many firecrackers detonated outside that Lane covered her ears against the sound's intensity. When the din finally did subside hundreds of explosions later, she could barely detect the doorbell's chimes from the ringing in her ears. Tentatively removing her hands from her ears, she heard first the maid's, then Chen's voice as she ushered him in.

"*Zao*. Good morning."

He beamed, his autocratic face softened by his wide smile. White teeth flashing from his perennial tan, he looked like an attractive hybrid of a South-Seas pirate and a wall-street broker.

"And right back at y'all," said MacKenzie, pumping his hand enthusiastically.

Turning toward Lane, Chen stopped and caught his breath. Animation ceasing, he stared in open admiration. She stood poised, waiting for him to come to her. Though too exhausted to fully appreciate her self-possession, her terror had vanished. She looked at Chen with a Mona Lisa smile, mysterious yet satisfied, complete within herself. When he approached, he leaned toward her in their first kiss. She turned her head and formally offered her cheek. Admiring her dress, he referred to her *qipao's* design.

"The crane among chickens has become the phoenix among cranes."

Then he took her arm and led her outside through the firecrackers' remnants to his limo. Wide red ribbons festooned the car from its hood to its taillights, while its front grill sported a red silk wreath encircling bride and groom dolls. Deep in thought, MacKenzie trailed behind at a discreet distance.

They drove to Chen's condo in *Neihu,* a suburb known for its glorified apartment complexes. "Beverly Hills of Taipei,"

Iris had said when Lane told her where she was moving. As they drove into the exclusive compound, the guard opened the gate with a crisp salute. Chen's men set off hundreds of firecrackers, announcing their arrival to all.

Dogs barked, and children scampered to see the excitement. A small coterie of people swarmed them as they left the limo. Iris opened a large, black umbrella and held it over their heads as they walked along a red carpet, trampling the firecrackers' still-smoldering residue.

"It's not raining," Lane said. "What are you shielding us from?"

"Evil spirit."

"Another tradition?"

Lane took the girl's embarrassed shrug and nervous giggle as a yes. She recognized the wizened face of Chen's aunt as they passed and nodded. The old woman grinned back, exposing a gold tooth. As Chen led her to his home, she saw a familiar silhouette outlined against the marble entrance.

Lane stiffened. It's my imagination, she told herself, her high Mandarin collar suddenly tight, constricting her breathing. She adjusted the neckline and swallowed.

But attentive to her slightest change, Chen questioned her solicitously.

"Is anything wrong?"

"No, nothing," she said a beat too quickly, then looking behind her, she added, "I thought I saw someone I knew, that's all. Was that your aunt?"

"Yes, you met her at our engagement."

She turned back, and suddenly Li's face was in front of hers. Lane gasped and felt Chen's grip tighten on her arm. His tone was sharp as he waved them into his condo.

"Glad you could join us, Nephew. And where's your mother? Why isn't she with you?"

"She isn't well. She's back in the hospital." Reserved, he answered respectfully.

"Sorry to hear that," said Chen, marking their territories. "And the lovely Mei-ling? Where's she?"

"She's . . ." he stole a glance at Lane before concluding, "indisposed."

Lane wondered whether the butterflies she felt were due to Li's baby or his nearness. Determined the pregnancy would not show, she sucked in her stomach, creating as long a vertical line as possible in her *qipao*. The traditional garb hung loosely, concealing her rounded belly, offering her refuge.

Now she tried to hide her feelings as well. Once the initial longing had passed, she eyed Li objectively. How could he have married Mei-ling? She remembered MacKenzie's vindictive words. Was he right? Was Li a two-timing liar? A mama's boy? Her lip curled cynically as she swore he would never learn about their baby.

"How unfortunate she couldn't join us," Chen answered sympathetically, the pupils of his eyes round and small as a rat's. He gauged her response. "Lane," he prompted, "wasn't it kind of Nephew to attend our wedding when he has so much on his mind?"

"Yes," she said hoarsely.

Her mouth as dry as uncooked rice, she suddenly remembered an ancient method for detecting liars. Suspects were given raw rice. Those who could chew it, salivate, were freed. Those with dry mouths were killed. She shuddered and looked away.

"You must visit us when your wife feels better," said Chen, a brief smile tugging at his lips. "Your aunt and I look forward to it."

"Thanks for your hospitality." Li's bloodshot eyes glared.

Then chuckling bitterly, he turned toward Lane. "Congratulations . . . Auntie. I hope you're happy."

Her stomach felt like a flock of birds had given wing. Even her voice was gone.

"Don't you have two reasons to celebrate today?" Li asked.

Too caught up in her thoughts to concentrate, her puzzled expression was her only answer.

"Fourth Thursday in November?" he hinted. When that evoked no response, he said, "Happy Thanksgiving!"

"How could you possibly remember that?" She gave a dubious laugh.

"Americans don't have a monopoly on gratitude." His face took on an earnestness that gnawed at her skepticism. "The pilgrims' story of going to the New World has special meaning for me."

"You?" She snickered uneasily.

"I can relate to it," he said, nodding. "When my father immigrated from mainland China, he thought Taiwan was the land of opportunity, of religious freedom. Sound familiar?"

She blinked in surprise.

"I'm Chinese," Li said, catching her eye, "but Taiwan is my homeland." Then turning, he stared at Chen, his gaze piercing. "Where's your home, Uncle?"

"You're standing in it." Chen's expression silently acknowledged the bait, but he answered evenly.

"I believe that just as much as you do." Li turned to Lane, his question catching her off guard. "Which country will you call home?"

Unsure, she looked to Chen for an answer. Not having had time to discuss their future privately, they were obliged to publicly.

"Where *will* we settle?" she asked. "Here? The States?"

"China?" Before Chen could answer, Li's eyebrows arched defiantly as he challenged his uncle to contradict him.

Nonplused, Chen smiled malevolently, answering with a chuckle.

"Why, Nephew, you surprise me. Have you forgotten? This *is* China. The Republic of China. The provisional capital of all of Ch. . . ."

"Don't quibble with semantics. You know what I mean. Are you planning to live in The *People's* Republic of China? The mainland? I'm sure Auntie's anxious to know."

Lane shot Chen a worried glance. She had not considered China. Feeling the baby quicken, she bit her lip, as much to keep from blanching as from questioning him about her child's fate. Noting her pallor, Chen's eyes bored into Li's.

"There's no reason to upset my wife. This is her wedding day, the happiest day of her life. Help us celebrate. Have something to eat. Have some *jiu.*" Chen's scowl relaxed into a smile. With a genial wave, he led her away from Li, calling over his shoulder, "Join the party, Li. Mingle, but don't stray too far. I have something to ask later."

"Thanks again for your hospitality, Uncle." His jaw clenching, Li gave a terse nod and stalked away.

Chen took Lane's hands in his and whispered, "Don't let him upset you. We'll live wherever you please. . . ." She smiled, relieved that was settled. "Taiwan or Macao."

Her smile shriveled as she recalled Macao's impending restoration to the PRC. Her eyes searched his.

"What about the US? I thought we might. . . ."

"Time enough to discuss that in Thailand," Chen said smoothly, referring to their honeymoon. "We have guests to attend to now."

Her mouth fell open at the words' similarity. Am I marrying my father? Am I leaving one bondage for another?

Anger at her father, Li and Chen intertwined, braided together, forming a rope which she suddenly wanted to tie around Chen's neck.

"No, we'll discuss it *now!*"

"Is it that important to you?"

"It's crucial," she hissed, not caring that people were beginning to stare.

Turning away from the curious onlookers, he paused, then became very conciliatory.

"All right," he said softly, "if it means that much to you, we can live wherever you choose."

She drew a deep sigh, not aware she had been holding her breath. Relaxing, her body swayed against his, so tense had she been until he answered. Relieved, she laughed nervously.

"I don't know what came ov. . . ."

He shushed her, interrupting her apology with a shake of his head. Pleased she was leaning against him, he gently squeezed her cold hand.

"Where I live doesn't matter, as long as it's with you."

His aunt appeared silently, grinning, offering Lane a bowl. Lane smiled unsurely, as skeptical of her future as she was of the bowl's contents. Beige globules floated unappetizingly in a milky liquid. Lane made such a sour face, Chen chuckled. He took the bowl from his aunt and handed it to her.

"It's our custom for the bride to eat lotus seed soup," he said. "It's good. Try it! It ensures the early birth of a son!"

At that Lane blushed, widening the grin on his aunt's face as she moved off and making Chen laugh out loud. The guests looked on approvingly, relieved the couple's first argument had ended. Lane sat down and tasted the soup gingerly, expecting a salty or bitter flavor.

"It's sweet!" she announced, her eyes opening wide in surprise.

Sitting beside her, Chen smiled affectionately. "Of course. At weddings, everything's sweetened." He pointed to the table full of cakes and sweet dumplings.

"Another custom?" she asked, looking at him through her dark eyelashes.

He nodded. "To ensure an agreeable marriage."

She took another spoonful of the soup, then put it down and reached for what looked like a flat, crisp, oval cookie. "What's this?"

"Ox-tongue cake."

"What?!" She put it down immediately.

"It's just in the shape of an ox-tongue." Amused, his eyes crinkled as he explained, his finger tracing its outline. "See? It's a popular snack from *Lukang* and has no ox meat at all." Then he broke off a piece and popped it in her mouth. "How is it?"

She chewed and chewed the light, flaky pastry, then finally took another spoonful of soup to wash it down.

"Delicious but dry."

"These," he said, pointing to small pastry squares, "are pineapple shortcakes, a specialty of *Taichung*. And smell these." He waved a plate of fluffy cookies beneath her nose.

"What is that?" Her eyes lit up at the fragrance.

"Almond powder, but try these."

He passed her a bowl of watermelon seeds. She sampled them, again expecting a salty taste but discovered a unique, sweet one. She raised her eyebrows questioningly.

"Star-anise, although the seeds come in many flavors. Have more, or try these. These also ensure the early birth of a son." His eyes twinkled as he handed her a bowl of boiled peanuts.

"Does everything here ensure an early birth?" she asked, gesturing to the food.

"That or an agreeable marriage. We Chinese are very superstitious." He paused, looking at her bashfully, then stood up. "I know these aren't your customs, but would you humor me with one more?"

She tilted her head questioningly.

"Would you help me pray to my ancestors?"

"I'm not Taoist, David, I'm Christian."

As her forehead wrinkled, he smiled reassuringly, his eyes appealing to hers. "You don't have to believe. Just stand next to me, that's all I ask."

He held out his hand. She took it hesitantly, then followed him toward his ancestral tablets. Calling the people to attention, he lit three sticks of incense and whispered to Lane.

"Bow when I do."

She frowned, whispering back, "No!"

"Then just nod," he said furtively.

"I said I'd come with you, but that's all I promised." Her eyes flashing defiance, she resented his asking her to do one thing and then telling her to do another.

Visibly irritated with her, he muttered, "Don't make me lose face in front of the guests!"

When she shook her head, he scowled, then held the incense to his forehead and kowtowed three times, doing *bai bai*. He placed the incense in a holder and spoke under his breath.

"Nod politely to our guests."

She refused to move. Gruffly taking her hand, he spun her toward the onlookers. Squirming, Lane searched the small crowd and spotted Iris pantomiming an exaggerated nod. Silently, her friend mouthed the word *bow*.

Out of the corner of her eye, she saw him bow deeply, the

tip of his tie sweeping the floor. With Iris' prompting, Lane nodded formally to the people. He then turned toward her.

"Watch me," he whispered tersely. "Do as I do."

He bowed to her three times, bending from the waist. She reluctantly gave him stiff nods in return, the headdress weighing heavily, swaying dangerously. She tilted her head to keep it from toppling, then squinted with pain, feeling a headache coming on.

Smiling, Chen cordially invited the people to help themselves to the desserts and wine. When the guests had scattered, Chen dropped his jovial smile.

"Why did you deliberately embarrass me?"

"Why did I . . . ?"

Too flabbergasted to continue, she took a deep breath. The beads of her headdress shaking, her head beginning to throb, she started again.

"Why did *you* mislead me? At the very least, you could have coached me on your traditions."

"I did," said Chen. "I explained. . . ."

"Asking me to go with you and then barking orders at me in front of the guests is hardly 'explaining.' " Pursing her lips, she jutted her chin at him.

Breathing deeply, he pulled himself up to his full height and planted his hands on his hips, a belligerent pose he had long ago learned to feign. It struck terror in his employees, and he fully expected the same response from his wife. Her tacit disregard confused him. After a moment's fuming, he dropped his arms to his sides, as if tired from the struggle of wills. Giving an amused snort, he thoughtfully rubbed the side of his nose.

"You're right. I assumed you knew more about our customs than you do. You're not essentially Chinese, are you?"

MacKenzie sauntered toward them wearing a wide grin.

Then muscling his way between the couple, he pumped Chen's hand.

"Do I call you son now?"

"Not yet. There's one more ritual before we're married. And regarding *son,* I'm not sure who's the elder, you or me."

The senator forced a wry laugh, his eyes grimly thoughtful. Turning to Lane, he leaned over, trying to kiss her cheek. When she remained stiffly erect, he bent his head to avoid her headdress and settled for brushing his lips against her cheek. He started to speak, cleared his throat, then spoke lamely, formality replacing feeling.

"Congratulations."

She acknowledged him with a cool nod.

He clenched his jaw, then turned back to Chen, clapping him familiarly on the shoulder. "I wonder if I might have a word with you." MacKenzie turned back to his daughter, his words more a statement than a question. "You don't mind if I steal your husband a moment, do you. . . . Now, let me get this straight, Chen. You said the Trade Commission would. . ."

Before she could answer, he had guided his soon-to-be son-in-law away, his words drifting out of range.

Lane stared after them, wondering if it were too late to change her mind. Her father's and prospective husband's similarity made her uneasy. She edged her way to a quiet corner, then closed her eyes, gathering her thoughts, trying to regain some of her earlier confidence, trying to rid herself of her headache. When she felt a hand on her arm, she jumped.

"Sorry." Iris' voice was contrite. Smiling tentatively, she meekly held up four red ribbons imprinted with gold characters. "It time to wear."

"What are they?" Lane studied them, her headache making concentration difficult.

"Badge to wear when Mr. Chen colleague make marriage."

The words sounded so final, Lane panicked. Shaking, her hands reached up to massage her pounding temples. Then her eyes brimming, she began hyperventilating.

"Iris, I don't think I can go through with this."

"Relax." With a lilting laugh, the girl grabbed Lane's shoulders in reassurance, then finished with a perky smile. "It normal to be scary for marriage day."

"But you don't understand, I. . . ."

"You just have cold foot."

It took a silent moment to register. Then Lane began giggling through her tears, her shoulders shaking.

Confounded by her friend's odd reaction, Iris fussed about, trying to be of service. She attached her maid-of- honor's ribbon to her own lapel while waiting for Lane's tears to subside.

She offered a tissue, warning, "You spoil make-up."

She pinned the bride's badge on Lane's *qipao,* not knowing what else to do, then smoothed her hair and straightened her headdress. When Chen and MacKenzie returned ten minutes later, Iris was unnerved, feeling personally responsible that Lane was still snickering and sniffling.

MacKenzie took one look and muttered, "Women!"

"And what does *that* mean?!" His comment jerked Lane from her emotionalism.

Iris intervened quickly, stepping in front of MacKenzie, handing Chen his groom's badge. She smiled innocently.

"You need help?"

Chen shook his head as he pinned on the ribbon. "Does the best man have his badge?"

In answer, Iris held up the remaining red strip. "Should I give to her . . . *him?*" When Chen nodded, she looked puzzled. "Who is?"

"My nephew."

Discovering a speck of lint on his lapel which suddenly deserved his full attention, Chen fastidiously brushed it off, managing to miss the shocked look Lane exchanged with Iris.

"Li?! You can't mean Li?!" Lane's red-rimmed eyes blinked in disbelief.

"Who better to be the *best* man?" He coolly met her stare.

"This is impossible." Lane gasped as the full impact of his words sunk in. "I won't go through with the wedding." Then she started off, her tassels swinging.

"Aren't you forgetting something?" Chen caught her arm and spun her around. He looked pointedly at her waistline.

Clearing his throat, MacKenzie offered a solution. "Maybe someone else could fill in? Perhaps . . . well. . . ." He fell silent, adjusting his cufflinks under Chen's withering stare.

"No, I'm not forgetting *any*thing." Lane shrugged off Chen's arm as she pulled off the badge, letting it flutter to the floor. After taking two steps, she struggled for the worst insult she could imagine. Turning back, she screamed at him. "And to *hell* with your ancestors!"

Then she stomped off, her Mandarin sleeves flapping in her wake. Now it was Chen's turn to gawk, slack-jawed, as an angry red crept over his face. He abruptly recovered, snapping at MacKenzie.

"Do something!"

MacKenzie pivoted toward Iris. "Don't just stand there. Run after her!"

Iris retrieved the ribbon, squeezing between the two men. As she scurried out of hearing, Chen's low voice began.

"If you want that agreement. . . ."

She found Lane in an empty bedroom. Automatically reaching for her tissues, expecting more tears, Iris was surprised to see Lane's eyes bright and dry. So instead of tissues, she held out the badge.

"You drop."

"I don't want anything to do with Dav . . . Chen!"

As she pushed the ribbon away, Lane almost bit her tongue catching herself using his given name. She gravitated toward a mirror, unconsciously tucking in a strand of hair. Then she turned back to her friend.

"The man's infuriating! He's fiendish—no, inhuman—no, insane. No one in his right mind would make his rival the best man." She finished by plopping on the bed.

Iris chewed her lip, wondering how to begin. Finally she sat next to Lane.

"Mr. Chen clever. He businessman."

Iris straightened up proudly, as if that explained it. When Lane scowled, she tried again, grasping the air with her hands, struggling for the right words.

"She . . . *he* arrange thing. He make person *mind* to see. She . . . *he* want you to say good-bye to Li. Now. Forever."

"You mean like at a funeral." Lane's ears perking, she nodded thoughtfully. "A ceremony for a final farewell."

"My vocabulary not good." As Iris shrugged, Lane squeezed her hand affectionately.

"You explain better with a few words than most do with many. Do you give him that much credit, though?" To Iris' puzzled expression, Lane asked again, "You think that's his reason?"

The girl nodded enthusiastically. "He wise man."

"And you're a trusting soul." Her voice skeptical, Lane shook her head slowly. "He's not that wise or considerate. He reminds me too much of my father." Her eyes narrowed. "I think he's a slippery opportunist."

"Another way to say he good businessman?"

"Yeah, I guess it is." Chuckling, Lane conceded.

"He be good husband," said Iris, underscoring her point.

"You mean a good manipulator." Lane's sarcasm weighed as heavily as her headdress.

"Yes," Iris agreed vehemently, "good *man*."

"No, not man, *manipulator*. Forget it." Lane sighed, annoyed by the language barrier. Then suddenly catching their reflections in the mirror, she saw the humor and began giggling. "We're some bride and maid of honor. Look at us!"

"Nothing change since you say you marry Mr. Chen, not him, not ancestor, not Li." Speaking to their images, Iris smiled but remained serious. "Why you want to stop wedding?"

"I've changed."

"Nothing else."

Lane glumly looked at herself in the glass. Then thinking aloud, she forgot Iris was listening. "That's right. Li's married, my father needs Chen's support, my baby needs a name."

"You to have baby?" Iris gasped. When Lane nodded uneasily, Iris hugged her so tightly, the *qipao* wrinkled. "*Zhen de ma?!* Really? Oh, Lane, nothing matter but baby. No one else matter, not even best man. You understand?"

Her eyes shining with new fervor, they held Lane's until she saw assent. Then Iris jumped off the bed, took a compact from her purse and dabbed Lane's face, repairing her smudged make-up. "You have lipstick?"

Lane reached inside a pocket sewn into her long Mandarin sleeve, then held up the tube. "You do it. I'm a little shaky." Lane waited patiently as Iris applied the traditional red color, once again gathering her strength for the ceremony.

"You very luck to have baby. . . ."

Her expression looked so wistful, Lane started to question her, but Iris quickly resumed her serious, practical expression.

"Mr. Chen be good father. You see." Pinning the bride's badge on her, she smiled brightly. "Ready?"

Lane stood up. Taking a deep breath, she shyly smiled back, until she heard a knock and saw Chen open the door.

"I must to help outside." Iris tactfully sneaked behind Chen. Eyes glowing, she held up her thumb in a winner's pose, then left.

Awkwardly Lane realized she was alone with Chen in a bedroom. She clasped her hands together tightly, the sleeves covering them and draping gracefully to her knees. Though the only exposed skin was her face, Lane felt naked and vulnerable.

He closed the door and took a step toward her. She took a step back, in the process stumbling against the bed. To cover her clumsiness, she pretended she had meant to sit on the edge.

"I'm relieved to see you wearing the bride's ribbon," said Chen. "I thought I might be left standing at the altar."

He chuckled nervously as he walked toward her. Though he was smiling, his eyes watched her anxiously. Lane realized they were both uncomfortable, and that encouraged her.

"Iris has a way of looking at things that puts them in perspective."

She considered asking why he had chosen Li as best man but thought against it. Her resolve was too shaky to chance a disappointing answer. At least Iris' logic made the wedding acceptable.

Chen's touch brought back the immediacy of the situation. Standing in front of her, he reached into her sleeve and took her hand.

"Lane, will you be my wife?"

She looked up through the fringe of her eyelashes, swallowed hard and slowly nodded. Before she could resist, Chen lifted her to her feet and hugged her as tightly as Iris had. Loathe to admit it, Lane found the moment not altogether unpleasant. When he loosened his grip, they smoothed their clothes and walked out hand-in-hand.

Chen introduced her to a large man named Ho Yu-lin. Again language was a barrier, but through Chen's translations, she learned Mr. Ho was his superior or boss. Though both words were used, the explanation was unclear, and Lane was unsure of the relationship. All she knew was that he was important to Chen's career and, as such, would witness their wedding.

Chen called the people together. After seating Lane, he presented her with another ring. This one had a central band of the greenest jade with a circle of diamonds above and below. She softly drew in her breath for courage as he placed it on her finger. Then she presented him with a heavy gold band imprinted with the *xi* character of double happiness, the symbol of married bliss.

Helping her up, he led her to Mr. Ho. Iris stood beside her, and Li took his place on the other side of Chen, making it difficult for Lane to see his face. Though she remained impassive, she bitterly wondered what personal reasons had compelled him to participate. Did Chen buy him off? Did his mother make him? Did he want to humiliate her? Did he feel the need to say good-bye?

Because Mr. Ho spoke in Chinese, Lane had little to do but think and watch. As the minutes passed, she began analyzing the wedding members. When they laughed often at Mr. Ho's words, she imagined the man witty. Iris was beaming so widely, guests might have thought she was the bride. Lane hid a gentle smile, then wanting to share the moment, stole a shy glance at Li. He was staring at her so intently, she blushed under her heavy makeup. From the corner of her eye, she peeked at Chen to see his reaction. As usual, his face was inscrutable. Then he turned toward her so quickly, she realized he had witnessed the little drama. Though he said nothing, he took her left hand in his and began toying with her ring, twisting it round and round her finger.

As Mr. Ho droned on, the incessant fingering became annoying. When she pulled away, Chen grabbed her hand so tightly, the diamonds cut into her skin. She bit her lip to keep still, but not before a small sound had escaped, making Li turn his head. His expression as dark as his hair, he eyed Chen mutinously.

Mr. Ho finally concluded, much to Lane's relief. Without further incident, the four signed the wedding certificate. Then the guests engulfed them with congratulations. Chen played the perfect host, all the while keeping her hand in his. When Iris gave her another warm hug, Lane looked for the best man, but he had disappeared. Probably sneaked away, she thought, now that his role's complete.

After her father had bussed her cheek and shaken hands with Chen, he toasted them.

"And what about a wedding cake? It's an American tradition. You know, cutting the cake together, feeding each other? Do they do that sort of thing here?"

Chen nodded. "Only instead of cake, we eat *tang yuan,* a sweet dumpling made from glutinous rice."

Leading them to the dessert table, he smiled tolerantly at their dismayed expressions. Then he picked up two dumplings, handing one to Lane.

"It's gooey," she said, peeling the dough from her fingertips.

He smiled at her like a patient parent, then popped one in her mouth. "Now feed me yours."

As Chen was eating from her hand, Li appeared.

"Perhaps you could tear yourself away from your bride long enough to explain a Chinese adage to me, Uncle. It's said that in marriage, a man takes and a woman's given. I understand how a man takes, but 'given' has two meanings." He shrugged philosophically. "She could be given away, as in *discarded*—or *sold* at discount, or she could be given her husband's love and respect. Which is it, Uncle?"

"I'm surprised someone as smart as y'all needs advice," said MacKenzie, fielding for Chen who was still chewing the sticky dumpling. Li bowed in mock deference as he watched his uncle swallow the last of the chewy confection.

"But as a man respectful of the past generation, I must listen to my elders. Could you explain, Uncle?" asked Li, tongue-in-cheek.

"Such a dutiful boy," said Chen, "so much filial devotion."

First addressing MacKenzie, Chen took Lane's hand in his and turned to Li. The creases around his eyes deepened as his expression became more intense.

"Each relationship should be judged on its own merit, but if you're using this marriage as an example, I'd be glad to explain. My wife was given to me in wedlock. And as you can see, she was given my love and will continue to be given all I can provide."

Wearing a caustic smile, Chen pointed to Lane's heart-and-*mei hua* necklace. His arm reached around her waist possessively, while Lane yielded, unsure how to resist gracefully.

"Now, Nephew, you won't mind if I ask you a question. What more could a wife be given? Or perhaps I *should* ask," he rubbed the side of his nose with his free hand, pausing dramatically, "what more could *you* give?"

A quick estimation of Lane's jewelry told him it would cost several years' salary. Li swallowed his feelings of inferiority.

"A gold heart isn't a man's heart. Love can't be measured in grams." Li turned toward Lane. "In fact, love often isn't what it appears. Unlike gold, it's transmutable, changeable."

Lane felt curious and imperious at the same time. Chen tightened his grip on her waist in a silent warning. Angry with Li for not marrying her, yet for not letting go of her, she pressed.

"Don't give us philosophy. Answer the question. What would *you* offer a wife?"

"*Jiang xin bi xin*. Imagine my heart were yours, and you'd know."

Not a muscle moving on his chiseled face, he turned and left. Suddenly the rushing in her ears and the throbbing at her temples blocked out all else.

His arm still around her, Chen caught her as she slumped.

# CHAPTER 5

Lane woke in a strange room. Overhead, red paper lanterns cast a cozy yet sensuous glow as she wondered where she was and why she felt so lightheaded. Groping for her headdress, she felt it was gone. She touched her neck, reaching for the Mandarin collar, but felt only skin. Except for a chemise, her chest was bare. Startled, she realized she was practically nude.

But not alone. Chen dozed in the chair beside her, snoring, the ends of his bow tie dangling onto his chest.

She looked at her hands. The rings were there. Yes, she was married. This was no nightmare. She gasped, and Chen groaned in his sleep. Afraid to breathe, she lay as still as possible. The last thing she wanted was to wake him. Trying to keep calm, she recalled what had happened.

She reconstructed the events, remembering she had fainted, then been carried into another room. Only half conscious, she had been crying as she heard Chen calling for a doctor and felt Iris chafing her hands, slapping her cheeks. Slowly she remembered Iris helping her out of her *qipao,* and then, later, someone giving her an injection.

Now here she was in her bridal bed. She looked at the festive lanterns, hung for the occasion, and shuddered involuntarily. Chilled, she pulled the covers around her shoulders.

"Good, you're awake. Feeling better?" Stretching, Chen stood up and undid the top two buttons of his shirt.

Lips tight, she gave a terse nod, then pulled the covers higher, embarrassed by his presence. "What time is it?"

"Two. Good morning, Chen *Taitai.*"

After checking his watch, he leaned over and kissed her. Lane shrank from his touch, cowering beneath the sheet. He looked amused as he took off his jacket and unbuttoned his shirt. When he had unfastened his cufflinks and undone his belt, Lane modestly turned away from him.

"Don't worry," he said with a chuckle, "You're still sedated, and I'm too exhausted for anything but sleep."

With a relieved sigh, she snuggled under the covers, yawned and went back to sleep. The next time she woke, she peeked cautiously across the bed. It was empty. Grateful for the privacy, she dressed quickly and found her way to the kitchen. Mildred, the Filipino housekeeper, jumped up from her chair.

"I didn't know you were awake, Miss. Do you want anything? Coffee? Tea? Breakfast?" She looked at the clock, Lane's eyes following. "Lunch?"

Three o'clock? What did that doctor give me? Lane was too surprised by the time to keep up with responses. Instead she struggled with semantics, debating between Chen's familiar and formal names.

"Where's Mr. . . . Dav. . . . Where's Chen?"

"He had an emergency meeting and won't be back until late." Lane hid her annoyance as the woman added, "He's already postponed your flight to Thailand."

Lane felt her headache returning. Rubbing her temples, she began to feel sorry for herself. Though she dreaded keeping the marriage contract, she had been looking forward to getting away. Now the honeymoon was as much a disappointment as the marriage.

"Why weren't you at the wedding? I clearly instructed you. . . ."

"Li's crazy!" Mei-ling's shrill voice interrupted him, rising in pitch. "He locked me in the *yu-shi*. First he spilled tea on my dress. Then when I went to rinse it, he locked me in the bathroom. He's lost his mind!"

Chen's tone was a sober contrast. "You said you could handle him. If you can't. . . ."

"The man's. . . ."

"I'll get someone who can." Chen finished despite her interference. Then he added a warning. "Brush up on your communication skills, Mei-ling. If you're as articulate with him as you are with me, I might as well sky-write him my messages."

"But he. . . ."

"You've got what you want. You're married to him and half-owner of the Juliet Club for your efforts. Now give me what I paid for. Keep Li occupied. Make him forget Lane." His voice took on a sharpness. "Can you do that?"

Seething, Mei-ling bit back a shrewish answer, thankful he could not see her reaction through the phone. When she remained silent, Chen continued.

"Why did you agree to this if you couldn't deliver? The partnership or spite?"

"You wouldn't believe it was for love, I suppose?"

As her mouth trembled, she was glad again of the anonymity of phone calls. Chen laughed until she interrupted him.

"I told you, I already was married to him."

The laughter continued.

"I *was* married to him, damn it."

"Sure you were." Though still laughing, he spoke in conciliatory tones.

"Chen, I have witnesses."

"Who? Two friends too drunk to remember what really happened?" His voice lowered an octave, registering his disbelief. "If you *were* legally married, why would you have needed 'another' certificate of marriage for last month's wedding?"

"I . . . it wasn't a formal wedding," she stuttered. "He . . . he, that is, we wanted to wait until. . . ."

"Don't bullshit, Mei-ling. Your alibis are like ripe sushi. Both smell." He sighed, his tone softening. "But if it helps you to believe this story, stick to it. Anything to make you more convincing. What about his mother? Does she buy it?"

"I'm carrying her grandson," she snapped. "She believes whatever I say."

Chen heard the false bravado in her voice. "The question is, does Li?"

Lane was stretched out on the bed. He watched her from the doorway, admiring her dark hair spreading out from her delicately-featured face. With her almond and peach-blush complexion, she reminded him of a cameo. Trying not to disturb her nap, he shuffled across the marble floor into the dimly-lit room.

She woke with a start, brushing the hair from her eyes. Genuine fear in her voice, she called, "Who is it?"

"Your husband." He answered with forced nonchalance, still having trouble believing this beautiful creature was his wife. "I see your color's returned. Are you feeling better?"

She tried not to appear as startled as she felt. Recovering her presence, she arranged her hair and wrapped her collar tighter about her neck.

"Yes, thank you," she said stiffly, turning on the lights.

Her polite distance chafing him, he hid an annoyed moue.

"Would you like to go out for dinner? A new Mongolian barbecue opened nearby, or maybe you prefer vegetarian."

When she did not answer, he tried again.

"Of course, if you don't feel up to it, we could eat at home."

She visibly shuddered at the word *home,* wondering why she had locked herself into this marriage. She studied him through critical eyes, reevaluating him now that the deed was done. Under the bright light, she noted the faint lines around his eyes, the slight jowls, the soft paunch of his belly.

Her scrutiny not lost on him, his cheeks blotched a mottled red. Discomfort gave way to anger. Then covering it with forced civility, he shot her a coy look.

"Maybe you'd prefer to eat in our room? Dinner for two, a romantic way to celebrate our first meal alone as man and wife."

He emphasized the last word, rolling it over his tongue, the sound menacing and sibilant. She stood up to face him. In his slippers, he was shorter than she. He must wear lifts, she thought, gaining self-confidence from the knowledge.

"That's something I wanted to discuss. Until we're more . . . comfortable with each other, I'd feel better having separate rooms. After fainting yesterday, I need my strength."

She noted his eyes were level with hers as they darted left and right, taking in every nuance of her expressive face. Gaining courage, she continued to stare back. But when he took a step closer, she held up her hands as if fending him off. Before he could object, she spoke quickly .

"And I need more time."

He breathed deeply, reassessing the situation. Finally he gave her an abrupt nod.

"I'm a patient man, but remember, you are my wife—in every sense of the word." His voice took on a new edge. "How long will it take you to feel 'comfortable'? A day? A week? A month? What about our honeymoon? Did you want separate rooms for that, too?"

Annoyed, she looked away, staring at the wall sconces. Sarcasm hung from his words like the prisms from the light fixtures. Then she turned her eyes toward him and watched him coolly, not intimidated by his outburst.

"Let's wait until Phuket to . . . get acquainted. When's the flight?"

"I left it open until you recovered from yesterday's illness."

Although his heavy lids veiled his eyes, Lane caught his tone, his sarcastic emphasis on the word *illness*. That's not consideration, she realized. It's jealousy.

"If you've recovered from our nephew's bad manners," he continued, "My aide'll book us flights tomorrow."

She agreed with a nod. "But until then and after we return, I want separate rooms."

He looked at her animated face, at the snug fit of her blouse over her swelling breasts. *Aiiee,* he thought, the farther she pulls away, the closer I want her. He nodded reluctantly, then put on a pleasant face.

"So," he asked affably, "where would you like dinner?"

A tap at the door interrupted them. "Chen *xian-sheng,*" called the aide, *"dianhua."*

Chen picked up the bedside phone. *"Wei."*

Sitting down, he began a conversation in Chinese. Lane watched him get more agitated with each exchange, his face hardening. When he put down the receiver, he turned to her with a wry grin.

"I'm afraid our honeymoon will be delayed again. Wong Xiaoping has had a stroke."

"What has that to do with us?" she asked innocently.

Though Lane saw no connection, Chen could not believe her naiveté. He began to repeat her question, then swallowed his sarcasm and resumed in a patient voice.

"Wong's health is vital to the Hang Seng Index. If he dies, Hong Kong's markets will plunge, destabilizing the entire finance, commerce and business sectors of southeast Asia. My company's at risk. I have to leave on the next flight."

He stood up abruptly and started for the door.

"When are you coming back?" she asked peevishly.

"I don't know. I'll call."

"If he dies before appointing an heir, who'll succeed him?" asked Ho Yu-lin, sweating, visibly shaken by Wong's comatose condition.

"Zheng, of course," said Chen, nodding affirmatively in the President's direction.

"Can you guarantee it?" Zheng asked.

The three men sat in one of the Fangshan Restaurant's private dining rooms, overlooking the artificial hills and pavilions of Beijing's Beihai Park. Because the eatery specialized in the Dowager Empress' preferred entrees from her infamous 120-course meals, it was President Zheng's favorite restaurant. But today he was too tense to enjoy the food. Sending mild karate chops to his upper shoulders, he waited impatiently for Chen's answer as he used shiatsu to relieve his stiff neck and indigestion.

"The People's Republic of China needs three things for super-power status," Chen said, reviewing their goals, "improved international trade, Taiwan's reunification and Tsai's political 'passing.' These accomplished, as Speaker of the People's Congress you're as good as nominated."

"That's merely the line of accession, not news," barked the President. "Tell me something that is."

"Because of my marriage to the Senator's daughter, the PRC has vastly improved US and international trade relations. The trade agreement's all but concluded, and China's

MFN status is an accomplished fact."

"You've done well," Zheng said, his brief nod recognizing Chen's coup, "*so far,* but the US Congress still hasn't ratified the agreement, and you've done nothing in the other two areas. Taiwan's clamoring for independence, and Tsai's accepting kudos that are mine! What about my opponent?"

"Why not kill two birds with one arrow?" asked Chen. "Speed both Taiwan's reunification and Tsai's demise."

Chen leaned back, basking as easily in his interrogator's spotlight as Thai sunlight. He was a survivor. He came out on top whether in a hot seat or a honeymoon suite.

"How?" asked Zheng with renewed interest.

"Taipei wants to exchange high officials, upper-echelon administrators with Beijing."

"Why?" asked Ho Yu-lin suspiciously, his wide nostrils quivering as he sniffed danger.

"The ROC wants to renew cross-strait talks, improve trade relations." Chen paused, savoring the moment. "Send Tsai."

"No!" shouted Ho Yu-lin. "He'll *gain,* not lose, popularity. You know the KMT supports Tsai, branding him the moderate and Zheng the hard-liner. The Kuomingtang'll make concessions for Tsai it wouldn't ordinarily consider, just to give him face. The KMT Nationalists are chafing to show the People's Republic how accomplished a leader he is. No, it's political suicide for Zheng to send him!"

Chen waited for Ho Yu-lin's bluster to pass. "It's not suicide," he said. "It's manslaughter. And not Zheng's, but Tsai's."

"How do you mean?" Zheng's eyes flickered like charcoal catching fire.

"Taiwan's Democratic People's Party is set against any official cross-strait exchanges," said Chen. "The DPP's staging independence demonstrations, rallies and marches on a weekly basis."

"So?"

"I have infil-traitors," Chen said, sneering at his private joke, "who'll incite the rabble to violence. It doesn't take much to rouse those disgruntled taxi drivers—a few words, a little wine, and they're ready to fight anyone, from the crooked clerks at the taxi-licensing bureau to Chiang Kai-shek's old guard."

"Demonstrations won't touch Tsai," said Ho Yu-lin. "If he visits Taiwan, he'll gain popular support at home."

"Maybe Tsai'll gain face, but he'll lose his head."

Zheng eyed Chen caustically. "How so?"

"Assassination," said Chen, rubbing the side of his nose. "We incite—or bribe—one of the ruffians to kill Tsai."

"What if the plot fails?" asked Ho Yu-lin.

"No matter," said Chen. "Either way we win. Even an *attempted* assassination's an international incident. The PRC will be rightfully outraged, and world opinion will be on China's side."

"For what?"

"Retaliation," said Chen. "If Taiwan strikes the first blow, China has every right to stage a counter-attack on its renegade province." He spoke under his breath. "When subdued, the wayward wife succumbs to her husband."

"So by sending Tsai, I can't fail," said Zheng slowly, rewording the plan as he assimilated its possibilities for personal success. "If Tsai's killed, I'm unopposed as Wong's successor. If the assassination fails, Tsai looks like a bleating sheep for his foolish "one country/two system" liberalism, and I ride the tiger." Then remembering their discussion was about China's victory, not his own, President Zheng added, "Either way, Mainland retaliates for Taiwan's aggression and regains the island."

Chen left the dinner-meeting feeling satisfied. Self-assured of his role in the political accession, he suffered neither indecision nor indigestion as he strolled leisurely to the East Gate and hailed a cab.

"Sorry, Mr. Chen," said his aide, meeting him at the trade company's office, "but the archives had no record of Empress Ci-xi's *Special Edict* deeding the Tiaoyutai archipelago to Sheng Hsuan-hui or his descendants. I spoke with the Minister of Antiquities at the Chinese National Archives, himself, but he believes the paper never existed."

Chen rubbed the side of his nose thoughtfully. "That, or it was destroyed during the Cultural Revolution."

"So many records were burned," agreed the aide, the quintessential yes-man, "especially documents from the Imperial era. If the paper ever existed, it's not likely to have survived the purge."

"No?" Chen reached for a cigarette as his aide lit it. "Mao was thorough in his repression of the past, but not its total obliteration. Keep searching."

Each night Chen phoned Lane with the same message: "I don't know. I'll call."

A week later she heard on the six o'clock news that Wong had passed away, still in his coma. When Chen called that night, she listened dully, fearing her reprieve was over. As Phuket loomed on the horizon with its scenic beaches and promised accountability, she realized she dreaded his return. Assuming he would announce his ETA, she let her mind wander as she rehearsed how she would tell him their marriage was a mistake.

". . . so I've been delayed another ten days," he said, "until the funeral's over and the market rebounds. My aide'll take care of the Thailand reservations."

"What?"

Drawn from her reverie, she could not believe her ears. He repeated his message, vexed at her lack of concentration.

"I hope that doesn't inconvenience you," he added.

Breathing a silent prayer at the postponement, she answered civilly, vaguely wondering why he never suggested she join him in Macao. But she kept her thoughts to herself, exulting in their delayed union.

The ten days stretched into three insufferable weeks. Though relieved by her continuing freedom, Lane's anxiety level continued to climb. She never knew when her single lifestyle would end. Since Macao was only an hour's flight away, she expected to see Chen each day, yet each night he called with another temporary respite. The suspense caused her a nervous stomach and sleepless nights.

And Li. After tossing for hours, she could not get him out of her mind, married or not. Insomnia and indigestion were her constant companions. Still she would not have complained at all, except for the disturbing cramps and spotting. When she mentioned it to Iris, the girl gasped.

"Hang up! I call to doctor."

After the examination, the obstetrician met with Lane in his office. He spoke somberly, drumming on his desk for emphasis.

"Two weeks in the hospital. Complete rest, or you could lose the baby."

It was December twenty-third. Chen still was not back, and Lane did not want to spend the holidays alone in a hospital ward. She reflected for a moment.

"Couldn't I get as much rest at home?"

"You should be under constant observation," said the doctor.

"Even if I promise to stay in bed?"

She bit her lip to keep it from quivering. As he watched her eyes well up, he relented.

"Only if you promise to stay off your feet *entirely* for the two weeks."

Her depression continued into the next day. She listened to Christmas carols on ICRT, then angrily switched off the radio, opting instead for television. Even old reruns sabotaged her. Everything made her homesick. Her feet propped up under the covers, she called her father, wishing him a merry Christmas. The twelve-hour time difference caught him just as he was getting up, and his flat conversation only deepened her depression. Iris called to say good-bye. Her friend was driving her to *Ilan* for the long weekend.

"While West celebrate Christmas," she said with her characteristically dry humor, "Taiwan have Constitution Day. Chiang Kai-shek Christian. He sign document on December 25. Only way Buddhist country to make Christmas national holiday."

When they hung up, Lane felt lonelier than ever. Sighing, she flipped through a magazine, then halfheartedly started a letter, and finally opened a book. As she was getting into the plot, the housekeeper tapped tentatively at her open bedroom door.

"Mrs. Chen?" Lane scowled at the name, but the woman continued, oblivious. "I said you were ill, but you have a visitor who insists on seeing you."

Lane's pulse jumped, but she tried to remain calm, telling herself Li would never visit her there. Yet who else could it be? She pinched her cheeks and drew the covers closer to her neck, smiling for the first time all day.

"Show him in," she chirped.

"Not him, *her*."

With a laugh, Iris swept into the room, carrying a bulging plastic bag. Lane's expression drooped, but only for a moment. Then glad to see her friend, she brightened, motioning to the chair by her bed.

"I thought you were on your way South."

Iris pulled three paper-wrapped bundles from the bag and handed them to Lane. The lumpy packages made crackling sounds when she squeezed them.

"What is this stuff?" Lane asked.

"Chinese medicine. My friend father *traditional* doctor."

Lane unwrapped the first bundle and looked at the shaved bark, sliced roots, leaves and dried berries. She smiled uncertainly.

"I don't mean to sound ungrateful," Lane said, "but what do I do with this?"

"Boil and drink."

Iris' lilting laughter did more good than any herbs or medicine. Lane laughed with her for no reason at all, just glad for her company.

"Make you and baby strong."

"You mean if the western medicine fails, this is the substitute? Like chicken soup, it can't hurt."

Iris nodded enthusiastically as she gave directions. "Since three day, you be right as ran."

"Right as rain."

But as Iris stood up and squeezed her hand, Lane's smile disappeared. "You have to go so soon?"

"My friend wait in car." At the door Iris turned and smiled sheepishly. "I maybe to have surprise. I phone you." Before Lane could answer, she called, "*Sheng-dan kuai-le!* Merry Christmas!"

"Happy Constitution Day!"

Lane chuckled to herself, warmed by her friend's concern

and curious about her mystery. With a sigh, she returned to her novel. Later when she heard the housekeeper's tentative knock, she picked up the packages and spoke without taking her nose out of the book.

"Can you take these into the kitchen?"

Looking up, her eyes met Li's, and she dropped the bundles on the bedspread. Lane blinked, blushed, then modestly yanked the covers up to her neck, scattering the shaved bark and sliced roots. Though Mildred rushed to help, Lane motioned her off.

"Is this a bad time?" he asked tactfully. "I could come back later."

"No, no, I'd probably be just as klutzy then, too."

She grinned self-consciously, pulling twigs from her hair. After brushing herself off, she motioned to the chair beside the bed. The herbs kept her from acting as uneasy as she felt with him.

He gently reached over and picked a leaf from her bangs before he sat down. It was so natural, so intimate. She never knew she had nerve endings on the tips of her hair, but his simple gesture made her blush to her roots. For an awkward moment, neither spoke. Then both began simultaneously.

"Ladies first."

He laughed uneasily, his large white teeth glistening. Then he cocked his head to one side, almost shyly. Though her eyes danced, she folded her arms across her chest and hugged herself tightly.

"No you. Guests first."

"I called your office to wish you merry Christmas, but Iris said you were sick. It's nothing serious, I hope."

Though he had tried to contact Lane dozens of times since the wedding, he bit his tongue to keep from mentioning the refused calls and unanswered messages. His finding out about her illness had been purely accidental. Because the embassy's receptionist was on another line, Iris had picked up the phone. He suspected the rude brush-offs from Mildred and the office secretary had been courtesy of Chen's orders or bribes, but he was still unsure. After his behavior, he could not underestimate Lane's contempt, and with her crossed arms Lane's defensive posture did little to reassure him.

Blissfully ignorant of his dilemma, Lane debated how much to divulge of her own secrets. She shook her head, smiling tightly to keep her mouth closed. He laughed in exasperation.

"Is this a guessing game, or are you going to tell me what's wrong?"

Embarrassed, she tried to think up a plausible fib. Shrugging her shoulders, she concluded innocently, "The doctor just thought I was overdoing it and needed a rest. That's all."

He studied her thoughtfully. Seeing the skeptical tilt to his eyebrow, she changed the subject.

"How's your mother?"

Hesitating, he answered, "She's dying."

As his eyes clouded, Lane ducked her head, embarrassed she had asked. Then peeking through her lashes, she saw the pain in his eyes.

"Oh, Li, I'm so sorry. I didn't know. Is there anything I can do?"

"There's nothing anyone can do, just make her comfortable, make her happy." He smiled to break the melancholy. "But 'tis the season to be merry, right?"

"You don't have to pretend with me. If I'd known. . . ." She stopped speaking as a maverick thought entered her head. Was it possible? "Li, does your mother's illness have anything to do with your marrying. . . ." Unable to speak the name, she finished lamely, ". . . *her?*"

"She . . . the one had nothing to do with the other." He blanched a sickly white as he stuttered.

"Oh, Li! Why didn't you tell me?" She reached for his hand.

Then she remembered their phone conversation the night she accepted Chen's proposal and how she wouldn't listen. Regret swept over her, then as quickly was replaced with rage. How could he be so stupid?! If he hadn't married that girl, neither of them would be this miserable.

Silence reigned as they both sat alone with their thoughts, biting back mutual recriminations. Lane heard the phone ring, but it wasn't until the housekeeper tapped on her door that she flinched.

"Mr. Chen would like to speak to you." The woman looked at Lane still holding Li's hand. Her jaw fell open. "Should I tell him you're asleep?"

"No, that won't be necessary. Thank you."

Lane jerked her hand away, then waited until Mildred left, using the time to gather her thoughts. She excused herself coolly, picked up the receiver and answered Chen in the same tone. As they spoke, Li tactfully walked to the other side of the room, apparently lured by the watercolors.

"I had hoped to be home by Christmas," Chen said with a tired sigh, "but the market's still jittery. Between Wong's death, the new leadership's power struggle and the PRC taking control of Macao, investors are skittish." His tone warmed. "Sorry, but with the market as unsettled as it is, I won't be able to get away until New Year's."

"So, you'll be arriving next Friday?"

Lane's heart sank, knowing the showdown was near. She tried to be polite, as much for Chen's sake as for Li's, who she sensed was listening, even though his back faced her. After a moment of silence, Chen realized the communication problem.

"No, not the western New Year, the *Lunar* New Year. I can't return until February."

Lane's face lit up. Her eyes danced as she thought of all the possibilities another month offered. Then she remembered her manners.

"Oh, that *is* too bad."

"Yes," he answered dryly, hearing her pause. "I'd better let you rest. Goodnight, Lane. I'll call again tomorrow."

" 'Night."

She listened for the click of his phone before she put down the receiver. Uncomfortable that Li had listened to her husband's call, Lane balked at making conversation. Li began for her in a gloomy monotone that stated, more than asked.

"So Uncle's returning next week."

"Not really. He's delayed until February."

She tried to keep the glee from her voice. Their eyes met in a jubilant recognition, then she looked away modestly. Again a silence.

"Are. . . ." He wanted to invite her out but was afraid of being presumptuous. Clearing his voice, he started again. "Would you meet me for lunch New Year's day?"

He watched her reaction cautiously, not wanting to reveal how much he feared her rejection. Weighing the risks, she considered it slowly, inadvertently adding to his anguish.

"I promised the doctor not to get out of bed for two weeks."

Relieved, he said, "Is *that* all?" Then as he caught her shocked expression, he tried again. "I meant, *that's* something I can fix. Leave it to me."

January first. Lane looked from the new calendar to the mirror. Taking inventory of herself, she tried to be objective.

Because of the enforced rest, her eyes looked clear and relaxed, neither scowling as they had after the wedding, nor ringed with dark circles. Her hair softly framed her face like undulating silk. The gold tones of her silk hostess pajamas warmed her pale complexion, while the festive red *dai ichi* design on her quilted satin bed-jacket contrasted with her emerald eyes. Not bad, she told herself, smiling at her reflection.

She looked at her bedroom transformed into a chic suite. Upholstered chairs on rollers pulled up to the antique cherrywood bed. A narrow linen-covered table separated the bed from the chairs but was in easy reach of both. Seven-color-jade urns of flowers filled the room, creating the scent and feel of a subtropical garden. And a traditional, 'old-man' tea service rested on the hand-carved mahogany drainboard.

Twelve hours earlier, as 1999 chimed in, she had done some soul-searching. In her solitude, she had come to terms with herself, deciding to ask Chen for an annulment when he returned in February.

To start over, that was her New Year's resolution.

Her decision made it morally easier to meet Li. This way, she felt she was not deceiving Chen. Still her conscience nagged, and she found herself justifying their dinner-date.

It's just lunch. Period. What's the big deal? She caught her reflection in the mirror. Nothing, except that my red cheeks and glistening eyes look like I'm running a temperature, and I feel as nervous as a sixth-grader at her first dance. This is ridiculous. I'm a married woman eighteen weeks pregnant.

At noon exactly Lane heard the front doorbell. She primped involuntarily, tucking her hair behind her ears, straightening her collar. Moments later her housekeeper tapped at her door as she wore a prissy, disapproving frown.

"Mr. Yang's outside." Mildred's voice rose an octave, anticipating hopefully. "Should I tell him you're resting?"

"Whatever for? Send him in."

Lane struggled not to show her annoyance with the woman as Li came in, carrying several bags with him.

"*Xin-nian kuai-le!* Happy New Year!" he said, carefully handing her the packages, one by one.

"Happy New Year!" Smiling now, she pretended to weigh each in her hand. "What's in these? Gold bars?"

"Lunch. Hungry?"

She stared at him, starved for more than mere food. He looked so handsome with his hair swept across his temples, his jawline firm, showing more strength of character than she felt in his presence. She stared at his mouth, remembering its taste, its insistent pressure on hers. Looking into his dark eyes, she suddenly realized he was waiting for an answer. What was the question?

"Yes, I'm famished. How about you?"

They ate *dim sum,* a smorgasbord of bite-sized dumplings made with pork, shrimp, steamed turnips and glutinous rice. Then they finished with traditional New Year's red bean and rice cake and washed it down with steaming thimble-sized cups of chrysanthemum tea.

During dinner they talked of the year to come, carefully avoiding the past. They kept to neutral topics, veering away from the personal, relying instead on current affairs. Hong Kong and China's '99 takeover of Macao headed the agenda.

"What'll happen now that Wong's gone?" she asked.

"That's what everyone's asking. If I had the answer, I'd never have to work again."

Thinking aloud, she said, "Chen told me the market's explosive, what with everyone so unsure of the future."

"You call your husband by his surname?"

He stared at her skeptically, not bothering to mask his belief that hers was a loveless marriage. Trying to recover gracefully, she laughed.

"It's a hard habit to break. That's what my father calls him." Then returning to the less volatile subject of politics, she asked, "Do you think Macao's takeover will affect Taiwan?"

Like a good guest, he played along, answering her question as if he had not seen into her private life.

"Economically it might, but I don't think the PRC'd be foolish enough to spring any military maneuvers." His frown returned briefly. "Still, you never know. China has a history of swooping down on lost provinces like a duck on beetles."

"We're not in any danger, are we?"

"Of course not. Today's China is totally different from yesterday's."

"Somehow your words are less than comforting since you've just compared 5000 years of history to a day." She chewed the inside of her lip. "How long does China hold grudges?"

"Smile when you say that, stranger." Li's face broke out in a toothy smile. "This is the East, not the wild and woolly West."

"You're right, and this is supposed to be a celebration, not a Mainland Affairs Conference." She laughed, then gasped in mock horror, again changing the subject. "It's New Year's, and we haven't even drunk a toast yet."

Stretching for the teapot, her jacket pulled open to reveal her silk-sheathed tummy. Li stole a swift glance and did a double-take. Unaware that her blossoming belly was outlined, she poured two doll-sized cups of tea before she felt his eyes on her.

"What?"

"You never told me why you had to rest," he said casually. "You seem healthy enough. What could cause you to stay in bed for two weeks?"

The pause lengthened uncomfortably. In the stillness, they heard the fax machine whistling mechanically in Chen's office. When the silence continued and she still offered no explanation, he insisted gently.

"How long?"

"How long *what?*"

She stiffened, willing herself calm as she discreetly drew her jacket around her. He grabbed her hand away.

"Don't cover up." His eyes seemed to pierce the silk. "Why didn't you tell me? How long have you been pregnant?"

"I haven't announced it yet, because it's too soon to be sure." She marveled at her self-control, managing to speak in an unruffled, patient tone.

"Don't give me that crap! Mei-ling says she's six months pregnant, and compared to you her stomach's as flat as a model's. *This* is a belly."

He gestured toward her middle. Then his eyes narrowing, he took on an accusing tone.

"You've been married a month. This baby's, what, four, five months old? Don't try to tell me it's Chen's! It's our baby, isn't it?"

He turned her face toward him. When she didn't answer, he tilted up her chin.

"Isn't it?!"

Lane played the odds. He can guess, but he can't be sure. She jerked away his hand.

"It's Chen's."

"Chen's?"

He stressed the word sarcastically, then laughed louder

than necessary. Lane worried the housekeeper would come running.

"Chen's?!" he shouted. "The 'father' of your child and you don't call him by his given name? Not likely."

"Keep your voice down." Whispering, she glanced at the open door.

"Then give me the truth, Lane." He lowered his voice as his anger escalated. "Who *is* the baby's father?"

She stared blankly on the wall, debating whether or not to confirm what he already surmised. She remembered him walking away from their engagement. She thought bitterly of his marriage to Mei-ling and his behavior at her own wedding. Then focusing numbly at the ring still glittering on her left hand, she recalled her father's debts and alliance with Chen.

As the lull stretched into another pause, he realized she would not answer. He moved the table aside, sat on the edge of the bed and covered her hands with his. No longer questioning, he stated a fact.

"It's ours," he said.

"Now what do we do?" she said, looking straight ahead as if in a trance.

"Start over."

His words woke her from the reverie, echoing her own New Year's resolution. She watched as he motioned to the roundness that was their baby.

"We belong together, the three of us."

He slipped off her ring, gently laying it on the table, and nuzzled her hand. They discussed the obstacles, the alternatives. He reluctantly agreed with her decision not to tell Chen until February, ending with a caution.

"Just be ready to move at any time."

"What about Mei-ling," she asked, "and *her* baby?"

He shook his head, focusing on their hands—long, pink fingertips resting in blunt, squared palms.

"It's not my child she's carrying. I've suspected that for some time, deep down, but I wasn't able to admit it 'til now. I've been living a lie, so a dying woman can cling to her dreams. I only meant to do the right thing, but I've hurt so many others in the process." Turning his eyes to hers, he said, "Lane, I'm sorry."

As she stroked his hand thoughtfully, she hesitated voicing what would sound like an accusation.

Finally he prompted her. "What?"

"Things would've been so much easier if you'd told me sooner."

As she sighed, he reached around her shoulders and gently pulled her close. They hugged wordlessly, enveloped in their arms' cocoon, contentedly breathing in the familiar security of the other's scent, hearing nothing but their heartbeats and wistful, unspoken regrets.

The housekeeper rapped loudly on the door.

"Mrs. Chen," she said sharply, stirring them from their daydream, "do you want me to clear away the dishes now?" The woman had an indignant, self-righteous air about her, as if she had caught them committing adultery.

"No, that won't be necessary." Lane tried to down-play the incriminating scene as Li's arms slowly dropped to his side.

"Perhaps if Mr. Yang is leaving soon, I. . . ."

Coldly formal, Lane interrupted. "I'll call when you're needed."

"I'll get more hot water." She moved toward the tea service.

"No *thank* you!" Lane's voice rose in tandem with her temper.

When the woman scuffled out, Li's brow furrowed skeptically.

"Maybe I should go. Mildred's been here for years. She thinks this is her house, not yours, and she'd be only too happy to exaggerate our 'infidelities.' "

"No, I'm tired of being manipulated. Now that we've admitted the truth, I hate to keep up any pretenses."

She looked so forlorn, Li reached over and smoothed her hair behind her ear.

"It's only for another month. In February, we'll tell Uncle, Mei-ling and Mother. Until then, remember I love you." As he brushed her temple with his lips, she caught her breath.

"I thought I'd never hear those words again."

The days passed slowly. When the spotting didn't subside, the doctor insisted on a hospital stay. Again Lane stubbornly refused, promising to rest in bed. The doctor finally relented, but the hours dragged as slowly at home as in a ward.

She hadn't seen Li in three weeks. Not surprisingly, he had been transferred to Macao the day after their New Year's dinner. Although he called each night, as did Chen, Lane felt lonelier than ever. Iris stopped by occasionally, but the visits were short and less frequent.

"Too much works," she complained. "Every night consul stay overtime. Type this, fax that," she mimicked, crossing her arms scornfully. "Macao takeover *ma fang*."

"I'm sure it's more than 'inconvenient' to Macao." Lane chuckled at the description, then tried to cheer up her overworked friend. "Be glad China's not taking over Taiwan."

"You hear something?" The girl looked up quickly, her face a blank mask hiding her fear.

A sobered Lane said, "No, why?"

"Oh, nothing."

Iris changed back to her sociable tone, her face again becoming as animated as water coming to a boil. Lane marveled at the mood-swing. Still she couldn't help but get caught up in her friend's dynamic energy.

"Did I tell about Iming?"

"No!"

"Remember when I bring herb?" Lane nodded, remembering only too well. "Iming father make. They work?" She looked up expectantly.

Lane nodded, despite the fact they had made her gag and vomit. She homed in on more important issues.

"Is this Iming a friend or a *friend?*"

*"Friend!"* Bubbling over with pent-up excitement, Iris' tone meant serious boyfriend.

"Was this your surprise? How long have you kept him secret?" Lane stopped, caught her breath, then said, "No, *first* tell me how you met him."

Iris blinked, remembering far more than she told of their first meeting. "It Asia blind date. My parent, his parent, Iming and me."

"What! That's not my idea of a blind date."

"Well," she explained, "after age thirty. . . ."

"You're not thirty, are you?" Lane stared hard at the girl, taking in the unlined forehead and petite figure. "You look about twenty-two."

"Thirty-three, almost past age to marriage." Iris shook her head, flattered, blushing as she forced a smile. "Iming mother think I too old for childrens. My parent arrange. They want grandson."

She glossed over their first meeting, laughing at her fears, keeping back cultural codes of behavior. She did not tell Lane it was understood that if Iming liked her, they would marry. Their first meeting had been as simple—and complex—as that. By arranging it, their families had already preapproved. She and Iming were the same age. With her education—the two-year secretarial course at Ming Chuan College—she was considered a relatively good catch despite her age. Iming was a high-school educated cab-driver, but he was a male, an unwed woman's admission ticket into Chinese society.

Considering what her life had been without a husband, Iris' fragile smile trembled. As an unmarried daughter, she had no social status in the Chinese family-centered culture. Peer pressure had been mounting each year, but her own clock had ticked louder than relations' taunts. She was tired of being the only single girl at extended family dinners, at annual class reunions. She was tired of the Japanese euphemism *single-noble,* tired of being alone, tired of not fitting in, and she would do whatever it took to change her position, even if it meant being nice to the old crone who was his mother.

But retelling the story, Iris kept her insecurities to herself, sharing instead a rosy rendition with Lane, laughing at the trials.

"Tonight Iming take me for *Yang Rou Ru,* hotpot of winter herb and mutton. Very romantic, with spark from charcoal fire." She blushed. "She . . . *he* propose maybe. New Year good lucky for wedding!"

She giggled, familiarly holding onto Lane's hand. Then with a bright smile, she held Lane at arm's length, studying her as if for the first time.

"This your first Lunar New Year?" Before Lane could answer, she continued, "Big Chinese festival! With weekend, five day off, firework, many food, family dinner, *hong bao,* red envelope of money, two-month bonus. . . ." She squealed. "You very much like!"

Iris' enthusiasm was infectious, but after she left, something gnawed at Lane as she mentally reran their conversation. Glad for her friend's near engagement and obvious delight, she wished her luck. Yet Lane realized her flip remark about China had disturbed her. Why? Had Iris heard anything? Her brow puckered thoughtfully. Then she tried laughing it off, knowing how consulates are rumor mills. They thrive on sour grapes and grapevines.

But try as she would, she could not dismiss it. She considered calling Chen; he would separate rumors from facts. Then she remembered his office had closed hours before. She searched for his Macao home number but, paging through her directory, realized she did not have it.

"That's odd," she mused out loud. When he called an hour later, she asked, "Where can I reach you at night?"

The pause was nearly imperceptible. "Why, you can turn over and nudge me. I'm flying back tomorrow."

She shuddered, and not from the damp weather. Lane knew February was approaching—January had certainly crawled—but she was still not prepared to broach the annulment. Phone calls were one thing: impersonal, no reaching out or touching. She had learned to handle them, talking with Chen as she would a colleague from work. But face to face, sternum to sternum, would be another matter entirely. Wrapping her robe tighter, she switched topics.

"Iris just left. She acted very mysteriously. Is Taiwan in any danger?"

He paused before answering. "From what? Unseasonable typhoons? Earthquakes?"

"No, nothing like that. It. . . . Oh, I'm probably just imagining things." She regretted mentioning it, especially after his voice took on such a serious timbre.

"What did she say?"

Reluctantly she answered, "It wasn't what she said as much as her reaction. I joked about the PRC including

Taiwan in its Macao takeover, and I thought she'd choke."

He took a deep breath. "You shouldn't make reckless jests, Lane. Exercise more discretion next time. Working in a consulate, you should know that."

"I haven't been to the Institute in over a month. I don't know what's going on."

She chafed against his lecture. Then sensing more than a paternal scolding in his criticism, she felt goosebumps on her arms.

"Taiwan's not in any danger, is it?"

"Of course not. At least, no more than usual since it's along the Pacific 'rim of fire.' Did you know *Neihu*'s built beside a volcano? With all the mudpots, fumaroles and hotsprings, there's enough thermal activity to frighten any geologist." Chuckling, he laughed at her fears.

"That's not what I meant," she said in a small, injured voice.

"Has anyone ever mentioned you worry too much? See you tomorrow night."

Li did not return with Chen. When Lane questioned her husband, he feigned indifference.

"Someone's got to mind shop."

"What do you mean?"

"He's being groomed for the family business." Chen's polite smile fading, he tossed his jacket over the chair and walked toward the bed. "Your concern for our nephew's touching. Yang's returning on a later flight."

Appraising her coolly, he reached over and brushed her lips with his. She tensed and turned away.

"Is that all the greeting you have for your husband?" he sneered.

With Li out of the country, she felt too vulnerable to mention an annulment. Just being in the same room with Chen made her nervous, made her skin crawl, but she forced a smile. At least one thing was working in her favor. Diagnosing it as "complications," the doctor had cautioned against marital relations. Gently rubbing her large belly, she unconsciously sighed with relief. Since she had nothing to worry about, she tried flirting.

"After what the doctor said, I didn't want to start anything we couldn't finish."

"Don't play the coquette, Lane. It doesn't become you."

Eyes taut and judgmental, he watched her sourly. Then sitting on the edge of the bed, he took her face in his hands. She tried to pull away, but his grip tightened.

"I heard about your performance with Li. Don't be coy. If you'd been more modest in the past, your lover might not be in Macao now."

"He's *not* my lover."

She wedged her arms between them, pushing him away.

"I'm sure he's not, at least in the physical sense, or I'd have done more than fly him to Macao. It's immaterial to me who has your heart, as long as I have your body," he caressed her belly, "and your son."

"Who said it was a boy?"

She shrank from his hand, but her voice was strong. Watching her, he threw his head back, laughing.

"The same source who told me you were pregnant."

"Me? I couldn't have told you. Until you mentioned it, I didn't know myself."

"I never said you did." As his hands flew up in exaggerated innocence, his dark eyes mocked her. "Think! Who else knows?"

"No one."

He raised his eyebrows, silently disputing her. "When did you last visit the doctor?"

"Yesterday when I had the ultrasound."

He caught her eye, hinting she had made the connection.

"But I told him I wanted it to be a surprise," she said, regarding him warily. "No one knew the gender."

"Someone did. The same source that informed me of your pregnancy." He watched as comprehension crept into her mind.

"You knew before I told you?" Her mouth sagged.

Examining his manicure, he announced smugly, "Ten minutes after you tested positive on the morning of our engagement."

"But why?" She was incredulous. "What possible difference could it have made to you?"

"You were the link to the trade agreement." His eyes meeting hers in their first understanding, he smiled gleefully. "Now China has direct access to Mexican and American markets. No sanctions, no tariffs, no duties."

His treachery reminded her of the Pacific Ocean. The first time she swam in it, she had stayed near shore. Then finding the knee-high water too shallow, she had paddled out to the thigh-high water beyond the ropes. It looked safe, even tame. Unfamiliar with the surf, she had been caught in the undertow, narrowly escaping drowning. She felt that way now. The danger wasn't visible, but it was viable.

How could I have been so stupid? She mentally replayed his words, punishing herself. Then she stopped, her eyes clouding thoughtfully.

"You said China, not Macao."

"Did I?" He stiffened. "Simple error. In a few months Macao will *be* China."

A new thought pushed that aside. "And if you already have your trade agreement, you don't need me anymore. I'm getting an annulment."

Squaring off with him, she started to get out of bed and out of his life. Then she pulled off her ring and threw it at him. Reflecting like sunlit ice crystals, the jade and diamond ring spun through the air and ricocheted off his silk suit. He caught it before it bounced on the marble floor. Then grabbing her arm, he forced her back onto the pillows, holding her in a vice grip.

"You're right. I don't need *you* anymore, but I need your connections, and I need an heir."

"I'm not your pawn!"

"Let's say you're a precious vessel to me." He spoke through clenched teeth as she struggled to break free. "One I wouldn't want to break."

Then he gave her arm a painful twist, bringing her close enough to force the ring back on her finger. His inflection changing, it took on honeyed tones as his lips pressed against her ear.

"You're like a beautiful Ming vase, decorative *and* functional. You'd grace any china cabinet—or China Cabinet."

He laughed so loudly at his private joke, he frightened her. She fought harder, pulling, pushing, finally lunging at his eyes and delivering a bloody gash to his cheek. No longer laughing, he angrily wrenched her arm.

"No, you're my American wife, the daughter of a US senator with all the contacts and privileges that implies, and you're carrying my heir. I'll never let you go."

# CHAPTER 6

Despite her husband's return and the resulting conflict, Lane's strength gradually increased. The doctor even encouraged daily walks along with his prescribed mountains of calcium-rich tofu. Buttoning her jacket as she prepared for her afternoon stroll around the compound, she heard the doorbell but paid no attention. It was only Chen's man who doubled on her outings as her bodyguard. Her husband took every precaution for his unborn son. Moments later the housekeeper announced an unexpected visitor.

"Mr. Yang," she said with a disdainful sniff.

"Li?"

She would have jumped to her feet, but the baby interfered with her balance. Using her hands to push herself up, all she could manage was an awkward lift off the sofa. He was shocked at how she filled out her black and white maternity dress, his look of surprise turning into a chuckle as she wobbled toward him.

"All this in a month? You look like a penguin in that outfit, black and white and round in the middle."

"Gee, thanks."

She took the bouquet of orange and purple bird-of-paradise flowers he held out with a wry smile. Though his words were not comforting, his presence was. She would have loved to throw her arms around his neck and bury her head in his chest. Instead she shyly accepted the flowers and inhaled their subtle scent. Looking at him through up-tipped eyes, she wished she could stand on tiptoe and kiss him. But even frustrated, she was happier than she had been in weeks.

"When did you get back?"

"This morning. I stopped in *Yangmingshan* for those," he indicated the flowers with an endearing tilt of his head, "then came straight here."

A frightening thought made her shiver. "Does Chen know you're in Taipei?"

"He will soon enough." Li spoke gruffly, then regretting it, gave her a disarming smile. It did not ease her apprehensions.

"How did you get past Chen's man?" Looking for the plain-clothes man who stood guard, she peeked out the window.

"He got an urgent call on his cellular phone. Five minutes ago he drove away on his girl friend's scooter. They'll be occupied for some time." While Li laughed at the thought, she looked at him with new respect.

"How did you ever manage that?"

He shrugged modestly, then reached for her hands. Wilting at his touch, she wondered why the flowers didn't also. Smiling lazily, he caressed her arms and gently guided Lane by her elbow toward the other room.

"Why don't you put those in water?"

"I'll just call Mil . . ."

"Let's not get her involved again. I don't want to share you with anyone."

Then why did you let me marry Chen? she wanted to ask—but didn't. She decided not to waste precious time together quibbling.

"OK, be right back," she said, tottering off.

Not wasting a moment, Li slipped into Chen's office, pressed the "print log" button on the fax machine and waited impatiently as the summary sheet of incoming fax numbers printed out. He read it quickly, smiling sourly to himself. Then hearing Lane's voice, he folded the sheet into his pocket and darted into the hall.

"What did you say?" he called.

Pretending to come from the guest bath, he adjusted his tie. Then with a challenging grin, he took the vase of flowers from her and set it on the glass coffee table. She eyed him skeptically.

"How about seeing the real thing?" he asked quickly. "*Yangmingshan* Park's blooming with azaleas, *cha hua,* tea flowers, cherry blossoms and *mei hua.* It's the height of the season. Come on, you can't miss it."

His eyes sparkled as they dared her, but she shook her head. "Chen wouldn't like it."

Undaunted, he coaxed, "We'll be back in an hour. Besides, he'll be glad you saw it. For only a day or two each year, the park bursts with pink and white blossoms. Today's the day."

He persisted until he saw the corner of her mouth lift in a grudging smile. Then he dangled the car keys in front of her like a carrot. She finally gave in with a reluctant smile, but Li took no chances. Before she changed her mind, he grabbed her hand, whisking her away as fast as she could wobble.

"By the way, happy Valentine's Day!"

"I'd forgotten."

Touched by his thoughtfulness, she stopped in her tracks until he tugged at her hand, hurrying her through the compound to his car. Then they drove up *Yang Te Ta Lu,* a two-lane, twisting road, focusing on each other and the scenery. At one hairpin curve, they swerved on the shoulder to let an oncoming 260 bus pass. Lane held her breath as the speeding bus careened by, their car narrowly missing a 200 foot vertical drop down the embankment. As Li rounded one tortuous curve after another, he skillfully dodged speeding motorcyclists and slow-moving grandfathers pushing strollers. Lane's growing admiration showed in her eyes.

"How can you be so calm with these curves and drop-offs and traffic?"

He raised his right eyebrow. "What traffic? This is Tuesday. You should see it on Sunday!"

They passed the Chinese Cultural College perched on the mountainside like a white-washed monastery, its traditional, terra-cotta-tiled roofs piercing the mist. Then they drove by *Chungshan Lo,* the Citizen's Conference hall with its impressive rotunda.

"That's only open once a year for the annual congress."

She craned her neck as she turned to watch. "What a waste of space!"

"Maybe, but it's imposing, impressive. That's the important thing."

When they rounded the next curve, she forgot the human selfishness behind the unused classical building. Gasping at nature's generous floral display, she spoke in an awed whisper.

"It's lovely, a fragile fairyland!"

After they parked, he opened the door for her and would have taken her hand if Lane had not pretended absorption in the flowers' beauty. Side by side, their jacketed arms discreetly brushing against each other, they meandered along a winding path. Blooms on both sides exploded from the bushes. Blossom-laden branches hung low overhead. Unable to keep her eyes on where she was walking, Lane tripped on an uneven bit of pavement. When Li grasped her elbow to steady her, she leaned into him, smiling up at his face. Then she noticed the blue sky, his white teeth gleaming in the bright sunlight.

"I thought the sun didn't shine in Taipei."

"Only on special occasions."

They walked over a half-moon bridge, admiring the waterfalls and its rushing rivulets beneath them. Farther down the path they recrossed under an overhanging rock ledge, the same cascading water splashing past them, the mist leaving behind glistening water beads in their hair. At the path's base, the falls emptied into a motionless lotus pond, with only goldfish breaking its placid surface. Lane looked up at the path's crest where the water tumbled down the mountain in a torrential deluge, and then, tracing the stream's course, she smiled at its tranquil conclusion.

Fragrant blossoms everywhere, they slowly climbed the serpentine path until they came to a pagoda. There they rested several minutes, chatting, looking at the view, breathing a mixed scent of flowers and sulfur. Lane sniffed suspiciously.

"The hot springs. *Yangmingshan* sits on top of an ancient volcano."

Li's explanation made her uneasy. Concentrating, she scowled.

"It's like hell." When he did a double-take, she clarified, adding, "The Old Testament's brimstone was sulfur, so *Yangmingshan* smells both heavenly and hellish!"

His face contorting into a quizzical smile, he broke out laughing. Unable to resist, Lane joined in, feeling freer than she had in months. With only flowers to hear them, they laughed like tickled children.

Still grinning, Li held out his hand, and they started back down the path, passing beneath gnarled branches laden with delicate white blossoms. Li reached up to pick one.

"This is the hardy *mei hua,* the national flower. It blooms even in the harshest conditions, just like Taiwan." Then seeing its five-petaled image on Lane's heart-shaped necklace, his eyes hardened into two black pearls. "This is the real thing," he said, holding the blossom close for her inspection, "not a twenty-four-karat-gold imitation."

He dropped the flower, crushing its petals under his feet as he turned away. Stunned by his outburst, she fell into step, not knowing what else to do. They walked in awkward silence a few minutes, Lane suddenly wishing she had not come.

"Look," she said, facing him, "maybe this wasn't such a great idea. I think I'd better go back now, before Chen finds out his son and I are missing."

"*His* son?"

Li's tone was derisive. Then the true meaning dawning, he pulled at her elbow, drawing her nearer.

"It's a boy? Why didn't you tell me we're going to have a son?"

"I . . . you haven't called since Chen got back."

"Never mind. It's enough that we know now."

He hugged her to him, belly and all. After several moments, she broke away first, feeling equally cozy and guilty. But without his warm arms' support, she shivered at the first chill of the day and drew her jacket close. Though barely five o'clock, the winter sun was setting. She stared glumly as the mountains cast long shadows in the early twilight. Starting down the path, Li silently reached for her hand.

After returning to the car, they had only driven around the bend when traffic came to a halt. Men wearing white headbands imprinted with Chinese characters shouted and pushed, blocking the way. Some carried pickets and chanted slogans. Others taunted the drivers of stopped motorcycles and cars. She watched nervous policemen speak animatedly into their radio-transceivers. Long rows of parked yellow cabs lined the road beside *Chungshan Lo*.

"What's going on?"

"A demonstration."

"What are they protesting?"

"The wrong thing," he said curtly.

Backing up, he sharply cornered and U-turned at breakneck speed. The impact of the brakes forced her to hold onto the dashboard to keep from toppling forward. Without explaining, he backtracked, driving recklessly along the twisted road. It frightened Lane as she gulped for air, one hand holding onto her stomach, the other balancing herself against the dash.

"Where are you going?"

Li paused to look at her and immediately slowed down. He squeezed her hand reassuringly.

"I'm sorry, Lane. I didn't mean to scare you, but I didn't want us to get caught in that demonstration. No matter how peaceful those things start out, they can turn violent in a minute. We'd be trapped in the car. I can't take any chances with your safety." Then with a beguiling smile, he added, "Let's wait this out over dinner. I know a quiet place with a panoramic night view of the city, and it serves the best *tu ji* you ever tasted."

"The best what?"

"*Tu ji* directly translated means mountain chicken. They run loose up here. Because the chickens aren't penned up, they graze off the land and have a special flavor all their own." Letting go her hand, he continued, "Actually it isn't a complete trip to *Yangmingshan* unless you try some. Maybe the demonstration was a blessing in disguise."

Lane looked dubiously at the sun setting behind the mountains, wondering what she would tell Chen, but minutes later found herself seated at a small table overlooking the first twinkling lights of Taipei. A hushed twilight surrounded them on the mountainside, broken only by the sound of the waitress taking their order. When she saw Lane's swollen belly, the girl told Li she would add extra *dong quoi* to the chicken.

"An herb especially good for women," he explained, "it's called angelica in the West. In Taiwan, no distinction's made between seasonings and medicine. The same herbs are used to flavor and heal."

They talked in the deepening dusk until the waitress brought the food and a single-burner stove. Its flame gave off flickering light as well as heat, keeping the chicken bubbling enthusiastically in its dented pot. Lane breathed in the pungent aromas.

"It smells delicious!"

"But it's the flavor that makes it so special."

Nodding, she had to agree, and she ate heartily. Then with a contented sigh, she looked out over the mountains' basin, watching the winking lights of the city. After a poignant moment's silence, Li reached under the table for her hand and whispered in her ear.

"The way wild chicken tastes sweeter than caged, love's more tender with free choice."

For an instant she grasped his hand then quickly let go. It would be too easy to yield to the moment. Her pulse speeding up, she remembered their New Year's resolution. Then she recalled Chen's reaction to an annulment. Until she was free to make a choice, she did not want to complicate their lives any more than they had. The lump in her throat ached, but she answered evenly.

"We'd better be getting back."

When he didn't respond, she turned to watch his expression and saw he was staring at her mouth. Never taking his eyes from it, he reached over and kissed her. In the shadows of the mountains, she answered that kiss hungrily, clinging to him, kneading his arms with her fingers, drawing him closer. Then abruptly she pulled away, feeling dizzy, compromised. Unable to look at him, she stared straight ahead, speaking in a thin voice.

"Do you think the demonstration's over yet?"

They drove back to *Neihu* unimpeded, passing only a littered area where the rally had taken place an hour earlier. Uncomfortable with her thoughts, she strained to fill the drab void of silence.

"What were they protesting?"

"The KMT government."

"Why?"

Politics interested her, having been around it all her life. She also preferred his conversation to dwelling on her confrontation with Chen. Never taking his eyes from the serpentine road, he answered vehemently.

"The people you saw want independence for Taiwan. They want *taidu*."

"What's that?"

"*Taidu* is complete separation from mainland China. The *Kuomintang* or KMT party has been ruling since 1949. That's when Chiang Kai-shek named Taiwan the provisional capital of the ROC—the Republic of China. The KMT believes mainland China and Taiwan can be reunified into one China. Their goal is coexistence between Beijing's PRC and Taiwan's ROC, but they want equal status despite the size and ideological differences. Remember, mainland's communistic; Taiwan's capitalistic."

Confused, she squinted at the idea. "I still don't understand why they were demonstrating."

"Beijing believes it rules all Chinese provinces, including

Taiwan. The KMT believes Taiwan's the true capital and the KMT's the lawful government of all China."

He took his eyes from the narrow road to see if she understood. She didn't. He took a deep breath and tried again.

"The protesters you saw were DPP, the Democratic Progressive Party. The fools are calling for independence. Advocating independence from the mainland is begging for trouble. Not only is the idea treasonable here, but if the PRC believed Taiwan would declare independence, it could blast this island right out of the China Sea."

Lane felt another chill at the words. "What's to stop China—I mean, the mainland—from doing that anyway?"

"We share the same heritage, the same culture. All we have to do is put the pieces back together, join forces for a stable economy."

His anxious expression relaxed into a smile. She smiled back ruefully.

"But what if mainland China doesn't think Humpty-Dumpty can be put back together again?"

"Then all the KMT's horses and all the KMT's men couldn't stop Mainland from attacking again." He hid his concern with a laugh. "Did you hear the joke about the *Kuomintang?*"

She looked up expectantly.

"A new building just opened on *Tun Hua Nan Lu,* and its elevators announced each floor in English: first floor, women's apparel; second floor, ladies' lingerie. All went well, even though most people couldn't understand the English, until the elevator announced, *Going up* or *Going down*."

He started laughing, waiting for her to join in. Lane scratched her head.

"What's so funny?"

"Don't you get it? 'Going down.' "

She smiled politely, shaking her head.

" 'Going down,' sounds like *'Kuomintang.'* " He sounded it out phonetically for her. "Gwo-ming-dong. Everyone wondered why the building was promoting the KMT party."

Lane joined in Li's laughter all the way through the *Ta chih* tunnel, but as they approached *Neihu,* she abruptly sobered.

"Li, maybe you should let me out at the guard's gate. I don't want a scene with Chen."

"We have nothing to hide. We went for a walk, then because of the rally, we had dinner. There's nothing to be ashamed of. We're going in together." Turning toward her, Li gave an affirmative nod before parking and opening the door.

"Where have you been?"

Still wearing his impeccably-cut jacket, Chen met them at the front door. Though his expression was courteously restrained, he could not hide the accusation in his voice.

Feeling defiant in Li's company, Lane countered coolly, "And hello to you, too."

Li's right, she quickly reassured herself, we've done nothing to be ashamed of. Unprepared for her assertive tone, Chen chose another line of offense and gently took her hand.

"I was worried about you," he said. "You look so tired; sit down."

Chen's concern apparently genuine, Lane relented, letting him lead her to the sofa.

"We were delayed by the demonstration," Li said. "We got back as. . . ."

"Hope it didn't inconvenience you, Nephew. You take such a filial interest in your aunt."

As Chen's eyes narrowed to calculating slits, Lane spoke quickly. "The road was blocked. Cab-drivers were protesting in front of *Chungshan Lo*."

"For once the DPP's doing something right," said Chen. "Getting those old KMT soldiers out of office would be a public service."

He thoughtfully rubbed the side of his nose. Then watching Li's reaction, he snorted indignantly, waiting for what he knew would come.

Li's jaw clenched as he struggled to remain polite. "Though some of the members are experienced. . . ."

"Experienced?" Chen smiled as he studied Li. He had him right where he wanted him. "What a politic way of putting it. They're old. Half of them are octogenarians appointed in '49. Not elected, appointed. It's time to oust those yes-men. They're nothing but rubber stamps for the KMT. Time for a new government."

Ashen with anger, Li rose to the bait and crossed to Chen, their nearness emphasizing the height difference. Looking down on his elder, Li feigned surprise.

"What do you want? Insurrection? Independence?"

*"Ni hao,"* called a woman's voice.

The three heads turned sharply at the interruption. Mei-ling appeared in the doorway, perfectly groomed, looking as though she had come from the hair salon instead of the guest bath.

Instantly assuming the cordial speech of a host, Chen said, "Li, your wife was so distressed concerning your whereabouts, I invited her here."

Lane drew in her breath sharply, shocked at seeing the smartly-dressed woman for the first time since her engagement party. Lane noticed her tastes seemed more polished, less flamboyant, as if a sliding scale existed between her raised status and lowered hemlines. Although the dress Mei-ling wore was loose-fitting, it was too fashionable to be called a maternity gown.

Giving Lane a sly smile, Mei-ling slunk toward Li. Then standing on tiptoe, using his arm as leverage to brush her lips against his cheek, she spoke in Chinese.

"I've missed you, Li. Welcome home."

Standing erectly beyond her reach, he neither bent toward her chaste peck, nor returned the kiss. He simply stared at her sternly until Chen spoke.

"What? No greeting for your wife? You must be choked with emotion."

"Surprised, perhaps," Li said dryly, turning his gaze on Chen. "How did you know I was back?"

"Taipei's small, a natural basin nestled in the mountains, no bigger really than a fishbowl—and just as transparent. Very little goes unnoticed, Nephew."

Simpering, Mei-ling let go Li's arm and produced a beautifully-wrapped box from its matching shopping bag, a well-known bakery's name emblazoned in gold on a red foil background. She cast Li a syrupy smile, peeked shyly at Lane, then murmured to Chen in Chinese.

"Mei-ling wants you to try a local confection popular with pregnant women, candied lotus seeds." When Mei-ling whispered again, Chen added, "It eases the baby's birth."

Wearing a composed smile, the girl set down the bag, slunk toward Lane with the grace of a runway model, bowed slightly and offered the beribboned box with both hands, the polite form for gift presentation. Lane glanced uneasily at Li, took a deep breath, then forced a grimace as she accepted the gift.

"Thanks," she said stiffly, tossing the box ungraciously on the coffee table.

Mei-ling protested in Chinese and pressed it back into her hands.

"Try a piece," Chen snapped, losing patience.

"I'm not hungry. Li and I just finished . . . eating."

The innuendo hit its mark. As Lane met her husband's gaze evenly, Chen's eyes glittered like obsidian. Again Mei-ling spoke in Mandarin, while Chen translated.

"She's anxious to see if you'll like it."

Lane stifled a deep sigh, retrieved the box and began removing the ruffled ribbons and multi-layered red-foil wrappings. She had difficulty hiding her distaste for the girl, remembering only too well the previous time they had met. Now here she was, Li's wife, offering her candy as if nothing had passed between them except pleasant conversation.

After Lane had removed the layers of outer wrapping, she opened the box to discover two more layers of cellophane. These candy shops really make a big production out of a small box of candy, Lane thought, irritated at the wasteful packaging. Finally she discovered one centered piece of candy used as a decoration on the final layer of wrapping paper. Deciding to be civil, she offered it to Mei-ling.

"*Bu shi!* No."

Mei-ling politely refused it, gesturing palm up that Lane should try the first piece. After she exchanged an annoyed grimace with Li, Lane begrudgingly opened the individual wrapper and popped the white candied seeds into her mouth.

"Mmm," she grunted, nodding approvingly but wincing, thinking it tasted like bitter melon. She swallowed it with difficulty. Then she removed the box's final ribbon, lifted the tissue paper and offered the wrapped candies to Mei-ling. The girl's eyes sparkled like effervescent cold springs. Smiling sweetly, she took a piece, and passed the box first to Chen, then to Li.

Playing the congenial host, Chen gestured for everyone to

sit down and ordered Mildred to bring oolong tea. Conversation was stilted, Mandarin being spoken alternately for Mei-ling's benefit, English for Lane's. Poised on the arm of Li's chair, Mei-ling watched them all with a tiger's alertness. Though she added little to the conversation, she missed nothing, even seeming to follow the English.

During the strained silences, Mei-ling played hostess eagerly, pouring tea, passing the candy. The three helped themselves liberally. Only Lane refrained, wondering how they could stomach the confection's tart, metallic flavor. A bitter aftertaste still coated her tongue.

Inevitably the conversation returned to politics, Li and Chen barely disguising their antipathy for each other's party, let alone personality. The discussion became a debate, then degenerated into thinly veiled hostility.

"You never did answer the question, Uncle. If you're so fed up with the KMT's system, what do you want? Insurgency? Independence from Mainland?"

"No. I want an end to this corruption. No Taiwanese voter likes being duped, I least of all. Betrayal in government is like deception in marriage." As Lane shot Li a nervous glance, Chen stifled the urge to chuckle. "Only ethical lawmakers will win back the people's faith in government."

"You're obviously not pro-KMT, Uncle, and if you don't favor independence, you're not DPP. You must be New Party. Spreading dissension will only bring chaos, not a new order. By dividing, do you hope to conquer?"

Li's dark eyes snapping, he paused, letting his words sink in before continuing.

"Whether a country or a couple in love, by introducing a third party, you weaken the system. If the vote's split between the KMT and New Party, the DPP will win by default. It's like a love triangle, wouldn't you agree?"

"More like a *menage a trois*." Chen's voice intense, his and Li's eyes locked in a conflict having little to do with political theory.

The air was so thick with dissension, Lane found it difficult to breathe. As if a weight were pressing on her chest, she gasped in short, quick breaths, panting. A cold sweat broke out on her forehead, and she felt suddenly light-headed. Her eyelids fluttered, momentarily showing the whites of her eyes. Though she tried to speak, the sound strangled in her throat.

Then Lane felt a sudden cramping in her stomach. A flash of pain pierced her and left as quickly, leaving behind a warm trickle of blood. She rose unsteadily to her feet, intent only on getting to the privacy of her room. Then the pain slashed through her abdomen again, and she fell back on the sofa with a moan. Li turned to his wife, loathing in his eyes.

"You! Did you do this?"

"How could I?"

Li glanced at the half-eaten box of candies. Then he shook Mei-ling's shoulders.

"What was in those?"

"Nothing, Li. You ate them yourself. We all did. None of us is sick. Besides, each piece was individually wrapped. It's the baby, not the bonbons."

Li shrugged off his wife's cloying hands, slipped a candy into his pocket for later testing and rushed toward Lane, calling her name. Chen tried to intercept by fending off the younger man but was no match. Li easily pushed him aside as he knelt by her.

"What's wrong? What's wrong?"

Wincing, Lane held her stomach and tried to explain as Chen bellowed for Mildred to call the ambulance and for his aide to remove Li.

Mei-ling watched from the sidelines, a self-satisfied smile playing at her lips. No one heard her chuckling as the sirens wailed and the aide strong-armed Li out of the way.

# CHAPTER 7

"It was close," the intern said, "but I've averted the miscarriage. Now rest is the best medicine. Under no circumstances are you to go for extended walks or take Chinese medicine. Used incorrectly, even natural herbs can be poisonous. And no more excitement."

He issued orders as he reviewed her chart, frowning at her phone call from Li. She paused, her hand covering the receiver.

"Then it *was* something I ate."

"Maybe, maybe not. What had you eaten yesterday?"

She told him, remembering the chicken with *dong quoi* and the suspiciously bitter candy.

"Something reacted in your stomach. Without pumping it, we can't be sure, but that'd have been too invasive for the baby. Have you taken any *strong* Chinese medicine?" Peering at her skeptically, he added, "Some are potent agents of abortion. You haven't tried to terminate the pregnancy, have you?"

"No!"

Too outraged to retaliate, she fumed, wondering where medics found the gall to insult their patients at their most vulnerable moments. The man shrugged his shoulders noncommittally and left.

"Don't worry," Li said, overhearing the verbal exchange. "I'm sure it wasn't the *tu ji,* and I had the candy analyzed at a lab. It tested fine, just sugar and lotus seeds." What he did not tell her was his suspicion or the row he had had with Mei-ling.

"I've already told you," Mei-ling said. "Everyone ate the same candy, and no one else got sick. I had nothing to do with it."

"The piece Lane ate was different, apart from the rest. I swear, if you hurt her or the baby, I'll have you. . . ."

"Have me what?! Are you threatening me? Think again! Your mother won't allow a hair of my head harmed." She pulled her arm from his grasp. "Besides, do you think I'm so stupid I'd poison her in front of Chen? He's crazy about her and that little bastard she's carrying."

It took all his self-restraint to keep from slapping her jeering red lips. Instead he gripped his hands into fists and started for the door, until Mei-ling's shriek stopped him. Turning back, he saw her double-over and collapse against the sofa's back. Her eyes wide with fear, her hand reached out to him.

"Li! The baby. . . ."

After a week of rest, Lane returned home from the hospital. Time passed slowly until Iris' visit. Then over *bing cha,* iced tea, Lane told her friend the news.

"Mei-ling had the baby."

"How Li feel?"

"Confused," said Lane, gesturing helplessly with her hands. "Though Mei-ling swears the baby's his, Li doesn't believe her."

Iris watched cautiously, her eyes lidded. She blinked, digesting the information before offering a suggestion.

"Could test for blood type?"

"They already did—without Li's mother knowing. It matches his." Lane grimaced. "But half the people in Taipei have type O blood."

Iris concentrated again, pursing her lips. "If question, another doctor could test them?"

"His mother won't hear of it." Lane shifted her position as she spoke. Her lower back seemed to ache dully all the time now.

"He . . . she still in hospital?"

"The doctors give her only a few months. And now that Mei-ling's presented her with a grandson, Li's mother thinks she can do no wrong. She refuses any blood tests for the child." Shaking her head, Lane adjusted the cushion with a sigh. Uncomfortable from the back pain and the injustice, Lane felt irritable. "Why are babies so important in Taiwan?"

"Not baby, son."

The women exchanged resigned looks.

"This Tao society. Only son and grandson to do *bai bai*, pray for ancestor. Giving son best thing daughter-in-law to do. It keep bloodline and make her place in family. Li mother grateful."

"Even if the baby's not Li's?" Lane was incredulous.

Laying a light hand on Lane's, Iris agreed with a nod. "Yang *Taitai* to die soon, and baby answer to prayer. She want to believe it her grandson. Now old woman best friend to Mei-ling. Li do nothing to make mother unhappy."

Watching Lane's eyes redden, Iris gave her an encouraging smile.

"Don't worry, truth come out."

Suddenly feeling close to tears, Lane blinked and sniffled. Not finding a handkerchief nearby, she quickly wiped her nose with the back of her hand.

"I'm sorry. I don't know what's wrong with me lately."

"Nothing wrong. You have pregnant."

"I *never* cried until . . . until this." Looking at her belly, she began to smile, her green eyes still glistening with unshed tears. "Maybe it does have something to do with hormones."

They laughed together so loudly, Lane shushed them.

"Mildred will report I'm getting too 'excited.' Chen has her tattling on me."

She tried to cover the sudden pall of depression with a laugh, but it rang hollow in the stillness, and she sank back dejectedly on the cushions. Iris' dark eyes registered empathy, then they brightened with mischief. She smiled so widely, Lane could see her perfect set of teeth.

"I know something to make you feel better. Iming propose."

"He did?" Sitting up, Lane squealed and grabbed her friend's hands. "I'm so happy for you!" Then she stopped and looked deeply in Iris' eyes. "It is what you want, isn't it? I mean, do you love him?"

Still smiling, but not quite as widely, Iris bobbed her head and glanced at their hands.

"It *is* what I want. Love will come. Chinese way. Even now I to falling in love."

Then again full of smiles, she looked shyly into Lane's face, her eyes hopeful and sincere. Lane saw the unmistakable signs of infatuation.

"Yes, I think you are. You're going to have a happy marriage. I can feel it." As they discussed Iris' wedding plans, Lane pushed her envy deep inside.

Three weeks later she attended Iris' engagement, a small ceremony held in her parents' modest home. A picture of the goddess of mercy *Kwan Yin* covering one wall, a household altar filled another. Red flame-shaped lightbulbs lit the prominently-displayed shrine to *Kuan Kung,* the god of war and business. Tablets bearing names of the family's ancestors lay stacked on the altar.

Iris demurely served sweetened tea to her in-laws, keeping her eyes cast down chastely for the occasion. She had been tutored on proper behavior. Her hair had been elaborately styled and her make-up professionally applied. She wore a pale blue, diaphanous ball-gown that looked made for a duchess in Louis XIV's court. Gesturing with her hands, Iris whispered she felt uncomfortable but stylish.

"*Cheongsam* or white bride gown so-so, but evening gown very fashion."

Lane smiled and, instead of correcting her grammar, hugged Iris.

"You look beautiful, like a fairy-tale princess, but you haven't introduced me to prince charming yet. I want to meet this mystery man."

"He not handsome like Li—or Mr. Chen," she hastily added.

"I'm sure he's the most handsome man in Taipei."

Though Iris' brow furrowed slightly, Lane understood the customary exchange of compliments. She knew it was courteous to pretend your own dress, house, husband less worthy than your guest's. Iris shook her coifed head.

"No, she not good-looking." She waved him over, whispering to Lane, "She . . . he speak not much English, too."

But Iris' face lit up when he appeared at her side, and her eyes snapped with anticipation when he brushed her hand. Finally remembering her reason for calling him over, she introduced him.

Lane silently agreed he wasn't much to look at, but she saw the expression of raw love in his eyes when he stole side-long glances at Iris. A lump caught in her throat as she wished she could see that same look in Li's eyes. Swallowing quickly, she said hello to the short, red-faced man across from her. She noted his feet were weathered and bare, even in February at his own engagement party.

She also saw his intelligent eyes that met hers honestly

without pride, without deference. Traveling in the worlds of politics and international business, she knew it was a rare person who tried neither to impress Senator MacKenzie's daughter nor flatter Chen *xian-sheng's* wife. Iming earned Lane's immediate respect.

Iris translated as Lane congratulated him, then asked politely if he had taken his fiancee to see *Yangmingshan's* flowers. Iris gradually lost her smile as their conversation lengthened into a hushed but heated discussion. Wondering why a simple question required such a long debate, Lane finally spoke.

"Did I say something wrong?"

Before she could answer, Iming's smiling father joined their group, nodded politely, said something in Taiwanese and whisked his son away for a toast. Iming and Iris' eyes watched each other until his friends surrounded him, blocking their view. Subdued, Iris turned toward her friend, speaking in a low voice.

"Iming go same night as you and Li."

As Iris' chin dejectedly pointed toward her chest, Lane joked, trying to break the somber mood.

"He wasn't there with an old girl friend, was he?"

"No, she . . . he demonstration."

"So?"

"He get arrest." Iris hesitated, chewing her lip nervously.

Lane's smile vanished. "Why? I thought protests were legal."

"They say she hit police."

"Did he?"

Her shoulders slumping, Iris shook her head. "But they say. Now he have police record."

"Taiwan's a democracy." Lane struggled to say something to relieve her friend's anxiety. "They need proof. They can't just convict him of an offense without evidence or a trial, can they?"

"Not like US. He have record, and nothing we can do."

Iris spoke with such finality that a long pause followed as each was caught in her own thoughts. After a frustrated sigh, Lane forced a resilient smile, then put her hands on the girl's bare shoulders.

"In that case, don't let it spoil this special day. If there's nothing you can do to change your situation, you might as well enjoy it the best you can." They shared a grim, conspiratorial smile before Lane added, "It's what I do."

In an excited chatter of Taiwanese, Iris' mother burst into their conversation, stole her daughter away and seated her in front of the guests for the traditional exchange of gifts. Though the bride money was conspicuously absent and the gold jewelry scant, Lane watched enviously when Iris put bashful arms around Iming's neck as she clasped the gold chain. She saw the look they exchanged. She remembered her own engagement and how comparatively luxurious but poor in love it had been.

Afterwards the families organized a car caravan to a local restaurant. Since Lane had come alone, she felt uncomfortable staying for dinner, so she made her excuses, blaming her early departure on the baby.

"Oh, I jealous!" Iris gave her a tight hug.

"Why?" Lane was genuinely perplexed, knowing Iris was impressed by neither Chen's wealth nor their strained marriage.

"Because you have pregnant!" Smiling, she blushed and whispered in Lane's ear. "Me, too, as soon as I can. Our son play together."

Taking the limo back to *Neihu,* Lane was honest with herself. She had not left because of her baby's health. She left because she could not bear watching Iming's naked love for Iris. Happy as she was for her friend, Lane's envy gathered into an ache in her chest, and as she thought of Li tears welled up in her eyes.

When she arrived home, she learned Chen was still shut in his office with members of the Ministry of Economic Affairs and the Mainland Affairs Council, or big MAC as she irreverently called it. Still feeling keyed-up, she asked Mildred for a cup of herbal tea and settled into a cozy chair in the den, as far away from the group's cigarette smoke as she could get.

Smoking in Taiwan was a national pastime, she had learned. Though the smell had never bothered her until her pregnancy, now it made her nauseous. Since Chen's return, he had held daily meetings with CETRA, MOEA or MAC members until his office reeked of stale cigarettes. Walking past the room made her retch. Sometimes when he had been cooped up for hours in the smoke-filled rooms, his clothes smelled like a cheap bar. Just being near him gagged her.

When Lane heard shuffling footsteps, she roused herself from her thoughts and automatically thanked Mildred for the tea. Looking up from her seat, she was mildly shocked to see Chen. He smiled as he leaned over to kiss her cheek, but his scent preceded him.

"Ugh! You stink."

Speaking in muffled tones, she turned her head to avoid the smell. Then pinching her nose, she covered her mouth with her hand. He straightened up as quickly as if she had slapped him.

"What an endearing way to greet your husband."

He sneered as he took a pack of cigarettes from his coat pocket. Then as she raised herself off the chair, he lit a cigarette and exhaled. She stepped past him, holding her breath.

"Leaving so soon? Remember," he called as she stalked

from the room, "this is my house, and I'll do as I please. And after you have our son, I'll remind you that as my wife, *you* will do as I please."

The threat reverberated in her ears as she marched to her room. At least, she thought, slamming the door, we have separate rooms. Then she recalled Iris and Iming, again comparing their relationship to hers and Chen's. She ached to call Li but blanched at the thought of Mei-ling answering. Instead she slumped into an easy chair and morosely considered her situation.

If I find nothing in it to enjoy, she thought, rewording her advice to Iris, I'll have to do something to change it.

Chen returned to the meeting, walking into a room blue with smoke. He immediately snuffed out his cigarette, angry with himself for behaving as he had with Lane. He found it increasingly difficult to keep his attention on the issues at hand until Yin, director of the Hong Kong and Macao Affairs Department, confronted him.

"Will Beijing agree to send a delegate to our Mainland Affairs Conference?"

Chen rubbed the side of his nose, trying to gather his thoughts.

"Mainland wants reunification with Taiwan. Even though it feels dissident secessionists here are interfering, Beijing is open to upscale negotiations and exchanges. When Macao reverts, Mainland would like nothing better than to see Taiwan return to her husband."

At Yin's confused expression, Chen smiled ruefully.

"Beijing's always felt Hong Kong, Macao and Taiwan were like *xiao taitai,* little wives, concubines. Mainland wants Taiwan to come home."

Wu, chairman of the MAC, looked skeptical.

Afraid he was waxing too poetic, Chen reworded his reply.

"So will Beijing send a representative here? Yes, I think so, if we can guarantee the delegate's safety . . . and make certain economic concessions."

"What kind of economic concessions?"

Wu's hand in his pocket, no one saw him press the record button of his microcassette-recorder.

"As a businessman, I know one thing." Focused on commerce, Chen smiled confidently. "To make money, you have to spend money. By the turn of the century, Mainland will be Taiwan's largest trading partner and its biggest target for investment. Our job is to make Taiwan look attractive as a builder and supplier in developing the southeastern provinces of Mainland." His lip curled into a sneer. "A good *taitai* knows how to seduce her husband."

"Yes," said Fan, the negotiations director for the Board of Foreign Trade, "but a *xiao taitai* must profit from her caresses, not give any away." He added shrewdly, "She should be compensated for her fickle husband's infidelities."

"But first she has to win his attention," stressed Chen.

"It's not that easy," said the political vice minister of MOEA, "You predict economic growth. For this to happen, Mainland and Taiwan need a stable environment. Stability requires more interdependence between Taiwan and China."

"You're right," Chen conceded, "a *xiao taitai* has to do more than just turn China's head. As a mistress, Taiwan needs to strengthen her relationship. To do that, she needs better access to her husband's bedroom." Sensing he was becoming too lyrical, he added, "Better access to China's boardrooms. In commercial terms, the two countries need a more open-door policy, more mutual visits by senior-level officials. The Taiwanese business community doesn't want to lose its $20 billion investments along the mainland's southeastern coast. It wants to increase them."

His eyes swept the room, focusing briefly on each man present. Then addressing the vice minister, Chen summed up. "First *xiao taitai* has to win her husband's attention. Only then can she gain his loyalty. Once Taiwan attracts the mainland with tempting propositions, China will agree to cross-strait exchanges. Stronger ties will follow."

"Instead of opening a door, what about shutting it? Gaining more independence?" asked Hsieh, deputy secretary-general of CETRA. "There are those of us who feel our Taiwanese *taitai* should get a divorce from her 'husband.' "

"Taiwan's goal is to establish a democratic, free and equitably prosperous China," said Wu. "The unification of China should not be subject to partisan conflict."

"What are you doing? Quoting from the guidelines for national unification?" Hsieh hawked and spit in the garbage can.

Wu fastidiously removed his glasses, folded them and placed them in his pocket. "As it happens," he said, "the guidelines' short term process for reunification calls for exchanges and reciprocity. Both sides must gradually ease restrictions and increase contact in order to prosper."

Hsieh kicked the garbage can, knocking it across the room as it spewed out debris. Talking ceased as the men jumped out of the rolling can's way.

"The exchanges have all been one-sided," said Hsieh. "We give, and China takes. Give any more, and you might as well hand over Taiwan on a platter."

Wu's jaw tightened as he spoke through pursed lips. "We're not giving anything away. We're only establishing official communication channels on both sides of the Strait. The guidelines' medium term process calls for mutual trust and cooperation. If dissident elements of Taiwan's political system jeopardize joint development of the mainland's southeastern coastal area, it'll mean economic disaster."

In answer, Hsieh lifted a chair above his head and sent it crashing onto the desk, wood splintering in all directions.

"Where do you think you are?" shouted Chen. "In the Executive *Yuan?* There are no TV cameras here to televise your play-acting."

The crowd laughed as Hsieh's face turned red.

His eyes shined zealously as Wu looked from one man to the next. Quoting from the guidelines for national unification, Wu licked his lips as his tongue darted. "If we follow the guidelines, especially the section promoting visits by high-ranking officials, both sides will prosper. And ultimately we'll achieve reunification."

"The Conference shouldn't be a debate of pro-independence or pro-unification," said Chen. "For now, its goal should be pro-status quo." His patience beginning to wear thin, he repressed a deeply felt sigh of frustration as he turned to Hu, the chairman of the External Trade Development Council.

"Let's get back to the matter at hand," Chen continued. "We want to encourage China to cooperate in the economic development of *Guangdong, Fujian* and *Zhejiang* provinces. Now how does *xiao taitai* sweeten the pact? What concession could Taiwan offer without actually giving anything away?"

Chairman Hu frowned as he considered the plan. "It could allow duty-free capital imports," he said slowly, thinking aloud. "With Hong Kong and Macao no longer buffers, all trade with Mainland will be direct. Instead of imports and exports going through neutral harbors, Taiwan and China will trade directly. New tariff codicils will need to be defined and created since Taiwan has no *official* precedence of trading with the mainland. If Taiwan allows duty-free capital imports, Mainland will view it as a concession."

Hu paused thoughtfully, then smiled at the simplicity of

his plan. Turning, he acknowledged the grunts of agreement coming from all corners of the room.

Juang Fang-Rung, Director of the Department of Finance, said, "The Finance Ministry could relax requirements on Mainland letters of credit to smooth business across the Strait."

"Or," said Fang, director of the Commerce Department of the Ministry of Economic Affairs, pausing dramatically to gain attention, "Taiwan could renounce its claim on the Tiaoyutai Islands."

An angry chorus of "No, never," met his idea. The meeting erupted into pandemonium, each faction disagreeing for different principles but concurring as a whole on the absurdity of the plan. Chen stepped into the fracas.

"Perhaps *xiao taitai* could keep that up her sleeve for future negotiations," Chen said loudly. "Fan's right. Taiwan doesn't want to give too much away at the opening discussions of the Mainland Affairs Conference." Then as the others argued heatedly, he addressed Fang in a low voice. "But an excellent suggestion!"

His expression discreetly confirmed his support as surely as a handshake. Fang beamed as Chen continued in a loud voice, calling the men to order.

"Relaxed requirements on letters of credit should be enough of an incentive, at least initially." Order restored, Chen swiftly changed the subject. "But what about guaranteeing the safety of a representative from Mainland? Remember Taiwan must assure China that its man will not only be safe from dissidents, but safe from disgrace, loss of face. Every reassurance must be given that he'll be treated royally, so Mainland can't accuse Taiwan of being offensive."

"He'll have the usual," said Wu impassively, shrugging as he rattled off the diplomatic privileges. "Motorcades with police escorts and sirens, street-light regulation—safety precautions so he doesn't have to stop for red lights and risk injury from radical demonstrators—full military honors, international media coverage, financial and political support, power lunches, red carpets, white-tie dinners and blue balls from prostitutes. He can have whatever he wants."

Chen nodded his agreement, then conducted the rest of the meeting with his customary aplomb, hearing recommendations for the representative's well-being, directing fractious members, coordinating so subtly as to bring about unanimity without appearing to supervise. Chen was a master strategist, and he knew it, except where Lane was involved.

When the meeting finally broke up, Chen retreated to his room, showered, then helped himself to a glass of X.O. Still unable to relax, he picked up the television remote, flipping disinterestedly through the channels. Bored, he punched the off button and paced around his room, wandering toward the window. Chen knew it was full moon; every shopkeeper in Taipei had been burning paper money to the gods. The air was still laden with the acrid scent. Searching for the cause of his restlessness, he wondered if it were the moon's influence.

On a whim, he lifted the curtain, and in the silver light he saw his wife standing on the balcony, her face angled away from him, her profile backlit. Riveted to the marble floor, he stared at her, transfixed. With a pent-up groan, he realized it was not the moon making him sleepless.

How do I deal with her? The tighter my grip, the more she struggles. The longer the leash, the farther she strays. Her head turned as she heard a movement, the moonbeams highlighting her exquisite face. He stepped back. For a moment, he considered letting the curtain fall before she noticed him. Then, true to form, he decided to confront his challenger in this contest of wills. Tossing down the drink, he reached into his top bureau drawer for a silk pouch. Then secreting it in his robe's pocket, he slid open the glass door to their connecting balcony.

She gasped, pulling her robe tighter around her, snugly tying the sash. Though annoyed by her modesty, he forced himself to overlook it and addressed her pleasantly.

"Enjoying the night air?"

She sniffed peevishly. "I can still smell the *bai bai* burning. Why do they pollute the air with that paper money?"

"They're praying. The merchants ask for better business, better luck." He smiled. "The smoke's a blessing; if you can smell it, the gods will smile on you, too."

"Breathing carcinogens isn't my idea of lucky. Smoke inside and out. Smog, pollution everywhere. It's so oppressive, I can hardly breathe." She put her hands up to her sinuses. "Isn't there any fresh air in Taipei?" Then she turned her back to him.

"Which atmosphere is smothering you? The ventilation or the lifestyle?" He looked perturbed, but his voice held only concern. Moving closer, he asked, "Are you so unhappy here?"

She turned to see if the sincerity she heard were reflected in his eyes. It was. Chen had cut to the heart of her problem. Embarrassed now by his directness, she wanted to avoid a confrontation, delay it until she knew what she wanted with her life. She tried to think of some excuse, but without directly lying, Lane could think of nothing plausible. So she waited for his lead.

He also waited. Long pauses ruffled him not in the least. It was a stratagem he often used in negotiations. He watched her expectantly but waited patiently, as if merely being polite. Silent minutes passed.

Finally in frustration, she turned toward her door. "It's

chilly out here. I'm going in."

Silently cursing his ploy for not working, he tried another device. He gave her two options, both of his choosing. That way either decision would still be his.

"Perhaps you could describe your feelings where it's warmer. Which is more comfortable, your sitting room or mine?"

Deciding her room would seem too inviting, she chose his. That way she could leave whenever she felt inclined. She nodded curtly toward his.

"Yours is closer."

He hid the smile at his successful coup and slid open the door for her. She crossed the threshold gingerly, looking around the sitting room with its western style furniture and leathered upholstery. Wrapping her robe even tighter, she felt as if her presence were somehow improper.

"I've never been in here."

"Please," he said, motioning to an easy chair, again hiding his irritation at her reticence.

She sat down warily, poised to rise again at the slightest provocation. He saw her hands fumble uneasily with the tie belt and thought she might feel more comfortable with something in her hands.

"Would you like something to drink or eat? I can order. . ."

She interrupted with a shake of her head, her hair still tumbling loosely, mussed from sleep. He thought she never looked lovelier.

"No, thanks. I'm fine."

"But are you really?" he asked. "You never told me if you're unhappy here."

"Unhappy?!" Her eyes widened into angry green orbs. "That's like asking if the tropics are hot! If I'm not kept in the hospital or confined to bed because of this unending pregnancy, I'm spied on and made to feel a guilty prisoner in what should be my home, too. I feel I'm being crushed. If the baby isn't pressing down on my lungs, the pollution is. It's like I'm gasping for air and never able to fill my lungs. If life with my father were stifling, life with you is oppressive." Shouting, she concluded, "Tonight I watched Iris and Iming, and I'm so jealous, I could scream!"

"I don't suppose it would improve your disposition," Chen said, watching her expression slyly, "to learn that Li and Mei-ling are the proud parents of a son."

"No, it wouldn't." For the first time she reined in her emotions and stared coldly into his eyes. "But then it wouldn't surprise me, either."

Chen tucked that little piece of information away for future use. "Pregnancy is never an easy time, Lane. Under the circumstances, maybe it's too much pressure for you to bear alone. I've been busy with the company and the Mainland Affairs Conference, maybe too busy." Looking sheepish, he sat down across from her, moving his chair closer. As he took her nervous hands in his, she pulled away. "No matter what you believe, I truly care for you. . ."

"You care about the trade agreement with my father!"

He shook his head. "That's not all. . . ."

"That's right. That's not all." She pretended a laugh, sneering in his face. "You also care for the son I'm carrying, which isn't yours! You don't care for *me* at all. You told me I was nothing more than a vessel to you, a thing."

When he tried to deny it, she pressed on, the anger mounting as she recalled his words.

"Me, myself, I," she said, thumping her chest, emphasizing each pronoun, "mean nothing to you at all. Thanks for helping me make my decision. After the baby's born, I'm going back to America and getting an annulment."

She stood up to leave, taking a step toward the balcony door. But digging into her arm with his stubby fingers, he caught her and swung her around.

"Don't you ever turn your back on me again! You'll never get an annulment. I'll swear that's my son you're carrying, and no court in Taiwan would grant you an annulment."

"I said America, and they grant annulments there, especially when DNA testing proves it's *not* your son."

Pulling away, she rubbed the red welts on her arm and narrowed her eyes to hateful slits. He began laughing louder and louder as her anger grew, his eyes staring hers down.

"How are you going to leave Taiwan without an exit permit?" he asked. "With my influence, the police will never grant you an exit permit, so an American annulment's out of the question."

"Taiwan grants divorces."

He rubbed the side of his nose, his habit annoying her. Then he raised his eyebrows as if having given her words thought.

"That's true," he conceded, "but in Taiwan the children always go to the father. . . ."

"You're not the father," she shouted, "and the DNA will prove it."

"DNA testing can distinguish between two men of separate families, but with the same bloodlines? It'll never be able to tell Yang's DNA from mine."

Shaking his head, he smiled at her glazed expression, her mind focused inwardly. When she did not resist, he gently took her arm.

"You are carrying my son, Lane. Get used to the idea. If you really can't bear living here after the child's birth, leave. But the boy's mine." Then using her arm as leverage, he swung her toward him roughly. He peered into her green eyes before she shook free. "Mine and *taitai's*."

"What are you talking about? Much as I loathe it, I'm your *taitai*."

"You are my *xiao taitai*." He smirked as he shook his head.

Her eyes widened in recognition. "The story you told my father about Li was your story, wasn't it?"

He shrugged noncommittally. Understanding came like a wave of nausea. She could see his plan now.

"I was your green card to US citizenship. Marry me, and keep your other wife tucked away, where, on *Huahsi* Street?"

"Not other wife, *taitai*, first wife. You are the other woman." He watched her pale as he continued sarcastically. "And she doesn't live in Taiwan; she lives in Zhuhai, China, across the border from Macao."

"I don't believe you."

Her eyes looked glassy, her pupils dilating like those of roadside animals shined by car headlights. Stunned, she couldn't take her eyes off him.

"Now you know why I didn't give you my home phone number in Macao."

"What . . . Who . . . Does she know about me?"

Lane had so many questions, they garbled together, while Chen laughed, enjoying the upper hand.

"No, not yet."

"But she . . . she'll despise you when she finds out." Lane had trouble focusing as she looked into his sparkling eyes.

"Not if she gains a son from this. It'll raise her status as nothing else can."

"This isn't the Ching Dynasty," she said, gathering her frayed dignity about her like an old dressing gown. "I'll have our marriage annulled and see that you're charged with bigamy."

"Don't be so sure. Though you're not my only wife, you're the only one in Taiwan. Even my passport states that." He smiled maliciously. "Wives are like flags, only recognized in their own countries."

"This isn't my country."

She raised her chin level with the floor, turned on her heel and walked away. Light-footed, he caught her and spun her around.

"I told you not to turn your back on me."

Lane had never seen him so angry. His rage palpable, he seemed poised to strike, but rather than frighten, the idea repulsed her. Her green eyes challenging him, she spoke in a low, controlled voice.

"Take your hand off me. Now!"

Chen pulled away as if bitten by a dog. He backed toward the wall, stung by her words. Still he pretended to dominate.

"Don't you ever touch me again," she warned him in slow, intense tones.

"Don't take that tone of voice to your hus. . . ."

"Shut up, shut up, shut up," she screamed, covering her ears. "I can't stand the sound of you anymore than I can stand the smell!"

Finally when her words had finished ringing through his room, echoing off the cement walls and marble floors, she unplugged her ears. He opened his mouth to speak, and she shrieked.

*"Shut up!"*

Another silence ensued as she collected her thoughts. She took a deep breath and focused unrelenting eyes on him.

"First of all, *never* put your muddy paws on me. Second, you threaten me again about my son, and I'll have my father and the whole US Senate breathing down your back. Third, if I want to leave Taiwan, I sure as hell will." She held her finger in front of his attenuated nose, threatening. "Though I'm married to you, I'm a US citizen, and I don't *need* an exit permit." Then she thumped his chest. "Don't ever underestimate me. And if you want that trade agreement, you'd better not breathe a word about another wife, or I'll have you indicted as a bigamist. I believe there's still the issue of China's Human Rights policy holding up the pact. Wouldn't that make headlines!"

In control, she felt confident enough to laugh in his face. Ashen, he rearranged his robe, assuming first a stance of wounded pride, then bravado. While she stood solidly, he visibly quailed. Whether he shook from fear or rage, she was uncertain, but she was satisfied with her retaliation. Now was not the time to wonder how much her father or her government would back her. Instead she watched smugly as he moved about the room affecting poses, then discarding them as if the correct posture would win his battle for him. With a disdainful sniff, Lane realized he wasn't used to anyone, especially a woman, calling his bluff.

Finally he approached her but still maintained a respectful distance. He looked into her eyes, an easy task since hers were roughly his height, a difficult one since he felt culpable.

"Lane, you're right. I behaved badly. I'm not sure how to say this. I'm sorry. I meant to tell you how much you mean to me, and I ended up threatening you." He gestured with his hands, palms up. "I don't know how to act around you." Then his open palms became fists, and some of his anger returned to his voice. "I want us to be man and wife. I want you to return the feelings I have for you, but when you don't reciprocate," his voice rose to a crescendo on the last word, then died to a whisper, "I act uncivilized. Lane, I apologize. I . . . I don't want to lose you."

His shoulders sagging, he dropped his hands to his side.

She stared at him warily, the distrust evident in her eyes.

"Lose me? Or lose the trade agreement?" She sneered. "Don't make me respect you any less than I already do."

He sniffed thoughtfully, his chin sagging, his middle age showing. After a pause, he looked into her face.

"That hurt. More than anything else you've said to me, that hurt."

He stuck his hands dejectedly into his pockets and touched the silk pouch. Fingering it, he debated whether to offer it now or not. Then with a wry smile, he handed her the bundle.

"This is for you."

She pushed his hand away.

"No, please, it was meant to be a reminder of my affection." He shrugged. "Now let it be a peace offering."

She opened the zippered pouch gingerly and touched a cold circle of jade. Holding it up to the light, she noted its deep green color.

"Burmese jade," he said, "the highest quality I could find." With a dry laugh, he added, "It matches your eyes."

"I can't accept this. I'm sure it's too valuable to wear, anyway."

When Lane handed it back to him, his expression became serious.

"No, that's the point of it. You should wear it all the time. The Chinese believe jade protects its wearer from harm. Please, just keep it on it until you have the baby. It'll guard you both."

His eyes met hers again, but with sincerity, not affectation. When she made no move, Chen hesitantly molded her hand to a narrow point and slid the bracelet onto her wrist. She gave him a wary glance, then pulled away and turned to leave. As she opened the balcony door, he called to her.

"Wear it in good health."

Giving a faint nod, she left, more confused than when she had entered his room. Lane paused on the balcony, studying her wrist in the moonlight, thinking the jade more a manacle than a bracelet. She stared at the moon, feeling lonely, feeling alone in an alien land. She thought about going back to America then dismissed the idea. Who did she have to go back to? Home is not so much a place as a person.

The only one she cared about was in Taiwan. Suddenly the urge to speak to Li overwhelmed her. She strode into her room, bolted the door behind her and checked the time. Ten o'clock, not late by Taipei standards. Taking a deep breath, she decided to call him, despite Chen, despite Mei-ling. She had to hear Li's voice.

She dialed his number, praying he would answer.

"*Wei,*" said a masculine voice.

Not sure if she recognized him, she hesitated, then whispered, "Li?"

At the same moment, Mei-ling picked up the extension, listening. Although the sound was imperceptible to Lane, Li heard the receiver's click and quickly covered, hoping his wife would not guess the caller's identity. Forcing a casual tone, he said, "Sorry, wrong number," and hung up.

Li clenched his hands to his forehead and inwardly groaned. He wanted nothing better than to talk to her, hear her voice, but he did not dare take the chance with Mei-ling telling Chen his every move. Shutting his eyes, Li pictured Lane, smelling the sweet coconut scent of her shampoo, feeling her hair cascade over his face when she leaned over him, seeing the soft gleam of her eyes after they made love. Thinking about her caused an ache in his groin and a loneliness that tore at his chest.

Mei-ling stayed on the line, waiting for a clue. She heard a surprised gasp that ended in an unmistakable sob before the line went dead. Smiling, Mei-ling silently replaced the receiver. Smirking gleefully, she sauntered into the living room, her frothy negligee barely skimming her slim hips. She seductively slipped her arms around Li's neck.

"Aren't you over her yet?"

She nipped his ear gently with her small, pointed teeth. Recoiling, he shrugged her off and crossed to the liquor cabinet. As he poured a drink, she came up behind him, walked her fingers up his back, then twisted them in his hair, not so gently pulling his head close to hers.

"Don't you know Chen's crazy about her?" she asked, licking his ear. She sized him up before adding, "He'll never let her go."

Li started at the words but faked disinterest, refusing to believe her. Chen thought of Lane as a trophy or a means to an end, but the man was incapable of affection. Li's nostrils flared in disgust at the idea. Mei-ling was a liar and a fraud. He automatically discounted anything she told him, yet her news stabbed his heart like a syringe of adrenaline.

Sensing she had hit a nerve, she rubbed her body against his, squeezing his sinuous arms, massaging his shoulders. Sliding her body around his, she undid his shirt buttons while pressing against his groin. When Li responded with a stiffening erection, Mei-ling laughed in her throat. Again he pushed her away.

"Aren't you aggressive for a woman who's just had a baby?"

She laughed again, this time a clear, tinkling sound like wind chimes, as she approached him frontally, stroking him through his clothes.

"It's been a month. Really, what's so wrong with this arrangement?" Cupping his sex with one hand, she tucked her other arm inside his shirt, around his back for leverage, and suggestively rode his knee. "You have a son; you've done your filial duty." Flicking her tongue in light circles around his nipples, then licking her way up his chest, she whispered, "Your mother has a grandson to do *bai bai.* You've made her happy." She raised her lips to his and breathed, "Now let me make you happy."

He debated only a moment, then kissed her with all the pent-up passion he had been harboring since October. Silently cursing her for not being Lane, he rasped her mouth and neck with his teeth, pulling her against him with a ferocity that brought an excited squeal from her throat. She skillfully undid his belt and zipper, then slipped her hand inside his shorts and massaged him to a full erection. His eyes closed as he imagined Lane caressing him, fondling him. Still palming him, Mei-ling slid off his trousers and knelt, lowering her lips over his sex. Her rhythmic movement freed him from his last restraint, releasing them both from his self-imposed celibacy.

# CHAPTER 8

His heart thumping like temple *jihn* drums, Li stopped at the gate to Lane's house. Since he followed Chen's departure by only moments, the guard eyed him suspiciously, speculating whether he had planned it that way. Scowling, the aide recognized Li as the cause of his disgrace. Even after a month, he was still chafing from Chen's reprimand for misconduct. Vowing not to make the same mistake twice, he questioned Li sullenly, ushered him into the atrium and waited, arms akimbo, as Lane greeted her guest.

"What a surprise," she said sarcastically.

Self-consciously finger-combing her hair into place, she tried to draw attention away from her red eyes. Unable to forget Li's rebuff, she had been up most of the night, debating whether or not to return to the States. She knew it would be easier to leave before the baby came, both legally and logistically, but the pregnancy had sapped her strength. As the sun rose, she had fallen into a disturbed slumber, dozing fitfully, waking more exhausted and confounded than the night before.

"I wasn't expecting anyone so early," she finished with a weary sigh.

To Li, she looked as fresh as a lotus unfurling its petals on the pond's surface. He instantly felt as murky as the water's depths and hid his guilt behind a phony smile.

"I stopped by to see my uncle," he said for the guard's benefit, "but apparently I've just missed him. Is that coffee?"

Sniffing the air, he looked from her cup to the guard and

back again. With an understanding nod, Lane instructed Chen's man to get another *beizi*. Watching his reluctant retreat, she waited until he was out of hearing range, then turned to Li in an anxious whisper.

"Why did you hang up last night?"

His voice was contrite. "Mei-ling was listening on the other line."

Though relieved not to be compounding his deception with lies, he winced. Li regretted his fling like an alcoholic rues a binge. That his wife had manipulated him did little to ease his conscience. He had responded willingly enough. That thought made his next move more difficult. Unable to meet her eyes, he held up the envelope in his hand.

"My excuse for being here. I'd better leave it in Chen's office."

"The aide can do it."

"No need. I'll only be a second."

She struggled to get up from the wobbly wrought iron chair. "Here, let me take it for you."

He jumped up nimbly. "You take it easy. I'll be right back."

Before she could argue, he was out of the room and standing beside Chen's office. He cautiously checked for the aide, then slipped in silently, shutting the door behind him. He printed out the summary sheet of incoming fax numbers, folded it and hid it in the envelope.

Halfway to the door, he paused at the trill of an incoming fax. He debated, certain the wary aide would investigate if he were gone too long. Breathing heavily, Li glanced furtively from the door to the fax machine. He decided to wait, knowing the risk if caught. As he mentally rehearsed an alibi, a trickle of perspiration slid down his back, another down his cheek.

Finally the fax finished printing. He ripped it out and glanced over it quickly, not forgetting to press the reprint button. With each word, his pulse quickened until his heart beat like the drums at Lunar New Year. He crushed the fax into his coat pocket and hurried along the corridor back to Lane.

Hearing muffled voices, he ducked into the bathroom, flushed the toilet and meticulously washed his hands, humming loudly while the water ran. As he opened the door, the guard met him with a distrustful stare. Still humming a broken melody, Li nodded coolly and stepped past him, rushing down the hall and into the bright atrium where Lane was pouring coffee.

After the darkness of the corridor, he blinked, adjusting his eyes. His heart skipped a beat. Surrounded by the white morning light, she seemed ethereal, as if the glow came as much from within as without. Backlit by the sunlight, her head seemed encircled by a corona. An optical illusion, he told himself, blinking again. His imagination must be playing tricks on him, but he wanted nothing so much as to confide in her, touch her, end this unreality they were living. Instead he primly accepted the coffee and sat down, feeling despicable in her presence. Neither did it put him at ease that the aide had followed him and resumed his cross-armed sentry behind Lane.

At least the man's blocking the sun's glare, he consoled himself, but the aide's scowl was nearly as harsh. His undisguised contempt made Li wince. "It's so bright in here," Li said, squinting, changing seats, seeming to move out of the light but actually moving from the aide's line of vision. "Doesn't it hurt your eyes?"

Lane wondered why he was acting so skittish. A disturbing thought crossed her mind, bringing with it a frown. Was it her imagination, or was his conscience bothering him? She wished she could speak to him alone, get some answers, but her husband's man stayed as close to her as a visor on a cap. Every way she turned, she saw him hovering over her.

Sighing, she tried to make the best of Li's visit with monitored small talk, though another thought nagged. Why had he wasted their few private moments with a petty errand?

As she set her cup on the glass tabletop, the bracelet gracefully slid down her arm, shimmering into view. An admirer of jade, Li recognized fine quality when he saw it. Using it as a conversation piece, he reached for her wrist.

"That green's so clear, it's extraordinary. Is it mainland Chinese?"

He saw the guard move forward, and Li quickly withdrew his hand. Lane looked at it for the first time in daylight.

"No, Burmese." Surprised that it did match her eyes, she added for the guard's benefit, "My husband gave it to me last night."

Then unable to look Li in the eye, she pretended to study the jade. Too late she remembered his financial rivalry with Chen.

Biting back his questions, Li could only guess the reason for the gift, wonder if it had prompted her phone call. The aide's presence kept him from asking, from listening to her needs, from explaining his situation or confessing. Then his shoulders drooped as he mentally replayed the scenes from the night before. After an abashed silence, he drained his cup.

"I really should get to work. Sorry to have missed my uncle."

With effort, Lane lifted herself from the chair. Still keeping up the courteous act for the guard, she said, "I'll mention you left a letter in his office."

Li's jaw dropped. He saw the aide's folded arms fall to his

sides as the man started toward the other room, and he spoke quickly.

"No need." Producing the envelope from his jacket, then tucking it safely away again, Li added, "I'll just hand it to his secretary at the trade company." The aide looked undecided whether to inspect the office or monitor the conversation. Li relieved him of the decision by choosing for him. "If you could show me out, I'll be on my way."

Genuinely perplexed, Lane felt her suspicions compound as she watched Li. Though her aloof smile did nothing to alert the aide, her words were rife with meaning.

"Good-bye, Li. I hope next time you find my husband here . . . instead of me."

With that she sat down and resumed reading the morning paper, her back stiff and her resolve firmer. Calling him had been a mistake. She understood that now. If his hanging up had not proven his indifference, his terse explanation had. No apology, no consoling words, his stilted conversation had been as impersonal as a PC newsletter.

Facing facts, she took a deep breath. It was over. His preoccupation today confirmed it. New Year's dinner, the phone calls and *Yangmingshan's* walk must have all been irrational lapses. Maybe he didn't know what he wanted—or who.

Frowning, she wondered why he had come. If not out of concern for her, then why? She replayed his words and actions, always returning to his conflicting stories of the letter. With an indignant sniff, she decided his visit had been a ruse for some private agenda, maybe something to do with Chen. Suddenly she felt used. Determination replaced any self-pity or doubt she might have had as she grimly realized the only person she could rely on was herself.

She sat for several minutes, planning. The idea she had debated all night finally took shape. Inhaling a deep breath, she resolved to board the next plane for the States. Why not? Li was gone from her life. Chen? Her lip curled in distaste. What was he but a pompous bigamist who cared only for himself.

"Mildred?"

Lane called for the housekeeper to help her pack. Grumbling, she slowly pushed herself up from the glass-topped table, in the process knocking over her coffee, shattering the cup and splashing coffee on the waxed marble floor. Using the wrought iron chair as leverage, she tried to stoop to wipe up the mess, but halfway down, she realized her belly simply would not allow it.

"Mildred?" she called again, then mumbled, "Where is she?"

Using the rickety chair as a brace, Lane leaned her weight against it, pushing herself up. This time the slim wrought iron legs slipped on the wet marble and sent Lane sprawling. She landed with a crash on her stomach, her wrist breaking her fall but splintering the jade bracelet into a thousand green fragments. Laying in the green crystals and porcelain shards, Lane blacked out, her last memory being an overwhelming urge to urinate.

Chen met Mei-ling for coffee at the Juliet Club. Too early for business, the karaoke bar was empty except for them, the cleaning woman and two "princesses" chatting at the bar. He noticed Mei-ling's insufferable grin as she watched him from across the table, languidly stroking her coffee cup with red-enameled fingertips.

Finally he asked, "How's married life?"

She laughed, tilting back her head, showing her small white teeth. "Pure pleasure." Her sparkling eyes told more than her red-glossed lips.

After last night's unsatisfactory confrontation with Lane, he needed proof his wife was not renewing her affair with Li. Bending his head close, he hissed, "Is this another of your stories, Mei-ling?"

"Do you want evidence, Chen?" She laughed bitterly this time. "Do you want a gynecologist's exam, semen analysis, or," pulling aside her high neckline, she showed the love bites on her neck, "will these do?"

Her strong personality compelling, Chen sat back in his chair, surprised but relieved at the sight. An inveterate businessman, he was new to the insecurities of the heart. Eager to be convinced, he nodded, accepting it as proof. "Speaking of doctors, has Li pressed you about the baby's DNA testing?"

Rearranging her clothing, she shook her head. "His mother won't hear of it." Then flashing an arrogant grin, she added, "He'll accept this son as his own, just as he's embraced me as his wife."

As their eyes met in a silent pact, he grudgingly admitted his approval with a terse smile. "Either way," he said, "genetic testing isn't a problem."

Li parked on *Heng Yang* Street and hurried to the Presidential Office Building. Glancing over his shoulder, he approached the red-brick colonial building through the rear. He walked past the roped tire spikes and military trucks spilling out coils of razor wire. Then he showed his papers to the armed guards at the back gate. After a quick salute, they waved him in, and he took the stairs two at a time.

A special agent for the National Security Bureau in the Subversive Activities Control Department, Li reported directly to President Fu. Since Chiang Kai-shek had made Taiwan the provisional government in 1949, all subsequent presidents had been appointed—until this one. In nearly half a century of quasi democracy, Fu was the first elected president. A man of the people who spoke Taiwanese, not Mandarin Chinese, he was popular with the masses. Yet he had made enough enemies to maintain strict control of the NSB. He needed to be kept informed, and Li was his primary informer.

When Fu's personal guard admitted him into the presidential suite, Li said, "This should brighten your morning." He passed the crumpled fax to Fu, then added, "Silkworm's cocoon is unraveling. Here's the loose end." Li smiled. "All you have to do is pull."

After reading the fax, Fu handed it to Wang, his aide, then flashed a toothy grin. Fu reminded Li of old newspaper photos of FDR. All the Asian president needed was a monocle and cigarette holder. As if reading his thoughts, Fu reached for a cigarette, never pausing as Wang rushed to light it. He took a long drag.

"Now we have proof that Silkworm works for the CCP Central Committee, operating under Zheng," said Fu, clapping Li on the shoulder. "Good job."

Wang hesitated but asked anyway. "What difference does it make who he works for?"

Both heads spun toward him. Li gasped at the young man's ignorance, wondering which official had bribed his son's way into this position.

"Zheng's the Speaker of the People's Congress," said Fu, straining not to lose his patience. "He controls the legal system in the mainland and is head of the Chinese Communist Party." As Fu sucked deeply on the cigarette, Li took over.

"If Zheng succeeds Wong, the ROC's security will be severely compromised. We've suspected he used Silkworm to influence Taiwan's policies, but until now we had no proof.

Connecting Zheng to Chen is the first step in balancing the power between the two Chinas."

Stuttering, the ill-informed aide continued, "Why don't we just arrest Silkworm?"

Li waited politely for Fu to answer.

"The man's our bait. Isn't that a simple enough concept for you?" As the president spoke, he waved his hands, flicking ashes on the marble floors. He motioned at Li. "With his previous information, we traced six fax numbers to known sympathizers in Hong Kong and located another twenty partisans in Taipei, all members of the Bamboo Union."

*"Dui bu xi,"* said Li with a self-satisfied smirk, handing him the envelope, "here's another fax summary sheet."

Their minds meeting tacitly, the two exchanged gratified smiles. Fu opened it, glanced at the page, then passed it to Wang.

"You see?" Fu asked. "More numbers, more names. The longer Silkworm dangles on the hook, the more fish we'll catch."

Feeling himself falling in his commander-in-chief's disfavor but unable to stop, Wang persisted, "But we could never indict the biggest fish of all, Zheng, so what difference does it makes whether Chen's his agent or not?"

"An enormous difference!" The president snuffed out his cigarette angrily.

Li played peace-maker, explaining, "Mainland politics has been going through a transitional period, ever since Wong's death. It's a power struggle between Zheng and Tsai. Zheng's a hard-line Communist, who'll never accept equality between Beijing and Taipei. Tsai's more moderate—but he has two strikes against him. Because he's only in his sixties, he was too young to take part in the revolution. The party doesn't want to back him."

"What's the other reason?" The aide blinked innocently, as if learning a history lesson.

"The man has no charisma," said Fu, partially regained his patience, taking on the role of mentor. "Taiwan wants to endorse Tsai, strengthen his credibility. If he can consolidate his power, stability can be maintained on both sides of the Taiwan Strait. If Tsai were purged or overthrown by another faction in China—Zheng, for instance—there would be chaos! Then Taiwan's security would be in danger."

"By coming here," Li added, "Tsai hopes to gain public support at home through Taiwanese concessions. Then he can flaunt his 'successes' in Beijing." He pointed at the fax. "You read it. Zheng knows the KMT wants to help Tsai, and he's furious Taiwan's backing his adversary."

"Then why is Chen organizing Tsai's visit?" Wang's confusion showed clearly in his pained expression.

"You *do* understand Taiwan needs stable cross-strait relations to keep the status quo, don't you?" asked Fu, obviously irritated with his assistant. At the aide's nervous nod, he continued. "Zheng wants an incident to occur during Tsai's visit that will destroy diplomatic relations between the two Chinas. Since Silkworm is Zheng's agent, we have to watch him, use him. . . ."

"As bait," filled in the aide, hoping to score points.

Fu eyed him harshly. "As a barometer for the political climate," he finished.

Li arrived at the trade company moments ahead of Chen. He went directly into his uncle's office, delivering an unimportant letter in case Lane should mention the envelope. Li was thorough; he might forget weddings, but he never forgot details.

He noticed the office was buzzing, and with a heart-fluttering smile he asked Chen's personal secretary, "What's all the excitement about?"

Before she could answer, Chen strutted in, rearranging his lapels, smoothing the buttons of his jacket, acting very self-impressed, Li thought as he watched his uncle approach.

"Mr. Chen," the secretary called in a thin, tense voice, "your aide just called. Your wife's been taken to the hospital."

Chen went pale. Li's Adam's apple bobbed as he swallowed his cry of concern.

Turning on his heel, Chen shouted over his shoulder. "Phone my driver to meet me out front."

"I'm going with you," said Li, stepping quickly to catch up.

"The hell you are!"

As Chen pushed brusquely past his nephew, knocking him against the wall, Li watched him disappear down the hall. Then Li rushed out the side exit and caught a cab.

The streets were jammed. A legislator with a police escort had had the green lights adjusted to speed his way through town, bringing traffic to a halt. In a city of nearly six million, his action cost each commuter an extra ten minutes as grid-locked side streets slowly squeezed overheating cars onto *Chungshan* Road.

Cursing loudly in Taiwanese, Li's cab driver condemned the politician. "Look at that," he said, nodding toward the black motorcade. "Just because the pimp's father was a general in 'forty-nine, he's appointed to office." He spit red beetlejuice out the window. "Damned KMT," he grumbled.

Li was too fraught with worry to take offense. Sick with guilt, he blamed himself for Lane's condition. He should have stayed with her, explained himself. Mentally replaying the morning's visit, he shook his head, realizing he should never have gone there in the first place. He pounded his skull with his palm. Why am I doing this to her?!

The cab's blaring horn shook him from his reflections. Still seething at the dignitary's role in the traffic jam, the driver shouted, "Cocksucking KMT mainlanders fucking up politics, fucking up traffic!"

Li's eyes narrowed to angry slits. "You're right. Without the KMT, there'd be no traffic jams. Taipei would still be a rice paddy." He noted the cabby's identification number as the man eyed him warily through the rear-view mirror. "Remember that when it's time to renew your license."

As the sullen driver swerved between two lanes, creating a third narrow one of his own, Li sniffed contemptuously. The bastard had answered his question. The ROC was the reason he was mistreating Lane. Duty. If not filial duty, civic duty. Duty, it was his reason for everything.

When the cab finally pulled into the hospital drive, Li wordlessly paid the driver and rushed inside, shouting to the information desk for Lane's room number.

"Chen *Taitai*'s just gotten out of surgery," said the acne-pocked assistant. "Have a seat in the waiting room." He pointed the way with a dismissive wave.

"Damn it, what room number?" Li looked ready to explode.

The man's face paled behind the red bumps and scars. "Are you her husband?"

Li hesitated only a moment. "I'm the baby's father."

"Room five-one-four." Li about-faced as he heard the last syllable, turning left into the corridor, then catching an elevator just before its doors closed. The young man was still staring after him when Chen confronted him.

"What room is Chen *Taitai* in?"

Looking him over, assessing his age, the assistant debated,

then made his choice. "Are you her father?" he asked deferentially.

"I'm her husband!" Chen shouted, his eyes flashing angrily as his face turned a bright pink.

The man flinched. "Room five-one-four," he said, pointing out the elevator with a shaky finger.

"What are you doing here?" asked Chen, arriving only moments after Li.

Before he could respond, the nurse walked in, noted their anxious faces and made a snap judgment. "Your wife's resting now," she told Li.

"Thank you," said Chen, looking apoplectic. "She's *my* wife."

A second nurse appeared, removing her mask. Taller and more politic, she asked with a compassionate smile, "Who's the lucky father?"

Both men spoke simultaneously. "I am."

The nurses exchanged discrete looks, as Chen elbowed his way to the front. Remembering his dignity, he channeled his emotions. "When can I see my son?"

Li felt the nurses' eyes on him but was unable to meet them. He studied the scuffs on his shoes as he heard the second nurse speak.

"There are complications."

"What?" demanded Chen. "What's wrong with my son? It's nothing serious, is it?"

"Is Lane . . . is the mother all right?" Li's dark eyes snapped anxiously as he looked up, watching the nurses step aside for the doctor.

The doctor removed his mask and addressed Chen first. "Your son's in an incubator. . . ." Chen gasped, then stopped, nodding silently to the man to continue. "As you know, he's premature." The doctor smiled encouragingly. "It's still early to make any prognosis. We'll know more in a few days, but don't worry. His vital signs are excellent."

Addressing Li, he said, "The mother's experiencing some trauma. Though she didn't break any bones, the fall caused severe internal bleeding."

"Fall?" Li asked too quietly to be heard.

The doctor continued uninterrupted. "She's sedated now," he turned to Chen, "but you can visit her, one at a time." He turned back to Li. "Just don't excite her, and stay no longer than five minutes apiece."

"What about my son?" Chen asked. "When can I see him?"

"Now, if you like. He's on the third floor."

He shook his head vehemently. "First I want to visit my wife, make sure she's all right. Then I'll meet my son." A shy smile flickered at his lips. "I've waited this long; I can wait five minutes more."

The doctor motioned for the tall nurse to accompany Chen. She led the way to the adjacent room, saying, "If it weren't for the jade bracelet, your wife would have lost the baby and broken her wrist."

"What?!"

"Her wrist broke her fall," explained the doctor.

With a knowing smile, the nurse countered, "The *jade* broke her fall."

Annoyed, the doctor said, "This hospital's no place for superstition."

His patronizing tone silenced her, but when her eyes met Chen's, the two tacitly agreed it was the jade that had protected Lane. With a contented sigh, Chen felt the bracelet's exorbitant price money well spent.

He was unprepared for the sight as he entered the room. Lane lay deathly still on the bed, her dark hair clammy with perspiration, her cheeks chalky. Glazed and slowly rotating, her eyes would not focus. When he called her name, she looked through him. Chen glanced at the nurse for support.

"She's heavily sedated," the woman said, inspecting the intravenous tubes. Then she lifted Lane's bruised hand. "See? The jade shielded her and saved the baby."

The words caught Lane's attention. She whispered in an odd, childish voice, as if in a dream. "Baby. Go home." Her eyes focused for a moment on Chen, then began spilling over. Tears streamed down her cheeks unchecked. Then she began sobbing, the tones coming deep from her chest. Chen's initial reaction had been to reassure her, but the primal moans made his skin crawl.

The nurse came to his rescue. "She needs rest. Come back tomorrow."

Gratefully Chen nodded and escaped, still hearing Lane's eerie wails as he got into the elevator. The awaited moment was not turning out as planned. Only the thought of seeing his son lifted him from the unexpected melancholy. He stopped at the third floor and with heart palpitations eagerly asked directions to the incubator. He smiled at his fears as he approached the apparatus, anxious to see the son he had been anticipating for forty-nine years.

However, the brown shriveled being in the glass box looked like a hairless monkey. Chen shrank from putting his arms through the holes and touching it. Though he did try to smile at it, talk to it, its eyes were tightly shut, and it mewed piteously. After five minutes, the nurse suggested he let the baby rest. Disappointed, Chen stumbled away, suddenly exhausted.

Li had heard Lane's cries from next door but waited until he saw Chen tiptoe away. Then he cautiously approached her room, his eyes silently begging the nurse for permission to visit. She opened her mouth to say no but was unable to refuse his troubled eyes. "The doctor said five minutes," she reminded him. Then with a sympathetic smile, she slipped out, leaving him alone with Lane.

He sat on the edge of the bed, speaking in a soothing voice. "Lane, I promise I'll make this up to you." Though she did not appear to comprehend, her sobbing gradually stopped. "I'll make you happy. Lane, look at me." He took her bruised hand gently in his. "Lane, try to listen." Her head still wobbled and her mouth hung slightly open, but she seemed to be watching him, so he continued. "I love you. When this is over, I'll make it up to you." He kissed her hand. "That's a promise."

# CHAPTER 9

The next morning Iris visited with a golden bouquet of miniature orchids and yellow flowering dill. Lane was still sedated but conscious. She smiled as Iris enthused, "You very luck girl! You have beautiful son."

"You saw him?" Her voice cracked.

"Just now." Iris was beaming. "She . . . he so cute!" Handing her the flowers, she added, "For you." Glancing around the room at Chen's grandiose floral arrangements, she added, "This garden room."

Lane warmly smiled her thanks, breathed in their heady scent, and asked the nurse, "Could you put these in water?"

The woman looked to Iris for a translation, then in Chinese told her the story about the jade. As the nurse started off with the flowers, Iris asked, "*Zhen de ma?* Did bracelet really break your fall?"

"Well, it's true my fall broke the bracelet." For the first time since the accident, Lane laughed dryly. "As to the superstitious part, I don't think so."

Iris looked serious. "Jade very luck. Protect you and baby." Then she smiled impishly. "Who give you?"

In a bored monosyllable, Lane said, "Chen."

"See?" she chirped, raising her finger to make her point. "Mr. Chen worry about you."

"He just likes to show off his wealth," said Lane glumly. "The jade was expensive, so he bought it. It had nothing to do with concern."

Iris shook her head. "You wrong. Mr. Chen protect you."

She cocked her head coquettishly and thoughtfully rested her cheek on her hand. "She . . . he love you."

"Because you're in love, you think everyone else is," Lane accused, her eyes sullen and ringed with fatigue.

Iris did not take offense. Instead, worried about tiring her friend, she said gently, "You rest. Iming take me to lunch." Then she gasped, clapping her hands together. "I almost forget. We moved in wedding date."

"When?" asked Lane, ignoring the faulty idiom. Iris' excitement was infectious.

"Sunday!" Her eyes leaped out like a three-dimensional picture.

Iris' smile contagious, Lane returned it, asking, "So soon? Why?"

"*Feng shui*. Iming mother ask *feng shui* master." She beamed. "Good day to wedding." She grabbed Lane's suddenly cold hand, whispering conspiratorially. "And we start family more soon."

Lane remembered the *feng shui* of her own engagement. Wilting now under Iris' sunny smiles, she sank back on her pillows, lapsing into a moody silence. When her friend's hand slipped from hers, Iris got up to leave.

"You tired. Get well. Come Sunday."

Lane's only response was a wan smile before her eyes closed, and she drifted into a drugged sleep. What seemed like moments later, she heard a knock. As her eyes focused, she saw Li standing at the door with a bulky bouquet of birds-of-paradise, passionflowers and red baby carnations. Tucked under his arm was an unwieldy stuffed animal. Between the two gifts, he had trouble making it through the doorway. Laughing, as the flowers' cellophane wrapper crinkled in protest, Li finally squeezed into the room.

"Hi," he said, setting the stuffed cow on the bed.

Though she could not remember the words he had spoken the day before, she recalled the peace of mind he had brought. Instinctively feeling safer in his presence, Lane relaxed. She looked at the plush black-and-white toy and smothered a giggle.

"Is that for me or the baby?"

Relieved at the change in her mood, he answered spontaneously. "It's for our son." Then as her smile drooped, he winced. Quickly changing the subject, he pushed the toy closer for her inspection. "What do you think? It's the biggest one I could find."

"Why did you buy a stuffed cow?" She tucked her hair behind an ear in a weak attempt at primping. "Why not a teddy bear or something cuddly?" Then she asked anxiously, "This isn't some religious thing, like worshipping golden calves, is it?"

This time Li laughed. "No, although there is a superstitious connection. According to Chinese horoscopes, this is the year of the ox. The baby will grow up to be a sincere, dependable person."

"Like a contented cow?" she asked, a teasing quality to her voice.

"Like a child who knows he's loved." His eyes latched onto hers a beat too long. Then embarrassed by his sentiment, Li shoved the flowers under her nose. "These are for you."

Lane pulled her head back from the bushy bouquet. Clasping her hands around its stem, she held the flowers away so she could admire them. "They're beautiful."

"Like you," Li whispered.

Knowing how disheveled she looked with her thick hair tousled from sleep, Lane blushed. She was still pale but with a fine porcelain quality to her complexion, not the chalkiness of the day before. Her skin seeming to glow from within, the pink tinge only heightened her delicate loveliness.

Li was entranced. He stared without meaning to.

When the morning nurse came in to check on her, Lane held out the bouquet, speaking to Li, "Would you ask her to put these in water?"

Li obliged, translating. The nurse smiled indulgently, then looked at the overcrowded tables.

"The room's blooming now," she said. "Where should I put them?"

Forced to see something besides Lane, Li dismally noted Chen's ostentatious arrangements. His looked cheap in comparison. Instantly seething with his long-felt competition, he snapped at her.

"Put them in the toilet for all I care."

They both caught their breath. After a tense silence, Li wiped his fingers penitently across his mouth, as if erasing what he had just said.

"Sorry, this is all new to me."

Rebounding, the woman said, "Fatherhood usually is." She took the bouquet from Lane but addressed Li, "If you want to make yourself useful, wheel your wife in to see your baby."

"Really?" A smile of wonder creasing his grim expression, Li did not correct the new nurse's error.

"There's a wheelchair in the hall."

"Thank you!" With a boyish smile, he reached around the bouquet and kissed the nurse's cheek. Lane watched with a half-dazed smile as he ran out, then rushed back in, pushing a wheelchair in front of him. "Your sedan awaits," he said with a gracious bow.

The nurse propped the flowers in a corner and helped Li assist Lane into the chair, carefully arranging the IV tubes and bag. Lane protested about the fuss but was anxious to see her baby. Wincing at the soreness, she eased into the chair. Then arranging her hospital gown and finger-combing her hair, she turned to him nervously.

"How do I look?"

"Like a new mother." Li chuckled as he began wheeling her down the hall.

"I suppose it sounds silly," said Lane, licking her dry lips, "but I want to make a good impression." Because her back was to him, she could not see his own panicked expression. "Have you seen him yet?" she asked, craning her neck in time to watch his Adam's apple bob. He shook his head.

The nurse rolled her IV stand behind them, forming the caboose of their excursion train. Lane's tension mounted as they took the elevator to the third floor. Approaching the incubator, she felt goose bumps. The moment she saw her son, she let out a small cry and looked from the nurse to Li, waiting for him to translate.

"Can I hold him?" she asked.

After a short discussion with the RN, Li relayed the message. "Not yet," he said gently. "He's still weak, but you can touch him through the openings."

As she reached out, he pushed her chair closer. Sliding her arm through the opening, she tentatively touched his hand.

"He looks tan," Lane said, addressing the nurse. "Why?"

Via translation, she said, "It's natural. The color will fade in a few days."

Lane examined the tiny fingers. "Look," her eyes widened with wonder at this little being she had helped create, "his nails need trimming." Her dewy eyes glowed with a new-born love. After exchanging a delighted giggle with Li, she lightly stroked the baby's arm. "He feels so soft." Then turning to Li, she added, "Touch him."

Li cautiously reached in and fondled a foot no larger than the Chinese women's of ancient times. Just as tightly as their feet had been bound, the bonds anchored father to son. He looked from the sleeping baby to Lane and silently renewed his pledge to her. Still holding his son's foot, he reached for her free hand.

When they connected, they formed a love triangle, each side necessary to the others, the baby the cherished vertex, the parents the solid base. It felt right. Looking up at Li, Lane smiled her satisfaction.

"What are you doing here?" shouted Chen, his fury tangible.

A sudden chill swept over Lane. She reflexively jerked her hand from Li's and in the process woke the baby. Instead of mewing, her small son bawled as loudly as Chen. At that moment, he even looked like Chen. Mouths wide open, both angry red faces demanded attention. She rubbed the baby's arm soothingly, a gesture as old as humanity, as instinctive as motherly love.

Li gingerly massaged his son's foot. "There's no need to shout. I'm only visiting," he told Chen, momentarily scowling at him. As the baby cried lustily, his concern returned to his son.

"You're intruding on my family," said Chen.

He motioned to his aide. The man stepped behind Li and none-too-gently tapped his shoulder. Li angrily took the hint, carefully removing his hand from his son and stepping aside.

"Keep your voice down," Li said calmly. "You're scaring the baby."

Chen's booming voice continued. "You're not welcome here. Leave!"

He took Li's place at the foot of the incubator and reached in. Awkwardly he grazed the baby's bony ankle, which set off a new round of cries.

"I don't know who's worse," Lane hissed, "you or my son." She gave her husband a sharp glance. "You're both behaving like newborns."

"You'll have to leave," the nurse said perfunctorily.

Glaring at Li, Chen nodded to his aide. When the man tugged at his arm, Li jerked away.

"Don't touch me," Li said, his words a frigid warning.

As the baby's cries increased alarmingly, he made choking sounds, gasping for breath.

"I'm sorry, you'll all have to go," the nurse informed them in Chinese. "The baby needs rest." Arms spread wide, she herded them out.

"My son," cried Lane, "will he be all right?"

Li translated for her. As Lane let go the baby's frail arm, his cries escalated, and she again tried to speak soothingly to the child.

"You'll have to leave *now,*" the doctor said in Chinese, stepping into the room. "You're wasting the baby's strength just when he needs all his energy to survive."

Subdued, everyone responded to his words but Lane, who didn't understand. When Li started wheeling her, Chen motioned his aide to man the chair, muscling Li out of the way.

"No, I don't want to leave my baby." Lane became agitated.

Chen walked arrogantly alongside her chair, his eyes hard as anthracite, while his aide wheeled her toward the elevator. The nurse followed, pushing the IV, the doctor beside her, prescribing a sedative for Lane. Li brought up the rear, feeling as useless as a fifth wheel.

His place was beside Lane, reassuring her, bolstering her, and he could not even join her convoy. His eyes stinging, he swallowed his pride along with the lump in his throat. In the elevator, Chen, his aide, the nurse and doctor squeezed around the wheelchair.

When Li tried to step in, the aide jammed the button, jeering, “No room.” The doors slammed, shutting Li out of Lane’s life like a deportee at the boarding gate.

Still hearing her son’s cries as the metallic doors closed with a hollow thud, Lane slipped into an insulated shell. Not understanding the Chinese spoken around her, she retreated even further inside her thoughts. Only when Chen and the nurse helped her to bed did she struggle, almost pulling out the tubes in her arm and hand.

“No, I have to see my baby.”

The doctor injected her IV with a strong sedative. Though she resisted, she felt herself drifting into a seductive languor. The nurse held her arms still until they went limp.

“Can I stay with her?” she heard Chen ask.

“Just a few more minutes until she’s asleep,” the doctor answered.

She heard footsteps as he, the nurse and aide left the room. Then she heard Chen speak, his voice high-pitched and whining, like cicadas. Irritating, it intruded on the numbing effects of the narcotic. If the medication had not made her legs marble columns, she would have physically escaped his droning words. Instead she was imprisoned by her own drugged body, forced to listen until the sedative mentally overpowered her, drowned out his words.

“Lane, don’t do this to me! Don’t turn my son against me. Don’t confuse him about his father.” He paced as he talked, his words a stream of consciousness that hummed and hissed in her weary mind. Then his voice sounded closer, as if he were whispering in her ear. “Give us time, you, me and Tian-syang. Let us be a family.”

Tian-syang? Had he named the baby? She tried to shout

*no,* but consciousness was slipping. Only a small moan escaped her lips.

She heard him cross to the door and breathed a sigh that he was leaving. When she heard him mutter to his aide, she closed her eyes. He would be gone in a minute.

Then a click of the door lock jarred her awake. Straining to open her drowsy lids, she saw the shadow of Chen's man standing guard outside the frosted glass door. Had Chen left? She rolled her eyes as far back as she could. He was standing outside her peripheral vision, so she could not see him. She could only hear him.

"You're my wife, Lane. You haven't learned that yet," he laughed through his narrow nose, "but you will." In a dreamy state, she felt his hands on her. "You're mine, not Li's, mine. Do you hear me?"

He shook her, but even when her eyes flickered open, she did not realize what was happening. He slapped her cheeks until her eyes dully focused on him. In a disturbed limbo between anguish and peace, she felt him rip the covers off her and push up her hospital gown. His hands tearing off her panties shocked her into semi-consciousness, but she felt too frozen to move, to speak, to even think clearly.

Through half-lidded eyes, she watched him lift a tube of lubricating jelly from the hospital cart's tray. Leering at her as he squeezed the container, his hands roughly forced her thighs apart, and he slathered her with gel. In detached fascination, she watched his hand come away from her smeared with blood. He wiped it on the sheets, then reached at his belt buckle, unzipped his pants and masturbated his dick to a pathetic erection.

As at her engagement, she felt she was watching a video. None of it seemed real. Groggy from the IV, she felt only mild discomfort when he entered her. Falling into a deep hypnotic state as much from the drugs as from her own mind protecting her from the rape, she was aware only of his fetid cigarette breath and the shaking bed until he climaxed. Then his piercing grip woke her with spasms of agonizing pain. The seeping spread of red from her vagina was her last memory before she slipped into unconsciousness.

Smiling with satisfaction, Chen gloated. She's mine, he thought, as he washed himself at the sink. Comparing her blood to red ink and the rape to a signet's imprint, he felt his mark of ownership was on her as if stamped by his chop. Before he left the room, he took one last look at her head on the pillow, its tangled hair radiating from her wan face, and felt a conquering thrill surge through his groin. He unlocked the door and strode away, his aide at his heels.

Minutes later the nurse came to check the IV. When she routinely lifted Lane's arm to take her blood pressure, the covers fell away, revealing the blood. It had pooled, saturating the sheets, wicking onto her hospital gown. The nurse felt Lane's pulse, then rang for help. Noting the torn panties, her eyes narrowed as she deduced the facts.

After they injected Lane with coagulants to staunch the flow, the doctor examined her. Quickly diagnosing the bleeding as complications from delivery, he scheduled an emergency operation. Orderlies lifted her onto a gurney and wheeled her into surgery. As the doctor rushed after them, the nurse stopped him.

"May I have a word with you?"

"Is it necessary?" he snapped, irate at the interruption.

Nodding her head, the woman threw back the covers, exposing the gore. Then she retrieved the torn panties from the bed's recesses and pointed out the bloody fingerprints. He stifled his reaction, asking,

"How did those get there?"

"That's what I'd like to know," the nurse said. "There was no blood under her nails."

"Meaning . . . ?"

"Meaning she didn't tear the stitches herself. Someone else did."

He took a deep breath, analyzing the situation. "Who else was in this room?"

"Only Mr. Chen." Her eyes pierced his as her tone accused.

He studied the woman's expression, then nodded in tacit agreement with her conclusions. His manner again brusque, he warned, "Keep this to yourself."

The nurse stared at him, mouth open, ready to speak. Instead she blinked, closed her mouth and gave a quick, deferential nod.

"Change the bed," he called over his shoulder, leaving for OR.

As the doctor stitched Lane's wounds, his suspicions were confirmed. "What's the cause of the bleeding?" asked an intern, filling out the exploratory surgery report.

The doctor hesitated only a moment before answering. "Complications of labor." Then he peeled off his rubber gloves and pushed through the swinging doors, telling the nearest orderly to call Chen's office.

When his personal secretary answered, she said, "Mr. Chen's in a meeting. I'll have him return your call."

"Tell him his wife has suffered another severe trauma," said the doctor in his most authoritative tone. "Unless he wants to assume responsibility, he'll take my call now."

Chen was speaking with the China External Trade Development Council Chairman, Cheng, and Hsieh, deputy secretary-general of CETRA when the call came through. After listening to his secretary's nervous relay, Chen excused himself, angling his chair away from his guests.

"Put him through."

"Mr. Chen, your wife has suffered a setback. She's experiencing severe vaginal hemorrhaging." He paused skillfully before posing the question. "Do you have an opinion as to how this could have occurred?"

Chen rubbed the side of his nose thoughtfully. "It was a difficult birth for my wife, her first." Swinging his back to his guests for more privacy, he added quietly but reproachfully, "Apparently more difficult than either you or your staff realized." He let his words hang in the air.

"Before you insult me or the hospital staff," said the doctor, his voice icy, "I should mention the suspicious circumstances surrounding her sudden relapse." Again he paused shrewdly. "I'm sure the hospital administrators would be most interested."

"Doctor, you misunderstand me." Chen's eyes as unperturbed as lotus ponds, his visitors sensed no undercurrents. "Perhaps your facility's ill-equipped." A goldfish broke the surface of his serene ponds. Chen let the undulating waves break and dissipate before continuing. "I was thinking of making a modest contribution to the hospital. Of course, you could dispense with it as you see fit."

The long silence did not embarrass Chen. His eyes placid pools again, he waited for what he knew would come.

Slowly the doctor answered, "Your wife will require special care. . . ."

"Exactly," said Chen, seizing the initiative. "Would three hundred thousand NT take care of the expenses?"

The doctor breathed in sharply. "Five hundred would ensure my personal attention."

"I'll send my aide over with it immediately." Chen smiled, his eyes as inky and unfathomable as reflecting pools. "And doctor, see to it that my wife recovers rapidly." He laughed crudely. "As a man of the world, you understand I want to claim my conjugal rights as soon as possible."

He hung up and waved his aide to him. After excusing himself, he unlocked his wall safe, withdrew several bundles of bills and dispatched his man. Returning to his guests, he smiled unctuously.

"Sorry for the interruption, gentlemen." He directed his question to Cheng. "You had asked if Beijing will send a delegate to our Conference?" The chairman nodded. "The China Council for the Promotion of International Trade is as eager to increase Taiwan-Mainland economic cooperation as your China External Trade Development Council. Offer it a rostrum to exchange views on present trade policy expansion." He chuckled reassuringly. "It won't pass up an opportunity to improve commerce across the Taiwan Strait. Tempt it, and the CCPIT will endorse sending a delegate to the Conference."

"But is the CCPIT powerful enough to influence the Central Committee?" asked Cheng.

Chen shook his head, an amused twinkle in his eyes. "No, but if it can show the Cabinet the benefits from improved trade with Taiwan, China's Association for Relations Across the Taiwan Strait can persuade them to send Tsai."

"Tsai!" echoed Hsieh incredulously. The two CETRA men exchanged glances. "I never suspected."

"As Beijing's party chief, he's the highest-ranking official in the capital," said Cheng. "Would the Communist Party's Central Committee approve it?"

"With enough support from the trade sector, it would." Chen felt the thrill of dominance for the second time that day. "In fact, with a little grease to turn the wheels, I can personally vouch for it." He stared at them slowly. "*Guanxi*, gentlemen, you scratch my back," greed flashed in his eyes like a torch flickering in a cave, "and I'll scratch yours."

Lane was good for him, Chen thought to himself, mentally estimating his bribe. She brought him luck. Why hadn't he taken her sooner? A small murmur of regret whispered in his ears, but the power rushing through his temples drummed out the sound. Not only was he moving to a point where the two Chinas were one, but where he and Lane were one. Reunification for the PRC; coupling for him. Husband and *xiao taitai*. With a substantial profit. He grinned, feeling a gratification too long delayed.

Lane woke sore and weak. Her throbbing headache blotted out her nightmare, yet tendrils of the memory remained. She was trying to knit it together when she heard voices.

"She's coming out of it, doctor."

"Increase the morphine."

The memory vanished like fog in sunlight as she drifted into a never-never land.

When Iris phoned, she was told Lane had had a relapse and could take no calls. Li called hourly, each time getting the same response.

"No change in her condition."

The second day Li went to the hospital, demanding to see her. Chen's man stood outside her door, arms crossed, mouth sneering. When Li tried to get past him, he radioed for assistance, and a second guard appeared, helping him escort Li from the building.

That afternoon Li confronted Chen at the office.

"There's nothing to discuss," said the older man. "Lane suffered a relapse after the disturbance you caused. If you want to help her," his eyes pierced Li's like obsidian spearheads, "stay away!" Then Chen pushed past him into the conference room, leaving Li staring at his wide back.

"One question, Uncle," Li called after him. "If you despise me so much, why do you keep me on at the trade company?"

Chen hesitated as if considering an answer then strode into the meeting.

The third day Lane woke groggy and disoriented. Her mouth felt like she had been chewing dry rice. She tried to speak, but her throat was so parched, it scratched. She tried to sit up, but her throbbing headache returned, and her stitches pulled. Finally she settled for opening her eyelids, even that effort requiring all her strength.

Looking around the hospital room, she tried to get her bearings. Snatches of memory haunted her, tugging at her mind like naughty boys pulling braids. When she heard voices, she closed her lids, pretending to sleep. Breathing shallowly, she listened for clues to jog her memory.

As someone checked her pulse, Lane willed herself to relax to slow her heart rate. Apparently it was normal because her wrist was lowered again.

"Decrease the morphine," said the doctor in Chinese. "She's going home tonight. Give her fruit juices and *dou hua.*"

Then she heard retreating footsteps. Though she could not understand, she thought she heard the word *jia,* home, but it might have been *jiu,* the word for nine. Then she felt hands begin to bathe her face and brush her hair. Cautiously she opened her eyes and saw the smiling image of her nurse.

Lane tried to talk to her, but her voice came out a croak. "Do you want some juice?" asked the nurse in Chinese. Lane saw her reach for a glass and nodded. The woman put a straw in it, so Lane could stay semi-reclined and still drink. "You're going home," the woman said in Chinese. As Lane swallowed, she again heard *jia.*

"Home?" she asked in a hoarse whisper.

"*Dui, jia,* home," said the nurse.

Jigsaw fragments of memory churned in her mind, tumbling past each other but not connecting. Lane's first reaction was panic.

"Where's my baby?" She spilled the juice as she tried to crawl out of bed. "Where's my baby?"

The nurse caught her by her arms and held her down, speaking Chinese in a soothing voice. Pinned to the pillows, Lane stared intensely at the woman, trying to remember why this seemed familiar. For a moment the nurse's face seemed to be Chen's. Then she had a flashback to her nightmare, and her headache returned with a blinding cluster of lights.

She moaned and sagged limply against the pillows. The woman tentatively let go her hold as Lane covered her eyes with her hands, massaging her temples. Suddenly she heard Li call her name. She peeked through her fingers, not believing her ears, thinking it was another dream.

Ignoring the headache, she whispered, "Li, ask her about my baby. Where's my baby?"

Li tried to hide his worry. Lane's face looked drawn, dehydrated. She was so pale, he could see the fine blue veins at her temples.

"What happened?" he asked the nurse.

"She's had a relapse," she said guardedly, mopping up the spilled juice.

"Why's she so white?" Li tried to make eye contact with her, but the woman refused to meet his eyes.

"She's lost a lot of blood."

"The baby?" Lane whispered anxiously.

Li translated and the nurse smiled, relieved of answering more questions by Lane's interruption. "I'll bring him in."

Then she added in a warning tone, "If you promise to keep her calm."

"What day is this?" Lane asked hoarsely when the woman left.

He tried to avoid the question by pouring her more juice. "Here, drink this."

She drank greedily, watching him over the glass rim. "What happened?"

"What do you remember?" he countered.

She squinted, mentally searching for clues. Shaking her head, she said, "Only parts of a nightmare."

"What parts?" His eyes pierced hers.

She gestured futilely, touching air. Then she pressed her hands to her forehead, massaging.

"If this headache would only go away, maybe I could remember."

Tentatively Li sat on the edge of the bed, reached over and began rubbing her temples with his cool fingertips. With a grateful sigh, Lane leaned back, responding to his healing touch.

Chen's man was returning from his break when he spotted Lane's open door. Rushing in, he saw Li on her bed and bounded toward him, arms outstretched, hands ready to grab Li's throat. Lane opened her eyes in time to see him and screamed hoarsely. The man lifted Li off the bed by his lapels and punched him in the stomach. Pressing the buzzer, she continued screaming until two attendants came running into the room and pulled the men apart.

"Keep him out of here," she shouted hoarsely, pointing to Chen's man.

Chen's guard shouted to Li, "I'll be waiting for you right outside." Li was explaining the situation to the attendants in Chinese just as the nurse came in with the baby.

The sleeping infant sensed the anger around him and began balling his tiny fists and waving his thin arms. His small, flat face turning red, he opened his mouth in silent protest, then vented his frustration in loud wails.

Still visibly upset, Lane tried to gather her composure. Seeing the baby brought a sparkle to her eyes and color to her pale lips. They parted in a half-smile as she held out her arms.

"Let me hold him."

She gingerly took the baby from the nurse, afraid to hurt the small bundle. Her own emotions running high, Lane tried to calm herself as she soothed her son. She tried talking to him, but her words came out a hoarse stage whisper that frightened him more. Finally she just held him against her, rocking him gently. Gradually his cries died to a whimper, and he fell asleep, curled in her arms. Only when his dimpled fists relaxed did she look at Li. She caught him gazing at the baby, a gentle smile tugging at Li's lips.

The nurse discreetly left the room, closing the door behind her, much to the guard's annoyance. With the newfound privacy, Li leaned over and fondled the tiny fingers, now limp with sleep. Then studying the baby's face, he traced the bridge of the nose.

"He has your western nose."

Lane looked at the work-of-art in her arms, surprised to see a mini version of herself, and felt a faint stirring of pride. She smiled from one to the other, comparing Li's face with the baby's.

Feeling unselfish, she added, "He's got your wide forehead."

Their eyes met in an exclusive intimacy as they shared the moment. Lane broke the gaze first as a disturbing thought crossed her mind.

"What day is this?"

He told her reluctantly, trying to soften the blow.

"I've been asleep three days?!"

Startled at her outburst, the baby made mewing sounds, the prelude to crying. She began rocking him instinctively, willing her distraught mind to calm down, consciously checking her temper.

"What happened to me?"

"That's what I've been trying to find out." He smiled ruefully. "All they'll tell me is that you've had a relapse." He stared into her limpid green eyes. "What do you remember?"

She frowned, trying to mesh the strands of memory together, like intricate Chinese knotting. "I can see vignettes," she said, motioning with her free hand, "like still frames of a film." Her eyebrows knitted together thoughtfully, then she shook her head, grimacing, "But I can't connect the frames into any moving picture." She sighed. "Why do I feel so drained?"

"Because you've just had a baby," said the doctor, clipboard in hand, as he opened the door, "and rather severe internal bleeding from the fall."

Startled, she looked up in time to see Chen's man peering in before the nurse clicked shut the door.

"But isn't this unusual?"

"Perfectly normal," he said in his most patronizing tone.

"Then why do I have flashes of memory?"

"Side effects from the morphine." Interrupting before she could ask any more questions, he motioned to the nurse to take the baby, telling Lane, "You've had quite a shock to your system." Addressing Li, he said, "I'm sorry, but you'll have to leave. If Mrs. Chen's going to be released today, she needs to be examined."

Li smiled obligingly, then tousled the baby's fine fringe of hair. He looked into Lane's wan face.

"We'll work this out."

She nodded, but before she could speak, the nurse reached between them for the baby, blocking their view. Li stood up to meet Lane's eyes in a silent good-bye. He gave her a parting wave and mockingly saluted Chen's man on his way out. Then he was gone.

Lane had misgivings about leaving the hospital. She resented the idea of Chen's house being home, but there was more to it than that. Not quite remembering why, she loathed being alone with him. Analyzing it, she realized it was fear she felt and began planning her escape.

When she arrived home with the baby, Lane called Iris, inviting her over. She needed someone to talk to. Chen ignored her as he bustled to catch his plane.

"I've called an emergency meeting in Macao," he said, popping into her room between phone calls and a visit to the nursery. "I'll see you when I get back."

He leaned over her to kiss her lips, but, as she pulled away from the tobacco smell of his breath, she was reminded of the dream. Before she could recall it, though, his wry laugh dispelled the memory. He kissed her cheek roughly, then lit a cigarette before he left the room.

"Don't smoke in here," she said, wiping his kiss off the side of her face.

"Remember, this is my house, and you're my wife; I'll do as I please."

He arched an eyebrow, put away his lighter and sauntered out, his left hand resting in his pocket, pulling his coat snugly around his arrogant shoulders.

Her lip curling in a sneer, she watched his retreating figure, vowing her escape. When she heard him leave, she brought the baby in with her and watched the news, listening to reports of Tsai's proposed visit. Lane and the baby dozed in front of the television as an angry DPP legislator reproached the KMT for giving away Taiwan to the mainland.

*"Tsai is China's Chairman of the Military Affairs Commission. Why improve relations with him if Taiwan's announcing its independence? President Fu's meeting with Tsai for one reason—to reunite with the mainland. This cannot be. Saturday the Democratic Progressive Party's demonstrating outside the Presidential Building."*

"DPP again," said Iris as the housekeeper tapped at the open door, "Always DPP. If not Iming, Channel Four talk about."

Alarmed, Lane sat up suddenly, waking the baby. She tried to hide her fear behind a nervous laugh but did not succeed.

"Iris," she gasped, relieved it was her friend, not her husband, waking her.

As the baby began to mew, then wail, Iris focused her concern from Lane to the tiny form in her arms. Quickly covering the distance between them, Iris reached out for the baby.

"Oh, let me hold."

Instantly the baby stopped crying.

"You're a natural mother." Turning to the housekeeper, Lane added, "Mildred, can you bring us tea?" Then she smiled warmly at Iris. Motioning to the chair beside her, she flipped off the TV with the remote.

"I'm so glad to see you. How are your wedding plans going?"

"Mother-in-law take care everything. She so helping. I very luck."

A small frown creased the girl's smooth forehead, then disappeared as quickly. Just then the baby caught his fingers in her long hair. As he tugged, her face lit up with a sunny smile. "And you have health son! You luck!" Thinking it was a game, he smiled back and pulled harder. "Oww," she laughed, extricating his tiny fingers from the tangles. Then she nuzzled him and kissed his neck, breathing in the scent. "He smell sweet." Hugging him to her, she added, "I very want baby."

"Something tells me you'll have one soon." Lane smiled at her friend's open yearning.

They talked until Mildred brought in the tea and took the baby. Then when the clock chimed eight times, Iris stood up to examine it.

"What beautiful sound. When you get?"

Lane shrugged. "My father sent it yesterday. Do you like it?" At her friend's nod, she made a mental note to give it as a wedding gift.

"Like wind chime."

"It's Swiss. He's always getting presents from lobbyists and importers, then he recycles them to me."

As Lane covered a yawn, Iris asked, "You tire?"

Lane shook her head, smiling through pale lips.

"Just a little drained. The doctor said I lost a lot of blood. It'll take a while to get my energy back."

"You need *qigong*." Iris' face became animated.

"What's that?"

Iris thought for a moment, then sighed. "Hard to explain." Gathering her thoughts, she tried again, gracefully motioning with her hands. "*Qi* energy in body. If *qi* low, master heal, give energy."

"How?" Lane was polite but skeptical.

"Through hand, like this." Iris put her hands near Lane but did not touch her.

Lane's smile was doubtful. "You mean something like faith-healing?"

"It help to believe, but not need." Iris smiled winningly. "Want to try?"

"They say a third of all patients can be healed, no matter what cure the doctor uses." Lane took a deep breath. "Would I have to drink any more of that Chinese medicine?"

Lane made a face, remembering the bitter taste. Shuddering at the memory, she studied her friend closely.

Iris laughed. "No, you do nothing."

"It won't hurt?" When Iris shook her head, Lane shrugged. "Okay."

"I ask Iming father."

"I thought he was an herbalist."

"Yes, but he *qigong* master, too." She smiled mischievously. "He at my house. Want me to call?"

Nodding, Lane pointed to the phone, saying, "Don't bother dialing; just press the redial button. Your number was the last I called."

Iris picked up the receiver and pushed the button. After a moment, Lane could hear the muffled sound of *"Wei"* as a man's voice answered. She heard Iris carry on a short conversation in Chinese, then stared as the girl abruptly hung up the phone, a worried expression etched into her usually serene face.

"Is anything wrong at home?"

"That not my number." Iris chewed her lip thoughtfully. "Mr. Chen make call?"

Lane sniffed, making a sarcastic moue. "He only got off the phone to catch his plane, but I thought I'd made the last call."

Iris shook her head. "That Phoenix pachinko parlor."

"So?"

"You not at work to hear."

Lane struggled to hide her impatience. "What's the problem?"

"Phoenix pachinko parlor is Bamboo Union . . . office."

Lane's expression was blank as she listened for more information. Frustrated, Iris sighed as she struggled for the right word.

"Triad."

Understanding flooded Lane's face as she filled in for her friend. "The way the Institute is the unofficial consulate in Taiwan, the Phoenix is the Bamboo Union's center for activities, their unofficial headquarters, right?"

Nodding solemnly, Iris' dark eyes watched her. "Consulate say mainlander triad criminal. . . ."

". . . like the mafia." Meeting her eyes evenly, Lane interrupted, remembering the rumors she had heard. She shuddered as a chill swept over her. "You don't think Chen's involved with organized crime, do you?"

Wearing a worried expression, Iris shook her head no and shrugged noncommittally. "Maybe."

Lane's eyes widened. *Qigong* forgotten, she and Iris discussed the possible consequences of Chen's connections.

"Maybe you and baby in dangerous." On the spur of the moment, she said, "Come home with me. You be safety."

"Maybe Chen's just gambling." Lane tried to laugh off the situation.

Iris shrugged doubtfully.

"Are you sure you haven't been listening to too many political intrigue stories at work?" asked Lane.

When the girl's dark expression conveyed her thoughts, Lane appealed again.

"Maybe you pressed the wrong button?" She shook her head. "Got the wrong number?"

In answer to the question, Iris silently pressed the phone's redial button and got the same number. Hanging up, she discussed the situation with Lane until the clock chimed nine.

"So late?" she asked, jumping up. "Iming DPP rally end

soon." Explaining, she added shyly, "Before he drive father, he meet me for snake."

*"Snake?"* Startled, Lane gave her friend a quizzical stare as Iris nodded.

"Oyster omelet in Shihlin night market."

Lane started laughing, as Iris looked on, perplexed. "You're meeting for a snack," Lane said between giggles, "not a snake."

Iris joined in the laughter, then became subdued. "You okay?"

"I'm fine. There's got to be a simple explanation behind this."

Lane used her most confidence-inspiring tone. Then grasping for a plausible reason, she smiled broadly.

"Chen's probably doing some import business with them. Don't worry so much. Just meet Iming and enjoy yourself!"

As Iris gave her a fast hug, she noted the time on the Swiss clock. Then she rushed off, calling, "See you Sunday!"

Lane rested the three days Chen was in Macao, thinking, planning her retreat, falling in love with her son.

"Justin," she said to herself, rolling the name over her tongue. "Yes, Justin," she repeated out loud to the baby, nuzzling him. "Since I had you just in time, Justin's perfect, just like you."

She kissed him good-bye and hurried into the waiting limo, not wanting to be late for Iris' wedding. Although she had slept most of the time since being released from the hospital, she felt weary, almost groggy with fatigue. When the car stopped in front of Iris' parents' home, Lane forced a smile, gathered the wrapped clock under her arm and tried to put a lilt into her step, instead of sleep-walking, zombie-style. She did not succeed.

"What happen? You all right?" Iris demanded the moment

she saw the dark circles under her eyes and the gray color in her cheeks. She stared into Lane's glazed eyes, the lids only half open, worried as much for her safety as her health.

"Of course," she answered too quickly, finishing with a wan smile.

"Now meet father-in-law."

Iris took Lane's arm and ushered her through a small crush of people to the sedate man sitting on the sofa's edge, smoking companionably with Iris' father.

After a brief exchange of Chinese, he nodded while Iris explained, "Come to my room. She . . . *he qigong* master."

Lane pulled away, not wanting to offend anyone, but equally unwilling to get involved with folk faith-healing.

"Thanks, but this isn't necessary. I'm fine."

Misunderstanding, Iris said, "Not hurt. Father-in-law not touch."

"I'm all right. Tell him thanks, but. . . ."

"You feel better." She firmly tucked her arm in Lane's and started walking her down the hall. As Lane held back, Iris said, "Like you say. Chicken soup not hurt."

Laughing, she let Iris guide her. In the bedroom, Lane set down the gift as the girl explained her father-in-law's actions. Making several wide circles with his arms, he began breathing deeply.

"He gather energy," she said before answering him in Chinese. Then translating, she said, "She . . . *he* want me to describe what happen. We must to be quiet." Lane nodded. Placing her palm near Lane, Iris said, "He give energy to you, like this, make *qi* strong."

"Will I feel anything?" Lane asked, trying not to show her skepticism as the man began moving his arms in a graceful parody of *tae kwon do*.

Iris spoke to him. "Maybe," Iris translated. "Not pain. Everyone different. Some feel heat, other feel nothing. Some feel exciting."

Too wrapped up in her own thoughts to correct the grammar, Lane said, "Iris, I don't think I. . . ."

"Shhhh," cautioned the girl. "Father-in-law ready."

Lane bit her lip and drew in a deep breath as the man approached her. He seemed to feel the air close to her body, as if sensing temperature differences or drafts. Time and again his open palm returned to the area closest to her abdomen. Then he held both palms two inches from her and closed his eyes, concentrating. Fascinated, she held her breath, not realizing it until she was out of air.

Then she became aware of a warm surge of energy throughout her body, a tingling in her stomach. As her adrenaline kicked in, she felt a rush, followed by an overall sense of well-being. It brought a strength she had not felt in months. She felt a flush on her cheeks and a sudden clearing of her thoughts.

When she looked at the man, he had backed away and was watching her, smiling.

"Thank you," she said with a polite bow. He acknowledged with a nod and left.

"How you feel?" asked Iris.

"It's hard to put into words." Lane tried to describe it but failed. "My stomach feels like pins and needles."

"You very pain!?"

"No, nothing like that."

"You feel better?" Iris looked perplexed.

Hesitating, Lane said, "Yes, but I'm not sure if I'm imagining it or not."

"It not matter," said Iris. "Only you feel better matter."

Again she bowed to the girl's logic with a smile. They started out the door, then Lane stopped.

"I almost forgot. This is for you." As she lifted the package, Iris' face lit up until the gift chimed. Watching the smile crumble, Lane asked, "What's wrong?"

"Superstition." Iming spoke from the doorway. Iris shushed him, pretending nothing was wrong, but he continued. "Old men think clock bad lucky."

"Why?" Lane was incredulous.

He used body language to show the analogy. "Time and dead."

"I'm sorry." Embarrassed, Lane looked from one to the other. "I didn't know. I thought you liked it." She grabbed the box from Iris' hands. "I'll get you something else."

"No," said Iris graciously. "Iming right. Only old men believe." She looked at her husband. "Not need superstitious for lucky. We have lucky. We have each other."

As their eyes met, Lane realized how true the words were. Feeling like an intruder, she tried not to stare but could not help it. Watching the new couple, Lane understood what mattered in life and vowed to confront Chen when he got back. She and Justin were moving out.

She did not have long to wait. Chen arrived home while she was in Justin's room, saying good-night. Holding the baby in her arms, she turned and saw her husband approach with his inimitable swagger, his need for domination like a diplomat's sash across his chest.

Feeling stronger than she had since marrying him, she said, "Justin and I are flying to the US."

Ignoring her, he spoke to the baby. "Tian-syang, come to your *baba.*"

"Did you hear me?" Her sharp tone drew his attention.

He took his eyes from the baby's face long enough to answer. "Yes, now give me my son, Tian-syang."

"His name's Justin, and he's not your son."

"Oh, but you're wrong. Read Chinese law."

He laughed through his nostrils, emitting small puffs of air. Unable to speak Chinese, she was even less able to read it. Chen knew that, but he wanted to watch his quarry's face when she understood her position.

"What kind of game are you playing, Chen?" She knew it irked him when she addressed him with his surname.

She seems more resilient than the last time we spoke. The doctor must be doing his job, he thought. Good, I like her feisty, but first I have to show her who's in charge.

"By law, children belong to the father. Go if you like, but Tian-syang stays here with me." He smiled broadly.

Her face lost its color. "What do you mean?" she asked, holding her son tighter.

"The mother can leave, but the children remain with the father." He chucked the baby under his chin.

"That's ridiculous. He isn't even yours." She took a deep breath while she counted to ten. Though she detested the man, she tried to be reasonable. "We can share him, of course, but I'm taking him home."

Without moving, he turned his obsidian eyes toward her. His face lost its virile charisma and took on the surreality of a mask, the light emphasizing the pores, shallow pock marks and small scars of a lifetime.

"He is home."

Chen's blatant confidence unnerved her. Though she tried not to show it, her conviction slipped a notch.

"He can have two homes, but since Justin's an American citizen, I want him to know his national home."

The mask smiled. Its lips repeated, "Read Chinese law. Children belong to the father. Tian-syang isn't American. He's Chinese," he paused, "like father, like son." He started lifting the baby from her arms. "And I say he isn't going anywhere."

"I'm American, he's American, and I'm taking him home." She pulled away from Chen's reach, hugging the baby closer.

It amused him to let her play the line before he reeled her in. Watching her, he felt he had a prize catch, but he had given her enough slack. Now it was time to net her.

"Go to the States if you like," he said nonchalantly, "but Tian-syang stays here."

"He goes where his mother goes." She glared at him. "You can't stop us."

He adjusted his lapels and rebuttoned his raw-silk jacket before turning to her. "The ROC government can."

"Stop posturing!" She stared at him with loathing, wondering what had possessed her to marry him. "I have a US passport. No government in the world can detain me."

He saw the disgust in her expression, and inside he toppled. He ran companies, he reassured himself. No, he ran countries. Only her gut reaction had the capacity to squeeze him into a wretched gel. Though he felt like toothpaste, he would never show it. He smiled, speaking in an unperturbed voice.

"You're right. As an American citizen, you can't be detained illegally." His voice became silken. "But if you kidnap my son, you'll be committing a crime. Even the US Senate couldn't help you then."

He forced her eyes to look into his. Though she felt herself losing, she put up a brave facade.

"He's not your son, damn it. He's mine."

"Not according to law." He watched her face working, knowing what she was scheming. "Don't try to escape with Tian-syang. Immigration will stop you at the airport."

"Quit calling him that! His name's Justin."

Flushed with anger, she was exciting to look at. He marveled at her feral beauty, determined to domesticate it. Her eyes blazed like green fire opals in sunlight. Her raised temperature heightened the fragrance of her woodsy cologne, mingling it with her natural musk.

Chen breathed in the aroma, catching with it the familiar scent of victory. He was a master at manipulating people. He smiled again, knowing it was the reason behind his success. It was what he did best. Feeling the stirrings of an erection, he knew nothing aroused him as much as winning. He remembered the thrill he had felt at Lane's conquest, and he wanted to feel it again. It was time for the *coup de grace*.

Changing his manner to one of scholarly discussion, he said, "Lane, do you know why I put up with your demonstrations of independence?"

His tone caught her off guard. Not trusting him, she stalled, trying to guess where he was leading. He ignored her silence, the question having been rhetorical, anyway.

"You amuse me." He watched her flashing eyes, reading her thoughts. "Like a trout or an inept business rival, you entertain me, offering just enough challenge to be enjoyable." He liked baiting her. It was the best part, almost. His tongue darted over his thin lips, anticipating. "But like all competitors, you finally yield."

"To what?" She looked at him contemptuously. "Your superior intellect?"

He sensed her scorn now was a cover, a sign of weakness. "No, to my superior skill. You're mine. You belong to me just as thoroughly as a fly rod or a trade company."

"You're crazy," she said. "I married you for convenience, but you'll never own me." She all but sneered. "You'll never have me."

"Really?" He spoke quickly, then paused, waiting until she met his eyes with an expression of supreme indifference. "I already have."

Her jaw hung open for a moment, then closed just as quickly. He relished the moment, watching her response change from insolence to confusion.

"You don't quite believe me, do you?" He laughed, his teeth punctuating the mockery. Then he sobered. "You belong to me in every sense of the word."

"In another lifetime, perhaps. Sorry, Chen, I don't believe in reincarnation." She turned her back disdainfully and began walking away with the baby.

"You weren't entirely asleep," he said, chuckling. "Surely you remember our embrace in the hospital."

She gasped. "So it wasn't a dream." Her eyes narrowing, she screamed, "You sonofabitch! My father's going to hear about this."

"And do what? Sue me? You're my wife, Lane. You're mine," he pointed to the baby, "and so is my son. Get used to it." He walked past her and out the door.

Gripping the baby tightly, she stared after him, determined to escape. She put the baby down, found her passport and picked up the phone, calling the driver. "Take me to the Chiang Kai-shek airport," she said. When she heard silence, she said, "Taoyuan."

Chen's voice came over the line. "Don't be foolish, Lane. My man isn't going to drive you anywhere. And even if you get to the airport, no immigration officer will let you leave with the baby." He paused, willing her to retaliate. When she did not, he added, "For that matter, no one in this house will let you leave with the baby. If you want to go, go, but Tiansyang stays."

"Justin," she corrected him, finding her voice, "and only for the interim."

Chen listened to her slam down the receiver, then he hung up slowly, making a mental note to have her watched. "New

Party headquarters," he told his driver, "on *Ho-ping Lu.*"

He smiled at the irony of the headquarters' location on the Road of Peace as he began rehearsing his speech, listing the points he wanted to make: reunification with the mainland but without the KMT's corruption, denouncement of Fu's high-profile quest for a UN seat, rejection of the DPP's plank for independence. Chuckling, he wondered what they would think if they knew his real ties. He sniffed contemptuously. They will soon enough, he thought. Everything in good time, even Lane.

"I pregnancy!"

"Three weeks after the wedding? Iris, are you sure?"

"I must to see doctor, but home pregnant test positive. Me, too. I know! Marriage wonderful!" she ended brightly.

Lane could imagine her friend hugging herself on the other end of the line, so she chose not to answer, preferring to leave Iris in ignorant bliss about her own marriage. Instead she warmly congratulated her.

"How does Iming feel?"

"As exciting as me."

Lane silently doubted it. Nobody got as excited as Iris. "And his parents, how do they feel about it?" She knew they were living with Iris' in-laws and that the period of adjustment had only begun.

Iris' voice lost its lilt. "We tell," she hesitated, then admitted, "after we move."

"You convinced Iming to get a place of your own?" Lane's eyebrow rose with her voice.

"She not oldest son," she said defensively. "She . . . *he* must not to care of them. Now he father. My husband say we need private."

Hearing the scrappy tone of her voice, Lane decided to

change the subject. "So your wedding gift can be a house-warming gift. Have you decided what you want?"

"You give beautiful clock." Iris brightened again, her innate warmth returning to her voice. "That enough."

"But it's unlucky."

"Superstitious of old men. No mind," she said, dismissing it. "How about you? *Qigong* help?"

"Yes, I don't understand it, but I feel great! Guess it works whether you believe in it or not." Lane laughed, missing her friend, missing the easy camaraderie of her colleagues in the diplomatic world. "How're things at the Institute?"

"Busy." Iris groaned. "With Tsai come tomorrow, nobody take rest. You to join banquet next week?"

Lane's brows knitted together angrily. Pursing her lips, she took a deep breath before answering. The dinner-party was a point of contention between her and Chen. He insisted she attend. Lane wanted nothing to do with him, but, until she devised an escape route, she thought it best to mollify him.

"Probably, are you?"

"Everyone at Institute get invite."

Lane's voice brightened. "Will Li be there?" Not having seen him since her release from the hospital, she especially missed him.

"I not know," Iris said distractedly. Lane heard her cover the receiver with her hand as she listened to muffled strains of conversation. Finally Iris put her on hold. When she returned, she said in a worried tone, "Sorry, something happen."

"More rumors?" asked Lane, trying for levity. "Come on, you can tell me. I still have security clearance."

"Police arrest Iming at DPP demonstration," said Iris, close to tears. "They keep taxi."

* * * * *

"The greedy bastards! The KMT's raped Taiwan. Look at the pollution, the land speculation, the corruption. No controls, no environmental protection. Just take, take, take." The cabby punctuated his words by pounding on the cell wall. "Look at the infrastructure: flooding along the *Tamsui,* bridges ready to collapse, the MRT subway a national disgrace. What have they given back for all their taxes and promises?" He spit a red stream of beetlejuice, then looked into each of the men's faces. "Nothing! And now, when Tsai sings, Fu dances. The KMT's ready to give Taiwan back to the mainland, anything for reunification." He paced, his dwarfish body a short fuse on a keg of gunpowder. "Somebody's got to stop it."

Waiting in the detention center, Iming listened to the inmate's rhetoric with the other arrested demonstrators, sitting on his haunches, smoking.

"What can we do?" asked one taxi-driver, shrugging. "Government's always corrupt."

"What can we do?" The squat dynamo cynically repeated his words. Then lowering his voice, he answered in a stage whisper. "We can kill the bastard!"

"Who? President Fu?" asked the frightened cabby.

"No, assassinate the mainlander, Tsai."

Repelled by the suggestion, Iming scrambled to his feet, started to speak, then changing his mind, walked away and leaned against the wall.

"Do I offend you?" the agitator snarled, sarcasm hanging in the air like stale cigarette smoke.

"Violence won't help." Iming tried to hide his distaste.

"You're a fine one to preach nonviolence." The man laughed. "You've just been arrested for inciting civil disobedience."

"It was a peaceful demonstration."

"Not according to your record. Why do you think the police impounded our taxis?"

"They were blocking traffic. . . ."

"They're making examples of us," the small man said, interrupting. "Tell me, how are you going to support that new wife of yours without your taxi? That regime's using the law against us for its own ends. We've got to take control! Open your eyes!" He waved his arms angrily, then focused his wrath on Iming. "What are you waiting for? Buddha's enlightenment?"

The men hooted loudly, relieved not to be the one singled out.

Li rushed from the trade company to President Fu's office. "Yes, sir, I heard the *'I am Taiwanese'* chants and saw the banners on my way over." He ventured a grin. "Caught in its traffic jam, I'm more familiar with the demonstration than I care to be."

"The DPP rally's causing public outcry. These embarrassing squawks for independence couldn't come at a worse time." Fu exhaled his cigarette, smoke curling from his mouth up to his nostrils as he spoke.

"It's only a counter-demonstration to the New Party's *'I am Chinese'* march last week." Li's tolerant smile died on his lips under the president's scowl.

"Keep close to Tsai. Rumor has it a secessionist faction's planning an assassination. Imagine the repercussions if Mainland's highest-ranking official were killed while visiting."

Li nodded gravely. "Or even if an attempt were made on his life."

"See to it this diplomatic tour goes without incident," said Fu, looking earnestly into Li's face. Motioning to his aide, he watched the young man hand Li a packet. "You're in charge. Here are tickets and passes for all the scheduled events. Take your wife along; she's your cover. Just don't leave Tsai's side."

"Mei-ling, my grandson's crying," called Yang *Taitai* from her bed.

The young woman continued watching her soap opera, ignoring cries from both the nursery and the sickroom. After calling a second time, the old woman rolled to the edge of the bed, easing her way into a sitting position. Slowly she struggled to her feet and scuffled her way into the baby's room. She had begun changing his diaper when Li turned the key in the lock.

Jumping up from her chair, Mei-ling met him at the front door. She threw her arms around his neck and planted a wet kiss on his lips before he realized what was happening.

"Li, I'm so glad you're home. I've missed you."

Grabbing her hands in his, Li disentangled himself and pushed her away. He was in the process of wiping off her kiss when he saw his mother shuffle into view.

"What are you doing up?" he asked, lines of concern etched into his forehead.

"I was. . . ."

"You know how she insists on helping with Teng-hui," said Mei-ling. "I can't keep her still." She put her arm solicitously around the woman's frail shoulders. "Let me help you back to bed, Mother," she said, a simpering smile playing at her lips as her eyes twinkled at her private joke.

"My grandson's not being cared for properly." The woman tottered on her feet as she shrugged off Mei-ling's offered arm. Her knotted hand stretched out to Li for support. "She's not a fit mother."

Wrapping his hand around hers, he placed his other arm

around his mother's waist and slowly led her back to her room, silently absorbing her complaints about his wife. He shuddered at the spider's touch of her chilled fingers as he helped his mother into bed.

"Here," he said, pouring a prescription bottle's contents into a spoon. "This'll help you rest." When he held it to her bluish lips, she took the medicine docilely.

"You're a dutiful son, a credit to your. . . ."

"Father?" he filled in for her hopefully as her voice trailed off.

Her mouth puckering from the bitter medicine, she shook her head. "Ancestors."

"Why don't you ever speak of my father?"

"He died before you were born. You never met him, and I hardly knew him." She shrugged and looked away. "What more is there to say?"

"For one thing, if you didn't know him, how could you marry him? Or how did he die? You've never told me anything about him."

Despite Li's compassion for her, he couldn't keep the pent-up frustration from his voice. Hearing the tone, she turned heavy eye-lids toward him. Then as her rheumy eyes appraised him, she nodded weakly.

"Yes, maybe it is time you knew." Though tiring, she motioned toward an old chest with fluttering fingers so frail, they seemed made of bird bones and parchment.

He brought over the wooden case, dusting it before placing it on the bed. Her fingers picked at its rusted latch until it creaked open, emitting a dank, moldy odor.

"This was your great-aunt's."

He nodded, recognizing the ancient chest, remembering the day three decades before when she had shown it to him. His mother's hand shuffled among several documents before she pulled a blurred snapshot from the bottom. Then she handed him the picture of an unsmiling girl and an elderly man.

"My wedding photograph," she said.

"So this was my father." His eyes searched his mother's. She broke the gaze, focusing instead on the photo.

"That's Yang Tzu-Chyang."

"I never realized he was so much older than you. How old . . . ?"

"I was fifteen."

Li's eyes blinked as he debated which question to ask first. His mother came to his aid.

"He was eighty-six. It was an arranged marriage."

"Why don't you ever speak of him?"

"I never knew him. We met on our wedding day, and he died a week later."

Delicacy prevented him from asking the obvious. Instead he ventured, "Did you love him?"

"I married him."

"Did he. . . ."

"I want to rest now."

Dismissing him, she closed her eyes wearily. As she sank down into the pillows, Li shut the chest and began lifting it off the bed. Then a thought jogged her memory.

"Wait, there *is* something else. Something your great-aunt, my mother's sister, wanted you to have." She sat up with difficulty. "This was to go to the oldest male in our family."

Li looked perplexed. "Wouldn't that be my uncle Chen?"

"No! This is my legacy to you and my grandson."

"But Chen's the older generation. By all rights, he should. . . ."

"No! He forfeited those rights years ago! This is for you and Teng-hui, not your uncle and not that good-for-nothing wife of yours, either!" She raised her voice, so it would carry into the other room. In answer, Mei-ling turned up the TV's volume, affording Li and his mother a privacy otherwise impossible. Pleased at the seclusion yet miffed by her daughter-in-law's rudeness, the old woman shouted hoarsely, "Mei-ling's an unfit mother."

A coughing attack made further speech impossible. Wordlessly Li opened another bottle, poured its amber liquid into the spoon and gently held it to his mother's lips. Even after the coughing subsided, her chest wheezed, and when she tried to speak, her breathing was raspish.

"Save your breath," he said.

She shook her head and motioned for him to put his ear close to her lips. "This is for you and your son, not your uncle or your wife. This is my legacy to you."

"It's too early to talk of legacies." He tried to shush her. "Wait until Teng-hui's old enough, then give it to him yourself."

Shaking her head feebly, she pulled a yellowed, dog-eared paper from an embroidered pouch, the cloth's stitching ornate but faded, and pressed it into his hands. "You give it to my grandson." Then rising up on her elbow, the woman nodded toward the other room. "Don't give it to *her* or my brother." Though the woman's breathing was labored, she struggled to speak. "And there's something you must know about your uncle . . . he's more . . . than. . . ."

A coughing spasm overtook her, leaving her too hoarse to finish. Li stayed with her, holding her in his arms until the medicine took effect and she fell asleep. In the dim glow of the nightlight, Li watched his mother, waiting until her labored breathing became steady and shallow. Only then did he notice the tattered document in his hand. Scanning it, he gasped as he recognized the Qing chop. Then he struggled to decipher the document's antiquated characters:

*In gratitude for his imperial service, the Empress Ci-xi grants this property to Sheng Hsuan-hui, his eldest son and his eldest son in perpetuity. The bearer of this deed is the sole proprietor of the Tiaoyutai Islands.*

With perfect clarity, Li recalled Ma's words as he had listened in on his receiver, hunching beneath the rafters of Macao's Chula Vista hotel. "Article four of the 1952 *Sino-Japanese Peace Treaty* states all agreements made prior to the 1941 Sino-Japanese Accord are invalid, even the Shimonoseki Treaty of 1895. Legal sovereignty goes back to 1893, when Ci-xi granted Tiaoyutai to Sheng Hsuan-hui."

So the family tale's true, Li thought, staring numbly at the crumbling document. He remembered his great-aunt's story of how she had torn down the prayer cloth from the family's shrine as Mao's troops had advanced, stashed a few family possessions into the chest and fled first to Macao, then to Taiwan with the Nationalists. The tattered cloth had disintegrated from the rough handling, and the concealed letter had fallen out.

The secret had been well-kept. When Sheng Hsuan-hui died with no male heirs, the Sheng name also died, and except for Chen no sons had been born to the female descendants of the Sheng family for three generations. But as a mere nephew, Li wondered if he met the document's qualifications.

Minutes later Li returned to the living room to find Mei-ling sitting on the sofa, watching television, her legs curled beneath her.

"This isn't working," he said.

Pouting, she turned up the volume on the remote.

"Mei-ling," he warned. She ignored him as she stared glassy-eyed at the set. He walked over and manually turned it off. Standing directly in front of her, Li said, "Answer me."

"Why do you always take your mother's side? Why don't you ever believe what I say?" She raised her voice, shouting toward the woman's room, "She's a crazy old woman who's never satisfied." She mimicked in a high, frail voice, "Do this, and get that." Her voice ringing shrilly, she ended, "I'm not an amah. Hire a nursemate for her and the baby."

"Remember, this is what you wanted," he said coolly. "Be careful what you ask for."

In a single motion, she was off the sofa and seductively fingering his lapels. "Li, why must we fight? Why can't we be like we were before?"

"When? Before we were married?"

He eyed her disparagingly, grabbing her hands to stop them from fondling his chest. She slipped her hands from his grip and, arching her back, ran her fingers through his thick hair.

"Not even that far back. A month ago, before your mother returned from the hospital." She pressed against him. "You loved me then."

Pushing her hands away, he eyed her cynically. "Wrong. We mated. You were a convenient outlet for my frustrations. Don't flatter yourself into thinking we made love." He pointed, his arm sweeping toward his mother's bedroom and the nursery. "She's the only one you fooled with the baby. Your penalty's living that lie, keeping her convinced until her dying day that he's her grandson. I went through with this for one reason only: my mother, so keep her happy." He turned away, then turned back, his eyes piercing. "But when this is over, so are we."

She stepped back as if he had spit in her face. Swallowing

the hurt along with the tears of rage, she promised herself he would never see her cry. Is he so blind he doesn't see I love him? A small voice warned: success through discretion. Her slanted eyes looked up invitingly as she approached him, sliding her talons along the side of his face. She held her head high, challenging him in a seductive voice with a Chinese endearment.

"You deserve death by a thousand cuts."

"Don't you understand?" Roughly grabbing her hand, he stared coldly at her up-tipped eyes. "You and I are through. We're divorced in principle, if not yet in fact." He let go her arm with a shove, snarling, "I'll even keep the child, whoever he belongs to. Don't worry about being burdened with a baby." His tone softened. "I'll bring him up as my own."

Her mind whirred like a hard-drive, selecting and discarding strategies as quickly as they surfaced. "Chen boasts to anyone in the Juliet Club who'll listen about *his* son." She drew her head closer to him confidentially. "He also brags of his wife's hunger for his jade stalk."

"You're lying."

She appraised him. "Would you like to know how she earned her latest piece of jewelry?"

"Were you there?" he shot.

"Chen bragged about his manhood. His own aide swore he heard her moans of delight." She smiled, flashing her small teeth. Seeing she had his undivided attention, she continued, gloating, "The old ox likes to chew fresh grass." Then she peered up at him slyly. "Is it true she whistles on the jade stalk?"

Li's face mirrored his disgust. "Is that all this is to you? A vent for your lies?"

She examined her nails, then flashed a smug smile. "Ask her if you don't believe me."

# CHAPTER 10

Iming drove cautiously, letting the faster scooters weave around him. He shook his head as the bus forced him onto the road's sunken shoulder, then shouted above the traffic's roar. When she didn't hear, he called again.

"Iris!"

This time, hearing him, she tightened her grip around his chest and leaned against him, holding him like the hero he was to her. She loved this red-faced husband of hers.

"Yes?" she shouted over the two-stroke scooter's whine.

Without taking his eyes off the road, he called into the wind, "This isn't a good idea. Let's turn around."

"The Realtor's waiting for us," she called into his ear.

He silently cursed as a BMW cut him off, and a taxi screeched to a stop behind them. "The apartment can wait a day. Tomorrow I'll get the taxi from the pound. You shouldn't be riding on a scooter when you're pregnant."

She laughed, happy with the world, ecstatic her husband worried about her. Squeezing herself against him, she shouted, "Tomorrow'll be too late. At this price, the place will be rented." She loosened her grip only long enough to brush her wind-blown hair from her eyes. "Besides, tomorrow I'll be busy at the Institute. As the new coordinator, I have to organize Tsai's banquet for the Institute."

"All right. Hang on."

He turned his head so the wind would carry his voice to her, then smiled tolerantly, proud of his wife at her recent promotion. Saying a quick prayer to *Kwan Yin* that they would always be so happy, he turned his attention to the Jaguar edging him into the double-parked Mercedes.

President Fu's orders called for strict monitoring of traffic signals. As the presidential limousine raced toward the Grand Hotel, lights magically turned green, speeding them along but bringing a sudden halt to all intersecting traffic. The driver, a young soldier from Lukang who had never driven a car until he joined the army, drove north, picking up speed as he whizzed by light after light. Loyal to the KMT, he was in awe of the leaders he chauffeured. Trying to catch snatches of their discussion, he eavesdropped, bashfully watching them through the rearview mirror.

At the corner of *Mintsu Lu* and *Chung Shan Lu* an oversized, double-decker tour bus ran the light. Brandishing his reflected power, the chauffeur stepped on the gas, planning to shave the bus' rear fender to make the driver think twice about delaying the country's leader. Silently he chanted the Ministry of Transportation's slogan.

"Keep Taipei Moving."

Bearing down on the gas pedal, he swerved at the last moment to avoid the bus' rear, then found himself face-to-face with an old man in a coolie hat, peddling his tricycle-truck with its cargo of used cardboard boxes. Hitting the brakes, the chauffeur broke into a sweat as he swerved toward the bus, narrowly missing the peddler.

Forced into the congested lanes of stopped cars and scooters, the bus skidded as its operator frantically pumped the brakes, trying to escape the limo. Cursing the worn brake pads, he careened away from the pedestrians, plowing into the collective vehicles instead. As his bus rammed the cars and motorcycles, it created a domino effect, slamming each displaced vehicle into yet another and another.

Iming heard the squeal of metal on metal as the bus' brakes failed. Then he revved the gas, trying to get out of the way. Too late he heard the crunch of fenders and bumpers as he felt the impact of the Jaguar rear-ending him. He screamed into the crash of splintering glass and twisted metal.

"Iris!"

Deep in conversation, the President and Tsai heatedly compared the countries' weaponry as they passed the scene, oblivious to the chaos. They had not noticed. The chauffeur breathed a nervous sigh of relief, fingered his prayer beads while mouthing *Amit'ofo's* name, then sped on through the next intersection.

Iming got up from the pavement slowly, his leg pinned beneath him. Straightening it out, he worked it, relieved it was not broken, only sprained. He called to Iris, looking toward the crumpled scooter.

"Iris," he screamed, frantic he could not locate her. "Iris!"

He began rummaging through the over-turned scooters and melee of people. Finally he saw her, apparently sleeping against the wheel of the Jag, her eyes closed, a serene expression on her lips, her head turned at an odd angle.

"Iris."

He walked slowly, stumbling, fighting the lump in his throat, the tears burning in his eyes. Still he reached her before anyone could stop him. Shaking her limp arm so ethereally motionless, he looked into her sweet face. Then swooping down on the ground beside her, he chafed her cheek with his rough fingertips, gently trying to revive her. Her faint breath felt warm against his hand.

"Iris," he whispered. Then he shouted, "Call an ambulance!"

Mei-ling carefully flipped the pages, trying not to smudge

the wet nailpolish. As she studied the latest fashions, favorably comparing her face and figure to the models', she heard a strange noise. Thinking it came from outside, she dismissed it, but five minutes later she heard a gargling sound and reluctantly got up to look at the baby.

Seeing he was sleeping peacefully, she returned to her magazine, poring over the skin-care ads. The whitening agents, in particular, caught her eye. Mei-ling prized her milky complexion as highly as her slim body. She heard a muffled sound but resolutely ignored it. A moment later she heard a loud, eerie rattling that made her pale skin crawl. Convinced the apartment was haunted, she shrieked, calling on *Amit'ofo* the Limitless Light Buddha to protect her.

Shaking, she checked the baby but found him asleep. While in the nursery, she heard the sound again. This time, she cautiously crossed to her mother-in-law's room. The woman was lying on her back, eyes protruding, her hand at her throat, gasping for breath.

Mei-ling watched, horror and repulsion reflected in her expression. The old woman silently appealed to her for help, holding out one withered hand, imploring her with her rheumy eyes. Mei-ling shrank from the room, breathing heavily, swallowing hard. Shuddering, she dialed 119, Taipei's emergency rescue number, as she heard the raspy voice call her.

Stifling the urge to scream, she whispered into the receiver. "Send an ambulance."

As she waited, the old woman continued calling her name, her throat rattling like windowpanes in an earthquake, but Mei-ling could not fight her fear of death and go to her. Instead she curled up on the sofa in a fetal position and covered her ears, waiting for the ambulance.

An hour later, the medics knocked at the door. Half-crazed with superstitious fear, she screamed, "What took so long?!"

"Traffic accident," one said monosyllabically, his face as expressionless as an ink sketch.

"She's in there." She pointed to her mother-in-law's room. Mei-ling followed behind, hanging back at the doorway. The men found the woman stiff in bed, her glazed eyes wide and accusing.

When Li returned home from work, Mei-ling ran to him. He crossed his arms, warding her off. But not seeming to notice the rebuff, she stared at him with haunted eyes.

"Li, your. . . ."

Though dreading it, he began to comprehend. "Mother?" he called, running into her room. When he saw her empty bed, he turned to his wife, peeking around the doorjamb.

"Where is she?"

The only auspicious time for funerals was the day of the banquet. Li walked somberly into the crematorium. Over his clothes he wore a hooded, white cloak, the ceremonial mourning garb. Though Mei-ling was not invited, she attended from compunction, timidly waiting in the back of the cavernous room on *Min Chuan* East Road, near the *Hsin Tien* Temple.

Mei-ling waited until the gongs and drums stopped their raucous dirge. After the musicians had departed and Li had finished performing the rituals for his mother, she silently approached him. Deep in contemplation, he was aware of no one else in the room. Finally she pulled on his shirt sleeve to attract his attention.

"Li, I'm. . . ."

She tried to tell him how sorry she was, but a lifetime of not assuming responsibility kept her from speaking. She licked her dry lips. A master at passive manipulation, her credo played like a radio jingle in her ear: do nothing, wait.

He answered slowly, his energy reserves low. "After the banquet tonight, I want you out of my life." Before she could protest, he added, "I've hired an amah for Teng-hui and reserved a room for you at the Regent."

She gasped in disbelief. "You're going to a diplomatic dinner *tonight?* Why?" When he did not answer, she played her trump card, hoping for a last-minute pardon. Though her smile was stiff and her lips quivered, she tried to play the coquette. "If you're so anxious to get rid of me, why do you want me with you tonight?"

"It has to do with responsibility and honor, things you wouldn't understand." He looked at her with loathing. Then turning, he walked away from her, his footsteps echoing hollowly in the hall.

Mei-ling felt a draft, sending sudden chills down her spine. A ghost? Stifling a scream, she glanced around furtively, looking for the source, but she saw nothing. Feeling unaccountably jumpy, she tried to laugh off her fears, deciding to go to her favorite fortune-teller in the underground pass. He would tell her what to do.

As she crossed under *Sung Chiang* Road, a red-faced man bumped into her, his eyes haggard and his hair wild. She gave him a withering look, but his rough appearance subdued her, and she hurried away toward the blind palm-reader.

Unaware of anything except the lump in his throat, Iming bought incense from a vendor, then went into the *Hsin Tien* Temple. Why, he asked *Kwan Yin,* doing *bai bai.* Why did you let her die? Tears came into his blood-shot eyes as he thought of his wife and baby, both gone.

He did not know how long he stood there, praying fervently, his lips moving numbly, but when his answer came, it blazed through his mind. Staggering under its weight, he ran crazily from the temple, the nuns watching him like a man possessed. Crossing beneath *Sung Chiang* Road, he raced past the soothsayers, diviners and palm-readers, drawing stares from all their customers but one.

Mei-ling was listening avidly to the fortune-teller. Spell-bound, she watched him through eyes wide with fear as he told her how to placate her mother-in-law's spirit.

"Burn ghost money for her," he advised.

"And my husband, how do I win him back?"

He consulted her right palm, lightly tracing her fate line, fingering the mount of Saturn. He noted where her fate line and relationship line intersected near the base of the Mercury finger. Then tapping the obtuse angle, the palmist said, "Your relationship line splits. This means you have a rival. Stay close to your husband. Attract his attention. Buy a new dress."

Her eyes lighting up, Mei-ling remembered the banquet, thinking it was a stroke of luck Li had invited her. She began planning her outfit.

"What else?"

The palm-reader felt between her mounts of Jupiter and lower Mars, following the curve of the mount of Venus. "Your life line is curving more toward Venus than it had been on your last reading," he said. "That means you are becoming more adjusted to the comforts of home, more domestic." He nodded his head approvingly. "You have made some changes in your life. Your nature is becoming warmer, more responsive emotionally."

"Yes," she enthused. "It is." Her voice died to an intimate whisper. "I like being married."

Still nodding his head in acknowledgment, the palmist continued tracing his finger down her life line. His blind eyes suddenly scowled. He traced the line twice more, pressing harder, pressing lighter. His finger slowed to a point halfway around the Venus mount where the life line ended abruptly. The two furrows between his eyes deepened.

"Is anything wrong?"

His brow became smooth again as he let go her hand. "The lines of the palm are constantly changing. Old lines may fade or grow clearer. New ones can appear overnight." In poignant tones, he added, "Change your behavior, modify your attitudes, and you can change your life."

She watched his bland face, trying to detect clues about her future. It showed nothing.

"Why did you stop the reading?"

"It's almost four. The police will come through soon." He smiled, holding out his palm for the money. "It's time to leave."

Mei-ling paid him, bought incense sticks and stacks of ghost money from a vendor across the passage, then hurried upstairs to the *Hsin Tien* Temple. After a cursory prayer to *Kwan Yin,* she burned the money in the special hearth, offering stacks of silver bills to Yang *Taitai's* spirit and gold bills to *Kwan Yin.* Satisfied she had appeased her mother-in-law, she caught a cab to the *Dayeh Takashimaya* department store. Her red lips drawn into a crafty smile, she eagerly anticipated the night to come, welcoming the challenge. Mei-ling knew just the dress for the banquet's battlefield.

Iming desultorily paid the fine and claimed his impounded cab from the police. He had not washed or changed clothes since the accident. His bleary eyes had trouble focusing, giving the police the impression he was drunk.

"Drive carefully, old brother," the officer said.

Iming growled a reply, then drove off, squealing his bald tires on the hot pavement. He pounded his head with his fist.

"Why? Why didn't I have the car yesterday?" he shouted. He left the cab-light off, unsure of his destination, but convinced he did not want any passengers.

After driving aimlessly for an hour, he found himself on *Chin Yu Lu,* at the corner of *Tien Mu Dong Lu,* its shady, tree-lined road offering a popular rest area for cabbies.

"Iming," called a fellow driver, relieving himself against a tree, "are you going to the rally this afternoon?"

Too weary to look at the man's face, he mumbled into his steering wheel.

"What rally?"

The driver zipped up as he approached Iming's window. Then after pulling a warm can of Taiwan beer from inside his shirt, he took a long draft.

"The protest against Tsai's visit. It'll be *renao,* loud and fun." He snorted a half-laugh. "We'll show the KMT. We'll never support reunification. Our solidarity's our strength!" He took another swig, then muttered, "Damn government's always trying to push us little guys around."

Iming's ears perked up. Like a speeding hearse, yesterday's black limo flashed through his mind. Shutting his eyes against the mental reruns, he tried to block out still frames of Iris' lifeless body.

"Where are they holding the rally?"

Lane played with the baby until it was time to dress for the banquet. Listlessly she chose a severely chic, black cocktail dress. As she was slipping it over her head, Chen entered her room. Fumbling to cover herself, she scowled at him, her green eyes as dark as black jade.

"I didn't hear you knock. Get out!"

He ignored her outburst, taking a velvet case from his vest pocket. Fondling it between his fingers, he spoke quietly.

"Wear your red dress tonight."

"What?!"

As she glared at him, he looked genuinely surprised.

"I asked you to wear your red dress."

"You *told* me. Don't push it, Chen," she warned, her eyes mutinous. Then setting her mouth grimly, she added in a whisper, "I'm only going to this dinner for the Institute, filling in for Iris." Her chin dropped onto her chest momentarily. To hide a trembling lip, she jutted her chin at him angrily. "What do you want?"

"What I always want, to make you happy."

Stepping closer, he held out the red box. When she did not reach for it, he tucked it in her hands.

"Open it," he urged, his eyes glowing with an inner light.

Her own eyes lifeless and sullen, she idly opened the velvet lid. Despite her apathy, she gasped when the light reflected off the faceted ruby necklace, its pigeon-blood red color catching and reflecting the light like a prism. The effect was dazzling. A ruby the size of a quail's egg hung from the center of the gold links, while four smaller rubies flanked it, two on each side. She snapped shut the lid, handing it back.

"I can't accept it, Chen."

The polite response hid his irritation. "Why?" Using his polished charm skillfully, he added, "I enjoy giving you gifts."

"You mean, buying my affection, showing me off." Turning her back on him, she stepped away, then did an about-face. "I don't want anything from you that isn't mine already."

Pretending ignorance, he asked, "What's that?"

"My son and my freedom." She faced him defiantly.

Chen thought she never looked more beautiful; motherhood had added a certain dimension to her allure. He groaned inwardly. How do I persuade her to stay, he asked himself, seeing in her the beauty of a gem, its perfection marred by a single occlusion, willfulness. How do I remove this flaw in my otherwise perfect consort?

"Whatever's mine is yours," he said, pressing the plush velvet box into her hand. "But as you say, I can't give what you already possess. You're free to do as you wish." He paused as his meaning penetrated, then he kissed the hand holding the box. "So please accept what I'm able to offer."

His speech caught her off guard. Raising an eyebrow inquisitively, she asked, "I can leave with Justin? You won't try to stop me?"

He swallowed the bile that rose in his throat and smiled, remembering an ad he had heard: Promise her anything. . . .

"He's your son," he said softly.

Hope, wonder, astonishment registered in her eyes, bringing a gleam Chen had not seen in months. He silently congratulated himself on his choice of tactics. Then a dart of suspicion pierced her bright bubble. Afraid to trust him, she peered into his eyes, trying to penetrate their flinty reflection, intuit his agenda.

"You mean it?" she finally asked. "You don't mind my taking Justin to the US?"

"If it makes you happy, no."

Blinking with disbelief at such unexpected generosity, she moistened her lips and whispered fervently.

"Thank you."

"Lane, my only wish is to see us a couple."

She shrank visibly. Seeing he had moved too quickly, gone too far, he smiled warmly, convincingly.

"Forgive my bluntness. I can't hide my feelings very well, but I would like us to be friends. Please, wear the jewels tonight as a sign of our friendship."

She hesitated. His blunder had renewed her distrust, but she was so relieved to be escaping with Justin, she nodded her agreement, anyway.

"Then you'll change into your red dress—to match the rubies?" he said.

Her smile drooped and was replaced with a defiant tilt of her chin. "I'm wearing black for Iris."

"Of course, it's only fitting," he murmured, smiling his encouragement. "But you'll wear the necklace?"

Her answer a terse nod, he breathed a sigh of satisfaction. Everyone would recognize the jewels as a sign of his virility. He would see to that. His eyes gleamed roguishly as he thought of the night to come. How he loved showing off his trophy wife!

He knew a gift's value was the yardstick for measuring the giver's wealth. Realizing it would give him added face, he had let the jewels' price be publicized. He had also let it slip that the rubies were a reward for her ardor, her sexual accomplishment.

Feeling younger than he had in years, Chen looked forward to the banquet. Why not, he asked himself? With a new son and a young wife, I'm in my second spring. I'll be the envy of everyone. Applauding himself, his chest expanded visibly, and with a stroke of boldness, he kissed his wife's cheek.

Lane's head snapped around, looking at him in shock and bewilderment. Her hand went to her cheek as if he had slapped her. Though her tone since she had learned of the rape had been cold, her voice now was sharper than icicles.

"Don't ever touch me again! You've forfeited any marital rights you had." She turned her back to him. "Now get out while I dress."

"Lane, I. . . ."

Reproached, Chen's face fell. He licked his suddenly dry

lips. She turned frosty eyes toward him, silencing him with her icy glare. Subdued, he tried to regain his dignity.

"I'll be waiting in the car," he said.

She nodded grimly, then sat down at her dressing table, angrily taking out her frustrations on her luxuriant hair, ruthlessly brushing it, oblivious to the breakage and splitting ends. Watching herself in the mirror, Lane stopped, brush in mid air. She looked hard into her eyes, wondering if she were the same girl she had been a year ago when she had fallen in love with Li.

Then ashamed, unable to meet her own stare, she shut her eyes against her reflection's critical censure. What would Li think if he knew? Would he be judgmental or compassionate?

When she opened them, her eyes fell on the velvet box. She knew it was not a simple gift. Dwelling on its implications, she wondered what his reasons were for giving it. Again she speculated what Li would think, wincing. On the other hand, Chen had volunteered to let her leave with Justin. Maybe he really did mean this necklace as a peace offering. Sighing in resignation, she opened the box, lifting the gems to her long neck, securing the clasp.

The necklace seemed like a millstone. Thinking of the night to come, Lane felt even more burdened with responsibility: the task of coordinating the banquet's events—thanks to the Institute's hasty request to fill Iris's post—the sense of loss, knowing she would never hear Iris's lilting laugh again, the strain of pubicly playacting Chen's wife, and the dual-edged anticipation and dread she felt at seeing Li.

Watching her reflection, she saw her matured beauty as if for the first time. Though it surprised her, it offered small consolation. What good was beauty without self-respect? It was like stained lingerie, exquisitely lacy but soiled.

*****

"The rally's at the Legislative *Yuan,*" said the cabby, taking a long swallow of beer. "At two o'clock." He polished off the can and focused his bloodshot eyes on the man behind the wheel. "You going?"

Iming shrugged laconically, grunted and started the motor. The cabby tossed him a warm can.

*"Pijiu,"* he said with a crooked grin. "Maybe it'll improve your mood."

*"Xiexie."*

Iming popped the top and watched the warm beer foam before he took a swig. He saluted with the can and drove off.

*Chung Shan* North Road was slow as always, even at one in the afternoon. He drove erratically, cutting off aggressive drivers with a cool twist of the wheel, then laying on the horn. At one-forty, he saw the long line of cabs parked on either side of *Chung Shan* South Road.

With new-found arrogance, he U-turned and double-parked at the intersection near the Legislative *Yuan*. Immediately a second line of cabs began forming behind his. Before he had opened his door, another taxi pulled alongside, starting a third lane of parked cabs.

Motorists were cutting each other off to squeeze through the one remaining north-bound lane still open. When he turned to look, cabs had filled the three lanes for two blocks and were continuing to pour in. The same was happening in the south-bound lanes. Of the eight lanes, only one was passable in either direction. Traffic flow was choked, just as surely as the exhaust fumes choked gathering pedestrians.

"Iming," called a cabby wearing a white headband. "Put this on." He handed over the white strip.

"What's happening?" he asked, tying the band around his head.

"Officially, we're protesting Tsai's visit." The thonged man grimaced.

"And the real reason?"

"What's always the reason. Independence from the mainland."

The protester scowled, his jet-black eyes getting darker. He pulled Iming toward the driveway's entrance where they had set up a platform with loudspeakers. As they got closer, Iming could hear the activist's inciting words.

"We're tired of polite demonstrations no one notices! By blocking the main thoroughfares, every commuter will know about our protest." His eyes swept the crowd. "Do you want to be heard?"

A rambling chorus of *yes* answered feebly.

"Do you want recognition?"

Gathering momentum, a louder chorus shouted back, "Yes!"

"Do you want independence?"

A unified *Yes!* rang from the throng.

"Then let's do something about it. First. . . ."

As the man's call to action agitated the cabbies, Iming became more distraught. He could not stop thinking of Iris. Images of her face, her twisted neck haunted him. Flashbacks of the accident tormented his mind, the Jaguar's crushing fender, the careening tour bus, the old coolie peddling his load, the speeding black limousine, the altered street lights, the political machine that ignored the rules, Mainland's leader, Tsai.

With each thought, his anger increased. Though he was not listening to the speaker's words, each solicited cheer from the crowd fed his frenzy, bringing him closer to venting his grief. He sensed the mob's indignation, felt its fury as he caught snatches of the rabble-rousing words.

"Mainland. Reunification. Tsai." The name exploded in his mind. His eyes burning with fervor, Iming had found his scape-goat, the object for his unfocused anger.

More words broke through his thoughts. "*Chung Shan Lo*, banquet, independence." He found himself cheering along with a mob, growing hoarser and more fanatical as the rhetoric became bolder. Like a cat ready to pounce, his pupils dilated, his eyes grew wide, gleaming feverishly. Thirsty from shouting, he drank deeply from the bottle thrust at him. The Taiwan rum made his throat drier, so he drank again and again, cheering more ardently after each draft.

*"Chung Shan Lo"* repeated over and over in his mind. Iris would have been there, coordinating the banquet, if it had not been for the accident. Correction, if it had not been for the traffic lights, for the presidential limousine, for Tsai. His eyes blazed with self-righteous zeal. He had been wronged. Iris had been wronged by the KMT. They would pay. *Someone* would pay. Thinking of Tsai, he hawked and spit, then reached for his friend's bottle.

As he drank, Iming took in the scene around him. All eight lanes of traffic were now blocked with long yellow lines of cabs. *Chung Shan* South Road was immobilized. The city's main thoroughfare was at a standstill at the height of rush-hour traffic. During the three hours he had been listening to the inflammatory speeches, the crowd had swelled to thousands. All he could see were nodding heads of black hair tied with white headbands.

Then at the south end of the boulevard, coming from the old East Gate, Iming saw a battery of shields reflecting in the afternoon sun. Carrying the shields, he knew though he could not yet see, was a riot squad. His eyes were not the only to notice. The assembly's vehement leader shouted through his megaphone.

"You see? We have the government's attention." As men standing at the crowd's fringe began to clear a path for the heavily armed soldiers, he commanded, "Stay where you are. This is a peaceful demonstration."

Iming watched the soldiers warily. Wearing riot gear that looked like updated feudal armor with Darth Vader helmets, they began shoving aside men who would not move.

"This is a peaceful demonstration," repeated the spokesperson. "We're doing nothing illegal."

The squadron forced a path with their shields, striking those who resisted with billy clubs. Within moments, the assembly had become a battleground between the armored and the defenseless.

As a soldier clubbed his friend, Iming rushed to his defense, breaking the rum bottle against the open grillwork of the man's helmet. The soldier dropped his billy club with a scream as he struggled to open his visor. The last image Iming had was of blood trickling from the man's face.

Not pausing, Iming ran for his cab. Only because it headed the line could he escape. Wheels squealing, he turned right onto *Chung Hsiao,* then right on *Lin Sen,* where he U-turned in front of on-coming traffic. Amid honking horns, he managed to make the light and speed across *Chung Hsiao,* heading north toward *Shih Lin*. Sweating, he looked behind him. No police.

In front of him was bumper-to-bumper traffic. The DPP's demonstration had succeeded. Traffic was at a standstill, but Iming knew that was dangerous for him. He watched through the rear-view mirror as he waited for the light to turn green. It changed three times before he crossed the intersection. Glancing nervously at the cars, he realized no other cabs were on the road. His taxi stood out like a fluorescent street sign at night. He had to get out of view.

Iming turned left in front of on-coming motorcyclists, darting into an alley. He pulled behind a garbage dumpster and jumped out, walking away as quickly as possible. Getting his bearings, he realized he was only blocks from his uncle's electronics store. His breath coming more easily, he relaxed, knowing he could hide there until the traffic let up.

Smelling of sweat and rum, he walked into his uncle's store. Only his two cousins were there, sitting on small stools in the back, sipping oolong tea. Tsung-wen jumped up. "Iming, I'm so sorry. Can. . . ."

He silenced him with a gesture. "Don't remind me. Change the subject." Looking at the teacups, he asked, "Have you got anything stronger?"

His cousin brought out the *shaohsing* wine, its proof nearly as high as the rum's. He poured it into thrce shotglass-sized teacups, handing one to Iming. With a quick gulp, he polished off the liquor and held out his cup for more before he described the incident at the Legislative *Yuan*. By the time they finished the bottle, Iming had related the details of the accident.

"Damned KMT," shouted Ming, his younger cousin, a DPP fanatic, pounding his fist on the table.

"Tsai's the one to blame," said his older brother, Tsung-wen. "The mainlanders are always responsible for Taiwan's troubles."

"Not all mainlanders," argued Iming, "only the leaders."

"That's my way of thinking," said Ming. "Get rid of Tsai, and Taiwan's free of the mainland."

"What better way to end talk of reunification than to kill the ambassador of good will?" said Tsung-wen. The three snorted with suppressed laughter. Then he added with a nostalgic sigh, "If only it were that simple."

Silence reigned as the three contemplated the situation,

each lost in his own thoughts. Iming recalled images of Iris before and after the accident. As life had left her body, animation had left her face. He shuddered, remembering how relaxed her expression had seemed, then how still.

Tsung-wen remembered a time when the Nationalists truly believed that returning to the mainland as its rightful heirs was imminent. Except for octogenarians who had fought with Chiang Kai-shek, that dream was as dead as his cousin's wife.

Ming, too young to recall the Fifties, thought only of the Democratic Progressive Party's rhetoric, total independence from the mainland, from the PRC, from the KMT.

"Why isn't it?" asked Ming.

"What are you talking about?" asked Iming, reaching for the empty bottle, forgetting it was empty.

"Why isn't it as simple as killing Tsai?" repeated Ming, pounding on the table for punctuation.

"You can't be serious," said Tsung-wen, images of the Nationalists' faded glory waving in front of his eyes like red flags.

"Get the other bottle," said his younger brother, "we have plans to make." Then he looked at Iming. "Where's Tsai now?"

He paused, remembering Iris' role in the banquet. "He'll be at *Chung Shan Lo* tonight. Why?"

When his question remained unanswered, Iming looked into his cousin's fierce eyes and saw the deranged blaze. It had always lurked behind Ming's pupils, but now fired by his political fervor it raged. Suddenly Iming understood, and his peaceful nature railed against his cousin's insane plan. Then tortured by images of Iris and provoked by the alcohol and rhetoric, his embittered alter-ego won.

"How do we get in the building?" asked Iming, his festering anger having found a vent.

"Simple." Ming downed his shot before explaining. "We drive there in the electrician's truck and tell them we're answering a repair call."

Iming's eyes lit up with excitement, then squinted suspiciously. "What'd be the reason for the call?"

"We'll change the start-up capacitors in the fans." Ming stood up and paced as the idea unfolded. Answering their stares, he added, "We were just there last month. The exhaust fans in the rest rooms never vent right."

"So what are we going to do, blow him across the Strait with a strong wind?" Tsung-wen laughed at the image.

"That's right," Ming said to the guffaws. "Blow him from here to China."

"What do you mean?" Iming asked. As the youngest dug behind the counter for a moment, finally surfacing with small metallic fuses, Iming watched him skeptically. "What're those?"

Ming's smile was diabolical. "A gift from friends." Sure that he had their undivided attention, he paused before adding, "Detonating caps for plastic explosives. Each one can blow up a concrete wall."

"So?" asked Tsung-wen, jumping up to refill their cups.

"So we hollow out the electrolytic capacitors and set caps inside." As his brother nodded, Ming smiled evilly. "When the exhaust vents are turned on, they'll spark, causing an explosion that'll rock *Yangmingshan*."

"And assassinate Tsai," said Iming, blinking his bloodshot eyes, "if we time it right." He stared into space, seeing images of Iris.

"Let's do it!" The youngest raised his cup.

They polished off their drinks as they hastily wrote up a work order. Then grabbing the bottle and detonating caps, they locked up shop and hopped into the truck. Because of the heavy traffic, they arrived at *Chung Shan Lo* only minutes before the guests.

All seemed well until they were stopped at the gate. Trying to control his shaking, Iming felt like vomiting from fear. He managed a stiff smile as he told the guards they were answering an emergency call.

"Exhaust vents?" the young guard sneered at their explanation. "What's so urgent about exhaust vents?"

"Do you want to be responsible when the toilets stink and President Fu loses face?" He waved the work order at the uniformed teen-agers, adding, "The longer you keep us, the more pissed Colonel Lee'll be."

The first soldier glanced at the form, then, grimacing, motioned to the other soldier to raise the gate. Pretending bored nonchalance, he waved them through.

"Park around back."

*"Xiexie."* Iming nodded nervously, trying to control his fear.

"Relax," said Tsung-wen, "I know my way around here. Ten minutes and we're done."

They parked and entered through the service entrance. Another pair of guards questioned them at the door. Iming took them aside, reached into his shirt pocket and pulled out a pack of cigarettes, offering them to the guards.

"It's a rush order. Colonel Lee doesn't want Tsai smelling his own sewage." After lighting their cigarettes, he brought out the work order. Slapping it for emphasis, he added in a confidential whisper, "Actually Colonel Lee doesn't want to lose his promotion."

They shared a laugh at the colonel's expense. Then Iming told a yellow joke that made them laugh louder. By the time they had finished their cigarettes, the guards believed him.

"Hurry, old brother, the guests are already drinking. It

won't be long before they'll be using the urinals."

Sweating, Iming nodded his thanks, then waved his cousins in.

"This way," said Ming, taking the lead.

Iming stood sentry as they installed the three electrolytic capacitors in the vents. When they finished, he was hyperventilating from holding his breath. They backtracked, hurrying to avoid detection.

"How will it work?" Iming whispered.

"When they turn on the vents, the electric spark will set off the detonating caps."

He stopped in his tracks, a feverish look in his eyes. "What makes you think they'll turn on the vents?"

"We turned off the water valves."

Laughing at Iming's distressed expression, Ming explained. "The toilets won't flush. They'll have to turn on the vents to get rid of the stink."

They chuckled all the way to the rear hall, congratulating themselves. At the door, a different guard stopped them. Eyeing them suspiciously, he nervously fingered his M-16.

"What are you doing here?"

Iming reached into his pocket for his cigarettes, and the guard pointed his rifle at him. Breathing heavily, Iming forced a smile. He raised his right hand and gingerly reached for his cigarettes with his left. Falling into his amiable routine, he offered the guard a cigarette. The man shook his head *no* but lowered his rifle. Reaching into his pants pocket, Iming saw the guard raise his rifle again.

"I'm just getting my lighter. See?" His movements jerky, he lit another cigarette and repeated his story.

When the guard asked to see his papers, Tsung-wen handed him the work sheet. He studied it carefully, then looked up.

"Where's the colonel's signature?"

"It was a phone order," Iming said quickly, beads of sweat sliding down his back like snipped hair in a barber shop. He shuddered as the perspiration prickled.

"Come with me," the guard said, unconvinced. Iming shared a grim look with his cousins as they followed the guard toward his lieutenant.

"Wait," shouted one of the earlier guards, running to catch them. "The light in the executive bathroom's flickering."

"The executive bathroom?" repeated Ming. Suddenly realizing they had sabotaged the wrong room, the three cousins silently exchanged panicked expressions.

"Lieutenant Chu wants it fixed immediately."

"We have an installation in *Panchao,*" Tsung-wen said quickly. "We don't have time to. . . ."

"Go on to the other job site. I'll do this myself." Interrupting before his cousin could finish, Iming took the toolbox from him.

A tug-of-war ensued before his cousin spoke for the guards' benefit. "I can't let an apprentice handle this," said Ming. "I'm the master electrician. I'll do it."

"It's something I have to do. You take care of the other call." Iming's somber expression won his argument.

As the guards eyed them warily, his cousin sighed. "You're sure?"

Iming nodded.

Taking a deep breath, Tsung-wen faced the suspicious guard, then tapped the toolbox. "The wrenches are in the truck, not in here. He'll be right back, *hao bu hao?* OK?"

Tightlipped, he nodded. They turned and hurried out the door, toward the truck.

"Get in the truck," said Ming. "We'll get away before anyone notices."

Iming shook his head. "I've got to booby-trap the executive bathroom. If I don't make the exchange, a lot of innocent bastards'll get blown up with their dicks in their hands."

"No! If we leave you here, how are you going to get away?" asked Tsung-wen.

"I'll think of something." Iming flashed him a wry grin.

"You're sure about this?" At Iming's nod, Ming said, "Then you've got to know how to change the capacitors because all three detonating caps are in the wrong room." Opening the toolbox, he picked up a capacitor. "Pull off the top like this. Reach inside, then carefully scoop out. . . ."

# CHAPTER 11

Li entered the banquet hall with his wife pressed snakelike against him, clinging possessively to his arm. That she turned everyone's head as she passed did not impress him. If anything, it annoyed him, making him higher-profile than his needs warranted. Her brassy conduct was helping neither his cover nor his grief.

Still blaming her for his mother's death, Li swallowed his hostility with difficulty. His eyes dark and deep-set, his mouth a resentful sneer, he watched her at his side. Nothing except *ai guo,* love of country, could make him attend a banquet with her on the night of his mother's funeral.

Mei-ling, however, was blissfully unaware of his mood. Wearing a gold lame sheath that fit like a second skin, she moved sinuously, every fluid motion rhythmically reflecting the chandeliers' light, making her the dazzling center of attention. When she spotted Chen, she nodded coyly at his smile of appreciation and pulled Li toward him. Her eyes flashed at the sight of Lane as she gleefully prepared for battle, her armaments well in place.

Speaking with Iris' assistant, Lane had her back to them as they approached. Only the sound of Chen's booming voice made her turn. "Mei-ling, you're a gilded statue of *Matsu* come to life. Only a goddess could be as radiant."

Her lips curled into a simpering smile, accepting the compliment. Chen turned to her escort.

"You're a lucky man, Nephew, to have such a woman as your wife." Not waiting for a reply, he caught Lane's hand

and drew her close, waving their clasped fingers like a fox tail before a pack of hounds. "Nothing's as important as family." Continuing in a lugubrious voice, he said, "I'm so sorry to hear about your mother." Then his tone rising, he added, "And surprised to see you here. I thought you'd mourn your mother longer." Before Li could reply, Chen looked at him sharply. "What convinced you to come tonight?"

"Only the pleasure of your company." Not a muscle twitching, Li hid his anger behind an inscrutable exterior. The four stared silently at each other, then nodding to Lane, Li stalked away, his wife's stiletto heels clicking on the marble floor after him.

Lane pulled her hand from Chen's. With an angry shrug, she resumed her conversation with the staff-member, inwardly seething at her husband's insensitivity. It was the first she had heard of Li's mother. Though she felt no personal remorse for the woman's passing, she shared Li's grief. His mother, Iris and her baby were all gone. Lane found the thought overwhelming as she tried to ignore her husband, while pretending to listen to the assistant's words.

Chen took the hint, joining a group of businessmen near the windows. Within minutes, they were lighting each other's cigarettes and laughing together companionably, though Lane felt their eyes trained on her. Without knowing why, she blushed and moved toward a group from the Institute.

As she crossed, Li's eyes followed her, watching her graceful gait, her black dress contouring sleekly to her body. He compared her elegant sophistication to Mei-ling's flamboyancy, the seductive starlight to the glaring sunshine.

Following Li's eyes, Mei-ling grasped the chance to belittle her rival. "The old ox was telling the truth. Did you notice her rubies?" Mei-ling hissed.

He had forgotten she was at his side. Daydreaming, he said, "What?"

"Chen *Taitai* must be persuasive in bed. Chen described in detail how she earned the jewels." Her eyes wide open, she looked up at Li with feigned naiveté. "Would you like me to repeat it?"

"Gossip somewhere else," he sneered at her. With that he turned and walked away.

Her crafty face lost its guile. Then recovering, she tossed her head in time to see Lane walk toward the refreshment table. With a disdainful sniff, she followed her.

"Lovely necklace," Mei-ling said, catching up.

Surprised the woman spoke English, Lane said, "Thanks," took a glass of wine and started away.

Stepping in front of her, Mei-ling continued in a saccharine voice, "Li's always trying to buy me jewelry, too, but I tell him to save his money for other things." She watched Lane's face closely. "Especially now that our second son's on the way." She noted Lane's green eyes widen, then she caressed her taut stomach, her feline movements implying more than her words. "Li can be so convincing," she purred, fingering her sleek gold dress seductively. "He always gets his way, but then, *you* know how he is." Her eyes narrowing to arched lines, Mei-ling smiled, slinking away like a golden lioness after a satisfying meal.

Her lips parted in astonishment, Lane watched the shimmering figure cross the room and sidle up to Li.

Taking in the drama, Chen smiled crookedly, congratulating himself on his choice of brides for his nephew. Judging from Lane's shocked expression, Mei-ling was more than earning her fee.

"Excuse me, gentlemen," he said with a smirk, "my wife's in need of me." The men chuckled coarsely as Chen swaggered toward Lane.

As he approached, Chen said, "I'm the envy of every man here."

Lane looked at him through dull, glazed eyes, knowing better than to acknowledge his flattery.

Undeterred, he continued, "You're *piaoliang,* the most beautiful woman, in the room."

Smiling lecherously so onlookers would think his wife's reception warm, he turned and asked the bartender for a brandy. She continued to ignore him until the Institute's assistant asked her help with the seating plan. Before her husband could object, she was in the next room, arranging name cards according to protocol.

Suddenly they heard a commotion as President Fu and Tsai entered the great hall. Everyone spoke at once, well-connected people scrambling for introductions, their aides clambering for better views. The people kept stony expressions, each trying to save face as they pushed and shoved in an odd mixture of composure and chaos.

Keeping safely in the background, Lane viewed the fracas. Chen, at the forefront of the melee, greeted Tsai like an old friend. Mei-ling seemed to be enjoying the chaos with the same exuberant stoicism as the rest of the throng, her glittering dress outlining her figure against the crowd like a gold pin on a dark suit. Then feeling eyes on her, Lane looked up and caught Li watching her. They shared an amused grin before each remembered why the other offended them. Lane was the first to look away as her husband led Tsai toward her.

"*Wo taitai,* my wife Lane," Chen said, his chest expanding. "Her father is US Senator MacKenzie, the man responsible for the trade agreement between Macao, Taiwan, Mexico and the US."

Tsai shook her hand, emulating western ways. Through a translator he said, "You're lovelier than I heard. Rarely do stories live up to reality." When she blushed at the unexpected compliments, she unintentionally encouraged him. "Chen, you and your wife must join our table."

Though she tried to protest, Tsai dismissed her objections. Finally Lane motioned to the assistant to reorganize the seating, quickly whispering the recent changes. Fu hastened to add, "Make room for Li, too," his invitation apparently spontaneous.

As they made their way to the head table, Lane stifled a self-indulgent smile. She saw Mei-ling fuming from the fringes of a less prominent seat, her small mouth pursed shut in an angry pout. Lane glanced at Li to watch his reaction. He passed by his wife without a word. Though relieved he did not ask Mei-ling to join him, Lane thought it strange he would ignore her, especially after her disclosure about the new baby.

A small frown dimpling her forehead, she asked herself, how could he make love to Mei-ling when he said he loved me. Then she squirmed with shame, remembering Chen's attack. That was different. It was rape, not love! Anger quickly replaced embarrassment, and she scowled at Chen, her eyes shooting daggers.

Suddenly Lane realized Tsai was waiting for an answer. She blushed hot pink. "I'm sorry. Could you repeat that?" she asked the translator.

"Do you like Chinese food?"

"Meals here taste nothing like the ones in American Chinese restaurants." She laughed nervously, trying to cover her discomfort. "In the US, Chinese food tastes like the trade agreement, Tex-Mex with soy sauce."

When relayed to Tsai, he threw his head back and laughed out loud. Chen looked at his wife proudly, gaining face by the minute.

"Your husband won't mind," Tsai said through his translator. "Sit next to me. Nothing aids digestion like a charming woman."

Through course after course, Lane spoke animatedly, amusing the guest of honor. Sitting on Tsai's right, she acted unofficially as hostess. Forced to focus her attention from Li to another, she welcomed the concentration it demanded, slipping easily into her role as dinner companion. Though she successfully avoided Li's stony stares, she marveled at his duplicity. How could he act so lovingly in the hospital, only to deceive her with Mei-ling? Then a little voice whispered, they're married. She's his wife.

That thought increased her social distance. Seated in an enormous dining room surrounded by hundreds of people, Lane felt alone. Though she played her role with the aplomb of an actress, chatting, nibbling, she felt segregated. Hiding behind a bright smile, she nearly choked swallowing the sudden lump in her throat. With blinding clarity, she realized that only Li could make her pain disappear. She had to speak with him privately, find answers to the unresolved questions. Only he could relieve her isolation.

In the meantime, she consoled herself by stealing glimpses of him as he ate. His simple actions seemed almost intimate when viewed in secret. Seeing his long, graceful fingers curve around chopsticks, gesture, reach, she remembered their dexterity only too well. Closing her eyes to it, a shudder passed through her body, creating instead of releasing tension. As he leaned forward, Lane watched his jacket strain against his torso, knowing beneath his tailored suit lay the crushing strength of his lean, muscular chest. What she did not know was that her own chest had begun to rise and fall as her breathing became deeper, clearly outlining her breasts against her snug bodice.

Unobserved, she studied Li's face, noting his wide masculine mouth ending in the vertical dimple on the left side. Only when Li smiled did it indent. She saw his strong jawline, firm with resolve, sometimes stubborn. She looked at his cheekbones, prominent and angular in his gaunt, chiseled face. Longing to trace his features with her fingertips, she caressed them instead with her eyes.

Not realizing it, Lane had been staring. Turning unexpectedly, Li abruptly met her eyes, lighting them up like two flashing lasers. Their eyes burned into each other's, holding them transfixed in a current, neither of them able to turn away. Mesmerized, he was lost in her incandescence.

As he opened his mouth to speak, Tsai's translator broke in, "Have you visited the Great Wall yet?"

Startled from the hypnotic trance, Lane's head snapped around, turning toward the voice, breaking eye contact with Li. Too distracted to think, she stuttered, "Excuse me?"

He repeated the question, and Lane responded, but cut off from their energy source, the lights in her eyes flickered and died. As she spoke to Tsai via his interpreter, she went through the conversational motions, nodding and replying, but her mind could focus on one thing only: Li. Sitting across the table, he was so close that had she straightened her legs, she might have kicked him, yet the gulf between them was wider than the Taiwan Strait.

When the final course was served, Lane peeked at him. Deeply engrossed in discussion with the man at his right, Li seemed oblivious to her. Her expression drooped as her heart sank. He couldn't have been serious in the hospital, she told herself; otherwise he wouldn't be ignoring me. Taking a deep breath, she sat up straight, lifted her chin and turned back to Tsai. Starting a fresh line of conversation, she decided to make the mood festive. Soon her pealing laughter could be heard across the table.

Caught up in one of Tsai's jokes, Lane laughed out loud, giggling into her napkin to hide her tears. Looking up, she noted Li's disapproving frown. Her humor changed as quickly as if he had thrown a glass of cold water, but she hid that behind the napkin, too. If he could forget her, she could disregard him. Still chuckling, she stared at him as she dabbed her tears, gave him a wide smile and turned back to her conversation with Tsai.

After dinner, Chen escorted her toward the great hall. As they passed, Tsai remarked in Chinese, "You must be an extraordinary man to have such a wife." Then his aide ushered him toward the lavatory.

Chen turned to Lane. "You've made quite an impression on our guest of honor."

But watching Mei-ling claim her husband, Lane was not paying attention to Chen. He followed her stare, taking in the scene, silently seething. His eyes narrowed to slits.

"Did you enjoy your dinner?"

Still gazing raptly at Li, she was too engrossed to answer. Chen grabbed her by her elbow and pulled her up sharply.

"I'm your husband," he hissed. "Look at me!"

The air crackled with unvoiced accusations. Lane turned her intent stare toward his hand on her arm. Her mouth pursed in a grim, narrow line, her eyes spoke for her as she looked from his hand to his face and back again.

Equally intense, he met her stare, then released her with a push, causing her to stumble backwards. Catching herself, she rushed at him, her hand poised to slap his face. Chen acted swiftly to avoid any public embarrassment, stopping her wrist mid-air and forcing it down. In the process he drew her so close, she could feel his hot breath on her face, reminding her of the rape.

"I told you never to touch me again!" she whispered hoarsely, her lips curling in disgust. She pulled her arm away, turned her back on him and started haughtily toward the ladies' room.

Before she had walked ten paces, an ear-splitting explosion rocked the building, knocking her against three *Yuan* members. Windows shattered, sending shards of glass through the crowd. Chaos descended along with pulverized plaster. Screaming people ran in every direction, blocking each other's escape. Soldiers carrying M-16s swept Lane from their paths, further separating her from Chen. She wrestled the crowd, finally reaching the relative security of the wall. From there, she inched her way forward to the door.

She watched wide-eyed as Tsai and President Fu were ushered out by a coterie of armed guards, brandishing their rifles. Within the circle she saw Li, his eyes furtively searching the crowd.

She screamed, her voice barely audible over the uproar, but he heard and pushed toward her.

"Are you all right?" Li asked.

She nodded, so relieved by his presence, words were superfluous. Grabbing her hand, Li used his body as a shield, fighting their way out behind the armed ring of guards.

Once outside, the pandemonium continued. To prevent the would-be assassin from escaping, soldiers had blocked the exits. As people rushed from the building, they only added to the crush in the courtyard, increasing the din and confusion. Finding the criminal in the crowd was like looking for a key on the beach.

Li searched her face, his mouth tight with apprehension, his lips barely moving. "You'll be safe out here," he said, his eyes coursing up and down her face, then locking on her ruby necklace. In an instant his tentative smile became a sneer.

Stepping back abruptly, his manner changed completely. In a scathing tone of voice, he said, "You're getting along well with your husband, I notice."

"What are you talking about?"

Though puzzled by his words, his belligerent stare made Lane feel like cringing. Keeping an anxious eye on the President and Tsai, Li's mouth curled sarcastically. He motioned with his chin.

"I'd better see to their security now," he said. "You obviously don't need anyone looking after you."

"What?" She watched him quizzically, but he was already out of hearing range, leaping into the foray as limos lined up with a police escort. Moments later she saw him jump into the front seat of the president's limousine.

Still wearing a baffled expression, she craned her neck, watching as the entourage drove away, its sirens blaring. Against the background of the din and confusion, Lane wondered what Li meant. And why was he involved with the president's safety?

As the crowd grew, the commotion increased exponentially. Shoved aside as more people emptied into the courtyard, she wandered about, looking for friends from the Institute. Though the yard was washed with floodlights, it was a montage of bright white areas, like overexposed film, against silhouettes and shadows. Visibility was low from squinting into the light, then stumbling in the darkness, but finally she spotted a group of coworkers near the back of the building.

"What happened, Steve?" she asked.

"An explosion of some kind." The political scientist shrugged his shoulders. Then seeing her impatient expression, he added apologetically, "That's all we know for sure."

"What do you think's going on?"

"From what I can make of it, it's a plot to kill either Fu or Tsai." With his index finger, he pushed his glasses up the bridge of his nose. "With cross-strait relations the way they are, either's a likely candidate for assassination."

Shouting drew Lane's attention as soldiers led a staggering, hand-cuffed man out the back door. Impervious to their rough attempts to hurry him, the prisoner plodded as if in a trance. Lane watched as a soldier jabbed him in the back with his rifle's butt. The man twisted in pain, then fell, his bloody face flooded with light. Lane gasped.

"Isn't that Iris' husband?" asked her assistant, moving closer for a better view, her face transfixed in her eagerness to see the drama. Then answering her own question, she added almost gleefully, "Yes, it is!"

Lane stared at Iming's motionless body. She wondered dejectedly what had happened to him since Iris' death. What must have gone through his mind? As she mused, she saw one of the soldiers kick Iming's hip.

Outraged, she screamed, "No!" and lunged toward him, trying to protect him from his assailants. A soldier raised his gun and pointed at her just as Chen rushed onto the scene, shouting excitedly in Chinese.

The soldier lowered his rifle, replied coldly, then helped his troop half-carry, half-drag Iming to an olive-drab car. Chen turned to his wife.

"What's the matter with you? If I hadn't gotten here, you'd have been arrested."

Grabbing her elbow, he ushered her to the front of the building, toward their waiting limo. He silently cursed his aide, furious with him for not getting back from the DPP rally in time to accompany them. Lane glanced behind her as the military car pulled away with tires squealing. Feeling limp with shock, she followed Chen without resistance, slumping into the back seat.

Before Li could turn the key, Mei-ling flung open the apartment door. Startled, he said, "Why aren't you at the Regent? I told you to be out of here tonight."

Still wearing her gold lamé dress, she pressed against him. "Li, why are you being so mean?" Tears beginning to stream from her eyes, she looked like a little girl in her mother's dress. "Is it because I never told you how I feel?"

He groaned. "Spare me the histrionics," he said, taking her arms from around his neck, "and get out." He walked away from her, crossing to the cupboard where he poured a drink.

She flung her arms around his waist, reaching up, under his jacket, her fingertips lightly massaging his chest, fingering his nipples through his shirt.

"Li, what happened to us? Once we were crazy for each other."

Again he extracted himself. "That's called lust, Mei-ling, and it ended long before you made up this ridiculous story about us being married." He turned toward her with the collective fury he had been controlling for months. "You've ruined my life."

"Ruined your life?!" She changed tactics, turning from victim to assailant. Her eyes flashing, only the tracks of her tears were a reminder that she had been weeping. "I gave you a son. I gave your mother a grandson. I gave you your place in posterity. I gave. . . ."

Interrupting wearily, he said, "If it hadn't been for you, Lane and I would be married, and I'd have my own son." He took another drink. Gesturing, he moved toward Teng-hui's room. "I don't know whose baby that is, and I don't care. Like I said, I'll raise it as my own, but we both know it's not mine."

"How can you be so sure?"

"You might have fooled my mother, but nobody else believes you gave birth to our child." He rolled his eyes in disgust.

Eyes narrowing, she paused, surveying him critically. "Want to bet?" When he did not answer, she pressed her point. "If I can prove he's your son, I stay."

"You know he's not my son." He laughed derisively. "What kind of scheme are you planning now?"

"No tricks." She shook her beautiful head, her gold dress shimmering as she moved. "I'll have him tested for your DNA. If the test says he's not yours," she swallowed, "I'll leave, and you're free of me." Then she smiled seductively as she approached. "But if the test proves he's your son, we stay married," she lightly stroked his fly, cupping his sex, "and live as man and wife." She looked up at him. "Deal?"

He squinted, trying to read the fine print of her mind. "I choose the doctor."

She nodded. *"Hao."*

He watched her suspiciously, trying to think how she could fake the DNA tests, then finally concluded she couldn't. His teeth flashed.

"Deal."

# CHAPTER 12

Holding the baby, Lane watched the news in the living room.

CNN: *"According to reports from the Central Department of Public Affairs in Beijing,"* said the newscaster, *"Tsai was recalled for security reasons after an attempt was made on his life in Taipei last evening. An article in People's Daily, the Party's official newspaper, stated the Military Commission of the CCP Central Committee is demanding a formal apology from Taiwan. Corroborated an administrator of the All-China Taiwanese Association, 'We Chinese are sensitive as to face.' "*

Entering the room, Chen listened distractedly as he read his contact's relayed fax:

'IT DOESN'T MATTER WHETHER THE CAT'S WHITE OR BLACK, AS LONG AS IT CATCHES MICE,' SAID WONG XIAOPING. WHOEVER ATTEMPTED THE ASSASSINATION ISN'T IMPORTANT. THE EVENT IS. IT'S SET OUR COURSE OF ACTION. THOUGH IT WOULD HAVE BEEN BETTER IF HE'D LOST HIS LIFE, HE LOST FACE, AND THAT ALSO SERVES OUR PURPOSE.

Chen smiled to himself, feeling complacent as he slipped quietly into his easy chair. Taking in the domestic scene around him, he congratulated himself. Yes, everything was falling into place. Soon the two Chinas would be reunited.

Soon he and Lane would be one. The newscast droned in the background.

CNN: *"Said Zheng, the Speaker of the People's Congress, 'The People's Republic of China is shocked and outraged that Taiwan would extend an invitation, then attempt an assassination.' Relations are particularly strained since the attempt on Tsai's life, with Beijing calling for retribution."*

*"Huang Iming hanged himself last night in his jail cell after an assassination attempt on Tsai, the highest-ranking. . . ."*

The fourth time she had heard the news item, Lane grabbed the remote, flipping through the channels, trying to find an English station that was not reporting on the *Chung Shan Lo* incident.

BBC: *"In an apparently related story, the PRC has announced its sudden plans to escalate its already extensive military exercises by testing missiles in the East China Sea one hundred and fifty kilometers north of Taiwan, off Taiwan-held* Pengchia *islet. The Chairman of the Military Affairs Commission was unavailable for comment when asked if it were a deliberate attempt at scare tactics since Taiwan lies just one hundred and forty-five kilometers across the Strait from the mainland."*

*"Trading was swift on the Taiwan Stock Exchange today as China's proposed testing of nuclear weapons looms on the horizon. The TAIEX dropped by over nine hundred points, slipping nearly eighteen percent. In brisk trading against the dollar, the NT declined sharply, plummeting to a ten-year low. Economists predict. . . ."*

Shuddering involuntarily, she turned off the television. After the previous evening's events and the news updates,

Lane felt more insecure in Taiwan than ever before. Depressed, she held the baby closer, protectively, yet drawing comfort from him. She sniffed, reflecting on the irony. Then taking a deep breath, she decided to test Chen's magnanimity.

"About your offer last night," she said, waiting for him to look up from his fax. When she had his attention, she continued, "I'm taking the baby to the States." He said nothing as he fixed his eyes on her in a stony stare. Lane forced herself to meet them calmly, willing her heart not to beat so fast.

'He who speaks first is lost,' he reminded himself. Pressing his fingers together, he sat back and waited for her to explain.

For several moments, they held a staring contest, seeing who would capitulate and talk first. Then angry with herself for playing his childish game, Lane stood up. Resting the baby's head on her shoulder, she announced, "Justin and I are taking the first plane out of here tomorrow." Then she spun on her heel.

Before she reached the door, Chen asked, "Do you think it's wise?" Purposely ignoring her use of the boy's English name, Chen avoided her challenge, appealing instead to her maternal instincts. "He's so small for a twelve-hour flight. Wait until his body weight increases. He'll be better able to survive it."

"I knew you'd go back on your word!" Her voice rose with her temper. She was all too familiar with his devious machinations.

"No, you misunderstand. Just wait until he gains a kilogram, another week, two at the most."

Chen stood and quickly crossed to her, positioning himself near the door. He gestured with his arms, holding them out innocently as if he had nothing to hide.

"I'm only thinking of our son's health. That flight's difficult for anyone, let alone a premature baby." He saw her resolve cracking and pressed his point. "A kilogram, that's all I ask. Wait until he gains a kilogram, then I'll see you off myself."

Though Lane did not trust him, she also had doubts about Justin's ability to handle a trans-Pacific flight. As badly as she wanted to leave Taiwan and take her son to the States, she recognized the benefits of waiting another week.

"A kilogram," she said in a tone that warned, "then don't try to stop us."

He smiled inwardly at her impudence, remembering Wong Xiaoping's dream, a seventy-two-hour blitzkrieg that wouldn't allow time for US intervention, time for emigration. Knowing it would be a short campaign, he only had to stall for a week or two. Responding deferentially, Chen caressed the small head laying on her shoulder, his fingertips brushing against her breast.

"I'll reserve your flight today if it'll make you feel better. By the way, the specialist's office called, reminding you to bring the baby in for his test work this afternoon."

President Fu sat on the edge of his wide desk and crossed his arms. "It's serious," he said, the nervous energy emanating from him like heat rising off pavement. "The PRC issued an official statement, calling the assassination an act of war."

"Tsai wasn't assassinated," Li was quick to point out.

"*Mei-you guanxi*. It doesn't matter." The president shook his head. "The People's Congress has an incident it can exploit to its advantage. Zheng wants Taiwan to squirm."

"You're talking about the tests in the East China Sea. China's tested missiles before," said Li, trying to reduce the tension. "Remember in 'ninety-six? That's its way of flexing muscle."

"This is more than posturing. It's a live-fire operation, and the PRC's not known for its accuracy. One slightly miscalculated angle, and they strike Taiwan." Fu gave him a disparaging smirk. "Accidentally, of course."

"But the Chinese warships are launching vessel-to-vessel guided missiles, not sea-to-land."

Fu appraised him sarcastically, sizing up his political acumen. "This morning two of our naval patrols were fired on by 'fishing boats.' How long do you think it'll be before surface warships are firing warheads at Taiwan?" Abruptly he changed his tone. "But that's not what concerns me most." He paused skillfully, heightening the drama.

Li waited respectfully for Fu to divulge the information, his impatience multiplying by the moment. Wishing the president were more a leader and less a politician, Li finally decided to speed up the process.

"Yes?"

"Reports from *Kinmen* and *Matsu* Islands indicate increased activity on the *Fujian* coast. The PRC's stepping up its military maneuvers. Hundreds of thousands of troops are moving to embarkation ports in not only *Fujian,* but also *Zhejiang* and *Guangdong* provinces." Fu's eyes burned into Li's like a torch into a fuse. "I've put the armed forces on the highest level of alert and mobilized the reserves. If the mainland's planning to invade those islands, it spells disaster."

"Strategically, you mean," said Li, knowing *Kinmen* was little more than a mile from the PRC and 82 nautical miles west of the *Pescadore* Islands.

Taken aback, Fu coughed, then quickly amended, "Yes, of course, but politically, too."

"I don't see your point."

"In 'ninety-four, the DPP chairman urged our government to withdraw the military from those off-shore islands, feeling it would be a temptation to mainland, a challenge." Fu's tobacco-stained teeth clenched. "If China takes those islands, the DPP would fight in the Legislative *Yuan,* screaming, 'I told you so.' "

"I still fail to see the connection." Li's brows furrowed in confusion. "What has China's possible invasion of *Kinmen* and *Matsu* got to do with the DPP?"

"Rivalry!" Fu shouted. "Rivalry between the ruling party and the opposition party. The DPP has totally different tactics. It would polarize public opinion. It'd hold a no-confidence vote and try to topple the KMT government by splitting its ranks. *That* would spell disaster for Taiwan. There'd be mayhem, social insurrection, especially if the DPP took control and declared independence."

"How? What would happen?"

Shaking his head, Fu chuckled in amazement. "Your naiveté astonishes me." He counted off the consequences on his fingers. "The TAIEX would crash overnight. Real estate values would plunge. Bank stocks would plummet. There'd be a run on the banks, panic in the streets." Exasperated, Fu threw his hands in the air. "Mainland wouldn't have to launch any military offense to destroy Taiwan. The Taiwanese would take care of that themselves."

Sobered, Li saw the dual threat to Taiwan, martially and politically. "So the danger of China invading *Kinmen* and *Matsu* Islands is greater than the missile-testing off the north coast, but the most deadly of all is local politics." He sniffed contemptuously. "And I always thought armed aggression, not in-house fighting, would pose the biggest threat."

Not stopping for lunch, he rushed from the Presidential

Office Building to the clinic. “Mr. Yang,” said the specialist, “the results of your blood samples are just in from the lab.” He reviewed the contents of the manila folder, then held out his hand, smiling knavishly. “Congratulations, you’re the father.”

Li ignored the extended hand, resenting the need to discuss his personal affairs with a nosy buffoon. His expression dark and intense, he asked, “How reliable are these DNA tests?”

The doctor’s smirk disappeared. Stuttering, he said, “I’m not sure of the success ratio, but the police routinely use this procedure in cracking criminal cases. It’s considered very dependable, even. . . .”

Interrupting, Li asked, “Infallible? What about paternity cases?”

He fingered the manila folder, then said, “In paternity cases, the differences in genetic make-up are such that it’s easily determined who’s the real father. The results are quite conclusive, even regarding disputes within family bloodlines, say, between cousins or uncles and nephews.”

Angry with the messenger for reporting bad news, Li argued, “If the results are always conclusive, then the success rate’s one hundred percent.”

The specialist hesitated uneasily. “There are exceptions, of course.”

Li’s hopes rose. He knew if there were a loophole, Mei-ling would have found it.

“Yes?”

Scratching his chin, the doctor contradicted himself. “Actually, the only exception I’m aware of was a paternity dispute several months ago between a father and son. Because of genetic correspondence, the results were inconclusive.”

Li's shoulders sagged along with his spirits. His speech clipped, he said, "In other words, this baby's DNA and mine are the same."

Regaining his professional poise, the doctor smiled convincingly. "Indisputably." Then enjoying the sound of his own voice, he added, "Beyond any shadow of doubt," but as Li's expression darkened, he amended, "of course, you're welcome to get a second opinion."

"Thank you, doctor," snarled Li, "I will."

He stomped out the door, stopping only to collect the papers on his way to the elevator. Though not convinced by the report, he was furious with himself for having made a deal with Mei-ling. When will I learn? He punched the down button, then waited dejectedly. When the elevator doors opened, he tucked the papers inside his vest pocket.

A pacifier dropped on his shoes. At the same time, he heard a baby's outraged scream. Li automatically leaned over to retrieve the toy, wiped it off, then presented it to the distracted child.

"Here you go," he said patiently, the baby's wide eyes bringing a weary smile to his tight lips.

"Thank you," Lane said stiffly.

Startled, Li looked into her face, then back at the baby's. She tried to decide if his confusion were amusing or sad.

"Don't you recognize your own son?" The words cut deeper than she knew.

"No," he said with a self-disparaging sniff, "I guess I don't."

Caught off-guard, he covered his surprise by defaulting to an angry glare. He was still irked at her. How could she sleep with Chen? The thought of his uncle touching her sickened him.

Then realizing the child in front of him was not responsible for his foul mood, Li relaxed his stern stare, a gentle gleam flickering in his eyes. Grateful for an unexpected moment together, he brushed the baby's fine bangs across his tiny forehead and smiled into the trusting eyes.

Watching them, Lane suddenly felt excluded. He doesn't care about me at all. Like Chen, he's only interested in his son. What am I, a baby machine? Then she remembered Mei-ling's admission of a second child. Is that all women are here, human incubators? He doesn't care who he makes love to, just so long as she conceives a son.

Her lip curling in disgust, she said, "We're late for our appointment." Pulling away, she added, "If you'll excuse us. . . ."

Not removing his hand from Justin's head, Li stubbornly stood his ground. A suspicious cast to his eyes, he asked, "What are you doing here?"

"Isn't that obvious?" She held up the baby as mute testimony. Then remembering his role in President Fu's safety, she decided to confront him with her speculations. "Or is this a formal interrogation?" When he visibly jumped, Lane sensed she was on the right track. Her eyes bored into his. "Maybe you should take me to the Bureau for questioning."

"What do you mean?" His Adam's apple bobbed as he swallowed.

As the truth became obvious, Lane's anger fanned. Her tone accusing, she asked, "How long have you worked for the National Security Bureau?" Before he could reply, she said, "Maybe that's the real reason you . . . pursued me . . . to get tip-offs from Senator MacKenzie. Inside information about America's role in the trade agreement." Her eyes narrowed. "Or did you spend time with me to spy on Chen?" She watched the surprised guilt on his face, clear evidence of his involvement. Bitter at his deceit, she shouted, "That's it, isn't it? You used me to get to them."

Trying to quiet her, he said, "Lane, you're jumping to conclusions." He touched her shoulder, attempting to calm her. Then in a patronizing tone, he began, "It's too involved to explain, but. . . ."

"Don't condescend to me!" she said, jerking off his hand.

"You don't understand." Wounded, his voice became sarcastic.

"Oh, I understand well enough." Summing him up, she studied him as if seeing him for the first time. Her aversion evident, she sneered. "You're no better than your uncle. You use people, manipulate them."

"Be reasonable, Lane." Li glanced around at the ring of onlookers. "Can't we go somewhere to discuss this?"

"Go to hell," she flung at him. Then she stomped away, her soft hair bouncing angrily with every step.

The day passed slowly for Lane amid reports of China's missile-tests and Hong Kong's take-over. Rumors of China's military build-up in the *Fujian* Province prompted hourly updates on ICRT, the only English-speaking radio station in Taipei, and special news bulletins on the BBC and CNN.

The driver had tuned the radio to ICRT as he drove Lane and the baby home from the check-up. When the DJ interrupted the music with a news flash, Lane strained to hear.

*"Mainland China has just attacked the* Kinmen *Islands off the southeastern coast of the* Fujian *Province. Surface warships bombarded the group of twelve islets with chemical warheads. Reports of casualties are pouring in. Apparently unprovoked, this has been denounced as an act of aggression by President Fu. China's Central Department of Public Affairs has defended the action, labeling it as restitution for the recent assassination attempt on Tsai. More news at the hour."*

Snatches of overheard conversations whirling through her mind, Lane stared out the window. If this is the front-line of an invasion, Taipei could be bombed with silkworm warheads. China proved its missiles could reach here from the Fujian Province. Now if they use *Kinmen* as a missile base, Taiwan's a sitting duck. It would be like skipping rocks across the water. As realization set in, Lane made her decision. Kilogram or no kilogram, she and Justin were going home.

Though her eyes had been staring into space, they gradually focused on the traffic at the Grand Hotel interchange. It seemed more congested than usual. Gradually more and more cars entered the highway. Within minutes *Pei An* Road was bumper-to-bumper in both directions, grid-locked with people jamming the streets, honking horns, ignoring traffic signals. *Neihu* looked like one big *shi-chang*, open-air market. Shoulder-to-shoulder, pedestrians competed with buses, cars, cycles and baby carriages, prolonging the ten-minute ride into an hour. It was only by taking a relatively unused residential alley that the driver got Lane home then.

"Wait here," she told him, "we'll be leaving again in ten minutes." Slamming in the front door, Lane called, "Mildred, phone the airport. Get reservations for the next plane to the States."

"I can't do that, Miss. Mr. Chen said. . . ."

Lane stopped in her tracks. "Damn it, I don't care what Mr. Chen said. I'm the mistress of this household, and if you won't follow my instructions, you can leave right now."

In an incensed contest of wills, they stared at each other until Mildred finally lowered her eyes. Her jaw clenched tightly, she hissed, "Yes, Miss," and turning, ambled into the kitchen.

Lane heard her muttering to the kitchen help, but it was not until she heard Mildred on the phone that she began packing enough diapers and shirts to accommodate a twelve-hour flight home.

From there, she went into her room, lay the baby on the bed and began throwing toiletries into an overnight case. Intent on moving quickly, she did not hear Chen come in.

"What do you think you're doing?" came a voice from behind her.

Turning, she continued tossing packets and plastic jars into the case. "Have you heard about China's invasion?"

"Yes," he said, his voice cold. "What I haven't heard is what you're doing."

She stopped, puzzled. "Isn't it obvious? I'm taking the baby to a safe place."

Her lack of guile softened his approach. "This is a safe place."

"Taiwan's going to war." Frustrated, she said, "I've got to get Justin to America."

He ignored her use of the baby's English name, still attempting diplomacy. "Are you sure he's strong enough to safely make the flight?"

"We just came back from the doctor's. He'll be fine." She tossed a hairbrush into her case and snapped shut the latches.

Chen hid his agitation with difficulty. Making one last attempt, he asked, "Has Tian-syang gained a kilogram?"

She turned to face him. "No," she said in a wary tone, her brows knitting together impatiently, "but under the circumstances, what possible difference could that make?"

"We agreed you'd wait," he said, appealing to her sense of honor. An astute observer of human frailties, he knew her vulnerabilities. "You made a promise."

Though her conscience nagged, her baby's welfare took precedence. "This is his life we're talking about. His safety's all that counts." Chen's canny expression stopped her. Suddenly she stood up straight, realizing he was the one about to go back on his word. "We're taking the next plane to the States."

Speaking in slow, dolorous tones, like a funeral director, Chen said, "I didn't want you to learn like this. I was hoping to spare you."

"Learn what?" Her eyes narrowed suspiciously. "What are you talking about?"

Silently Chen handed her an official looking document with a red-inked chop on it. She scanned it, then looked up at him abruptly.

"You know I can't read Chinese. What is this?"

He paused dramatically, remembering his credo, 'He who speaks first is lost.' It increased both her tension and irritability, but she knew his game and mentally forced herself to wait for his answer. Finally he drew a long breath and began.

"It says Tian-syang's my son."

As taut as a bow string, she laughed in a neurotic, high-pitched falsetto, his words bringing comic relief. "And my name's Chiang Kai-shek." She hurried to the bed and picked up the baby.

"Put down my son. You're not taking him anywhere." His face was stony, his voice coolly authoritative.

"Are you insane?"

"That certificate proves genetically that Tian-syang's my son." He held out several more sheets of paper. "These are the DNA analyses. Would you like to see them?"

He saw the peevishness in her eyes turn to apprehension. Though he remained expressionless, he smiled inwardly, enjoying the feeling of power it gave him.

Her eyes hollow, she stared without seeing, making no attempt to take the pages from his hand. With false bravado, she slapped his hand away.

"I don't believe you. Those papers are probably business reports from the trade company." She tossed her head. "Since I can't read them, they prove nothing."

"Ah, but they mean something in the courts of Taiwan." He smiled complacently. "They prove that, as my son, Tian-syang can't leave the country without my permission."

"You really are crazy." She laughed again, this time with more self-confidence. "You know he's Li's and my baby, not yours." She possessively brushed Justin's bangs with her fingers. "Even if you had falsified documents, I can prove you're not the father." As the baby clung to her, she stood at her full height, her body language challenging Chen. "There's nothing you can do to stop me from taking him home."

He held out the papers again. "If you'll look, you'll see they're in English."

She blinked then searched his eyes for the truth. His face impassive, he stared back blandly. Finally she took the sheets from him and read them, her expression becoming grimmer with each paragraph. Swallowing hard, she made another attempt at bravado.

"I don't care what language it's in. It doesn't prove anything. It's all a lie. Who'd you bribe?!"

"Ah, Lane, you never cease to amuse me."

Totally unperturbed by her words, he laughed companionably. His composure unnerved her, sending her into spasms of self-doubt.

"I'll . . . I'll. . . ." Angry with herself for stuttering, she concluded, "I'll get a second opinion from a doctor I choose."

"You do just that," he said almost inaudibly, so softly, so confidently, her hopes sank. Then his tone sharper, he asked, "Will that be before or after you leave?"

A flicker of optimism shone in her eyes. "I'll have him tested in the States."

"Remember, Tian-syang can't leave the country without my permission." He enjoyed squelching her expectation. Then pressing his advantage, he added, "But you're free to leave if you want." As if an afterthought, he added, "Of course, the courts call that desertion. Once you say good-bye, you'll never see Tian-syang again." With that, he gave her an evil grin and walked out of the room, leaving her to struggle with her options.

Inwardly fuming, Lane shut her eyes and clutched the baby closer, swaying gently, trying not to let her fear penetrate Justin's awareness. Planning an alternate escape, she crooned to the baby, whispering reassurances she far from believed. Locked in the embrace, Lane was in her own world when she felt Mildred pull the infant from her. Gasping, Lane struggled, trying to hang on without harming the child. The frightened baby began screaming at the tug-of-war.

"Let go! Stop it, you're hurting him," Lane cried.

"Mr. Chen's orders." With a smug smile of superiority, Mildred said, "I'm to mind Tian-syang until you're yourself again." With a harsh yank, Mildred forced Lane to let loose her grip or risk permanently damaging the baby's spine.

"Are you insane? Where's Chen?" Lane pushed past the woman, searching the house. "Chen!" His aide appeared, standing by silently, menacingly.

Finally one of the kitchen help said, "Mr. Chen's gone, Miss. He went. . . ." Seething with anger, Lane raced to the nursery. She heard Justin still crying, but when she tried the handle, the door was locked. Following her, the girl said apologetically, "Sorry, Miss, but Mr. Chen gave orders. . . ."

Furious, Lane banged on the door. She heard Justin's cries get louder. "Damn it," she screamed shrilly, "let me in!" When she pounded harder, Chen's aide physically restrained her, taking her wrists in hand, firmly bringing her arms to her sides. “Let go of me!”

She wriggled free, then slapped him across his face, leaving a white imprint of her hand against his dark skin. He roughly grabbed her by the elbow and hustled her into her room, slamming the door behind him. She made a dive for the door, trying to open it. Though it was not locked, the aid held it shut as she strained and pulled at the handle. Finally in frustration, she lunged for the phone and dialed direct to the US, calling her father. Though the lines were jammed, she kept redialing until she got through.

When he finally answered a sleepy hello, she launched into an excited barrage of information, beginning with a frenzied description of Chen’s holding Justin hostage.

“Just a minute,” he said, still incoherent from sleep. “What time is it?” She heard covers rustle as he fumbled for his alarm clock. With a deep sigh, MacKenzie said numbly, “Lane, it’s three o’clock in the morning. Can’t y’all call later?”

Stunned by his indifference, she asked hysterically, “Haven’t you heard a word I’ve said? Your only grandchild is being held here while Mainland’s getting ready to bomb Taiwan.”

“What?” Waking from his daze, he asked, “China’s doing what?”

“Invading Taiwan,” she said impatiently. “Chen’s got. . . .”

Fully awake now, he interrupted, “What’s the TAIEX doing?”

“Who cares what the market’s doing.” Lane exploded. “Justin’s in danger. I’ve got to get him off the island, back to the States.”

“I’ll send a military plane for y’all from Guam,” he said, adding acidly, “they can’t complain about saving US citizens from a war zone.”

"Who's *they?*" she asked.

"Never mind," he mumbled, "just get to the airport. Flying time's about three hours from Guam. It should give y'all enough time to get that grandson of mine ready."

Drained emotionally, Lane spoke so softly, she whispered. "That's what I've been trying to tell you. Chen won't let him leave."

"Won't let him leave?" he repeated indignantly. "What kind of bullshit is that?"

She pounded her head with her fist, then took a deep breath, deciding to explain in language he would understand: financial terms. "Chen's holding him as collateral. He said Justin's *his* son." Lane hesitated, wondering how much to divulge.

MacKenzie filled the momentary silence. "Of course Justin's his son. What's that got to do with getting my grandbaby to the States?"

Realizing it would take too long to explain, she simply said, "If I leave, I have to give up Justin."

"What are you talking about?" he asked, his tone irritated, impatient.

"He's using Justin to make me stay," she snapped, then relenting, she pleaded, "You've got to help me get him out of Taiwan."

"I told y'all I'll requisition a plane. What more can I do?"

She paced, feeling as hopelessly trapped as a mouse glued to adhesive paper. Though shackled, she had to think on her feet. She struggled to devise a plan.

"Can you come here?" Suddenly brightening, she said, "Your presence would stall China's offense," under her breath, she mumbled, "and shake up Chen."

He answered slowly. "This couldn't come at a worse time. I'm plum in the middle of an internal Senate investigation.

Sorry, Lane, but I can't get away."

"What are you investigating?"

His low-pitched voice deepened. "It's not *what* but *who,* and I'm the one being investigated."

"What for?"

"Possible censuring for taking kick-backs and bribes in the trade agreement."

Her breath escaped in a small puff, as if the wind had been knocked out of her. Though she had no more illusions of her father, she never envisioned him up on criminal charges.

"Are you guilty?"

Protesting too quickly, he said, "Those were all legal donations deposited to my fund for reelection."

His very glibness made him suspect. While she questioned his scruples, she wracked her brains for ideas.

"What about your cronies? Couldn't one of your friends in the Senate step in and act as mediator between Mainland and Taiwan? Any American presence here would change things."

"No 'friends' are willing to risk their necks by pushing a cause of mine." MacKenzie laughed dryly. "It'd be guilt by association. Right now I'm as popular as a cottonmouth."

Running her hand through her hair, she grasped at straws. "Look, security in the western Pacific will be destroyed if someone doesn't try to reconcile the two Chinas. If the US could. . . ."

MacKenzie picked up her train of thought. "Yes," he sighed thoughtfully, "if the US could ride herd, it'd rein in the conflict and build up the US position along the Pacific Rim." His voice took on the vibrato tones of a televangelist. "It's criminal to stand by and watch innocent people victimized by foreign aggression."

On a roll, he mused aloud, " 'Course, anyone raising voter consciousness'd get full coverage by the media. Nothing like a high profile to improve my image." He laughed gleefully, his tone becoming oratorical. "Whoever champions the American sense of freedom and justice captures the heartland vote. With a strong constituency backing me, I can earn the President's confidence, convince him to change his policy regarding the ROC and, in the process, earn his gratitude. Yes, Lane," he concluded with a satisfied sigh, "that's a shrewd, uh, humanitarian move." She could almost hear him rubbing his hands together. "I'll have my press manager issue a statement. Then I'll take the next plane for Taiwan."

"But . . . but what about. . . ."

"See y'all in about sixteen hours."

"Yes, but. . . ." She heard the click of his phone. Sighing, she replaced the receiver and ran her hands over her face, unsure if her father could reach Taiwan in time to halt any attack, let alone release Justin legally.

Thinking hard, she planned her strategy. I have to find another doctor to test the DNA samples. That bastard! Chen must have bribed the clinic to falsify the reports. She pounded her head with her fist. I should have known he'd do something like this.

What to do? What to do? She slumped into a depressed fetal position on the bed, thinking. Then suddenly she sat up straight. Li! She dialed his office number, heard the busy signal, then decided it wasn't worth the waste of time. The circuits were jammed, and even if she got through, it was no guarantee he'd be there. Despondently replacing the receiver, she remembered his cellular phone. In a burst of optimism, she dialed and redialed its number until she heard it ringing on the other end. About to hang up after the tenth ring, she heard him answer.

"Li?"

"Lane?" His voice sounded pleasantly surprised. She

could hear the high-decibel levels of traffic in the background, the drone punctuated by horns and motor scooter mufflers. Immediately his tone became concerned. "Are you all right?"

She almost laughed from relief, answering breathlessly, "I'm fine," then her tone darkened as she remembered her reason for calling, "for now, but I'm worried about Justin." She explained the situation, finishing with a synopsis of her call to MacKenzie.

Li's handsome features hardened as he clenched his jaw. "What clinic did the testing?" He asked, inching the car forward in traffic.

"The one where we met."

Lane glanced at the report in front of her, then drew in a sharp breath. A frightening thought rushed through her mind. Was Li in on this ruse? Could she trust him?

His anger unmistakable, he exploded. "Damn it! That explains a lot of things."

"What?" Anxious to believe him, his fast reaction helped reassure her of his innocence, but she needed confirmation. "What do you know about this?" Her tone was cool.

It hurt him to hear the distrust, but putting himself in her place, he rationalized, he'd feel the same way.

"When Mei-ling suggested a doctor's test to 'prove' Teng-hui's my son, I chose the specialist." Knowing it sounded too coincidental, Li tried again, anxious to strip himself of any related guilt. "But she knew his name."

His tone persuasive, his words were plausible. Convinced he was telling the truth, Lane nodded to herself, but he took her silence for doubt.

Frustration coming through his voice, he said, "I don't know what's going on, but I guarantee Chen and Mei-ling are working together."

"I should have guessed." Her voice small and tired, the words came out a sigh.

Lane's lack of energy concerned him. It was unlike her. He tried to be reassuring, but the traffic's turmoil broke his concentration.

"Don't worry. We'll work it out."

"Sure," she said flatly, responding to the inane words. "They've locked Justin in his room and won't let me near him. How am I supposed to get him to a doctor for DNA tests, let alone out of the country?"

Li thought quickly, his mind racing in two directions. Though he wanted to give solace, he needed information.

"You said MacKenzie's coming here, right?"

"Yeah."

"Chen's a tyrant, but he's not stupid. He wouldn't dare separate you from Justin in front of your father."

"I know that," she said irritably, "but it'll be another sixteen hours 'til he gets here. I'm worried about my son's safety. In the meantime, China could blow us to Hawaii."

His voice authoritative, Li said, "That's not even a consideration. Mainland's still posturing."

"Li, they're only a few miles off the coast." Frustrated, she wondered if she were the only one listening to the news. Her voice rose shrilly. "They've taken the *Kinmen* Islands hostage, for God's sake."

"Now who's condescending?" His eyes blazing, his tone challenged her. When she did not answer, he continued, "I have it on good authority that you, Justin and everyone else in Taiwan's safe at least for the next twenty-four hours."

Still smarting from his rebuke, she taunted, "Is that inside information?" Her sarcasm thicker than rice congee, she said, "Oh, that's right, I forgot. Working for the National Security Bureau, you're privy to intelligence reports, aren't you?"

A cab turned left in front of him, cutting him off. He lay on the horn, then took a deep breath, ignoring her invitation to quarrel.

"Lane, why did you call? To make accusations? To start an argument?"

Contrite, she closed her eyes and wiped her mouth, as if erasing the hasty words. "I'm sorry. You're right. Since I don't know which way to turn, I'm jumping to conclusions." Then she remembered his ride in Fu's limo. "But you never did explain why. . . ."

Not giving her the opportunity to think it through, he interrupted. "And as you pointed out, Taiwan's under siege." Slamming the conversational ball into her court, he demanded, "What do you want?"

The question made her sit up straight. Mouth open, she could not answer. In her desperation, she had instinctively turned to Li for help, but now she could not think of anything to say. Rightly interpreting her silence for confusion, he spoke gently.

"Don't worry about getting Justin out of the country. Taiwan's safe for the present. There's no immediate danger of invasion." Substituting a sarcastic snort for a laugh, he said, "When your father gets here, he'll convince China to back down."

Though relieved by his words, she confessed, "Actually I'm more worried about Chen using Justin as a hostage."

"Chen doesn't want to take on a US senator, any more than Zheng." His tone was ironic. The light turned green, but he sat still, waiting for the string of cars that had run the red light and now blocked his path. Placating her fears, he said, "If it'll make you feel better, I'll take a blood sample to another clinic. Tests will prove I'm Justin's father."

"Thank you."

She filled her lungs with air, breathing her first sigh of relief in days.

Her gratitude softened his cynicism. Feeling protective, he thought of confiding in her about the Bureau, explaining why he'd had to use her as a source of information. But there wasn't time. Instead, he only hinted at his involvement as he pressed for news.

"MacKenzie's due here in about sixteen hours?"

His question took her by surprise. "Yes," she answered hesitantly.

"Where's he staying?" As the light turned amber, the cars blocking his path cleared long enough for him to inch across the intersection.

She blinked, wondering what had prompted the change of topic. "I'm not sure; here, I suppose."

His voice suddenly businesslike, he said, "Heads of state always stay at the Grand Hotel. We'll call it a full-scale state visit. This'll add more prestige to the occasion, will give Taiwan face." Before she could ask the pending question at her lips, he added, "I'll make the arrangements. When he calls. . . ."

"Li," she interrupted, pausing as she selected the words, "how are you mixed up in this?"

He hesitated, again choosing between his two loyalties. He wanted to tell her, but he couldn't stumble in his duty. Swallowing, he fibbed, "I'm only interested in what's best for Taiwan. My contribution's small, but the least I can do is make MacKenzie comfortable while he visits."

She didn't believe hospitality was the extent of it, but sensing it was the only rationale she'd get, she didn't force the issue. Still, she couldn't resist a swipe.

"Who's paying for the suite, the Bureau?"

"I'll charge it to the trade company," he said glibly. "I'm

sure Uncle would approve." Then glad she couldn't see the smile lifting his cheekbones, he added, "Tell him, will you?"

"Who? Chen or my father?"

"Yes." He laughed good-naturedly. "Tell them both, especially tell MacKenzie if he calls before the welcoming committee meets him with the briefing."

He slammed on the brakes, just missing the scooter that zigzagged in front, then squeezed between two buses.

"What's he need a briefing for?" asked Lane. "His entourage includes a Sino-relations specialist."

"He'll need a Taiwanese slant for his press release." Her peeved sigh told him what she thought of his subjective bent. Defending his motives, he added, "At the very least, he'll need to be updated on late-breaking news."

"With KMT political analysts interpreting the events, right? How impartial." She rolled her eyes as she considered the logistics. "I'll tell him when I pick him up."

"No need," he said quickly, "I'll meet him with a limo and police escort."

"And what about his only daughter and grandson?" Anticipating Chen's objections, Lane began planning how she would get Justin to the airport.

"I'll pick you up," Li said. "We can talk on the way."

She tensed, remembering Mei-ling's story of a second child. Yes, she thought, we have a lot to discuss. "What time?"

He wove around a stalled car as he spoke. "One in the morning; traffic'll be heavy." Then his tone became testy. "If you want Justin to go with us, you'd better deal with Uncle tonight."

Lane couldn't stop the pent-up words. "Will you be dealing with Mei-ling?" The words hung in the air like incense.

"See you later." His unperturbed tone of voice didn't indicate if she had annoyed him or not.

"Good-night," Lane said with the clipped enunciation of an English teacher. Then she hung up, regretting it the moment the receiver touched the cradle.

Stopped in traffic, Li immediately dialed the Presidential Office Building, telling Fu of MacKenzie's unannounced visit.

Fu listened carefully, determined to wring all the advantage out of it he could. "Treat this as an official US visit." In a tone used to issuing orders, he said curtly, "Put together a media packet with news clips, military videos of mainland's takeover of *Kinmen* and dossiers on Tsai and Zheng." Speaking to his aide, he added, "Wang, get those videos from General Wu." He watched the young man leave the room, then spoke into the receiver. "Wang'll be working closely on this with you."

"Wang?" Li snorted with contempt as he inched the car forward. Then two uniformed students on a scooter dashed in front of him. Sweat broke out on his forehead as he hit the brakes, narrowly missing them. His tires squealing, the cab driver behind also slammed his brakes and honked the horn impatiently. "I need someone I can rely on. He's barely out of intelligence school."

"He comes from one of the island's best families," said Fu, struggling for flattering words. "Wang's . . . dependable."

Despite the chaos in the streets, Li's voice remained calm, his logic flawless. "He may be punctual, but is he reliable for top-secret assignments? Sir, we need someone both experienced and *loyal,* especially if my hunch is right."

"Refresh my memory." Fu flicked a switch and began recording Li's conversation.

"It's no coincidence Taiwan's being attacked as Macao reverts to China. This aggression ties in with the Macao takeover," said Li, ignoring the traffic lights now as was everyone else. He spoke as he inched along. "The temptation to repossess both territories was too much for the mainland. It was just waiting for an excuse to recoup Taiwan."

"Do you have any evidence?"

"You heard Wu's tape of Chen's meeting." Li's lip curled at the memory as he spit out the words verbatim. "Beijing's always felt Macao and Taiwan were like *xiao Taitai,* little wives, concubines. Mainland wants Taiwan to come home." Thinking of the parallel between Taiwan and Lane, he angrily sucked air between his teeth. "The man isn't in touch with reality. He's a self-centered, narcissistic megalomaniac, and I don't want to be toilet-training some junior agent when dealing with him."

Livid, Fu's face went white. "You may be my best operative," he said, jumping to his feet, "but it's obvious you're too involved in this assignment to be the best choice for the job."

"What do you mean?" Provoked, Li's temper flared. "As Chen's nephew, I have access no one else has."

"That's just it," said Fu, regaining his poise. "You're too close to the players emotionally." Returning to his authoritative tone, he said, "Step down. Wang's taking charge."

"Wang?! He's barely out of military school. He doesn't even know why it matters that Chen is Zheng's accomplice."

Fu sighed, then used a conciliatory tone. "I realize that, but his father's active in the Legislative *Yuan* and wants to see. . . ."

Exasperated, Li interrupted, "Nepotism's no substitute for experience or nationalism. MacKenzie's visit is crucial to Taiwan's political stability." Battling the traffic, he clashed with the president. "If you care for Taiwan's welfare, don't take me off this case."

Fu astutely considered the alternative, finally asking, "Aren't you and the senator on less than friendly terms?"

Li hesitated before answering, choosing his words carefully. "We've had our differences, but our relationship tops any Wang could build in the next few hours."

Lighting another cigarette, Fu thought it over. "All right," he said, exhaling, "you're still in charge, but only as long as you don't jeopardize your judgment with your hormones. Keep your distance from the senator's daughter, *hao bu hao?*"

"Yes, sir," said Li, angry yet aware the President spoke from political, not personal motives. Swallowing his pride, he concentrated on logistics. "Should I reserve the Presidential Suite at the Grand Hotel?"

Fu grunted his consent.

"Then I'll also arrange a limo, police escort and welcoming committee to brief him. Of course, I'll greet him myself when he arrives at the CKS Airport."

"Li," said Fu, his tone a warning.

His breathing labored, he answered slowly. "Yes, sir?"

Fu considered admonishing him against seeing Lane MacKenzie Chen but thought better of it. "Keep your priorities straight."

Li was still fuming from the call when Mei-ling greeted him at the front door. He dodged her kiss as he pushed past.

"Now do you believe Teng-hui's your son?"

When he ignored her, she smugly took his silence for assent.

Her voice velvety, she said, "I've lived up to my part of the bargain." Following him, she threw her arms around his back, hugging him closely. "Now live up to yours. Treat me like your wife."

Sighing, he pulled away. "Not that I don't trust you, Mei-ling, but I'm getting a second specialist's opinion."

Turning to face her, he watched her reaction. She seemed nonplused, her only change of expression an amused tilt to her lips. Aggravated by her calm reception, he added abruptly. "Until a consensus of opinions states that baby's mine, I want you out of here." He pressed a stack of thousand-dollar NT bills into her hand.

She did not refuse them, but her eyes hardened. A beat later they brimmed with tears.

"Li," she pleaded, kneeling in front of him, wrapping her arms around his shins, "how can you treat the mother of your son like this?"

"I admit your tears-on-tap are good, but they don't work with me anymore." Shaking his head, he spoke with a grudging respect.

Immediately she stood up, her eyes dry, her small mouth puckered in a tight bow. Stamping her tiny foot, she said, "You always think you're so honorable. You're as bad as the MRT officials, going back on your word, lying to me, drooling after another man's wife. You disgust me!"

"Fine," he said coolly, "then leave."

She rushed to him again, placing her dainty hands on his chest, her eyes misting. "Oh, Li, you know I love you." She alternately wheedled, demanded and crooned in a breathy voice. "Why won't you let me be a wife to you?"

"Because you cheated me of my future," he said without emotion, "and for that, I can never forgive you."

Absentmindedly she fingered his shirt. "Yesterday you were willing to accept me if I proved Teng-hui was your son. I did that," she said, tears escaping. "What more do you want?"

"The truth about Teng-hui's DNA." His voice as sharp as volcanic glass, he asked, "Who's the father?"

"You are."

"Damn it, I said the truth." He pushed her hands from him while his fierce gaze held her firmly.

She dropped her eyes, looking away, afraid he would read her thoughts. A hundred answers came to mind, all of them lies. She swallowed, debating which part of her credo to follow: Don't admit mistakes. Instead lie, brag, slander. Don't take responsibility. If the sky falls, a taller person will stop it from falling on me.

Playing a hunch, Li said, "I know all about your little scheme with Uncle."

Wide-eyed, she stared at him gratefully. Li had chosen for her and rightfully so. It wasn't her responsibility. It was Chen's.

"You're not angry?" she asked in a plaintive voice.

Realizing he had stumbled onto something, he tried not to show his surprise. He would have to pry skillfully to learn her secret. He consciously softened his tone and stern expression.

"I was, but then I realized you were just a pawn in Uncle's game."

She expelled a sigh and with it, all the tension in her body. Mei-ling went limp with relief, brushing lightly against his arm. She grabbed his biceps to steady herself.

"You understand why I had to do it?"

He nodded. "Uncle can be convincing," he said soothingly, "but I don't see why he faked the DNA tests." She blinked, staring at him quizzically. Realizing he had fouled up, Li quickly covered. "He must have known I'd get a second opinion."

Anxious to gain Li's trust, Mei-ling filled in, "Yes, but since the DNA's so close, he didn't worry," she tossed her thick hair over her shoulder, "especially since there was no reason for other genetic comparisons."

Li's mind reeled. Feeling dizzy from the unexpected news, he stumbled back a step. Forcing his shocked brain to function, he tried to piece the information together. When he finally spoke, his voice was calm, reasonable, matter-of-fact. He willed his face to remain impassive while inwardly seething.

"Uncle never thought I'd suspect the baby was his."

She nodded, her eyes watching him warily. "You're not angry with me, are you, Li?"

Answering her question with one of his own, he asked, "There's just one thing that puzzles me." His tone acid, he said, "Why did you fuck him?"

"I didn't," she cried, "I . . . I swear it!"

He sneered. "A baby doesn't just happen."

"No, I . . . I . . . he had me artificially inseminated."

"That isn't Uncle's style." Li stared at her, not believing her gall at lying so blatantly. Then he combed his hand through his hair to keep from strangling her. "Try something new, Mei-ling. Be honest."

"It's true, he. . . ."

Li's smoldering stare silenced her. "Why'd you do it?"

Playing with the hem of her skirt, she focused on it, unable to meet Li's eyes. After a drawn-out pause, she said, "Your uncle bought me when I was seventeen."

"What?!" Li whirled around, grabbing her arm, forcing her to look at him. "What kind of lie are you telling now?"

Slowly shaking her head, she whispered, "It's not a lie."

As sobs began wracking her petite body, she began crying real tears. Her expression was not the pretty pout her manufactured tears produced, but the pinched face of a frightened child.

Despite his reluctance, he opened his arms, waving her toward him. As the tears came harder, he led her to the sofa and held her. When the worst of the crying jag passed, he tried again.

"Tell me about it."

Sniffling, she described her childhood. "My father was a KMT soldier who fled here with Chiang Kai-shek in 'forty nine. My mother was his second wife," she lowered her eyes, "since he'd left his *taitai* behind in the mainland." Her lip curled scornfully. "I grew up near *Hualien,* not *Tainan* city," she said, her limpid eyes looking woefully into his. "My mother belonged to the *Ami* tribe. She was half aborigine and half Chinese." She paused, letting its meaning sink in.

Then taking a long breath, she lifted her chin and continued her story in a monotone. "My mother had been sold into a brothel on *Huahsi* Street when she was fifteen. By the time was thirty, she was too old to work, and my father bought her."

Though he struggled to keep his face impassive, Li's fingers tightened around her shoulders. Mei-ling shook her hair from her face and continued. "My mother was sick as far back as I can remember. She died when I was sixteen, and my father's drunken bouts tripled. One night he raped me."

Focusing on a distant memory, she stared into space. "I thought that was the worst that could happen. It wasn't. He sold me to a pimp on my seventeenth birthday."

Li's voice was compassionate when he asked, "Did you work in one of the 'barber' shops?"

Wearing a disgusted half smile, she shook her head, remembering. "No, I was never a prostitute. My father was greedy. Wanting a higher price, he told the pimp I was still a virgin. That tag protected me until we got to *Shuangcheng* Street."

Li shifted his position, so he was able to watch her expression. When convinced she was telling the truth, he asked,

"Why didn't you tell me this before?" Though she shrugged indefinitely, Li guessed the reason. "How does my uncle fit into this?"

"The first few weeks I was there, I worked as a waitress in a bar and was made to play breast-touching games." She looked up at him anxiously. Not recognizing the game, he shook his head. "You know," she said, demonstrating, "where the customers play rock, scissors, paper with the girls. If they win the finger-guessing games, the waitress has to remove a piece of clothing; if they lose, the customers have to buy a round of drinks and tip the girl." Again she shrugged. "It was a gimmick to attract customers."

"I still don't see how this connects with Chen."

"I was good, so good, in fact, I became an attraction. Everyone tried to win, but no one could. The bar made more money with me as a waitress than a prostitute." Almost boasting, she said, "After two weeks, I moved up to princess." She looked to see if he followed her. Again he shook his head.

"A princess," she began, "is a teen-aged hostess who 'dates' customers in karaoke bars. For the first time in my life I wore pretty clothes and make-up. It was fun flirting with those young men." Her eyes smoldered mysteriously. "That's how I met your uncle."

"Odd," he said stiffly, "I'd never characterize him as a young man."

Sensing the rivalry, she suppressed a smile. "I met him my first night as a princess. He thought I was special," she added shyly, "and he bought me. I was his favorite, almost a daughter. He tutored me, groomed me, taught me how. . . ."

"How to fuck?"

Her animated face went white with humiliation. For a long pause, she stared at him with the eyes of a hurt animal. Then she raised her head proudly.

"Yes," she hissed, "he taught me how to fuck, but he never treated me as cruelly as you." She stared him down.

Grimacing, he closed his eyes. "I'm sorry, Mei-ling. That was uncalled for. I guess I'm angrier than I realized." He squeezed her shoulder gently. "This can't have been easy for you."

She shook her head, tacitly agreeing. After another pause, she said, "I don't know if he planned for us to meet that night or not," she smiled bashfully, "but from that moment, his relationship with me changed. We stopped," she squirmed, "seeing each other. He kept me on as a hostess, but instead of wages, he gave me a percentage of the Juliet Club's profits."

Li began uneasily, then faltered. "I don't know how to ask this tactfully." He drew his palm over his chin thoughtfully. "When did he . . . ?"

"Get me pregnant?" she filled in. With a sigh and a grimace, she explained. "Right after you said it was over between us." As she watched Li raise his eyebrows doubtfully, she snapped, "Believe it or not, you hurt me deeply. I was heartbroken . . . and frightened to go back to your uncle. It wasn't easy to admit you'd left me for . . . Lane." She sneered as she pronounced the name.

Irritated, he asked, "What about that 'wedding' you staged between us? Was that his idea or yours?"

"Mine." She raised her head proudly, tossing back her thick hair. "It worked, didn't it?"

"Not the way you'd planned." His eyes met hers with cool spite. "Was he sleeping with you then?"

She shook her head, ignoring the tendrils of hair that brushed against her face. "That dinner was my last chance to get you back. I knew it. When it didn't work, I had no pride left. I crawled back to Chen, afraid of what he'd do to me."

Tears started again, but she brushed then away angrily. "Li, you have no idea what it's like! Your uncle *owned* me. Though we'd been lovers and he'd treated me like a daughter, I was still his property. I was afraid of him!" After her outburst, she sat back, exhausted.

"That's when he took you back in his bed."

Her eyes clouded as she paused, then nodded. "When I got pregnant, it gave him an idea, but it wasn't 'til he learned of Lane's baby that he put that idea in motion."

"What are you getting out of this, Mei-ling?" he asked as he eyed her critically.

She lifted her eyes. "Our marriage," she breathed.

"Nothing's for nothing with you." She hesitated long enough for him to prod. "C'mon, Mei-ling, I know you too well. What else?"

"If you ask that, you know nothing about me." She caressed his face with her small hand. "Why won't you believe me? I love you, Li."

Unmoved, he repeated, "What else?"

Her hand dropping into her lap, she said in a monotone, "Partnership in the Juliet Club."

"I thought as much. You see, I do know you, better than you think," he said, not unkindly. "But it doesn't make sense that he has a baby with you and trades it for my baby with Lane."

"That's easy," she said bitterly, her lip curling. "Lane's the daughter of a US senator. A relationship with her gives him face, while I'm one-quarter aborigine. He's ashamed of me."

"You're beautiful, Mei-ling, and smart." He watched her compassionately. "If things were different, I'd be proud to call you my wife," he hesitated, then added gently, "but I don't love you."

Her tiny chin dipped against her chest. Unable to meet his eyes, she bit her lip and tried to swallow the lump that caught in her throat. When she looked up, her lashes were damp with real tears. Sniffling, she tried to control her trembling chin.

"But I love you."

Li felt frustrated. For the first time in their relationship, he understood her motives and shared her pain. He still did not trust her, but he no longer despised her.

After an inner debate, he said, "Though I've hired an amah to look after Teng-hui, you can stay a few days, until this gets sorted out." Then a note of warning to his voice, he added, "But in my mother's room. I can't sleep on this sofa any more."

"Don't make me sleep in her bed." She looked at him horror-stricken, her almond-shaped eyes round with terror. "Her ghost's waiting for me."

"Mei-ling, be reasonable. . . ."

She shook her head indisputably. "I can't." Ashamed to tell him the whole truth, she whispered, "Li, she blames me for her death. No, I'd rather stay in a hotel than there."

"The choice is yours." Not knowing what else to do, he put his arm around her shoulders, silently consoling her. They sat like that for several minutes until his watch beeped. Stretching, he groaned. "The car'll be here for me soon. I've got to shower." He stood up. "But before I go, I've got to be sure of one thing." He looked into her eyes earnestly. "You're positive Teng-hui's my uncle's son, my *cousin?*"

Her pretty eyes flashed momentarily as she struggled with the truth, then looked back at him disconsolately. She nodded.

"There's no possibility he's mine?"

"None." Mei-ling looked away.

He started toward his room, then turned back, a puzzled

expression on his face. "I don't understand why you're not fighting me for him."

Slowly she raised her eyes to him. Very still and serious, she answered in a small voice. "You'll want me back."

# CHAPTER 13

Lane dressed carefully but automatically, her mind focused on what she would say to Chen and MacKenzie. Watching her reflection as she brushed her luxuriant hair, she saw not herself, but the future. She rehearsed her arguments silently and defended her positions, preparing for her contests of will with her husband and father. Unable to imagine debating three issues at once, she carefully excised all thoughts of Li. Then she concentrated on the task at hand: convincing Chen that her one AM drive to the airport was sensible.

She checked the time. Standing up, she gave herself one last appraisal, then strode to the door, her carriage displaying far more confidence than she felt. Though the aide had left his post at her door hours before, she knew she was still under the staff's scrutiny. She walked silently through the living room and peered out the window.

"Expecting someone?"

Chen's voice trumpeted from a chair behind her. The sound went through her like the squeal of brakes, metal on metal.

Turning, she composed herself and said simply, "Yes." Then she resumed her watch at the window.

Standing up to his full height, he smoothed his jacket and rebuttoned it, sucking in his belly, making his chest appear larger. Pretending to give it serious thought, he asked, "This person wouldn't be my nephew Li, would it?"

"I'd appreciate it if you wouldn't patronize me with every word you utter." She took a deep breath, then exhaled as if clearing her lungs of a foul smell. "Yes, it is Li," she said, refusing to justify her actions. She resented being made to feel like a child. "We're meeting . . . a diplomat at the airport."

He feigned surprise. "A late hour for that, isn't it?" She shrugged. Picking his words carefully, he said, "It might be difficult landing in this atmosphere."

She caught the innuendo. "Are you referring to the sub-tropical or political climate?"

"I was speaking meteorologically," he said lightly, his turn to shrug. "Though personally I feel it'd be a waste of your time driving all the way to the CKS international airport, just to turn around and come back home again." As if an afterthought, he asked, "You weren't planning on taking Tian-syang with you, were you?"

Though she had meant to originally, Lane had decided the trip would be too hard on the baby, even without the conflict. Yet Chen's words irked her, made her confrontational. Knowing it was a challenge, she wasn't in the mood to back down. She turned to face him.

"Maybe it would be good for him to meet his grandfather's plane." She left the sentence hanging, waiting for his move.

"Your father's coming here?" he whispered. "What time?" His eyes bulging from their sockets, Chen's sallow face blanched.

Lane was not prepared for his intense reaction. She had no idea her father's position carried that much weight. "In about two hours."

Chen's mind churned, wondering if two hours were enough time. His darting eyes betraying his distress, he asked, "Is it an official visit?"

She eyed him scornfully, despising his weakness when he wasn't in control as much as his arrogance when he was.

"Yes." The flash of moving headlights caught her attention. Peering out the window, she said, "He's here. Rather than keep Li waiting, I'll leave Justin where he is. His grandfather'll meet him in the morning." She looked at Chen icily as she walked out the door. "Don't wait up."

Before Lane had climbed into the limo, Chen made the decision. Hoping his warning would reach them in time, he raced to his office, scribbled a message and faxed it to his relay in Hong Kong.

DELAY TWENTY-FOUR HOURS.

As one of the police escorts held open the car-door, Lane climbed in beside Li. "Where's Justin?" he asked.

"I decided not to wake him. He can meet my father in the morning." She told a half-truth, not wanting to explain.

Li sighed, thinking about the two babies. After Mei-ling's disclosure, he had been looking forward to seeing his son.

To cover his disappointment, he said, "It may take us 'til morning just to get to the airport. The roads are jammed."

As they got under way, both fell into thoughtful silences. The closer their entourage got to the highway, the slower their progress. The streets had been crowded but passable. The highway was at a standstill. Just getting on the entrance ramp took twenty minutes. Though worried about her personal problems, Lane watched wide-eyed at the number of people trying to escape, the impact of China's aggression becoming all too evident.

The minutes ticked by slowly as the car inched along. The six lanes of bumper-to-bumper traffic made rush-hour stalls seem like a speed race by comparison. Despite her alarm, the anxiety eventually gave way to fatigue, and she dozed against the window.

Li watched her thick lashes droop, then close over her eyes. He stared at her creamy complexion, her skin as smooth and firm as Teng-hui's. As a wave of hair fell across her face, he swept it away with his fingertips, lingering long enough to caress her cheek. Gingerly he traced the outline of her lips with his thumb, remembering their taste all too clearly. Only when she stirred, moaning softly in her sleep, did he remove his hand, contenting himself with merely studying her.

When Lane woke, she rubbed her eyes and peered sleepily at her watch. Three o'clock. She craned her neck, looking out the windows. All she saw was a red sea of taillights.

"Where are we?"

"About three kilometers from where we got on the expressway." His voice sounded gentle against the background din of motorcycles and horns outside the car and radio static from the front seat.

"It doesn't take trigonometry to calculate that at this rate, we'll never make the flight. Any suggestions?" She saw his grimace in the reflected lights of the cars beside them.

"There've been some developments since you fell asleep."

She tilted her head and looked up questioningly.

"The mainland's lowered a blockade around the island. Ships can't leave or enter the harbors," he said. "More scare tactics. They're trying to break morale by stopping oil tankers from reaching Taiwanese ports."

"And aircraft?" she asked, her voice rising as her heart sank.

"From reports, some passenger planes are still arriving," his voice became businesslike, clarifying, "those that were in transit before the embargo, but none are taking off."

"What about my father's plane?"

He shook his head. "Your guess is as good as mine."

She looked at the nearby cars, wondering if their passengers knew. "Did you hear that on the news or car phone?"

"Phone." Following her line of vision, he caught her train

of thought. "These people will panic when they learn the airport's closed."

"What'll they do?"

"Emigrate south to relatives, probably. If they can't escape the country, they'll at least leave the county."

His head jerked as he heard a knock at the window. Lowering it, Li saw one of the police escorts. They spoke for a minute, then the officer saluted, and Li pressed the button, closing out the mayhem that surrounded them.

"What's wrong?"

"There's been an accident. The escort just received orders to monitor traffic about five kilometers from here."

"How can they get there?" Lane asked.

Laughing wryly, Li said, "Only cars get stuck in traffic. Haven't you noticed the scooters whizzing by?"

Lane watched as the eight police drove off on their motorcycles, zigzagging between the idling cars. Though the cycles did not maneuver as easily as the scooters, they still squeezed through. She watched them forlornly. Without the escort, Lane somehow felt deserted. Stuck in the middle of the highway, miles from home or the airport, not knowing whether her father's plane would be able to land or not, she felt claustrophobic. What about Justin? When would she get back to see him? And if her father's plane were not permitted to land, what then?

Sensing her agitation, Li moved closer. "C'mere," he said, placing his arm around her. "Try to get some sleep." He gently pressed her head against his shoulder. "Maybe this traffic jam will let up once the police clear the road of the accident. When you wake up, we might be in Taoyuan."

Anxious but exhausted, Lane tried to take his advice. She drifted into a troubled sleep, dozing and waking as the scooters' two-stroke engines squealed by. But after an hour, she abandoned the idea. Straightening up, she smoothed her hair, in the process creating a small distance between herself and Li. The close quarters made her uncomfortably conscious of his masculinity.

"Did we make any progress?"

"About another kilometer."

"Is this worth it? Maybe we should turn around." Lane sighed dejectedly. "We don't even know if the airport's open."

"It's a little early for that."

"Maybe we should radio a message. After all, my father doesn't know we're meeting him. Even if his plane lands, we might miss him."

"That's true." Li told the driver to contact the CKS airport. After several tries, they spoke in Chinese, and Li translated. "He can't get through."

"Is there anyone else you could call for information? If this is a wild goose chase, I'd rather be back in Neihu."

Li leaned forward and spoke to the driver again, issuing instructions to call the Bureau. Finally the call went through. The chauffeur relayed the information to Li, who, after sliding shut the tinted glass panel, told Lane.

"It's official. The airport's closed."

"Did my father's plane arrive?" she asked anxiously.

He shook his head. "They were contacted mid-flight, ordered out of Taiwan's airspace and redirected to Guam." He did not tell her how low on fuel the plane was from flying in a holding pattern, waiting for permission to land in Taoyuan. Nor did he mention China's threat of air strikes. All he said was, "They landed safely ten minutes ago."

"Now what?" Lane slumped against the seat with a sigh.

Moving closer, Li placed his arm on the upholstered headrest behind her.

"Wait it out, at least until the next exit. We can turn around there."

When he shifted, the scent of his cologne wafted toward her. She took a deep breath, its aroma triggering discomforting memories. As her pulse quickened, she felt a sudden wetness at her center. Appalled at her body's betrayal, she shrank away from him and huddled against the door, cowering from her hunger. Still the tension persisted between them. When he did not move away, she turned to look out the window, hoping to show her disinterest by changing the topic.

"Where are we, anyway?"

"In trouble." His words came back succinctly.

"What?"

She pretended not to understand, but his intent expression silenced her as he pulled her to him and put his warm lips on hers. At first she squirmed, reluctant to let go her social constraints. Then gasping, she clasped him to her as if he were an oxygen mask, breathing fresh air into her suffocating life.

Through half-closed lids, Lane noticed the windows were tinted a shade too dark for curious spectators. Shutting her eyes, she shut out the world, living only in Li's tight embrace.

He murmured endearments against her neck, into her ear, running his fingers through her hair, smelling its sweetness. His hands fumbled with her blouse, loosening it from her skirt. Then slipping his fingers beneath the silk, he lifted her breasts from her bra, feeling their cool weight in his palms. Slowly, gradually, with infinite patience, he kneaded their tips into swollen pink buds, then bent his head and sipped, tasting her milk.

She gave little cries of delight, gasping as his gentle suction began stirring a desire deep within the pit of her stomach. She writhed against him, reaching for his swollen manhood, sighing when she found it. She stroked him, as aware of his arousal as she was of her own.

They stayed locked in their embrace, nuzzling and caressing each other for what might have been minutes or hours, until they heard the intercom buzz. Gradually they pulled apart, still lapping at each other's lips, reluctant to return to the world of traffic jams, military aggression and responsibility. Li cleared his throat, then answered the phone, the driver tactful enough to avoid opening the glass separating them.

Brought back to reality, Lane adjusted her blouse and smoothed her hair as Li spoke excitedly into the phone. She felt caught somewhere between guilt, euphoria and fear as adrenaline pumped through her veins. Though she could not understand the words, Li's tone alarmed her.

"What?" she asked when he hung up.

"The government's declaring a national emergency. It's ordering a curfew to clear the streets, so military vehicles can transport personnel." He gestured to the cars surrounding them. "In a few minutes, the president will issue a statement. Then all these cars will compete for the exit lanes."

He picked up the phone, speaking in Chinese to the driver. Before he hung up, Lane felt the car swerve to the shoulder, kicking up gravel as it sped along the rough pavement. Even with the luxury suspension system, Lane bounced, knocking her head against the roof and window. Grinning, Li slid next to her.

"Hold on, it's going to be a bumpy ride."

They traveled that way for half a kilometer, narrowly missing an overheated cab that blocked their path, swerving to avoid a wide-bed truck and squealing to a stop as a scooter darted in front. Finally they came to the exit and turned right, taking a narrow road that led through a small town and up a winding mountain road.

"I know this area," Li said, leaning forward, sliding open the glass and giving directions to the driver in Chinese. At that moment, a shrill air raid siren shrieked its warning. Closing the glass, he settled back against Lane.

"We got here not a moment too soon. This road will be teeming with frustrated drivers as soon as they hear the siren or news bulletin."

"Will China bomb us?" She leaned against him, huddling for security.

Li shook his head. "This is more posturing. It's my guess they don't know your father's involved." He turned to watch her reaction. "Did you tell Chen about MacKenzie's visit?"

"Only a minute before you picked me up. Why?" She studied his face.

Tempted to explain, he stopped at the last moment, remembering his loyalties. He shrugged noncommittally.

"Just wondered."

The car lurched to a sudden stop, throwing Lane against Li. "Are you all right?" he asked. When she nodded, he slid open the glass and questioned the driver. No explanation was needed as a uniformed soldier tapped at the window. Li motioned not to worry, got out and spoke rapidly in the Taiwanese dialect, shouting over the siren to be heard.

When he returned, he said, "Get in the front seat." She moved slowly, suspiciously. "Hurry," he said, climbing behind the wheel.

"Where's the driver?"

"He's being requisitioned." To her worried expression, he said, "They need another man to help direct traffic."

As Li stepped on the gas, the limo leaped forward, peeling rubber on the pavement. Loud as it was, the squeal of its tires couldn't be heard over the siren's insistent wail.

The stretch fishtailed as Li steered it along the street that twisted into a mountain road. Trying to stay on the narrow path, he straddled the center line, weaving from one lane to the other as they climbed a steep grade.

"Where are we going?" she asked, catching her breath as she saw the drop-off in the early morning mist.

"We have to get off the road." He glanced at her, momentarily taking his eyes from the road. When he looked back, a mountain dog was in his path.

He swerved to avoid it, skidding, spinning the wheels on loose gravel. For what seemed like hours, the wheels slid, scrambling to pick up traction on the narrow shoulder. As they approached the chasm, she mouthed a quick prayer, thinking they were going over the ledge. Expecting to feel the weightlessness of the plunge, Lane squeezed her eyes shut and hunched over, bracing herself against the dashboard.

Suddenly she felt the wheels grab the pavement. Opening her eyes cautiously, she began breathing heavily, queasy with relief from missing the near dive. Li pulled out of the spin and sped up again, zigzagging along the winding road that had once served as a deer path. She looked at him accusingly but said nothing, too afraid he would take his eyes off the road again.

After another three kilometers, he abruptly crossed the road, swinging left, turning the wheel into the stand of bamboo at the roadside. Lane was pitched against the window. Bracing herself, she screamed and closed her eyes. The limo plunged through the trunks' green canopy, crashed through the tall grass, then reeled to a stop as the tires hit a boulder.

He drew a deep breath and turned to her. "I had to get us off the road."

She looked at him incredulously. "Yeah, but did you have

to throw off the alignment doing it?"

"No one'll find us here."

"I thought we just had to get off the road, not hide. Who are we running away from?"

His eyes sought hers. Wearing an amused grin, he pushed open his door.

"I want to show you something."

She studied him warily, finally deciding to trust him, no matter how erratic his actions. Did she have a choice? She opened her door, listening to the rustling bamboo scratch the limo's finish. Then she looked down at the heavy undergrowth as she got out, making mental wagers as to how many creepy-crawlies lurked beneath her high heels. Pushing aside the lush branches and fronds, Lane followed him through the jungle.

"Does Taiwan have any snakes?" When he nodded without replying, she asked, "Many?"

"You sure you want to hear?" His voice taunted as he tramped through the tall grass.

"No, but tell me, anyway."

"It depends who you talk to, but there are over a hundred varieties of snakes in Taiwan." She screeched, lifting her feet high with each step, watching the ground for any movement. Chuckling, he said, "Many of them hang from trees." She immediately looked up, frightfully checking each branch, and nearly tripped. "Bamboo snakes are particularly fond of dropping on their prey from. . . ."

"Bamboo," she finished sarcastically. "You're enjoying this, aren't you?"

His chuckle his answer, Lane forced herself not to think about it. Instead, she pushed on, keeping as close behind him as possible without getting slapped in the face with swinging branches.

A few feet farther into the jungle, they came to hand-hewn stone steps. Gazing up, she saw they continued as far as she could see before being choked from view by overgrowth.

"Where do they lead?"

"You'll find out," he said, smiling mysteriously.

She followed, climbing after him until they reached what she thought had been the top. There the steps turned at a right angle and again continued as far as she could see. This happened three times. Tiring, she lagged behind, breathing the fresh air, stopping to admire the remarkable vegetation. After two more sets of stairways, she rounded the corner to see yet another. Gazing up at the endless steps, she had only enough energy to put one foot numbly in front of the other.

The stairs were thickly-cut stone with wide gaps between where the mortar had worn away. From one of the deep crevices, a small blue flower bloomed. She bent to pick it, and a grayish black snake slithered in front of Lane's eyes. Straightening, she screamed and froze. The snake stood up as its hood slowly fanned out from its head.

"Stamp your feet," Li called from several steps ahead of her. Morbidly fascinated, she could not move. "Make noise to frighten it away."

The cobra's flared hood was hypnotic. After what seemed an eternity, Li came running down the stairs, pounding with each step. The vibrations scared off the snake. Retracting its sheathe, it slipped to the ground and undulated into the brush. Lane gasped for air, having been too afraid to breathe.

"Are you all right?"

She gave him a sickly laugh, still too breathless to speak. Leaning over, she put her hands on her knees and breathed deeply. Finally she stood up and stared him in the eye.

"This had better be worth it."

Laughing, he took her hand in his and began climbing

again. "Just another two flights—three, tops—and we're there."

After four more flights, they reached a large outcrop of rock. Totally out of breath, Lane asked, "Is that it?" He nodded as she studied the compelling formation. Staring at its phallic design, she said, "If it weren't so huge, it'd look like someone had carved it."

The place had a mystical quality to it. Though it was past dawn, the heavy vegetation blocked out the early morning light, enveloping them in the semi-gloom of a cathedral.

Forgetting how tired she was, she raced ahead of Li for the last few steps, noting a small cave beneath the rock. Several candle stubs had been stuck on smaller rocks with hot wax. The remains of half-burned incense sticks were still standing in small burners. She felt them. Though cold, they looked as if someone had just left them.

"What is this place?"

"The script's too old for me to read, but this character on the left says Buddha." Li pointed to three carved characters in the rock.

"It reminds me of Lover's Rock in Hong Kong. The ancients believed it cured infertility." She grinned. "Young couples still go there to pray for a baby."

Li looked at her curiously. "When I found this place, I had the feeling this stone was worshipped before Buddhism came to Taiwan." He ran his hand along its damp angles with shy reverence. "Call it superstition, but there's a magical quality about it." When he turned back to her, he saw she was rubbing her arms. "Cold?" Concerned, he put his arm around her shoulders.

She shook her head. "Goose bumps."

She could feel the hairs tingling on the back of her neck. A shudder passed through her, but she was not sure if it were from the eerie location or Li's closeness. Enclosed in their privacy, their eyes locked. For several moments, neither moved. Then looking away, Lane was the first to break the spell. She took a step toward the cave's incense burners.

"What gods are worshipped here?"

Following her, he put his hand on the back of her neck. Again she felt the hairs rise in a fight-or-flight genetic response. With all the excitement of the past day, adrenaline was coursing though her veins. He turned her toward him slowly, gradually drawing his arms around her. By imperceptible degrees, their mouths drew closer, until finally they met as predestined in a timeless merging of ancient and present, past and future, yin and yang.

Clinging to each other, they sank onto the cave's basalt floor, its ground hallowed by centuries of worship. Its flat surface an altar, its natural planes and fractures were a yielding bed. Conceived by the infinite, they offered themselves to the divinity of their love.

Lane felt the transcendence of time and space sweep over her as Li's hard muscles pressed around her, through her, mingling the juices of their bodies with the essence of their souls. In a ritual as old as life, they renewed themselves in each other's being.

Lying in Li's arms, Lane traced his shoulders with her fingertips, running her fingers down his well-defined chest, enjoying the symmetry of his body after feeling its power. She sighed, reaching to the downy pubic hairs, playfully entwining them in her fingers, lightly stroking his masculinity with an absentminded nonchalance, remembering the urgency of their caresses only minutes before. Again she sighed with satisfaction as she turned on her side to watch him. Tickling his ear with her hair, she woke him. He reached for her with a smile.

"The next one's for you," he said, raising up on his hip and fondling her breast with a singleness of purpose. He moved his fingers in a circular pattern, round and round her breasts as if they were satin ribbons wound about her areolas. Gently kneading her nipples to erection, he then laved them with his soft tongue, his fingers searching out her creamy center and arousing her to orgasm. As she moaned softly with delight, he entered her again, slowly bringing her to a higher ascendancy than their mountain-top aerie. They climaxed together, sealing their love with a bond surpassing marriage certificates or contracts of convenience.

When they lay spent, they dozed in each other's arms. Lane opened her eyes drowsily. Li was watching her, a gentle smile playing at his lips. Gone was the tension from his jaw, the bitterness from his eyes. He lifted her to a sitting position and pressed her to his chest, their hearts communing without words. They clung together, swaying imperceptibly to a tune only they heard. Then with a kiss, he said what was on both their minds.

"It's time we were getting back. The air raid must be over by now." He helped her to her feet. "We can radio from the car to see if the blockade's been lifted. Maybe your father's been allowed to land."

"Do you think we'll be driving to the airport?" She looked at her wrinkled clothes scattered on the rocks.

He couldn't restrain a chuckle at her forlorn face. "No, but stranger things have happened. China isn't known for its rationality."

His good humor contagious, Lane smiled at their situation, refusing to look at its dark side. So what if China were embargoing Taiwan, Chen were holding Justin hostage, her crumpled clothes were a give-away of her tryst with Li? She was a satisfied woman, a lucky, no, a blessed woman, she corrected, a contented woman, confident of the outcome, whatever it may be.

They dressed, then arm-in-arm they descended the stairs, returning to reality step by step. When they got inside the limo, Li leaned across the console, took her hand in his and kissed her palm.

"Lane, before we go back, I want you to know I love you."

"And I love you," she said fervently. Her hand still in his, she drew him nearer and kissed his lips. "Whatever happens."

Frustrated at the quickly-passing morning, Li said, "There's so much to tell you, but. . . ."

She put her fingers to his lips, silencing him. "There'll be time for that later, years." She kissed him, adding solemnly, "I promise."

He sighed, kissed her fingers again, then picked up the microphone and called the Bureau. Lane watched the tension return to his jaw as the muscles knotted in his neck and the vessels stood out against his temples.

"What is it?" she asked when he hung up.

Giving her a brief smile, he said, "Don't worry about your crumpled clothes; we're not going to the airport. Your father's still in Guam."

She returned his smile, both of them knowing that wasn't her cause for concern. "Does that mean the blockade's still on?"

He nodded. "The airport's closed." A plan formulating in his mind, he added, "There's nothing to do but go . . ." he hesitated, almost saying home, instead saying, "back to Taipei."

Lane caught the nuance in his words. Stiffening, she began to realize the new level of anguish their separation would cause. She threw her arms around his neck in a moment of weakness.

"Li, I can't go back to Chen," she nodded toward the

mountain, "not after this morning."

His heart aching, he pressed her to him silently as his resolve deepened. Then he gently loosened her grip and held her at arm's length. Squeezing her fingers so tightly, they hurt, he confided.

"I have a plan."

Her eyes misting, she looked up at him expectantly. He shook his head.

"I can't tell you yet." Correcting himself, he said, "I'm not sure of it yet. I haven't worked out all the details, but like I promised in the hospital, I'll make you happy, Lane. I swear it. Just be brave a little longer."

She took a deep breath, straightened her shoulders and sat back in her seat. With a perky smile, she said, "Let's go. I want to end this limbo as soon as we can."

Surprised at her abrupt show of independence, he gave her an admiring laugh. Still chuckling, he started the engine and backed out into the mountain road's traffic.

"This is why I raced here last night." He gave her a devilish grin. "I didn't want to share our parking space with anyone."

Looking at the passing cars, Lane was relieved no one had found them. Privacy was at a premium in Taiwan, especially during an imposed curfew. Snug in their nest, she had been oblivious to the thousands of desperate travelers searching for a road stop. Now that she saw the vehicles, she realized it was a small miracle no one has stumbled on them. She looked at Li with new respect, delighted with his foresight.

As they approached the town, they saw that the barricade had been removed. Slowing for a flashing amber light, they paused as a uniformed man ran toward them, waving his arms to stop. When Li double-parked, the grinning chauffeur opened the driver's door.

"Let's get in the back seat," Li said to Lane, smiling.

# CHAPTER 14

Though traffic heading into the city was light compared to the exodus from Taipei, the ride seemed endless. The closer they got, the more agitated Lane became. In the hours it took to drive back, they discussed the situation Chen had placed them in.

"He won't let me leave Taiwan with Justin," she said, small furrows beginning to show in her forehead. "The DNA analysis states he's the biological father. Without his permission, Justin can't leave the country." Rubbing her temples, she groaned. "He's so hung up on lineage. If he feels that strongly about a son, why didn't he have children before now?"

Li took a deep breath and looked into her eyes, wondering how she would take the news. "He did."

"What?" She whirled to face him, seeing if he were serious since she could not believe her ears. "When?"

Again he debated how much to tell. "Almost a year ago. Teng-hui's his baby."

"Mei-ling admitted it?"

His somber expression told her it was true. Still she grabbed his arm, needing reassurance. If his expression didn't convince her, his nod did.

After he had told her the story, Lane shook her head. "That man is deranged." Then as another idea flitted through her mind, she shuddered. "Li, does that mean his DNA is the same as Justin's?" Before he could reply, she slunk back against the seat, feeling defeated.

"Nooo." His speech reflected his misgivings about

telling her the whole truth.

Brightening, Lane sat up. "No?" Then his long pause irritated her. "What? This is important!"

Li relayed what the DNA specialist had told him, concluding, "So the genetic makeup of an uncle and a nephew are entirely different."

"Then Mei-ling was lying; Chen bribed someone to falsify the analyses."

Li's skeptical expression made her uneasy.

"Right?" she asked, needing his endorsement. After another annoying pause, she repeated, "Right?"

"Maybe." His face was noncommittal.

"Maybe?! It's yes or no. Which is it?"

He decided to tell her. "There's only one genetic exception to the rule in paternity cases. Testing's inconclusive between fathers and sons." He looked directly into her eyes, piercing her incredulity.

As she met his gaze with stunned understanding, her jaw went slack. She paused, letting his words' full meaning sink in. Then she put her arms around him.

"Oh, Li, is it possible Chen's your father?"

He shrugged his shoulders, his troubled eyes looking into hers. "He's my mother's brother." Pausing, he chewed his lip as he recalled, "They never got along. There was always an underlying friction, but . . . incest? Rape? The possibilities are unthinkable."

She tried to be sympathetic, but she did not know how to comfort him. The memory of her own rape was still too vivid, angering her yet causing shame, as if it were somehow her wrongdoing. She thought of telling Li, offering evidence of Chen's abusive behavior, but she was afraid Li might shrink away, feeling she was unclean.

To hide her crimson cheeks, she lay her head on his chest,

neither of them speaking, until finally she said, "It could happen in any family." Then knowing how weak that must sound, she tried again. "Was there anything else that might give us a clue?"

"The obvious, he's kept a position at the trade company for me, even though he must know I work. . . ." Li stopped himself too late before committing the cardinal transgression.

She stiffened, letting her arms fall from him. There it was again, that same irritating distrust.

"Who do you work for, Li?" When he did not answer, she pressed, "Why will you share your body with me, share your soul, but not tell me where you work? It's unfathomable."

"Lane, please don't."

"It's beyond reason. It's infuriating!" In the silence that followed, she swallowed her anger, pleading, "Do you have so little faith in me?"

He said softly, "It's not that I don't trust you. I. . . ." He searched for the reason. "I made a promise to myself that. . . ." Realizing anything he said sounded like a lame excuse, he defaulted to the truth. "It's what you already guessed. I work for the National Security Bureau." He chewed his lip, admitting, "I was afraid you'd think I used you."

"Did you?" she shot back.

Deciding to clear his conscience, he said, "Sometimes, yes."

She took a deep breath as she digested it, then paused. "Was that your only reason for wanting to marry me?"

Pulling her closer, he crushed her to him, kissing her roughly, angrily. Then their kiss mellowed into a turbulence of indecision and love, passion giving way to tenderness. The kiss blurring the lines of defense between them, Lane responded to his wordless confession, once again losing all sense of time.

As she felt the limo roll to a stop, she glanced through the heavily tinted windows and saw Chen's house. Not home, she thought with a dry laugh. It had never been home. Still in each other's arms, she and Li looked at each other joylessly, feeling the separation long before relinquishing their embrace. Disappointed that the moment was ending, she was glad, at least, for the privacy the dark windows provided. She disentangled herself from Li and rearranged her clothing, trying to smooth out the wrinkles, present some semblance of dignity.

He grabbed her arms again desperately. "Lane, don't go in. That man's sick. I'm afraid for your safety." He drew her closer. "Stay with me."

Waiting for the chauffeur to open the door gave her time to compose her thoughts. She studied Li. How can I leave him and walk back in that house? Struggling with the question, the answer came from within. If I want Justin, I have to. It's that simple. Her spine stiffened as her jaw set with determination.

"I love you, Li, but no matter how much I want to be with you, my first duty's to protect our son." She sat apart, anticipating the approaching driver. A wry smile at her lips, she added, "Chen won't hurt me if he knows my father's nearby."

As the door opened, Lane saw Chen coming towards them. She took a deep breath, bracing herself for the confrontation, and inadvertently caught Li's scent in her nostrils. It triggered so many memories, she almost tripped stepping out. Li emerged stiffly, standing only millimeters from her elbow. How can anyone not sense the animal tension between us, she wondered, still tingling from their embrace. She glanced at Chen, realizing he was no fool. Of course he knew. Anyone watching them together would. As his eyes probed hers, she stared back defiantly.

"Where's Senator MacKenzie?" he asked, his eyes crackling like blistering charcoals.

"The airport was closed," Li said, knowing that was not news to Chen.

Suddenly she wanted to spit out all her festering hatred. Without forethought, she launched into the topic at hand: fatherhood.

"Yes, my baba," she stressed the relationship, "has been delayed."

Wearing a smirk, Chen turned toward Li for male collusion. "Women," he muttered, as if needing no explanation for dismissing her remark. Then humoring her, he said, "Yes, Lane, we all know MacKenzie's your father." His tone smugly patronized her for stating the obvious.

She swallowed her rage though his unwincing chauvinism galled her. "Yes, we do," she conceded, raising her voice, "but do we know who Li's father is?" That got his attention. His head snapped as he turned toward her. She answered with a sickeningly sweet smile.

When Li also stared openly at him, he answered nonchalantly. "Is that rhetorical?" Met by direct stares and silence, Chen asked with a nervous laugh, "What kind of game are you playing?"

"Who's Li's father?"

Chen looked from her to Li and back again. "Why, Yang Tzu-Chyang, my sister's husband, of course."

Li picked up the gauntlet. "Then why do Teng-hui and Justin have the same DNA?"

Without flinching, Chen shot back, "Because they're both your sons!"

He said it with such authority that Lane was speechless.

Her jaw went slack as she considered the possibility. It was plausible, much more so than Li's story. Her eyes darted nervously as she thought it through. Could Li be playing her for a fool? Again?

"Not according to Mei-ling," Li said evenly.

Chen vowed to kill the whore, but later. Now he had to concentrate. Using the tones of one morally outraged, he demanded, "What lies are you telling my wife?"

"You knew when Justin was tested he would have your DNA because you and I have the same genetic make-up . . . Baba." He spit out the word as if it were venom he had sucked from a snakebite.

"What kind of nonsense is this?" Playing the righteously indignant victim, he continued, "If your mother were only alive to hear you now."

White with rage, Lane retaliated as the truth became clear. "What would she say? That you had raped her as you raped me?"

Both men looked at her in horror. Chen, because she had guessed his first secret and admitted the second. Li, because her disclosure shocked his sensibilities. Without a moment's hesitation, he went to her side.

"Is this true?" he asked gently.

She forced herself to meet his eyes, still afraid of his rejection, and nodded. Li took her hand in his, turned to Chen and repeated the question, his eyes fiercely challenging him.

"This is preposterous!" Chen said, sneering at them. "My wife and her lover are fabricating lies, plotting against me." Turning his back on them, Chen started for the house.

His eyes steely, Li said, "If it's so preposterous, let's have your DNA tested against mine." As Chen kept walking toward the safety of his house, Li called, "Turn around, you coward!" His gait never faltered. In two strides, Li caught up with him, twisted his arm behind his back and forced him to listen.

Chen's aide bolted from the doorway, racing toward Li with a personal vengeance. The driver quickly stepped beside Li, coolly standing sentry, his uniformed presence enough to stop the aide from interfering, though the aide stood within arm's reach, itching to do battle.

Trying to regain his dignity, Chen threw off Li's arm and casually lit a cigarette, motioning to his aide to relax. The man reluctantly crossed his arms, waiting like an attack dog for his master's signal. The last thing Chen wanted to do was lose face. Inhaling deeply, he filled his chest with false pride as he thought out a plan. He knew it would be weeks before Taipei recovered from the political morass and clinics re-opened for routine tests. He hid a smirk. By that time, Lane and Tian-syang will be in Macao with me.

Speaking with as much authority as he could muster, he said, "If it'd make my wife happy, I'd be glad to comply."

Struggling to keep from putting his hands around Chen's neck, Li demanded, "If you want to make Lane happy, why did you rape her?"

Chen's eyes opened wide as he spread his arms out in a gesture of innocence. "Since when is it rape for a husband to love his wife?"

Li sucked air through his teeth, unable to retaliate.

Lane answered for him. "You call it love when you raped me in the hospital while I was still recovering from delivery?!" Her anger kept her from caring that the driver heard. "And you," she said, turning to the aide, "stood by and listened, you perverted creep."

Though he spoke little English, he reacted to her tone, moving uncomfortably in his ill-fitting suit. Remembering the unexpected set-back Lane had had, Li realized her words were true. He also recalled the aide's actions in the hospital. Not waiting for more evidence, Li's right arm caught his jaw, knocking out two of his front teeth.

He turned to Chen. "Only family honor prevents me from doing what I'd like to you."

The older man dropped his lit cigarette, its tip burning a hole in his pants on its descent. Still Li's eyes burned deeper, knowing the truth yet unable to prove it.

"But when the analyses confirm my suspicions, I'll personally see to it you're never able to rape another woman. I'll rip off your motherfucking dick with my bare hands." Interpreting Chen's strangled sounds as his reply, Li turned to Lane. "Get Justin. You're leaving with me."

She paused to give him a supportive smile. Then her jaw tightened and her eyes squinted with loathing as she passed Chen, her nearness to him a challenge to reach out and stop her. She felt his hot breath as she passed close, daring him to touch her, prevent her from leaving. She stared down the aide as she walked toward the door and took Justin from Mildred's arms. The older woman spit on the ground, splashing Lane's shoes, then ducked inside. Lane saw Li make a move toward the house then check himself. As Lane passed Chen on the way back, he was unable to keep still.

"You're my wife. Don't act like a whore." He faced Li. "You'll never get away with it. You can't steal a man's wife, Nephew."

Li laughed mirthlessly. "Nephew! What a joke, Baba, but you have a valid point. You can't steal a man's wife, and by all that's right, Lane is my wife."

"Not legally," Chen taunted, "and that's all that matters." He grabbed Lane so quickly around the waist, the baby screamed with fright. "You're not going anywhere."

Tightening her grip on the baby with one hand, she

slapped Chen with the other, the sound intensified by the stunned silence that followed. Nothing could have wounded his self-esteem more. Stepping out of his reach, she watched him with mutinous eyes.

"You said it yourself, Chen. I'm your xiao taitai. I can't be your wife." Tilting her head toward Li, she explained. "His first wife's in China." Again facing Chen, she said, "I'm taking my baby and leaving. If Chinese law contests it, the US senate will have something to say, especially regarding China's human rights policies. When my father calls, have the message forwarded through Li."

She stepped into the limo as Li and the driver followed, neither of them turning his back on Chen until they were safely inside. Li leaned forward, giving the driver instructions. He then sat back, tentatively touching Justin's smooth cheek.

"Whatever the cost, having the three of us together's worth it." Allowing the stillness of the moment to subdue her rage, she nodded. "Can I hold him?" he asked softly, his eyes never leaving the baby.

She relinquished the squirming bundle with a smile. "You handle him like a pro," she said, watching Li calm his son.

With a wistful smile, he said "I've had practice." Then his tone bitter, he added, "Just with the wrong baby: my brother, not my son."

Lane shook her head, unable to comprehend what thoughts must be going through his mind. Looking out the window absently, she noted traffic was as bad as it had been for the previous twenty-four hours. Taipei's populace was still trying to escape, even if the CKS airport were closed. Her mouth twisted wryly at the parallel. She had just escaped Chen. For now that was enough. Too weary to think about escaping the island, she leaned against Li's shoulder, the three of them a family for the first time.

The peace lasted only a moment before Li's cellular phone rang. Lane took back the baby as Li spoke in Chinese to President Fu. Clenching his teeth, he hung up, gave the driver revised instructions, then turned back to Lane.

"I'm sorry, but something's come up." He rubbed his forehead thoughtfully. "I'd like to take you home with me, but. . . ."

As his words died off, she nodded her understanding.

"I'll get you settled in a hotel, then I've got to leave."

He slumped back, putting his arm around her and the baby, drawing as much strength from Lane as she did from him. The driver turned on the radio when the silence continued. Though Lane needed no reminder of Taiwan's grave situation, she listened uneasily to ICRT's report.

"Leading the news this hour is an update on the cross-strait tension. We have just received unconfirmed reports that combat planes are continuing to fire on the islands. Again unverified, the casualty count is high. ROC troops are reportedly returning the missile fire, while fortifying defenses for an expected beachhead attack as amphibious vessels wait offshore. According to our sources, People's Liberation Army paratroopers landed on Kinmen and Matsu Islands thirty minutes ago. More on that as the news progresses."

Lane whispered hoarsely, "Is this war?"

Li's mouth was grim. "Not if I can help it."

"On the business front, the TAIEX is closed today despite investors' angry protests. Juang Fang-Rung, Director of the Department of Finance, denied rumors that the market's closing is a response to yesterday's rapid devaluation of the NT when it slipped to its lowest point in twenty-five years. 'Power outages are the sole reason,' said Juang amid disclaimers of an air-raid, blaming the electric company for the recent black-out. 'Once the energy crisis has been corrected, the computers can go back on-line and the market will re-open.' Meanwhile depositors are losing confidence in other financial institutions as several investment and trust companies, notably the Export-Import Bank of the Republic of China, have not opened for business this morning. The bank's chairman is unavailable for comment."

"In the international news," continued the reporter, "the US is demanding that the PRC cease its air and naval blockade, allowing US citizens to leave and a peace-keeping mission to enter Taiwan. In a phone interview earlier this morning, ICRT spoke with US Senator MacKenzie. The US senator, whose flight has been delayed in Guam, had this to say."

Chills ran up Lane's back as she recognized her father's voice and rhetoric.

"The two China's must be reconciled. Though this is a departure from US non-intervention policy, we must put an end to the fifty-year-old rivalry. The PRC calls the attempted assassination an act of war, while Taiwan denounces China's blockade and pending invasion of Kinmen as acts of aggression. The US wishes to be a neutral yet benevolent arbitrator.

"Speaking on behalf of the president, America can no longer stand by passively when security in the western Pacific is severely compromised. The US is prepared to act as mediator in an attempt to de-escalate the situation and resolve the conflict," his tone became menacing, "even should it involve bringing in a carrier or several F-15s from Okinawa."

Lane's eyes met Li's over the sleeping head of their son.

Infuriated at losing face in front of his staff, Chen denounced his aide's incompetence, haranguing him long after the limo was out of sight. The gap-toothed man remained silent, merely working his sore jaw and staring forlornly at the bloody incisors in his hand.

"And see a dentist," Chen finished unsympathetically, "if you can find one who hasn't evacuated."

Chen slammed into the house, going directly to his office. Running his hand nervously through his silver-shot hair, he tried to forget Lane's accusations and embarrassing departure, concentrating instead on more critical issues.

How could he avoid Zheng's wrath? He reviewed his options, finally deciding he would blame the belated message on the Hong Kong relay, flatly denying any responsibility in the mix-up. Zheng will believe me, he thought, wiping his forehead with his handkerchief.

He quickly typed the manufactured explanation and faxed it to a different agent in Hong Kong, not wanting to alert the fall guy of his accusations. It's this indirect system that's to blame, he reassured himself. Zheng can't fault me for any misconduct. But even if he does, I have a scapegoat. Pai Pie-Ying will take the blame for not forwarding news of MacKenzie's flight in time to abort the blockade. He mopped his brow and neck, loosening his tie and unbuttoning his collar. His starched shirt was no longer crisp, and his trousers had lost their crease. Chen, the GQ exemplar, looked as unstrung as he felt.

He caught his reflection in the mirror. Who is that? His fingers traced the deep lines near his mouth, the jowls hanging more prominently than he recalled. His skin looked pale against the contrast of his hair. And, what's that? He touched his hairline gingerly. His forehead seemed to be growing as his hair receded. I look old, he concluded wearily, turning on the television to forget.

As a special news bulletin interrupted the program, Chen's forehead broke out in a sweat. My god! Hadn't they gotten the first fax at all? How could they launch this attack so quickly? Why didn't they allow negotiation? Sighing, he fell back against the leather sofa. His eyes bleary, Chen saw his future.

It's over. My career's over. The PRC will draw world disapproval. They'll lose face, and Zheng'll blame me for not informing him in time.

Li stormed into President Fu's office like an irate customer returning flawed merchandise. His adrenaline pumping, he had something to say before he lost his nerve.

"If we move. . . ."

"Sit down," said Fu, sitting behind his impressive desk.

"No, sir," said Li, still standing, "I. . . ."

Fu pointed to the chair, palm up, a polite but firm injunction to sit. When Li did as directed, he asked, "How much is the radio reporting?" Fu grunted when Li told him, momentarily resting his chin on his folded hands. In a somber voice, he said, "The casualty count's high." His eyes leveled with Li's. "All military personnel have been taken hostage on Kinmen and Matsu. The mainland deployed enough missiles to sink the islands."

"Was it an error? Did some young recruits get trigger happy?"

Fu shook his head, his exaggerated frown showing his disdain. "Their deployment was sanctioned by the PRC Central Military Commission."

Li closed his eyes as the words sank into his mind. "And Zheng has two key supporters in the army, the Chief of Staff and Defense Minister. They're the vice-chairmen of the CMC." He was beginning to understand.

"Apparently Chen didn't inform him of MacKenzie's visit. Why?"

"I doubt he knew, at least not until it was too late."

Fu stood up and paced. "I received a call an hour ago. The PLA has to protect its assault, controlling not only the Taiwan Strait, but also the skies. Using the islands as a base for attack, China can build up its military arsenal, reassemble its troops, then invade Taiwan."

Lines showed around Li's eyes that had not been there the day before. His voice a monotone, he said, "What are they asking?"

"They've demanded my resignation and Taiwan's surrender."

Li shot out of his seat. "We haven't declared war. How can we surrender?!"

Listing their defeats, Fu said, "Can you think of an alternative? With a naval blockade in force and tentative control of the skyways, the mainland has us cut off by sea and air. Do you have any ideas?"

Li incorporated the new information into his original scheme. Finally he said, "Yes, we have world censure on our side."

"But no time!" Fu thundered. "Zheng's calling for an immediate answer."

"So we stall Zheng long enough to generate global sympathy."

Not flinching, Li's bloodshot eyes met the president's serenely. His lips creased in a caricature of a smile.

Something in Li's quiet attitude made Fu sit down again. Not moving a muscle, he pressed the button under his desktop, recording the conversation.

"How?"

"We stall until the US Cavalry arrives with MacKenzie."

His skepticism evident in his expression, Fu said, "You know Beijing's threatened to deploy missiles across the

Taiwan Strait, aimed at Taipei, if we invite foreign interference." He lit a cigarette, his aide being nowhere in sight. "With a population of nearly six million packed into this basin, can you imagine the carnage if even one missile struck?"

Li's tired eye twinkled. "If all goes well, we may be able to pull this off without US intervention."

He exhaled quickly to answer. "I'm listening." He took a long drag, inhaling the acrid smoke through his mouth and nose.

Li also took a deep breath. "We stage your assassination."

Choking, Fu said, "What?!" He reached quickly for the alarm button, fear winning out over reason.

Li could not believe the response. "After six years, don't you trust me?"

"Of course," he said, in that favorite uncle tone he used, "you just gave me a start." Chuckling, he added, "It's not every day someone walks in and recommends my assassination." As his aide rushed into the room, Fu greeted him jovially. "Wang, you're just in time." Leaving his aide confused about the distress call, Fu nodded to Li. "Go ahead, explain your idea of staging my assassination."

Debating whether to voice his idea in front of the assistant, Li finally shrugged off his reticence. "All right, here's how we gain time and world empathy. First we hold a joint meeting of all the military forces on the building's grounds—to announce your resignation. We close the area to traffic and encourage media coverage."

"It's already sounding too dangerous," Wang protested. "The secret service police won't be able to control the crowds."

Conceding, Li raised his eyebrows and sighed. "There's a risk factor involved, but it's warranted." When he saw Fu about to interrupt him, he spoke quickly. "You'll be ready to announce your resignation, but just as you get to the podium, one of our men will pretend to shoot you." He raised his hands as if fending off another protest. "With blanks, of course."

"Li, that's crazy." Fu stood up again and paced. "The plan's got too many variables. Any one of a hundred things could go wrong."

"You'll be safe. The grounds will be crawling with your secret service men."

Fu stumped out his cigarette and lit another. "Out of curiosity, what'd be the purpose of this?"

Li's tired eyes never wavered as they met Fu's. "We accuse the PRC of attempting your assassination. We embarrass China publicly. With enough media coverage, the world will see it!" His eyes lit up in his enthusiasm. "Taiwan gains global sympathy and therefore time for negotiations. And," he continued, excitement mounting, "with proper handling of this incident, it's possible that one assassination attempt could cancel out the other."

Still concentrating on the earlier points of the plan, Wang was not listening to its consequences. Covering, he said, "What would be the repercussions?"

Li hid his impatience at the aide's short attention span. "Two things, loss of face for the mainland and a possible end to the conflict."

"I don't know, sir." Wang addressed Fu, drawing mental pictures with his hands. "Worst case scenario: this plan fails, you're wounded—or killed," he paused, letting that sink in, "and China launches an immediate air strike. The mainland has a combined naval air and air force of nearly 5500 planes. No matter that their MiG-19s are dinosaurs, they outnumber us. Even including our new F-16s and Mirage 2000-5s, that's a ratio of ten to one. As of our latest reconnaissance, China has more than sixty intermediate-range ballistic missiles. And if they should invade, their manpower's astounding. Regarding ground troops, the mainland's outnumber Taiwan's at almost seven to one." Wang's expression openly challenged Li. "China's military dwarfs ours! It's absurd to provoke them."

"You're missing the point," Li said, defending his strategy. "One attempted assassination would void the other. This would avert conflict, not invite it. Any military imbalance would be moot."

Warming to the idea, Fu thought out loud, punctuating his reflection with drags on his cigarette. "If we wouldn't need to retaliate, we wouldn't have to reveal the arsenal's condition. Once the mainland learns half our weapons are outdated, and the other half don't work, Taiwan's open to invasion."

Li's jaw worked angrily, though he kept silent. Saving face, that's all he really cares about, not resisting assault but saving face. Fu doesn't want China to learn the truth. We're safe only as long as they think we can defend ourselves. Li sniffed. Our defense system's a paper tiger, but all he cares about is saving face. Repressing a sigh, he struggled to maintain a bland expression.

"And should push come to shove," continued Fu, oblivious to Li's disapproval, "the US will do our fighting for us. MacKenzie's already threatened to bring in a carrier or several F-15s."

"Washington may be prepared to act as mediator," said Wang, "and MacKenzie may want to protect his family members, but the US would never jeopardize its trade agreement with China. Why should it defend Taiwan, especially when President Dawson's accepted so many PRC reelection contributions?"

"That's a good question," said Fu, sobering.

"Why? Because it's in Washington's best interests." Li met their narrowed eyes easily.

"What do you mean?" asked Fu.

Li refreshed their memories of the Macao fund-raiser tape, finishing, "US President Dawson will back any nation that can prove sovereignty over the Tiaoyutai islands."

Wang sniffed disdainfully. "So?"

"So if Taiwan offers irrefutable proof of its sovereignty, the US will scramble to its defense . . . even against the PRC."

"Why?" Wang's scorn was as patent as the shine on his Italian loafers.

"Ever since the Japanese began opposing the US presence in Okinawa, Washington's needed a secure naval base and a reliable fuel source in the Pacific," Li said, again hiding his impatience with the Yuan legislator's pampered son. "With its vast natural oil resources, the Tiaoyutai islands could provide both. The US considers the islands crucial to southeast Asian stability."

"Your summary's interesting, Li, but evidence of Taiwanese sovereignty is circumstantial, at best. Except for historical reference or US policy during the Fifties and Sixties, Taiwan's dominion of the islands is unsubstantiated." Though a cigarette burned in the ashtray, Fu held another to his lips.

Wang hastened to light it as he added, "Washington would demand irrefutable proof that Taiwan doesn't have."

"Until now." Li paused, then reached into his vest pocket, producing the yellowed paper from Ci-xi. "This document predates the Shimonoseki Treaty of 1895, referring to a land grant the Dowager Empress made in 1893. This proves Tiaoyutai belongs to Sheng Hsuan-hui . . . my great grandfather."

Fu and Wang both stared at him, open-mouthed. Wang found his tongue first. "Says you and who else?"

Li tossed the paper on Fu's desk. Ignoring the aide, Li addressed the president. "Read it for yourself, sir. This is the antidote to the PRC's aggression. With this document as proof of the ROC's sovereignty of the Tiaoyutai islands, the US would defend Taiwan, should it come to that. However, if we follow my initial plan, there'll be no need to seek US intervention. One attempted assassination would cancel out the other."

Fu unfolded the paper and read it thoroughly, his eyes darting suspiciously from word to word. "But even if this document's authentic. . . ."

"Which it is," said Li.

Fu continued despite the interruption. "Then the Tiaoyutai islands belong to you, not Taiwan."

Li shook his head. "Legally, it'd be difficult to prove. Possession of this document, not paternal descent, is my only evidence of ownership." He smiled wryly, thinking of the legal battles to be waged once his uncle—scratch that, father—learned of the paper's existence. "Besides, I couldn't afford the legal fees to fight the PRC in court. Taiwan can. If it's in the nation's best interests, I'll relinquish any rights to Taiwan."

"Mind if I keep this?" said Fu peremptorily, about to whisk it into his top drawer.

"Actually, I'd like to hold on to it a while longer." Li held out his hand, palm up, until Fu reluctantly passed it back. "This is the contingency plan, should tomorrow's strategy fail. I'd prefer not to use it unless it's necessary."

"With all the media coverage," said Fu, "it would be an ideal time to make the disclosure."

Li agreed with a hesitant nod. "All right, I'll turn the document over to you tomorrow if . . . if we need to make it public."

They finished discussing logistics, then Fu dismissed Li, clapping him on the shoulder. "Good plan. Plans. Creative—not the kind of thinking we're used to! We'll consider the Tiaoyutai document the alternate plan, and in the meantime we'll begin working on tomorrow's troop assembly."

When Li was out of hearing range, Fu turned to his aide. "Spearhead this campaign, Wang. You're in charge. Yang'll be your support. I want you to choose the marksman. Don't even point him out to me. I want this attempt to look realistic. Make arrangements to assemble the troops tomorrow, and bc sure to invite the press. We want total coverage for my—er, resignation. Remember, the world's our audience."

"Yes, sir."

"And find out what you can regarding the validity of his document."

"Yes, sir." Wang nodded and saluted crisply. Leaving the office, he sneaked out the building, hurried to a pay phone and dialed.

The ringing woke him from a restless nap. He yawned, drawing his hands across his eyes and through his hair. "Yes."

"There're several new developments." Wang described Li's document and explained the details of the assembly, finishing with the coup de grace.

"Xiexie," he said, his index finger stroking his small nose. "Call me in an hour for your instructions."

Hanging up in Wang's ear, he began chuckling bitterly. So Li had the family deed, the rights to the Tiaoyutai islands, the ring in President Dawson's nose . . . and Lane and Tian-syang. The chuckle devolved into sobbing, then into a hellish laugh as Chen swore revenge. Li would fall tomorrow, regardless of who accompanied him. The document was his death warrant. And whether Fu resigned or were killed, without its leader, Taiwan would collapse like a paper lantern. He faxed Zheng with his plan.

Traffic was still chaotic, but thanks to the mass exodus it was lighter and no longer grid-locked. Though he dreaded the confrontation, Li decided to drive home and tell Mei-ling the recent developments. Letting her stay had been a bad idea, he realized. It complicated things.

Unlocking the front door, he heard a piercing scream. He groped along the wall for the light switch.

"Mei-ling?!"

"Li?" Between tears, she whimpered in the dark like a frightened dog.

Switching on the lights, Li was not prepared for the sight. Mei-ling looked dazed, her eyes wide and glassy, her permed hair standing out in comical tufts. Her clothes looked as if she had slept in them. Scanning the room, he saw the apartment looked almost as bad. Magazines were strewn across the furniture. A chair was upturned on the floor. Near it lay a vase, fragmented among crumpled flowers and spilled water.

"What happened?" She tried to answer but was unable to speak coherently. Alarmed, he shook her. "Where's the baby?"

She gasped, trying to catch her breath but couldn't stop crying. Beside himself with worry, Li sensed he would have to comfort her before she would talk. He walked over to where she was kneeling on the sofa and gingerly put his arms around her.

"Oh, Li, she . . . she. . . ."

"Who? Teng-hui's amah? Is that who you're talking about? Did the amah take Teng-hui somewhere?"

"No. Yes."

Trying to communicate, Mei-ling shook her head no then nodded yes. She swallowed and forced her breathing to calm down. Then the fear reclaimed her, and she began twisting and pulling at his lapels. Looking up at him with terror-stricken eyes, she frantically explained.

"It's Taitai! She's back. Last night when you didn't come home, I slept in your bed."

Irritated she had not listened to him, he gave her a sharp look. She crumpled against him contritely.

"Li, I can't stay in Taitai's room. She . . . she comes to me in my sleep."

"Mei-ling, that's enough of this nonsense!" Angry with her for frightening him, he let go her shoulders with a shove. "Where's Teng-hui?"

Struggling to gain control of her emotions, she said, "He's at his amah's apartment."

"What's he doing there?"

She stiffly tried to control her facial mannerisms before admitting, "The amah was afraid for him and took him home with her." Looking up at him pitifully, she said, "Taitai came to me last night. She told me Teng-hui must be with his father, and I must be with her." She choked on the prediction for Li. "You must . . . must be. . . ."

Tears engulfing her, she struggled to finish. He impatiently got up from the sofa and started for the door.

"Where are you going?"

"To get the baby."

She ran to him, throwing her arms around him, pressing against him, crying. "No, don't leave me. She'll come for me, Li. She'll come for me!"

Incensed at her latest trickery, he pulled her arms from him like tentacles, one at a time. "Stop it! I'm sick of your lies. Did you think scaring the amah was a joke?" He studied her, his lip curling with disgust. "You'd be laughable if you weren't so dangerous. But jeopardizing the baby to keep us together is going too far."

"Let me come with you. I can't stay here alone."

He started for the door again, then did an about-face. "Since you don't like it here, get out. Take the money I gave you and go to a hotel. Don't be here when I get back."

The apartment resounded with the slamming door. Mei-ling dropped to her knees, muttering incoherently, her hands shaking, covering her mouth. She rocked back and forth, grieving for herself, for Li.

"Amit'ofo, Amit'ofo," she mumbled, "protect me."

The phone's incessant ringing lifted her from despair. She got off her knees mechanically, answering in a faraway voice.

"Is Li there?" inquired Chen.

Surprised, she whispered, "No, he. . . ."

"You ungrateful whore! What kind of double-crossing game do you think you're playing?"

She started muttering, small sobs interrupting her guttural sounds. Too vehement in his attack, he knew he had to check his anger before it ruined his plan.

"It's all right," he soothed. "Don't cry. It's all right." But when her mumbling did not subside, he grew impatient again, shouting, "Mei-ling, stop it!"

His temper shocked her into confessing. "I didn't mean to tell Li. I swear I didn't mean to." Her words tumbling out, she described what had happened, both the day before and moments earlier. "I can't stay here. Taitai will come for me."

Chen tolerated her superstitions, half-believing in ghosts himself. Then an idea formed as he listened. Using paternal tones, he outlined his instructions.

"Take a cab here. You'll be safe with me. Leave this message for Li. Tell him Lane's father and the Institute both called, wanting her to attend Fu's address." He relayed the phone numbers. "And bring traveling clothes for tomorrow."

"Why? Where am I going?"

"Never mind." His thoughts elsewhere, he dismissed her questions. "On second thought, hang up. I'll call back and leave a message on the answering machine. Li doesn't need to know we've talked."

# CHAPTER 15

The next morning Li, Teng-hui and his amah picked up Lane and Justin at their hotel. Lane marveled at how alike the boys looked. Except for a slight variance of Justin's eyelids, both sets of dark eyes looked at her with the same open expression. She laughed despite the circumstances, happy to almost be a family.

"They could be twins. It's uncanny."

As they neared the Presidential Office Building, the streets were barricaded as a security measure. Coils of razor wire were strung across the streets and sidewalks. Large metal frames of barbed wire on wheels effectively blocked traffic, the rusting vertical squares reminding Lane of tortuous-looking bed frames. The crowds funneled into one narrow approach, while sanctioned limos and government vehicles were allowed to pass through one access alley. The police were taking no chances with Fu's safety.

Though it had started to rain lightly, Lane noticed a number of men at the perimeter of the crowd standing without umbrellas.

"Why don't they move out of the rain?" she asked, nodding toward the trees.

He smiled at her naïveté with protocol. "They can't. They're plain-clothed policemen."

Pursing her lips at their stupidity, she said, "They can't be too bright if they don't carry umbrellas."

"They're not allowed to. Guns can be concealed in umbrellas." He leaned over and kissed her. "It's just another precaution."

Li made his way toward the president's chair on the raised dais. Wang met him with a curt nod. Along with the Institute's representatives, Lane sat on the scaffold's platform under an awning. The amah took a chair behind her, trying to keep Teng-hui from squirming.

During the introductory speeches, he became so cranky, Lane suggested she take him. They switched babies, and both boys seemed so absorbed in the novelty of the women, they fell asleep.

Accompanied by Mei-ling and his umbrella-toting aide, Chen took his place on the platform's section reserved for minor dignitaries, the exposed, outermost fringes. Her chest pushed forward, her hips thrust back, Mei-ling modeled in her bright red suit with its black, oriental frog trim. Her red parasol and affected posture made their group impossible to miss. When Lane's eyes tracked them, Chen nodded with exaggerated courtesy, and she looked away, disgusted by his duplicity.

It began raining harder. Mei-ling opened her parasol, holding it solicitously over her and Chen's heads. Though beneath the awning, the president was also getting rained on. Wang quickly produced a "five-hundred-thousand dollar" umbrella, an over-sized umbrella nicknamed for the comprehensive life-insurance policy. Lane smiled to see one of the plain-clothes men huddling beneath an umbrella. Someone obviously feared rain more than reproach.

As the introductions ended, Taipei's mayor called the president to speak. Fu waved Wang off, not wanting to appear timid regarding either the rain or the mainland as he addressed the crowd.

Suddenly Mei-ling felt Chen tense. Their heads close together, she saw him sit up straight as his backbone stiffened.

"What's wrong?"

Chen laughed lightly. "Soon," he said, turning to her, "nothing."

She got a chill and, shivering, looked away. She saw Li boldly standing by the president, no longer concealing his intelligence position. She swallowed the lump that caught in her throat. Then she saw a shadowy figure moving in the rain. As it began to take shape between Li and Fu, Mei-ling watched, fascinated, her eyes fixed on the point. The hazy figure seemed to be laughing, dancing in the rain. Then it became distinct and stared back at her gleefully.

Taitai!

Terrified, Mei-ling tried to act as if nothing were wrong. She blinked, hoping it were an optical illusion that would go away. But when the woman's ghostly figure continued to laugh, then jeer at her, Mei-ling began hyperventilating. Can't anyone else see her? Afraid she was losing her mind, she tried to control her panic, scared Chen would abandon her as Li had.

She looked at Chen cautiously out of the corner of her eye. Preoccupied, he seemed intent on Fu and his assistant. She peeked at Chen's aide, squeezed close beside her on the right. His expression cruel, his eyes were fixed on Li. When she looked back at Taitai, she saw the specter clutched a wavering beam of eerie red light in her fist. Taitai was dancing and brandishing the light as if it were a spear. She aimed the glowing beam at Li and poised to throw it. Then cackling, she turned and pretended to hurl its other end at Mei-ling, laughing each time the young woman winced.

"Quit fidgeting!" Chen ordered sternly.

Not wanting to break eye contact with Wang, he could not look at her as he spoke. Had he, he would have noticed her pale complexion, dilated pupils and sweating upper lip.

Mei-ling watched, horrified, as Taitai approached, still

jabbing the bright spear at her. The specter came closer and closer until it stood directly in front, mocking her.

Chen saw Wang signal. In turn, he rubbed the side of his nose with his finger. The plain-clothes policeman across from him took the gun from his umbrella, pointed it at Fu and fired.

Sensing something might go wrong, Li had followed Fu to the dais. Now standing just behind him, he saw the secret service man take aim. In a blur of movement, he pushed Fu out of the way with a flying tackle.

Simultaneously, Chen's man aimed his pistol's laser gun sight, the light reflecting in the raindrops. But Mei-ling saw something quite different. In slow motion, she watched Taitai brandish the lance of light as the red laser connected with Li, and the aide fired his pistol.

"Li," she screamed, throwing herself in front of the gun barrel and feeling Taitai's spear plunge into her.

"You fool," shouted Chen, grabbing her instinctively, then letting go as her blood splattered him and dyed her suit a deeper shade of red.

When she heard the first shot, Lane ducked, shielding Teng-hui with her body. She tugged at the amah's hand, pulling her and Justin down to the ground beside her. At the sound of the second shot, she lay on top of the baby, her hands covering her head.

In the commotion, Lane felt herself being roughly jerked to her knees. Chen's aide tore the crying baby from her while holding her at gunpoint. Then laughing devilishly, Chen grabbed her arm and pulled her to her feet. Struggling, she bit his wrist and squirmed away, in the process kicking the aide in his groin.

"Leave her," Chen shouted as the flinching aide took aim, and they ran off with the boy.

She shrieked and tried to chase them, but the amah pulled her back moments before the aide shot at her. Ducking in time, the laser beam passed over her head, and the bullet hit the man beside her. No one heard her amidst the other screams. Nor could the crowd understand her English.

"Stop those men. They're stealing the baby!"

While the secret service men swarmed around Fu, protecting him, the onlookers cowered or scattered. No one wanted to get involved. Somehow in the pandemonium, Chen, his son, his aide and Wang escaped, slipping past not only the terrified spectators, but also the military.

Lane grabbed Justin from the distraught amah and tried to calm them both. Still in shock that Chen had kidnapped the baby from her arms, Lane wondered if he knew he had Teng-hui, not Justin. She did not immediately notice Li lying still on the ground in the confusion of stampeding people. When she did, she stifled a scream, pressed Justin closer, then grabbed the dazed amah's hand and slowly pushed through the crowd toward Li's limp body.

Kneeling beside his head, she called him softly. He did not respond. She tried to turn his head toward her, and blood trickled from his left ear. Pulling her hand away, she screamed, scaring the baby, his cries discordant with hers. Forcing herself to think clearly, she put her purse beneath Li's head, trying to make him more comfortable.

The movement woke him. Recognizing Lane, he motioned for her to put her ear close to his lips.

"Hide this," he said, feebly tugging at a yellowed document in his vest pocket.

Nodding, she took the paper from him and tucked it in her purse. He smiled weakly then lost consciousness. Frightened and frustrated, she looked around to see how she could help.

Two paramedics were examining the president, who was

shaken but unharmed. She struggled through the melee, pulling one of the medics toward Li. Though guards tried to stop her, she convinced the paramedics to inspect Li. Within moments, they fastened him to a stretcher and carried him to the waiting ambulance. Despite the lack of communication, Lane persuaded the medics to take her and Justin along in the ambulance.

Wang led Chen, his son and his aide through the building to an idling car in back. The drab-olive station wagon escaped undetected, its dark windows concealing the passengers' identities as the guards crisply saluted them in their race toward the city's domestic airport.

"How considerate of the government to provide us with a getaway car," Chen said in English, so the driver would not understand.

"And getaway jet," Wang said wryly.

With a dry laugh, Chen held the baby closer. As they passed a sentry and the driver limply returned his salute, he asked, "Why don't the guards stop us?"

He snorted. "They're trained to salute every official car, not exhibit initiative. They can't see if we're generals or criminals through these tinted windows." Demonstrating, Wang rapped the pane with his knuckles. "But they take no chances. Unless they were absolutely convinced we were fugitives, they'd never stop us. If they detained a general, for instance, they could be court-martialed." He leaned forward and spoke to the driver in Taiwanese. "Sung Shan airport."

The driver half-turned to address Wang. Confused, he said, "The airport's closed, sir."

"Do as you're ordered." Sitting back, Wang turned to Chen. "The next half-hour's the most critical." His wrinkled brow mirrored his concern. "Though the military keeps a

Lear jet on stand-by, I might not be able to convince them I'm authorized to take it."

"Do it." Chen's tone was acid. "It's what you're paid for."

Sweating, Wang asked, "You have the 'friendly' IFF code to clear us into China's airspace? I don't want to get shot down as a foe."

"I told you everything's been prearranged." Irritated, Chen looked at him sharply. "Just make sure you can pilot that aircraft across the Strait." Cuddling the baby, he added, "I've got a lot riding on you."

As they drove into the barricaded city airport, Wang ordered the driver to park in front and accompany them. He pressed a signed release into his hand, directing the soldier toward the armed guards. Wang and Chen, still holding the baby, walked swiftly through the gates while the aide followed several paces behind, his hand discreetly on his gun. Wang watched the driver argue with the guards.

When one of them reached for the phone and dialed, Chen took charge. "Walk faster, but don't run."

Out on the airfield, Wang intercepted two armed sentries with another signed release. Saluting, they let the group pass. A skeptical sentry met them at the plane, his rifle in hand. Though Wang presented him with a third document, he argued, telling them to wait until he was cleared to release the jet. Chen saw a group of soldiers coming through the terminal's doors toward them, and he decided to take matters into his own hands.

"Shoot him," he ordered his aide, nodding toward the recalcitrant guard. As the aide fired, the man crumpled and fell from the ramp. The shot brought the others on a run.

"Get in here," Chen ordered as the baby screamed in fright. Wang raced to the pilot's seat and started the engine as the aide pulled the door closed. Within moments the jet was taxiing down the runway. When the control tower radioed they had not been cleared for takeoff, Chen yelled, "Turn the damned thing off!"

"Yes, sir," Wang muttered sarcastically under his breath, breaking contact with the tower and abruptly lifting off. The thrust forced Chen back in his seat and threw the aide against the cabin wall. The baby screamed louder as he banged his head against the armrest.

"Damn it, Wang. Be careful!" Peering into his son's angry, red face, Chen tried to calm the wailing baby. He looked at the eyes and gasped. Staring hard at the lids, he wasn't sure if the baby's eyes were squinting from crying or were almond-shaped from a purely Asian heritage. "It can't be. It can't be!"

The longer he gazed, the surer he became. The baby was Mei-ling's. First he lost Lane. Now he had lost Tian-syang. Dejected, he slumped backward as the baby's cries rose with the air pressure.

"What's the code?" asked the aide. "Wang said he needs to know before we approach Chinese airspace."

His eyes dull, his voice monotone, Chen told him.

The aide appeared again, the gaping hole in his mouth proof that the dentists had fled the day before. "Wang says I gave him the wrong code. He wants you to tell him yourself." He reached for the baby as Chen got up stiffly from his seat.

He walked into the cockpit and mumbled the code to Wang, who was sweating at the controls. "This is no time for games, Chen. What's the real code?"

The pilot's energy pierced his stupor. "I told you."

Wang swung around in his seat to face him. "What you gave me is a standard military code used by Mirage 2000-5 fighters. If I issue this, China'll scramble a pair of Su-27s to intercept us."

"Send the code," Chen said.

Wang took a deep breath and tried again. "The speed and radar profile of a Lear jet are similar to a fighter jet's but not identical. If they see us on the radar screen, they'll investigate, but they won't fire without visual contact." Wiping the perspiration from his cheek, he continued, "But if I issue this IFF code, identifying us as a foe, Chinese pilots'll think we're a hostile contact and fire before we're even in visual range. We wouldn't stand a chance."

"It's the code Zheng gave me personally," said Chen. "It'll clear us into Chinese airspace. Now send it!" When the pilot didn't move, Chen asked, "Do I need my aide to convince you?"

Wang eyed him suspiciously. He paused, bit his lip, and tried again. "The radar signature of a Lear jet parallels a fighter. On a screen, we look like a fighter jet. We have to radio signal that we're friendly." He shook his head. "If I issue this code, they're going to fire on us."

Chen called his aide. Wang gave a nervous laugh.

"You wouldn't shoot me. If the bullet ricochets, the cabin would decompress, and we'd plunge into the East China Sea."

"Shoot him."

As the startled aide fumbled with the baby to reach his gun, Wang said, "You kill me, and we all die. Is that what you want?" Wang watched, bug-eyed, to see if he'd judged Chen correctly.

"Shoot him."

Still holding the baby, the aide pointed the gun at Wang's head.

"All right, all right!" Hyperventilating, Wang issued the code, then sat back, sweat running down his cheeks and neck.

US Big Ear satellites intercepted the radio signal at the

same instant as the Chinese. Records on both sides of the Pacific showed it was a standard Taiwanese military code used by Mirage 2000-5 fighters. Moments later, the mainland ordered two Su-27s to intercept. As Wang had predicted, the jets approached head on, firing on them without warning.

Taiwanese AWACs planes, capable of detecting aircraft six hundred nautical miles away, lost the signal. "They were shot down over the Strait, sir," reported the officer in charge.

"Any survivors?"

"None."

Inhaling on his cigarette, Fu considered the possibilities. "Don't be so sure."

# CHAPTER 16

Waiting in Li's private room, Lane listened to TV as CNN aired a taped interview with President Fu.

CNN: In a rare interview with PRC President Zheng yesterday, we asked if he could help end the cross-strait conflict. His comments revealed a man who would find it hard to live at peace with his neighbors. President Fu, is the return of Kinmen Island to Taiwanese control a precondition for peace negotiations?

Fu: Chinese forces have to withdraw unconditionally and completely from both Kinmen and Matsu Islands before any accord can be reached. We are willing to begin negotiations, but we can't accept the occupation of any square millimeter of Taiwanese soil.

CNN: In our recent interview with him, Zheng drew parallels between this conflict and the Serbian/Croatian war. He claimed the reason for the discord was cultural preservation. What is your comment?

Fu: The mainland and Taiwan share a common heritage and common ancestry. Our differences stem not from cultural divisions, but from mainland aggression. It's interesting to note Zheng's now attesting that cultural heritage was the pretext for invasion. The original reason stated was retaliation for an attempted assassination by an isolated individual. Now that China has attempted to assassinate me, Zheng's revised the motive for the mainland's attack.

CNN: What difference has the Su-27 missile attack made?

Fu: The PRC has severely compromised security in the

western Pacific, in the process disillusioning many of its staunchest international allies. As you know, the PRC has effected a blockade against Taiwan. This interrupts sea and air traffic, violating human rights and disrupting global trade. Though Taiwan has shown considerable patience, the repercussions from the PRC's act of aggression may lead to war.

CNN: Has the People's Republic of China stopped all air traffic to and from Taiwan?

Fu: Yes, but thanks to the efforts of the ROC's Straits Exchange Foundation and a US peace-keeping mission, the PRC has temporarily lifted the blockade, allowing holders of foreign passports to evacuate.

CNN: How long will this temporary stay remain in effect?

Fu: Until midnight tonight.

CNN: What is your. . . .

"Excuse me."

She flipped off the remote as the white-coated doctor stepped into the room, an otoscope in hand. Giving Lane a peremptory smile, he walked toward the bed, looked inside Li's ear canals, lifted his eyelids and checked his pupils.

"His eyes were twitching before." Afraid the doctor might overlook clues to Li's recovery, she offered details from her own observation. "I thought he was waking up." The doctor gave her a wan smile and took his patient's pulse. "His color seems better today," she looked up hopefully, "doesn't it?" When he did not answer, she tried to encourage his response with tag questions. "These are signs he's improving, don't you think?"

Straightening up, he addressed her in a clear voice. "Concussion can demonstrate a wide range of symptoms. Depending on the severity of the injury, the loss of consciousness may be temporary, lasting only a few hours. Or the recovery period may take several weeks. When the bullet grazed his head, it caused a temporary state of brain dysfunction."

Lane stepped away from the bed, motioning for the doctor to join her. She spoke in hushed tones, so Li could not overhear, regardless of his state of consciousness. She did not want him distressed by words like dysfunction in connection with brain. Controlling the quivering muscles around her mouth, she voiced her worst fears.

"He couldn't have any permanent damage from this, could he?"

The man drew a long breath before indirectly answering her question. "You see, deep inside the brain stem is a group of cells called the reticular formation. This regulates the state of alertness. A sharp blow to the head can cause a brief derangement in the formation. This in itself isn't that serious." He paused. "However, if the injury caused a bruise or a tearing of the brain, lasting injury may occur."

She swallowed. Now that she was treading dangerous territory, she decided to pursue all the possibilities.

"When you say lasting injury, do you mean irreversible?" There, it was out. She had said it.

Cocking his head to the side, he watched her through raised eyebrows, deciding if she could handle all the facts. "Right now there's pressure on his brain tissue from swelling. How much, we can't ascertain. Worst case scenario: if there were hemorrhaging between the brain and skull, or edema, the skull couldn't expand to relieve the pressure. In that case, the pressure could cause further damage to the brain," he paused, "or even coma."

The intent look in her eyes wavered. Though carefully controlled, the held-back tears moistened her eyes. She swallowed. "Isn't there anything you can do?"

He shrugged. "Give him complete bed rest, keep him comfortable. . . ."

"But what can you do?" Frustrated at her own inability to help, she wanted the medical professionals to make an attempt. "He's been asleep since yesterday, doesn't it make sense to try to wake him?" She considered shaking Li into consciousness or, anger returning, shaking up the doctor.

He stepped away, sensing her hostility. "If it's reversible, and at this point we don't know, patients have been aided in their recovery by administering large doses of barbiturates." He scratched his eyebrow. "It might work."

"Barbiturates? Aren't those sedatives?" She frowned as she thought out loud. "Wouldn't those drug him into a sounder sleep?"

"Test cases have proved recovery takes place in stages: first stupor, next delirium and extreme agitation, then mental confusion, later automatism, where patients act automatically, and finally the return of the highest brain functions."

Instead of helping her understand, his explanation baffled her. "You say barbiturates will speed his recovery. Are you sure?"

He shrugged again. "As long as his condition's reversible. You want me to try it?"

She had her reservations but nodded.

"All right, I'll have a nurse inject his IV."

Lane kept silent, upset at the doctor's lack of initiative. She wracked her brain, wondering how she could help. Then she remembered Iris' father-in-law.

"Do you think *qigong* could help?" She looked at him expectantly.

His lips curved intolerantly. Lightly touching her shoulder, he said, "Let's leave folk healing to the ignorant."

"But it's like chicken soup. It can't hurt, can it?"

She took his shrug for assent, then left the room and called the Institute, asking them to contact Iris' father-in-law and explain the situation in Chinese. She knew from her colleagues' tone, they thought she was acting irrationally, but she was past caring.

Two hours later, Lane heard a timid knock at the room's open door. She recognized the caller as Iming's father and smiled her welcome, unable to voice it, except for *ni hao,* hello.

As he had at Iris' wedding, he began making several wide circles with his arms, the actions looking like tae kwon do. His breathing deepened as he focused his *qi,* his life-energy. The man appeared to feel the air close to Li's body, time and again his open palm returning to the bandaged areas on Li's forehead. Then he held both palms two inches from him and closed his eyes, concentrating his energy through his hands.

She watched hopefully but detected no change in Li. As the man stepped away, Lane tried not to show her disappointment. Embarrassed by her lack of Chinese, she tried to express her gratitude, finally resorting to offering him several bills. He refused them with a gracious smile and a jaunty salute, then left. Depressed more than she had been since Li's injury at the ceremony, Lane slumped into the chair and resumed her vigil. Nothing. She noted no change.

She reached into her purse for a tissue and felt instead the ancient document, its brittle edges crumbling at her touch. In the commotion of the past twenty-four hours, she had forgotten it. Now she unfolded the paper and stared at its artistically drawn characters, intrigued but unable to read it.

Still studying it, she flipped on the remote again, listening to news updates.

CNN: When asked if negative reaction from the US, the

UN and other international sources had forced the PRC to de-escalate its campaign, President Zheng was unavailable for comment. With us now is Jen Li-jen a spokesperson for the PLA. Mr. Jen, what is the status of the PRC's recent blockade of Taiwan?

Jen: The People's Republic of China was attacked yesterday at 13:26 by an invading jet, which issued a standard military IFF code, identifying itself as a Mirage 2000-5 fighter. This has been corroborated by the US, whose Big Ear satellites intercepted the radio signal. The PRC is wholly within its rights to defend itself against invading hostile aircraft and to retaliate against this deplorable act of aggression by the Province of Taiwan.

CNN: Taiwanese President Fu in a recent interview denied any knowledge of the attack, alleging that a Lear jet had been seized from Sung Shan airport shortly before being destroyed over the East China Sea. Fu claimed the aggressors were escaping assassins, whose earlier attempt on his life had been foiled. Fu further asserted the assailants worked for the PRC and were returning home after a failed assassination plot.

Jen: Assertions and claims are not truths. The facts are that an attempt had been made on Tsai's life while in Taipei on a cross-strait-affairs mission last week and that an identified Taiwanese jet fighter entered Chinese airspace yesterday at 13:26. President Fu can cast aspersions, but the facts speak for themselves.

CNN: Then despite global outcry the PRC is continuing with its plan to invade Taiwan?

Jen: The PRC is the *People's* Republic of China. Our goal is peaceful reunification of all the provinces, all the people. To accomplish this, it is necessary to rescue Taiwan from its secessionist minority.

CNN: Then incursion is imminent?

Jen: The media, diplomats and foreigners residing in Taiwan have been given twenty-four hours to evacuate. At midnight the blockade will again be enforced.

CNN: Will China invade Taiwan at midnight as rumored?

Jen: The blockade will be put into effect at midnight. No air or sea traffic will be allowed into or out of Taiwan.

CNN: Is it true an invasion is imminent?

Jen: A blockade is not an invasion.

CNN: But isn't it true that PLA personnel will be sent to monitor the blockade? And if so, isn't the landing of military forces on foreign soil a preemptive strike?

Jen: Taiwan is not foreign soil. It is a province of China. And let me remind you that Taiwan made the first incursion into Chinese airspace yesterday. I am simply stating the blockade will be. . . .

"An unfortunate time for your father to be visiting the ROC."

Lane looked toward the door to see who was speaking and gasped. Rising to her feet, she flipped off the remote, the ancient paper still in hand.

"An even more unfortunate time for Taiwan, President Fu. How kind of you to visit, especially when you must have so many pressing matters of State."

Recognizing the document as the Tiaoyutai deed, he motioned to his body guards to close the door and wait outside. So that's what happened to it, he thought, devising ways to get possession of it. Though his men had searched Li's apartment, car and office, it had eluded them. As Fu reached for her hand, she casually tucked the paper in her purse, then shook hands with him firmly.

"It was the least I could do for my best agent," he said.

Lane filed that piece of information away. Still eyeing her handbag, Fu neglected to mention that discovering the document's whereabouts had been his real purpose in visiting.

Instead he added with exaggerated courtesy, "I'm so sorry about your husband's accident, Mrs. Chen. It was a shock to us all."

Embarrassed that Chen had been involved with Fu's assassination attempt, Lane did not know what to say. But not for a moment did she think Chen was dead. Even if he were, she felt no regret, only relief. Mumbling her thanks, she changed the subject.

"I appreciate your allowing my father's plane to land at Sung Shan airport instead of Taoyuan. With the traffic, it would have been impossible for us to get to the international airport. I'll be so relieved to get my son to the States."

Her thoughts came out as a heart-felt sigh. Then as her eyes fell on Li, she was torn between rushing Justin to safety and leaving Li behind. It was a dichotomy she'd been struggling with since Li's shooting. Remembering his plight reminded her of the island's twenty-one million residents in similar or worse straits.

"I can't stop thinking of the people who aren't able to escape," she said. "Would it still be possible to initiate last-minute peace-talks to stall China's assault?"

"You're your father's daughter. I see you have a mind for international policy." His lips smiled although his eyes watched her shrewdly, wondering if she knew the document's contents.

"I had hoped cross-strait tensions would ease once Senator MacKenzie's peace-keeping mission arrived," he said, "but so far the PRC has refused all attempts at negotiation."

She shook her head sadly. "My father said President Dawson has authorized a policy of 'Partnership, not confrontation' with China, hoping to defuse the situation. Washington's eager for relations to be normalized."

Inwardly President Fu sneered. Of course Dawson wouldn't want conflict with his Chinese supporters. You can't kill the cow and drink the milk. But if Taiwan had sovereignty of Tiaoyutai, all that would change. President Dawson would scramble to the ROC's defense if he thought Taiwan would reward the US with a Tiaoyutai refueling station.

Unable to contain his curiosity, Fu said, "Incidentally, did Li mention an old document to you?"

"N . . . no. Was it anything important?" Though she tried to appear outwardly calm, his question surprised her.

"No, just some tedious paperwork."

Fu's face remained inscrutable except for a small throbbing vein on his forehead. His smile was perfunctory as his mind raced. Chen was dead. If Li were out of the way, that would leave Lane's son as the sole male descendent and inheritor of the Tiaoyutai islands. Legally that met the document's conditions; therefore, it was enough to win US support. He stared first at her purse, then at her face, still wondering how to get possession of the document. Then abruptly turning away from her suspicious expression, he walked toward the bed and addressed her in Chinese.

"Excuse me? I don't understand Mandarin."

"How's Li doing?" he asked, watching her closely.

Fu's presence made her feel uncomfortable about both the document and the irregularity of her keeping vigil in Li's room so soon after her husband's presumed death. Hiding her wariness as well as her concern for Li, she tried to sound optimistic as she reported his condition.

"They're giving him barbiturates to wake him from this . . . sleep." She hesitated, chewing her lip, unwilling to use the word coma.

"Barbiturates to wake him?"

Lane worried whether she had done the right thing by forcing the doctor's hand. She struggled to stay upbeat. "The doctor recommended the treatment, saying it's worked in the past."

"Let me speak to him." Emphasizing his coercive power, Fu tried to reassure her with his tone and expression.

"He just left," she said. "It could be hours before he returns from his rounds."

An amused glimmer in his eye, he called his new aide to fetch the doctor. They returned within moments. Fu dismissed the aide and questioned the physician in Chinese.

"Yes, the tranquilizers should help him," said the doctor.

Fu addressed him casually, assuming his man-of-the-people pose. "What if complications develop?"

Weary from making his rounds, the doctor was loathe to keep defending his prognoses, no matter who was asking. "All I can do is diagnose and follow through with treatment. I'm not the god of longevity."

"What if the patient didn't wake from his coma? Would it be your responsibility?"

He removed his glasses and peered sharply into the president's eyes. "Certainly not!"

As he scrutinized him, Fu grinned. "Good, since you'll bear no accountability, you'll have no moral objections to helping your country."

The doctor glanced about nervously. "What are you asking?"

"When you prescribe barbiturates, triple the dosage."

Nervous that Lane could speak Chinese, the doctor looked toward her guiltily. "Why don't we discuss this somewhere else?"

Fu's eyes rested on Lane. Unblinking, they returned to the

doctor's. "She can't understand. Can you?"

"You're asking me to be an accomplice in murder?"

"Is it murder to let nature take its course?" His eyes searched the doctor's, confronting him. "Is there any guarantee he'd come out of the coma, regardless of treatment?"

Scratching his eyebrow, the doctor answered slowly. "No. . . ."

His poise intact, Fu radiated reassurance. "You'd earn my gratitude."

Lane watched at a polite distance, concerned that both men chose to exclude her by speaking in Chinese. Though she tried to shake off the negative reaction, her instincts cautioned her.

*"Duo-shao?"* said the doctor suddenly. "How much is your gratitude worth?"

A disturbance in the hall drew everyone's attention, suspending the conversation. MacKenzie's deep voice boomed through the closed door. "Lane, tell these bouncers who I am."

She leaped forward, glad for the opportunity to break away from the room's tension. "It's my father," she called over her shoulder, swinging open the door.

Had he been wearing chaps and a ten-gallon hat, his commanding presence could not have been more impressive. Only the baby in his arms seemed out-of-place with his image of a cattle-baron senator. His aide Jeffrey, a belated yuppie wearing horn-rimmed glasses, followed closely, bearing a diaper bag instead of his customary briefcase.

Lane had to smile in spite of herself. "C'mere, cutie," she said, lifting Justin from his grandfather's arms. "Has he been a good boy?" But before he could launch into a description of the baby's antics, Lane turned to Fu. "You remember my father, Senator MacKenzie."

"A pleasure to see you again," Fu said. "Sorry I couldn't meet your plane last night to welcome you personally."

"Don't y'all fret. Nobody knew when or if the PRC'd lift the embargo long enough to clear us into Taiwan's airspace."

While the two men shook hands, Lane introduced the physician. "How do you do?" he said. Then turning to Fu, the doctor smiled unpleasantly as he spoke in Chinese. "*Yi bai-wan qian*. For a million NT, I'll triple the dosage."

Fu held his breath as he studied the others' faces for their reactions. When he was sure no one had interpreted, he answered gruffly in Chinese. "I'll see you outside."

Reverting to English, the doctor shook MacKenzie's hand. "Nice to meet you, Senator, but I should be getting back to my rounds. Hope your next visit to Taiwan's under more favorable circumstances." He turned to Lane. "I'll have the nurse administer the barbiturates immediately." Then he reached for the aide's hand but saw his hands were occupied, one still holding the diaper bag, the other sliding his glasses up his nose. Nodding politely, the doctor hurried out.

"I'm afraid I have to be getting back to my rounds, too," Fu said, chuckling. "As a politician, I'm sure you understand." He turned to Lane, his expression encouraging. "Don't worry about Li. He's getting the best medical treatment possible." Fu reached for MacKenzie's hand. "Senator, I look forward to seeing you at the dinner reception this evening at six. We have several new developments to discuss before your departure. What time's your flight?"

"Eleven," said Jeffrey, answering for MacKenzie.

President Fu nodded, started to leave, then turned back. Addressing both MacKenzie and Lane, he added, "Your roles in Asian history may be larger than you realize." With a yellowed smile and a wave, he left, his aide closing the door behind him.

"What a cryptic thing to say," said Lane, frowning as she tried to decipher Fu's meaning.

Though she saw no immediate connection, she remembered Fu's odd question about Li's document and couldn't help wondering if the paper had had anything to do with it.

"Y'all know what they say about the inscrutable Chinese, the mysterious Orient," said MacKenzie, shrugging it off. "East is east and west is west, but I'll say one thing for Fu. He sure does some mighty fine politicking."

"I beg your pardon," said the aide, setting down the bag, "but that was a line of bullshit."

"Exactly!" MacKenzie's good-ole'-boy laugh interrupted his aide's interpretation.

"Why? What did he say?" Lane sensed her instincts had been right.

Jeffrey adjusted his glasses with his index finger before answering. "The doc's collaborating with Fu. For a million NT, he's going to OD Li."

His words exploded in Lane's ear drums like fireworks. When the buzzing subsided, her plan was clear. "We've got to get Li out of here."

"Now just a cotton-pickin' minute," said MacKenzie. "This man's none of my responsibility. He ain't friend or family, and after the way that jackass treated you. . . ."

Lane didn't have time for finesse. "He is family, and more than just my nephew by marriage," she said, anticipating his argument. "I'll explain later, but for starters he's the father of your grandson." Reaching into her purse, she handed him Li's document. "I think this may have something to do with his shooting."

"What kind of hogwash is this?" demanded MacKenzie, passing the paper to his aide.

After struggling through its antiquated characters, Jeffrey

briefly translated, concluding, "If this says what I think, Li stands to become a very wealthy man—that is, if he survives." He addressed Lane. "Can you prove he's the father of your son?"

"What the hell are y'all implying?" demanded MacKenzie.

"Sorry, Senator, but should anything happen to Li, Justin's the sole inheritor of the Tiaoyutai islands if Lane can prove the baby is Li's. It also follows that, since Justin's Taiwanese, the KMT government will appoint itself guardian to protect its own interests."

"What do you mean?" The senator eyed him warily.

"It'd create a trust, setting itself up as his proxy until he's twenty-one, and by that time have established enough legal encroachments to steal his birthright out from under him."

"My grandbaby's American. As an American citizen, his rights'd be protected," said MacKenzie with patriotic bluster, a greedy glint growing in his eye, "and the islands'd become US territory. I'd see to that personally."

Lane shook her head. "You don't understand. Since his father's Taiwanese, Justin's Taiwanese, not American."

"Who are you talking about? Chen or Li?" asked Jeffrey.

"Li."

Then to her withering scowl, he added, "Wasn't Chen from Macao?"

"Yes, but he held a Taiwanese passport." She suddenly understood his meaning, sickened as she remembered Chen's PRC connections. "You don't think the mainland would try to declare Justin a Chinese citizen, do you?" She took a jagged breath as she looked over at Li. "No," she said, answering her own question, "Li's the father."

"But even if you can't prove Li's paternity," continued the aide, "Chen was Li's uncle, right? That should be enough to establish a familial line of descent and make Justin the sole inheritor of the Tiaoyutai Islands."

"Actually," she said, stashing the document into her pocket, "Chen was Li's father."

"What?" shouted MacKenzie.

"There's no time now. We can discuss genealogies on the plane," Lane said, avoiding her father's apoplectic stare. Passing him the baby, she started out the door. "Don't let anyone in 'til I get back."

Subdued, the red-faced senator regarded his grandson with new interest. A moment later a nurse carrying a syringe pushed open the door and strode toward Li's bed. "Sorry," said the aide, "can you come back a little later?" When she did not respond to English, he spoke in perfect Mandarin. "The doctor said to postpone the injection until after we leave." Turning her by her shoulders, he ushered the woman out the door, shutting it in her face the second time she tried to enter.

Only then did he notice Lane's purse missing from the chair. His face pale, Jeffrey ran out in the hall after her as Lane pushed in a wheelchair.

"She took the Tiaoyutai document."

Lane patted her pocket, smiling. "No she didn't. Now help me get him in here." They lifted Li from the bed and propped him in the chair.

"This won't work," said MacKenzie. "He can't support himself. He'll fall out."

Knowing the nurse would be back with reinforcements any minute, Lane chewed her lip as she thought. "Be right back." Opening the door cautiously, she sneaked into the hall.

Moments later, Lane returned, carrying a motorcyclist's rain poncho and a dust mask, two popular items on Taipei's wet and polluted streets.

"Where'd you get those?" asked her father.

"The gift shop," she said, slipping the vinyl poncho over Li's head. Its folds draped over him, covering him past his calves. When she arranged its hood over his head, the visor hid his eyes but left his mouth uncovered.

"It won't work," MacKenzie repeated. "Everyone'll recognize him."

Lane fitted the dust mask across his nose and mouth, looping its elastic strings around his ears.

"What about his feet?" MacKenzie hated being proven wrong, or worse, feeling unnecessary. "Where're his shoes?" Pointing to Li's calves, he added, "And his pajamas stick out."

She rolled up his pajamas above the knees. "He'll go barefoot, like the laborers." Then she turned to the aide. "C'mon, help me get him out of here." She lifted one of Li's arms around her neck, struggling to get him to stand.

"Here," MacKenzie said, handing her the baby. "Let me do that." Between them, MacKenzie and his aide got Li to his feet. "Now what?"

"We walk him out to your car," she said, "and get him to the city airport before anyone notices he's missing."

"The plane's not scheduled for takeoff until eleven," said MacKenzie.

"That's too late," she said, chewing her lip. "If Li doesn't leave soon, he won't get out alive. We've got to get Li and Justin out of the country before Fu knows we're gone."

"What if someone stops us?" asked Jeffrey, assessing Li's guise.

"Say he was in a traffic accident. You speak Mandarin." She studied Li, making sure nothing would give them away. Then as an idea struck her, she fumbled in the bureau's top drawer for Li's sunglasses and carefully tucked them under the top of his mask. "No one'll recognize him now." She peeked out the door and waved them through the hall.

As they waited for the elevator, a nurse joined them. Stiffening, Lane whispered through gritted teeth, "Keep Li's face turned toward the wall."

One of his pajama legs unrolled, drooping beneath the poncho. Lane ducked in front, hiding his legs. Finally the crowded elevator stopped at their floor. Lane held the door for the trio, then closed it before the nurse could squeeze in.

"Sorry," she said, her finger still on the close button.

On the ground floor, they struggled out of the crowded lobby toward MacKenzie's waiting limo. "How are we going to get him through immigration without his passport?" asked the aide.

Lane shared a smile with the senator. "My father has two things: charm and diplomatic privilege."

"Those and a poncho aren't going to fool airport security."

"You're right. We've got to transport Li in some kind of container, then scream diplomatic immunity if anyone stops us. As long as we can get him through the terminal without being seen, we don't have to worry about customs or immigration. Once aboard my father's plane, we're safe. It's like being on US soil."

"What then?" asked Jeffrey.

"Get Li to the closest hospital." Lane felt her bottom lip beginning to tremble. In the excitement of hustling Li out of his room, she had almost forgotten his concussion. This jostling certainly couldn't be helping him. Trying not to dwell on those thoughts, she asked weakly, "Where'd that be?"

"Guam, about a three-hour flight, not counting the drive to the airport."

They pulled out of the parking lot into heavy traffic,

turning right onto *Tun Hua* North Road. The streets were grid-locked. Though so many had fled Taipei in the past seventy-two hours, people were still bustling about, making last-minute arrangements to escape the beleaguered city. Refugees were frantically trying to sell their condos, eager to salvage even a small percentage of their property's value, rather than leave it for the Chinese. Speculators were buying, calculating the inflated prices if Taiwan changed hands but betting on an amicable cross-strait agreement.

If the locals couldn't find flights off the island, they could escape to the countryside in cars, buses, motor scooters and bicycles. The boulevard looked like humming streams of fire ants about to devour anything in their path. Anticipating traffic delays, MacKenzie called ahead to have his plane fueled and readied for takeoff.

"Good thing it's at the city airport and not Taoyuan," Lane said. "The roads are like a parking lot. It'd take days to reach the CKS airport."

Agreeing, MacKenzie ordered the driver to turn on the radio. "Let's hear what's happening."

ICRT: "Cross-strait mediation is at a new low following a statement made by the PRC's Association for Relations Across the Taiwan Straits, the mainland's semi-official institution responsible for cross-strait affairs.

Said Ho Yu-lin, 'There is one China, and the PRC is its sole legitimate government. Though the ROC has a small degree of autonomy in domestic affairs, Taiwan is merely a province. The PRC's goal is to liberate Taiwan from the secessionists through military force.'

With us today is Ren Fu-rong of the ROC's Straits Exchange Foundation. Mr. Ren, would you care to comment on the PRC's assertion?"

Ren: "The ROC concurs with the mainland that there is one China. However, it differs in its definition. According to the ROC's position, 'one China' refers to China's cultural, historical and territorial heritage, but within this China there are two political bodies of equal stature. The SEF urges both sides to agree to disagree and then move on in a spirit of co-operation."

ICRT: "Thank you, Mr. Ren. In the local news, the American Institute in Taiwan has announced it's air-lifting the 30,000 US citizens to Los Angeles, CA. Contact AIT for details. The German embassy is requesting that expats identify their blood types and update their registrations for emergency evacuation.

Despite the record number of airline-ticket sales recently, the Ministry of Interior announced there has been no increase in the number of Taiwanese leaving the country. However, anonymous sources allege that 'immigration companies are working 'round the clock to process all applications for persons wishing to emigrate to Canada, New Zealand, Australia and South Africa,' in that order.

DPP opposition member Yu Chin-fu confirmed this by claiming he personally knew of many people relocating their sons abroad to avoid the draft. 'There would have been an exodus,' Yu said, were it not for the strict controls foreign governments imposed on immigration."

Fine creases ruffled Lane's brow as they inched along the chaotic streets. Long queues lined the sidewalks as depositors waited outside the banks' gated doors to withdraw their New Taiwan dollars and exchange them for greenbacks. Guards stood sentry, transceivers in one hand, billy clubs in the other. When a jewelry store clerk partially rolled up the shop's metal grate, three women ducked beneath, pushing into the showroom. Many still considered gold the safest currency.

Alarmed, MacKenzie sat on the edge of his seat. "Is there a run on the banks?"

"The China Post called it a 'strong buying spree,' " said Jeffrey with a wry smile. "Ever since China's blockade began, customer demand to switch NT to US dollars has soared. With depositors making withdrawals of up to half a million dollars US, foreign banks have set a $3000 ceiling per transaction. And when the US dollar reserves run out, the Taiwanese'll buy deutsche marks and yen, all at inflated prices."

MacKenzie's ears perked up. "Inflation? Can the TAIEX handle it?"

"Don't worry about the market. Yesterday Taiwan's central bank released NT$63 billion into the local banking system to ease the crunch." Comfortable in his element, Jeffrey nodded reassuringly. "The TAIEX is stable. For now."

Across the street, a wary group congregated outside a supermarket's locked doors, while the open-air-market stalls along the nearby alley bustled, the dried-noodle sellers doing an especially brisk trade. One enterprising vendor sold bottled water as fast as he could unbox it.

Like a convenience-store clerk dealing with the after-school rush of students, the increased activity made Lane unsettled, alert for signs of trouble.

"Taipei's citizens are settling in for a siege, stocking up on the basics," she said, sighing deeply. "Anyone without a foreign passport, green card or immigration papers is stuck here. And if China begins an actual invasion, no one knows how food supplies, electricity, gas or water will be affected."

"They'd better get while the getting's good," remarked

her father absently, his thoughts on his stocks and the 350-point fall in Hong Kong's Hang Seng Index.

Lane's eyes rested on Li, reminding her of the immediate problems. She took off his sunglasses, removed the poncho and rolled it into a makeshift pillow. Then she tucked it under Li's head and helped him stretch out on the seat facing them. Watching his shallow breathing, she said, "Now all we have to do is get him through the airport without being . . . stop!"

The driver slammed on the brakes, causing the tail-gating taxi behind them to squeal to a rocking stop. The cabby, lax about replacing the worn shocks, now did what he did best: lay on the horn. Lane held the baby tightly with one arm, while she kept Li from rolling off the seat with the other. As their driver maneuvered out of bumper-to-bumper traffic to double-park, MacKenzie's irritation piqued.

"What the hell are y'all doing?"

"Here." She handed him Justin. "Be right back."

Then she reached across the aide and pushed open the door. He caught the handle before it swung into a scooter passing on the right.

"I'm coming along," said the aide.

They raced across six lanes of traffic to a combination shop and showroom. Wood shavings and chiseled slivers littered the floor. Halved logs lined one side of the shop, carved sarcophagi the other.

"What is this place? It give me the creeps."

"A casket showroom."

He grimaced as he looked to her for an explanation.

"This is how we'll get Li through the airport," she said in a calm voice.

Jeffrey stared at her open-mouthed until he was called upon for his Mandarin. Despite the shopkeeper's attempt to steer them toward western-style caskets in the back, they chose an ornately carved and painted Taiwanese coffin.

"It looks like an old-fashioned linen chest decorated with folk art."

She smiled at the image, improvising on her idea. "Yes, tell him that's what I want it for in the States, but he has to crate it. Loosely." Puzzled, he squinted at her. "Tell him to crate it but not nail it shut. Leave one end open. And drill air holes in it." She interrupted his Chinese translation. "But tell him we'll only buy it if he hauls it to the airport immediately."

Their limo pulled into the airport parking lot, the delivery truck so close behind, it seemed in tow. Lane held on to the baby while the two men helped Li from the back seat and into the truck's trailer. Working quickly, they gently lowered Li into the casket, placed its heavy carved cover on top, then slid it into the crate. To make it look authentic, they hammered the crate shut, barely tapping the nails in.

"Make it easy to uncrate. The moment we're boarded, we have to let him out." Lane's jaw worked nervously. "I don't know how much air he's getting in there."

While they hammered the last nails, Lane saw a military car screech to a halt beside them. "Quick, finish up." The baby sensed the anxiety and woke, its lusty cries attracting the soldiers' attention. As they eyed her suspiciously, Lane said to the aide, "Tell them our baby's sick."

"I'll handle this," said MacKenzie, struggling out of the back seat, all too willing to assume control.

"No, you won't." Lane stared at him until he sat back down. "They're looking for Li, you and your daughter. They might not be looking for a young married couple with a child." As they approached, Lane linked arms with the aide and lulled Justin.

The largest of the three soldiers had his billy club swinging from his wrist. The second hung back passively. The third and shortest seemed to be the one in authority.

"Can I see your passports?"

In idiomatic Mandarin, Jeffrey said, "Since when is it a crime to have a noisy baby?" His smile as genuine as his Beijing accent, he handed over his papers.

Though the soldiers smiled, the leader carefully checked the passport and visa before returning it. Then ducking his head to peer into the back seat, he noticed the senator's foreign face. "Who's that?"

"The tail of an ox—my boss," he explained with a grin. "Me? I'm only the head of a chicken."

The soldier swallowed a grin and turned to Lane. "Papers, please."

She smiled, whispering to Jeffrey through gritted teeth, "They were in my purse. Do something."

"I don't think these men know about Li," Jeffrey said, noting that their car had no radio antenna or cellular phone. "This is only a routine inspection." He pretended to check his watch and addressed the soldier, reverting to Mandarin. "I'm sorry, but we're already late for the plane because of our baby. We still have to check-in and go through customs. Look, we'll have to show them our passports, anyway. Couldn't you let us through? Otherwise I'm afraid we'll miss our flight." While he spoke, Jeffrey ushered Lane into the car, holding the door for her. Then as the soldier nodded reluctantly, Jeffrey gave him a friendly salute, hopped in, closed the door and told the driver to hurry.

The limo then drove to the loading area, the truck following in its wake. A welcoming party was waiting. Four armed KMT soldiers stopped their car at the gate. After identifying his passengers, their driver reported to MacKenzie in broken English that they weren't allowed to leave.

Jeffrey said, "Let me try."

Again speaking in Mandarin, he changed his story, explaining how it was urgent that they return to the States. Senator MacKenzie's grandson was ill and had to get to a hospital. Justin's crying was on cue but did little to convince them. The officer in charge demanded to see their passports.

"Senator MacKenzie has diplomatic privilege. Neither he nor his party has to go through immigration." When they asked to see Lane's exit permit, Jeffrey shook his head stubbornly. "As an American citizen, his daughter shares his diplomatic immunity."

MacKenzie had reached the end of his patience. "Damn it, what is this holdup? If I'm not out of here in five minutes, President Fu will have the United States Senate to contend with."

The soldiers could not understand English, but they heard the tone. Jeffrey translated, embellishing MacKenzie's words to rattle them further. Retreating a few paces to discuss it among themselves, the soldiers finally returned.

"You can go," said the officer, "but you can't take any luggage."

Jeffrey considered it, weighing the semantics. Technically, the coffin was not luggage. He nodded his head, and they let them pass. A convoy drove to the waiting plane: the limo, followed by the truck and the army jeep with four soldiers.

"We're playing cat and mouse," said MacKenzie after Jeffrey had translated. "All you did was postpone the inevitable."

Lane shook her head. "We're closer. Once we make it up that ramp, we're safe. Let's just bluff our way through the last few feet of red tape." As the tension increased, she began hyperventilating, gulping air. "But hurry. I don't know how much oxygen Li's getting."

As they got out of the car, the two men from the truck carried the crate toward them. All tried to remain expressionless when the soldiers stopped them.

"What's this?" asked the officer imperiously. "I said no luggage."

"It isn't." Jeffrey casually inspected his fingernails. "It's a souvenir."

"Open it." The three soldiers moved toward the crate. "Put it down," the officer ordered the pall bearers.

"Keep moving," said Jeffrey. The bearers uneasily continued toward the ramp.

After a string of expletives, the officer repeated, "Put it down." The two men looked at each other and began to lower the crate onto the ground.

"If you want to be paid, get that aboard immediately," said Jeffrey. The men raised it and walked toward the Lear jet, the incentive of money adding a bounce to their step. Jeffrey turned to the KMT officer. "The United States senator has diplomatic privilege regarding customs as well as immigration. Any more interference on your part will be viewed as a challenge."

Visibly intimidated, the officer tried to save face in front of his men. "My orders are to inspect anything suspicious."

MacKenzie was getting nervous. When he got nervous, it came out angry. Hissing at Lane, he demanded, "Why did you have to rope me into this side-show?" He strode toward his aide and addressed the officer. "Unless you step aside now, I'm holding you personally responsible for this delay, Mr. . . . ?"

Jeffrey translated, his tone supercilious.

The man stuttered. "Cheng." He struggled not to shudder.

"Expect US retaliation unless I have an immediate

apology," said MacKenzie, Jeffrey interpreting.

Shaken, the KMT officer said, "I meant no disrespect, but your flight isn't scheduled until eleven, and my orders are to. . . ."

"Detain us?" asked Jeffrey. "This is a serious breach of international protocol." Then he took advantage of the officer's stunned silence to interpret in English.

"Get out of my way," said MacKenzie in his most stentorian tones.

It needed no translation as he regally swept past the soldiers. The pallbearers and Lane followed in his steps.

Jeffrey stayed behind, watching the rear. Lane climbed the ramp, paying little attention to her surroundings, intent only on getting Li enough air to breathe. Suddenly she heard two muted thuds. The man in front of her screamed in pain and dropped his end of the casket. Blood streamed from his shoulder. Screaming herself, she crouched down, protecting the baby beneath her.

"Get down!" shouted Jeffrey in English. He ducked into the car as the copilot dashed from the jet, shielding MacKenzie with his own body until they were safely inside the cabin. The second pallbearer looked around him in confusion, still holding up his end of the crate.

"Get down!" Jeffrey repeated in Mandarin, motioning with his hand. "Set it down."

The man heard too late. Before he could lower the balsam crate, a third bullet sank into its soft wood, muffling the sound. Lane screamed, fearing for Li.

The soldiers hid in the jeep and radioed for backup. Looking in all directions for a gunman, they spoke excitedly. But not until a fourth shot ricocheted off the limo's bumper did they spot the sniper, crouching on top of the main terminal building. After calling in his position, they watched him climb down a fire escape.

During the time it took for him to jump to the ground and race to a waiting car, the soldiers scrambled to intercept. Their jeep and another cornered the drab-olive car at a blocked exit. Someone had double-parked, stopping all traffic from entering or leaving the loading area.

The escaping NSB car backed up, ramming the nearest jeep, then plowed through the barrier gate and careened onto the sidewalk. Swarming pedestrians either jumped into the hibiscus bushes lining the terminal or scrambled into the rolling, bumper-to-bumper taxi line. The getaway car drove over an obstacle course of bags and suitcases, in the process puncturing its right front tire on an abandoned luggage cart.

Though its pace never slowed, the drab-olive NSB car swerved into the bushes, veering into the wall. Its driver over-compensated, and the car swung left, sideswiping a row of yellow cabs. Two pedestrians, seeking cover between two cabs, were squeezed between the bumpers, their knees and thighs mangled. Still the military car charged down the sidewalk, the two jeeps in pursuit and closing.

In a last-ditch effort to escape, the driver crashed the NSB car through the sliding-glass doors into the main terminal building. A soldier from the pursuing jeep fired his M16, hitting the driver in the back of his skull. The getaway car lumbered into the currency exchange booth, then glancing off, catapulted into the ticket counters. There it spun out in the throngs of emigrating people, injuring dozens, killing four in the final count. The driver lay slumped over the wheel, the horn blaring his requiem, while the sniper turned his rifle on himself and blew his heart and lungs onto a turntable of travel brochures.

Unaware of the catastrophe inside the terminal building, Lane dealt with the issue at hand. Using one of the baby's diapers as a bandage and her belt as a tourniquet, she staunched the flow of blood from the hired man's shoulder. Jeffrey called 119 from the car phone for an ambulance, as the copilot helped the other bearer get the crate aboard the jet. They paid the man, waited impatiently for him to leave, then using a crowbar, opened the crate and gently lifted Li from his transient coffin.

Lane kissed him, her own method of checking Li's respiration. Breathing a sigh of relief that he had not suffocated, she examined him for gunshot wounds and found no bleeding. Next she traced the outside of the crate and found two holes. Then running her fingertips over thc thick coffin, she found the bullets lodged in the dense wood. Weak with relief, she laughed.

"I always heard an inch of wood was better insulation than four inches of brick," she said, "but I thought that applied to building materials. I didn't know a tree trunk could double as a bullct vest."

While the copilot monitored them from the cabin door, MacKenzie and his aide waited on the ramp as they watched the soldiers drive up. "Inform President Fu that the US State Department will be contacting him regarding the attempted assassination of Senator MacKenzie," said Jeffrey.

The officer quickly apologized but, gathering his courage, denied them permission to leave. "You'll have to follow me back to headquarters for questioning."

Via translation, MacKenzie said, "This plane is US territory and as such isn't subject to Taiwanese law. If you persist in this interference, the US will have no choice but to retaliate."

Before the officer could reply, the copilot called from the door, "We're ready for takeoff, sir."

They heard the whir of the engines spinning to life. Mac-

Kenzie and Jeffrey rushed into the cabin as the copilot secured the door. Before they had fastened their seat belts, the jet was taxiing down the runway. Within moments it had cleared the ground and begun its climb over Seven Star Mountain.

Lane watched out the window for a last glimpse, the sun reflecting off the Tamsui River like a ribbon of molten glass. As the Lear jet gained altitude, the view widened to include the river's mouth emptying into the East China Sea, the rocky north coastline and the Taiwan Strait, that narrow line of demarcation separating the two Chinas. Lane closed her eyes. She'd seen enough.

As soon as the seat belt signs went off, the copilot rushed toward MacKenzie. "Sir, we've just received an encrypted message from Washington."

"Have you decoded it yet?" asked Jeffrey, speaking for MacKenzie who was holding the baby.

The copilot turned to answer. "Part of it, the portion from CIA headquarters. However, it contained another intercepted message from Beijing that neither they nor we have been able to decrypt."

"This is Henderson," said Jeffrey, addressing Lane, "a CIA operative posing as our copilot. Washington thought it best to include him on our junket."

"With all the bureaucratic bullshit Beijing's been handing out," MacKenzie added, "the president thought Henderson should ride shotgun."

"His dual role is to assess Taiwan's position and try to decode any intercepted radio transmissions," said Jeffrey. "He's our ace cryptographer."

"A regular johnny-on-the-spot," said MacKenzie.

She nodded, realizing the situation was grimmer than she had imagined. As if reading her thoughts, Henderson explained, "Since the PRC's throwing a temper tantrum, President Dawson thought it best if I came along. Big Ears has been picking up messages regularly for the past few months. This afternoon's is only the most recent. The theory is that Beijing is communicating covertly with the PLA or operatives in Hong Kong and Macao, but no one's been able to break the code to confirm it."

"We're working 'til the last moment to decrypt their messages, but so far, no luck," said Jeffrey.

"What do you need?" she asked. "What's the key?"

Henderson raised his eyebrows as he took a long breath. "That's a good question. A keyword would 'unlock' the code. It's like a password into a computer. Once you know the word, you're in. But finding the word, especially when it's in Mandarin, is the hard part. That's where Jeffrey comes in. He's our bilingual specialist."

She looked at them with new respect. Neither man was what he appeared.

"Would you like anything to drink?" asked the uniformed steward, unlocking the trays and placing cocktail napkins and peanuts in front of them.

Lane shook her head, using the interruption as an excuse to check on Li. When they had put the chair across the aisle in a fully-reclined position for him, Li had seemed to be sleeping soundly. His breathing had been shallow and even. Now Li seemed agitated, distraught. He tried to raise his body into an upright position, and she gently forced him back down. He felt feverish to her touch.

"Steward," she called, "could you bring him some water?" She slipped another pillow under Li's head and massaged his temples, doing what she could to make him comfortable, but he would not hold still.

"I'll leave it here," said the steward, setting several glasses and a sweating pitcher of ice water nearby.

"Thanks." She poured Li a glass and held his head up to drink. The cool water roused him further, and he mumbled something. "More?" She held his head again, letting him sip from the glass.

Li's hand reached out and gestured as if writing in air, but Lane tried to calm him, thinking he was getting too agitated.

"Is he waking?" asked Jeffrey, unbuckling his seat belt and joining them.

"I think he's delirious," Lane said. "After the last few hours, he's had too much commotion for someone with a concussion."

But Li continued to move his hand excitedly, repeating the same symbol over and over. She tried to restrain him again.

"No, wait, I think he's trying to tell us something." Jeffrey got a pen and pencil from his vest pocket, but Li's hand couldn't hold the pen. It kept slipping from his grip. "We need something for him to write with," he said, glancing around the cabin.

Lane searched the pouch of the nearest seat for a writing tool but found nothing. When she turned back, Li was touching the pitcher, his index finger drawing on the collected humidity.

"What's he doing? Drawing a 'pitcher'?" Henderson asked, his eyes twinkling, his curiosity getting the best of him.

"A Chinese character," said Jeffrey, never taking his eyes off the water pitcher.

"What does it say?" she whispered, afraid to interrupt Li's concentration.

"I don't know. He hasn't finished the second radical, but so far it's a nine-stroke character . . . ten, and he's still writing," said Jeffrey, studying the glyph. "You see, every stroke changes the meaning of the character, and most Chinese characters are made up of two or more radicals."

"Radicals?" Henderson asked. "Do you mean mathematical or political?"

"No, the basis of the Chinese writing system is 214 radicals or elements. Each radical has from one to seventeen strokes. These can be used independently or in combination to form more complex characters."

Exerting great effort, Li drew another line. "That's eleven strokes," said Jeffrey. "It could mean *gei,* to give or allow, or *jr,* meaning paper, *shau,* to join together, or even *hung,* the color red."

Worried at Li's exertion, Lane watched him struggle still again. "He's drawing a twelfth," she said, wondering what was so important that he labored so hard. And then she knew. "He overheard us talking about a keyword to decrypt the Beijing messages."

Li nodded his head and became more agitated, his finger shaking as he struggled.

"My God!" Henderson wiped the smile off his lips and craned his neck as he studied the glyph with new interest.

Excitement mounting, the three pressed their heads together, moving in for a closer look. Jeffrey scrutinized the dripping character. "It's difficult to know if that's a slanting stroke or a symmetrical wing."

"It seems to curve down," Lane said, following the line with her finger, careful not to touch the pitcher's fragile drawing.

"No, that's just the humidity dripping, gravity pulling it down," said Henderson.

As the three stared, Jeffrey squinted, trying to read between the dripping lines. "It could mean *yau,* a coil, or *lei,* to be tired," he said, "or it might be. . . ."

"What are y'all looking at?" asked MacKenzie, picking up

the pitcher and pouring himself a glass of ice water. Gasping in unison, the three stared in horror. "What?" asked MacKenzie, startled, looking at his zipper. "Is my fly open?"

Lane found her voice first. "Don't touch the sides of the pitcher!" she said. "Daddy, don't touch . . . don't. . . ." Too late, her warning ended in a deep, frustrated sigh.

"What?" His hand rubbed against the sweating pitcher, further smudging Li's figure.

The three looked at each other before Jeffrey spoke. "Senator, you just smeared what might have been our only clue to decrypting Beijing's messages."

"Well, I'll be damned." He wore a surprised expression but seemed unconcerned.

Lane shot her father a sharp look, then noticed half the glyph was still visible, though quickly losing its shape. "Jeffrey, can you make anything out of this?"

He glanced at it half-heartedly, then saw the second radical was partially intact. Interest building, he said, "It could be *sz,* which has two meanings, silk or a little bit, a trace."

Lane picked up the pen and paper, handing them to Jeffrey. "Make a list of all the possibilities. We can read them off to Li, see if he responds to any of them."

Jeffrey spoke each word as he wrote it, but Li had faded out of consciousness again. "Now what?"

"Try each word," she said.

"What do you mean?" Jeffrey asked.

Turning to Henderson, she said, "Try each word with the messages. Maybe one will be the password."

He took the list and studied it skeptically. "All right, I suppose anything's worth a shot." Henderson sat at the computer and one at a time keyed in *gei, jr, shau, hung, yau* and *lei.* Scratching his head, he said, "Nothing. This is getting us nowhere."

"You forgot the last one," Lane said.

Rechecking his list, he saw *sz* and keyed it in. "Nope."

"Maybe we're going about this the wrong way," said Jeffrey. "The character Li drew could have been half of a phrase, but he was too weak to finish. Try to think of idioms. For instance, if *gei* means to give, perhaps give up or give in would be what Li intended to write."

Once again they worked their way through the list, thinking up phrases, while Jeffrey translated and Henderson keyed them in.

"You forget the last one again, *sz,*" Lane said. "What's that mean again?"

"Silk," said Jeffrey. "Think of how it's used in phrases."

"Silk road, silk route," suggested Lane. Henderson tried them and shook his head.

"Silk shirt, silk tie," said Jeffrey. Henderson shook his head.

"What about silkworm?" asked MacKenzie, nursing a bourbon.

Henderson keyed it in, and the computer lit up. Letters, numbers, ASCII symbols flashed and danced across the screen. A message slowly began to materialize from the computer's alphabet soup. Gradually the puzzle reworked itself into a phrase, as Jeffrey translated:

"Initiate Project China One at zero hundred hours CST."

"My god," said Henderson, grasping the significance. "China One's the code name for the PLA's reunification plan."

"What's it mean?" asked Lane.

Jeffrey exchanged looks with Henderson. Then as the agent radioed the decrypted message to Washington, Jeffrey explained. "The maneuver that begins at midnight is no blockade. It's an invasion. China plans to storm Taiwan tonight."

"It's always been Wong Xiaoping's dream," agreed Henderson, "a seventy-two-hour blitzkrieg that wouldn't allow time for US intervention, let alone emigration."

Lane thought of the twenty-one million people stranded on Taiwan, the island a ship that was about to sink. "How long 'til we reach Guam?" she asked.

"About fifteen minutes," said Henderson, radioing the base.

Planning as she spoke, she said, "Let's get Li to a hospital. After we drop him and Justin off, we. . . ."

"And you and the Senator," added Henderson. "I can't be responsible for your safety when China attacks."

"And I can't sit around waiting for Beijing to swoop down on Taiwan like a duck on a beetle," said Lane, parroting Li's words. "We've got to do something."

"We will," said Henderson, "after we get you civilians to safety." Responding to her sour expression, he added, "It's my job to protect the senator and his family. You and your son are his family."

"And Li," she added softly.

# EPILOGUE

Her father and Justin safe in a guarded hotel room, Lane waited in the coffee shop of the Guam Memorial Hospital in Tamuning. Over inky cups of acidic coffee, she thought of all that had happened since her engagement party, wondering how many things would have been different if she had married Li.

"Mrs. Yang?" A nurse watched her expectantly.

Startled at being called by that name, Lane said, "No, I'm Mrs. Chen."

"Oh, sorry. The doctor would like to see you now."

She followed the nurse into the office and was pleasantly surprised to see a female doctor. Her smile was genuine as she shook hands. "How is he?"

The woman answered slowly, picking the right words in a delicate situation. "The patient is in a state of coma." Lane drew in a sharp breath. "But the good news is that it's reversible."

Her breath left her in a deep sigh. Then Lane remembered the condition was difficult to diagnose.

"Are you sure it's reversible?"

The doctor exuded confidence from her smooth blond haircut to her crisp manner. "Of the five steps toward recovery, Mr. Yang has entered his fourth."

"I'm so relieved. I thought the trauma of the move might have harmed him." Her brow wrinkled as she remembered how pale and still he had been when they had boarded the plane, then how delirious he had gotten. "He was so excitable when we arrived; we couldn't control him."

"He was in stasis during the first part of the flight, which is normal. When you brought him in, he had entered the second stage of recovery, extreme agitation. You did nothing to damage his condition."

Putting her manicured hands in her pockets, Lane walked toward the window and glanced at the view outside. Situated on a cape overlooking Tumon Bay, the hospital had sea-views on three sides. She noted the coral reef, the dividing line between the deep navy-blue and shallow aqua water.

"Why did he go into a coma?" Lane asked.

"In this case, the coma was a defense mechanism which served him well." The doctor nodded her belief in the human body's ability to heal itself. "It's nature's way of shutting down the body, so it can regenerate." She smiled gently, her eyes crinkling in concern. "When you speak with him, his speech and reactions may seem a little stiff. That's because he's entered the automatism phase."

"But he'll recover fully?"

"Absolutely, his brain functions will gradually be restored to normal." Lane's eyes lit up then glazed over as the doctor cautioned, "Just don't overload him with information today. It's the reason his brain shut down in the first place, too much stimuli. Don't overwhelm him with what's happened since he was injured."

Lane thought about Teng-hui, Mei-ling, Chen, Taiwan's looming invasion. Those episodes could wait. Li would learn about them when his mind could accept it. She recalled Fu's attempts to have him killed in the Taipei hospital and airport. Could that wait? Chewing her lip, she wondered what he knew that was so dangerous to Taiwan's security.

"Will he regain his memory?" Lane asked.

"Gradually, as his recovery progresses."

Lane looked past the doctor, contemplating the beach

below. Noting the breakers' relentless chase and retreat, she thought of Fu and the NSB, wondering if Li would ever be free from them. She focused again on the doctor.

"When can I see him?"

"Now if you like." She led Lane down the hall, stopping in front of a nondescript door.

Lane's heart was thumping as she peeked in, watching him, wondering how much he recalled. Her eyes widened nervously, hoping he would remember her, but not really expecting it. Then he turned toward her, his eyes crinkling in recognition. As her eyes welled up with tears, she blinked them back and smiled.

"Hi," she said softly.

His whisper sounded like sheets rustling. "Lane." He struggled to hold out his arms, settling for shaky extensions of his hands, but his glistening eyes said it all.

Speechless, she took his hand in hers. She couldn't speak around the lump that caught in her throat.

He whispered again, "Taiwan?"

Lane looked at her watch: eleven o'clock.